PRAISE FOR THE WORKS OF RICHARD WAGAMESE

"Richard Wagamese is a national treasure." —Joseph Boyden, Scotiabank Giller Prize-winning author of *Through Black Spruce*

"Melancholy tenderness and spiritual yearning. Wagamese evokes each character's consciousness and history with compassion, deep understanding and a knowledge of street life." —*Vancouver Sun*

"Richard Wagamese is a born storyteller." —Louise Erdrich

"Wagamese writes with brutal clarity. . . . Odious content proffered with stark and gutting gravitas. You will blanch [but] Wagamese finds alleviating balance through magical legend and poetic swells of sensate imagery." —*The Globe and Mail*

"Wagamese grabs the reader . . . and envelops them effortlessly in the emotions and atmosphere of unfamiliar territory." —*Calgary Herald*

"Wagamese is one of Canada's outstanding First Nations writers. . . . A born storyteller who captures your attention from the first page." —*The Sun Times* (Owen Sound)

"Wagamese is capable of true grace on the page." —*Winnipeg Free Press*

BY RICHARD WAGAMESE

FICTION

A Quality of Light

Dream Wheels

Him Standing

Indian Horse

Keeper'n Me

Medicine Walk

Ragged Company

Starlight

The Next Sure Thing

NON-FICTION

Embers: One Ojibway's Meditation

One Native Life

One Story, One Song

The Terrible Summer

POETRY

Runaway Dreams: Poems

RAGGED COMPANY

RICHARD WAGAMESE

ANCHOR CANADA

Anchor Canada edition 2009

Library and Archives Canada Cataloguing in Publication data
is available upon request.

ISBN 978-0-385-25694-0

Cover design: Andrew Roberts
Cover image: Jennifer Chau / EyeEm / Getty Images
Printed and bound in Canada

Published in Canada by Anchor Canada,
a division of Penguin Random House Canada Limited,
a Penguin Random House Company

www.penguinrandomhouse.ca

20 19 18 17 16

For all the invisible ones in all the cities,
and for Debra, for seeing me . . .

Its inhabitants are, as the man once said, "whores, pimps, gamblers, and sons of bitches," by which he meant Everybody. Had the man looked through another peephole he might have said, "Saints and angels and martyrs and holy men," and he would have meant the same thing.

JOHN STEINBECK
Cannery Row

ACKNOWLEDGEMENTS

I am sincerely grateful for the help of all the workers in all of the drop-in centres, missions, shelters, and hostels I ever stayed in through the years. They showed me the way up when all I could see was down. Their work goes unrecognized, and unheralded, but I remember and I am always grateful. This story began in those rooms, bunks, and hallways. Thanks to my agent, John Pearce, and all the folks at Westwood Creative Artists, and to Maya Mavjee at Doubleday Canada. To Richard and Dian Henderson, Ron and Carol Dasiuk, Ed and Arlene Dasiuk, Merv Williams, Ann Sevin, Robin Lawless, Bonita Penner, Joseph Boyden, Blanca Schorcht, and Vaughn Begg, for the friendship, acceptance, and inspiration.

Is it you?

Yes.

Where have you been?

Travelling.

Yes. Of course. Where did you get to?

Everywhere. Everywhere I always wanted to go, everywhere I ever heard about.

Did you like it?

I loved it. I never knew the world was so big or that it held so much.

Yes. It's an incredible thing.

Absolutely.

What did you think about all that time?

Everything. I guess I thought about everything. But I thought about one thing the most.

What was that?

A movie. Actually, a line from a movie.

Really?

Yes. Funny, isn't it? Out of all the things I could have thought about over and over, I thought about a line from a movie.

Which one?

Casablanca. *When Bogie says to Bergman, "The world don't amount to a hill of beans to two small people like us?" Remember that?*

Yes. I remember. Why?

Because that's what I think it's all about in the end.

What?

Well, you live, you experience, you become, and sometimes, at the end of things, maybe you feel deprived, like maybe you missed out somehow, like maybe there was more you could have—should have—had. You know?

Yes. Yes, I do.

But the thing is, at least you get to finger the beans.

Yes. I like that—you get to finger the beans.

Do you ever do that?

All the time.

Me too.

Let's do that now. Let's hear all of it all over again.

Okay. Do you remember it?

All of it. Everything. Every moment.

Then that's all we need.

The beans.

Yes. The beans.

BOOK ONE shelter

One For The Dead

IT WAS IRWIN THAT STARTED all the dying. He was my eldest brother, and when I was a little girl he was my hero, the one whose shoulders I was always carried on and whose funny faces made me smile even when I didn't want to. There were five of us. We lived on an Ojibway reserve called Big River and our family, the One Sky family, went back as far in tribal history as anyone could recall. I was named Amelia, after my grandmother. We were a known family—respected, honoured—and Irwin was our shining hope. I was the only girl, and Irwin made me feel special, like I was his hero. *Love* is such a simple word, so limited, that I never use it when I think of him, never consider it when I remember what I lost.

He was a swimmer. A great one. That's not surprising when you consider that our tribal clan was the Fish Clan. But Irwin swam like an otter. Like he loved it. Like the water was a second skin. No one ever beat my brother in a race, though there were many who tried. Even grown men—bigger, stronger kickers—would never see anything but the flashing bottoms of my brother's feet. He was a legend.

The cost of a tribal life is high and our family paid in frequent times of hunger. Often the gill net came up empty, the moose wouldn't move to the marshes, and the snares stayed set. The oldest boys left school for work, to make enough to get us through those times. They hired themselves out to a local farmer to clear bush and break new ground. It was man's work, really, and Irwin and John were only boys, so the work took its toll.

It was hot that day. Hot as it ever got in those summers of my girlhood, and even the farmer couldn't bear up under the heat. He let my brothers go midway through the afternoon and they walked the three miles back to our place. Tired as they were, all Irwin could think about was a swim in the river. So a big group of us kids headed toward the broad, flat stretch below the rapids where we'd all learned to swim. I was allowed to go because there were so many of us.

There was a boy named Ferlin Axe who had challenged my brother to race hundreds of times and had even come close a few of those times. That day, he figured Irwin would be so tired from the heat and the work that he could win in one of two ways. First, he could beat Irwin because he was so tired, or second, Irwin could decline the challenge. Either way was a victory, because no Indian boy ever turned down a race.

"One Sky," Ferlin said when we got to the river, "today's the day you lose."

"Axe," Irwin said, "you'll never chop me down."

Now, the thing about races—Indian races, anyway—is that anyone's allowed to join. So when they stepped to the edge of the river there were six of them. At the count of three they took off, knees pumping high, water splashing up in front of them, and when they dove, they dove as one. No one was surprised when Irwin's head popped up first and his arms started pulling against the river's muscle. He swam effortlessly. Watching him go, it seemed like he was riding the water, skimming across the surface while the others clawed their way through it. He reached the other side a good thirty seconds ahead of Ferlin Axe.

The rules were that everyone could rest on the other side. There was a long log to sit on, and when each of those boys plopped down beside Irwin he slapped them on the arm. I'll never forget that sight: six of them, young, vibrant, glistening in the sun and laughing, teasing each other, the sun framing all of them with the metallic glint off the river. But for me, right then, it seemed like the sun shone only on my brother, like he was a holy object, a saint perhaps, blessed by the power of the open water. We all have our sacred moments, those we carry in our spirit always, and my brother, strong and brown and laughing, shining beside that river, is mine.

After about five minutes they rose together and moved to the water's edge, still pushing, shoving, teasing. My brother raised an arm, waved to me, and I could see him counting down. When his arm dropped they all took off. Ferlin Axe surfaced first and we all gasped. But once Irwin's head broke the surface of the water you could see him gain with every stroke. He was so fast it was startling. When he seemed to glide past the flailing Ferlin Axe, we all knew it was over. Then, about halfway across, at the river's deepest point where the pull of the current was strongest, his head bobbed under. We all laughed. Everyone thought that Irwin was going to try to beat Ferlin by swimming underwater the rest of the way. But when Ferlin suddenly stopped and stared wildly around before diving under himself, we all stood up. Soon all five boys were diving under and I remember that it seemed like an hour before I realized that Irwin hadn't come back up. Time after time they dove and we could hear them yelling back and forth to each other, voices high and breathless and scared.

The river claimed my brother that day. His body was never found and if you believe as I do, then you know that the river needed his spirit back. But that's the woman talking. The little girl didn't know what to make of it. I went to the river every day that summer and fall to sit and wait for my brother. I was sure that it was just a joke, a tease, and he'd emerge laughing from the water, lift me to his shoulders, and carry me home in celebration of another really good one. But there was just the river, broad and flat and deep with secrets. The sun no longer shone on that log across the water, and if I'd known on the day he sat there, when it seemed to shine only on him, that it was really calling him away, I'd have yelled something. *I love you,* maybe. But more like, *I need you.* It was only later, when the first chill of winter lent the water a slippery sort of blackness, like a hole into another world, that I allowed the river its triumph and let it be. But it's become a part of my blood now, my living, the river of my veins, and Irwin courses through me even now.

My parents died that winter. Those cheap government houses were dry as tinder, heated by one central stove that threw an ember through the grate one night and burned our house to the ground. Those who saw it say it looked like a flare popping off. I hope so. I hope my parents slept right through it, that there was no terror or desperation for either of them. We kids were with my Uncle Jack and Aunt Elizabeth at a winter powwow that night. Standing beside my uncle's truck the next day looking at the burnt and bubbled timbers piled atop each other, I felt a coldness start to build inside me. A numbing cold like you feel in the dentist's chair, the kind you're powerless to stop. I couldn't cry. I could feel the tears dammed inside my chest but there was no channel to my eyes.

We lived with Uncle Jack for a while but he was a drinker and it wasn't long before the social workers came and moved us all to the missionary school fifty miles away. I was six and the last sight I ever had of Big River was through the back window of the yellow bus they loaded us into. We moved from a world of bush and rock and river to one of brick and fences and fields. There we were made to speak English, to forget the sacred ways of our people, and to learn to kneel before a cross we were told would save us. It didn't.

The boys and girls were kept apart except for meals and worship. I never got to speak to my brothers at all except in mouthed whispers, waves, and the occasional letters all the kids learned to sneak across to each other. It was hard. Our world had become strange and foreign and we all suffered. But it was hardest on my brother Harley. He was eight and, out of all of us, had been the one closest to our parents. He'd stayed close to the house while the rest of us tore around the reserve. He'd cooked with our mother and set snares with our father. Quiet, gentle, and thinner even than me, we always treated Harley like a little bird out of its nest, sheltering him, protecting him, warming him. In the tribal way, change is a constant and our ways teach you how to deal with it. But we were torn away from that and nothing we were given in the missionary school offered us any comfort for the ripping away of the fabric of our lives. Harley wept. Constantly. And when he disappeared over the fence one February night, I wasn't surprised. From across the chapel the next morning, John and Frank nodded solemnly at me. We all knew where he'd gone. I still remember watching from the dormitory window as the men on horses came back that evening, shaking their heads, muttering, cold. If they couldn't figure out how an eight-year-old could vanish and elude them, then they forgot that they were chasing an Indian boy whose first steps were taken in the bush and who'd learned to run and hide as his first childhood game. They looked for three days. Uncle Jack found him huddled against the blackened metal of that burnt-out stove in the remains of our house, frozen solid. Dead. All he'd had on was a thin wool coat and slippery-soled white man shoes but he'd made it fifty miles in three days. Uncle Jack told me years later in a downtown bar that Harley's eyes were frozen shut with tears and large beads of them were strung along the crossed arms he clutched himself with. When I heard that I got drunk—real drunk—for a long time.

Life settled into a flatness after we lost Harley. But all three of us rebelled in our own ways. Me, I retreated into silence. The nuns all thought me slow and backward because of my silence but they had no idea how well I was learning their ways and their language. I did everything they asked of me in a slow, methodical way, uncomplaining and silent. I gave them nothing back because all I knew was the vast amount they had taken from me, robbed me of, cheated me out of, all in the name of a God whose son bore the long hair none of us were allowed to wear anymore. The coldness inside me was complete after Harley died, and what I had left of my life, of me, I was unwilling to offer up to anyone. I drifted through the next four years as silent as a bank of snow. A February snow.

John and Frank made up for my absence. They were twelve and ten that first year, and when they refused to sit through classes they were sent to the barns and fields. John rejected everything about that school and his rebellion led to strappings that he took with hard-eyed silence. The coldness in me was a furnace in him and he burned with rage and resentment. Every strapping, every punishment only stoked it higher. He fought everyone. By the time he was sixteen and old enough to leave on his own, the farm work had made him strong and tough. It was common knowledge that John One Sky could outwork any of the men. He threw bales of hay effortlessly onto the highest part of the wagons and he forked manure from the stalls so quickly he'd come out robed in sweat, eyes ablaze and ready for whatever else they wanted to throw at him. It was his eyes that everyone came to fear. They threw the heat in his soul outward at everyone. Except for me. In the chapel, he'd look across at me and his eyes would glow just like Irwin's used to. He'd raise a hand to make the smallest wave and I would wonder how anyone could fear hands that could move so softly through the air. But they did. When he told them he was leaving there was no argument. And when he told them that he would see me before he left there was no argument either.

We met in the front hallway. He was big. Tall and broad and so obviously strong. But the hand he laid against my cheek was tame, loving. "Be strong," he told me. "I'm going to get you out of here, Amelia. You and Frankie. Just as soon as I can. I promise." Then he hugged me for a long time, weaving back and forth, and when he looked at me I felt like I was looking into Irwin's eyes. Then he was gone.

Frank tried to be another John. But he wasn't built of the same stuff, physically or mentally, and he only succeeded in getting himself into trouble. No one ever feared my brother Frank. In those schools you learned to tell the difference between courage and bravado, toughness and a pose, and no one believed in Frank's imitation of his brother. That knowledge just made him angrier. Made him act out more. Made him separate from all of us. He sulked and his surliness made him even more of a caricature and made him try even harder to live up to what he thought a One Sky man should be. He got mean instead of tough and, watching him through those years, I knew that the river, the fire, and the cold ran through him, drove him, sent him searching for a peg to hang his life on. It was a cold, hard peg he chose—vindictive as a nail through the palms.

A year and a half after he left, we heard from John again. Uncle Jack had sobered up, left Big River, and settled into a job and a house in the city. They were waiting for papers to be drawn up that would release us to them. When I held that letter in my hands, they shook and they still shake today when I think of it. I suppose you only get a small number of chances to hold hope in your hands and it's a memorable weight, one the skin remembers. I allowed myself a little outlet after that. For the first time let them hear me utter complete sentences, talk of books and stories I had read, share my thinking. To say they were amazed is too easy. I was simple Amelia One Sky to them, the quiet one who sewed quilts and cooked. To find that I could quote the Bible was beyond belief to them, and I enjoyed the depth of the surprise.

Uncle Jack and Aunt Elizabeth came and got us a month later. Frank and I walked out of that school with one small duffle bag apiece, all we had of our lives after six years, all they'd given us to prepare us for the world. But it was more than enough, really. The ride into the city was a small glory. Uncle Jack had a good car and Frank and I sat in the back watching the landscape skate by. I felt like I was flying.

"Thank your brother John for this, you kids," Uncle Jack said. "But don't expect too much from him when we get there."

I didn't know what he meant but found out soon enough. Leaving the missionary school hadn't changed John at all. In fact, it had made things worse. In the school he'd had targets for his anger but in the outside world he didn't. So he settled in with a fast downtown crowd of bikers, ex-cons, and drug dealers who were as much like himself as he could find. And he'd earned a reputation as a hellish fighter as well as someone who not only lived by the code of that world but also fought to defend it, protect it, honour it. Everyone was afraid of him. Everyone but me. For me, he always had those eyes. Bloodshot or not, they always held a smile for me and there was a big rough hand to tousle my hair. I had a hero again.

Life was good. Frank and I got into a school that a lot of other Indian kids attended and our aunt and uncle were pretty free with rules so we got to run around a lot. Frankie still tried to emulate John and he got away with it because he was John One Sky's brother. Me, I tried to learn to be a little girl but it was hard after all those years. Still, I played the games and ran around like all the rest, content to be with family again.

The year I turned fourteen someone killed John. They shoved a big knife into his back while he was taking a pee in the washroom of the Regal hotel. When they found him he was laying in a pool of blood and piss, one hand behind his back clasping the handle of that knife. He died trying to pull it out. Always the fighter.

I didn't come out of my room for a week. All I remember of that time is a crack in the ceiling. I lay there and stared at that crack until time was lost to me. I shivered from the return of the coldness and that ceiling became a bottomless pit I felt myself tumbling into. In that crack were voices. Voices of the dead, and I could hear Irwin telling me, *The water's great, Amelia, come on in.* I heard my parents say, *The fire's warm, there's tea, come on, little girl, come.* Harley's soft little voice told me, *It's not that far from home, Amelia, all you gotta do is try.* And John, my tough, strong, fearless brother, said, *Don't let them take you by surprise, little girl.* I heard them all, over and over, and if I slept at all it was the dreamless kind you're never sure you had. They wanted me. I wanted them. I was tired and the only thing that brought me out of that room alive was Frank.

Three days after John died Frank had disappeared. He was eighteen, and when I tracked him down at the Regal hotel drinking with John's crowd, he'd changed. Frank One Sky, he told me, stressing the last two words and poking a thumb against his chest.

John's brother, he said to the nods of a table of new-found friends. I sat with them a while and they made me welcome but wouldn't let me drink. Frank sat there drinking in the notoriety of being John One Sky's brother as much as he drank in the beer that came his way from all across that hotel bar. I left him looking like a minor lord, fawned over and protected. As far as I know, he never left the Regal again.

Word had got out that two people were responsible for John's death. When they showed up at the Regal, Frank walked over to their table with a baseball bat and crushed both their skulls. He was given two life sentences and sent to a prison a few hundred miles away. When I got the letter telling me he had hung himself in his cell soon after, I sat on the back stoop of Uncle Jack's house late into the night tearing that letter into small pieces, flicking each of them away and watching the breeze take them skittering across the ground and out of the halo of light beyond the stoop. With each torn shred of paper I felt a piece of myself tear away from whatever held it. Each shred ripped away from me too, until finally I sat there alone, surrounded by death in a place far beyond anger or sadness—a cold universe, empty of stars and silent. Then I walked away. Just got up and walked away. Walked to a table at the Regal and a place on the street.

John's crowd surrounded me like angels. I was fifteen. When I reached for dope or drink, they kept it from me. I was a One Sky and that was all that mattered. There's a code of loyalty on the street, and no matter what the normal people say, that loyalty is strong and deep. I moved around, stayed with hookers, dealers, bikers, and all the other rounders who'd known my brothers and chose to honour them by sheltering me. The Regal became my home. I witnessed beatings, brawls, stabbings, overdoses, seizures, arrests, releases, people shunned, and people accepted like me. Through it all I was shielded by the burly bodies of bikers and their women, and somewhere in that strange and quirky shelter I learned to live again. Not well, not in the accepted normal way, but I found a place in that world and I stayed there. Until I found love.

Ben Starr was a tall, good-looking Blackfoot from Montana. He'd been on the street for years and when he joined our crowd at the Regal with his long braids and black leather he was accepted as the known rounder that he was. He was twenty-two and I was sixteen. He'd smile at me and nod each time we saw each other and soon we were talking. Ben wanted to be a writer. He wanted to take everything he'd seen and done and turn it into poetry. He'd slip me pieces of paper and I'd run off to the toilet to read them. A lot of it was beyond me, but somehow knowing that it mattered to Ben made it matter to me, and I was in love long before I knew it as love.

I guess it happens that way. That's why it's such a mystery, such a force. Because you find yourself in the middle of whatever kind of life you have and suddenly there's an edge to all of it that wasn't there before. Expectation. Hope, you'd call it. You find your life surrounded by a quiet kind of light that warms everything you touch and see. At least that's how it was for me. And for Ben. I know it was that way for him, too. We moved in together after two months and when we finally united ourselves as man and woman the pain was sharp but elevated me somehow. When he entered me I felt opened up, raised to the world, and presented as a whole new being, freed from the cold and numbness, embraced by a bolder fire than I knew existed before or since. We lay there stoking the blaze and he told me stories. Some of them I knew from books but most were his, told spontaneously, magically, like something unfolding.

And so we lived. Not in a way most people would call well, but we got by. Ben took the odd day job, and because I didn't drink or do dope the Regal hired me as a maid. We had a room on the fifth floor with two large windows right beside the big orange neon sign, so that at night our loving was bathed in the soft orange glow. I can't see that kind of light anymore without a sense of celebration or loss for Ben. See, he had the monkey. Heroin. Morphine. Needles. I knew, of course. Everybody knew. But what a rounder chooses is what a rounder chooses, and only when that starts to affect other people badly is anything said. Most times you'd never know. He was careful, knew his limit, and never went overboard. But monkeys climb and Ben's was more agile and clever than most. He started to get sick in the mornings and if we didn't find him some more pretty quickly he'd just disappear and return in the early afternoon, strolling into the Regal calm and unaffected. No one asked him what he did for the money, not even me. It's one of the things you learn on the street—to never ask. Me, I was just glad to see him.

He started doing more. Secretly. But he was still loving me hard and being there for me and I guess I believed then that love itself would keep us above it, keep us floating, raised up, safe. But even love's power has limits and Ben was soon far beyond the border of ours. They found him in the same washroom where they'd found John, the rig still hanging above his elbow, a thin trickle of blood like a tiny river down the muscle of his arm. I know because I saw. Small as I was, there wasn't anybody big enough to keep me out of there and no one even really tried. I rocked him back and forth in my arms, cradling him, telling him it was going to be okay, to not be afraid and that my family would take care of him. I said it like a prayer and I believed it. When they took him from me I felt something—a warm thing, pliant, round, and complete—leave with a silent tug, and when I walked back into the Regal lounge all that was left was a hole. No cold, no numbness, no ache, no pain, just a hole. I walked over to the bar and started to fill that hole.

I was drunk for years. Years. Time, when you don't consider it, has a slipperiness, an elusive quality you feel in the hands but shake off fast like water, and I was in the pit a long, long time. Because I was John One Sky's sister and Ben Starr's woman they let me go. At first it was out of sorrow for my loss, my losses, the story I would tell in long garbled sentences as long as the pitchers kept coming. Then, it was out of pity for a drunken young woman. Later, when I became untrustworthy and a pest, they let me go completely. So I wandered from party to party, bottle to bottle, man to man. I sold myself along the way, and that was the cruellest thing, betraying my beloved Ben for enough money to keep on drinking. But finally, the years, the miles, the parties, the puke, the jails, and abuses broke me down and no one wanted me that way anymore. I stank. I slept in parks, doorways, abandoned buildings, and hobo jungles, stumbling into a world fortified by shaving lotion, mouthwash, rubbing alcohol, or whatever was handy. If there was a God in the world, he'd overlooked me and I became a crier, a weeper, tearfully begging change from passersby. Until the shadowed ones came.

I started seeing them everywhere. At first I'd rub my eyes, shake my head, and gulp down a mouthful of whatever I had to chase away what I thought for sure were DT's. But they stayed. Not real people, not even what you'd call ghosts, just hints, vague outlines I saw everywhere. Alleys, parks, windows of buildings, on the street, everywhere I looked I saw them—felt them, really—not able to disbelieve fully or convince myself of their presence. Shadowed ones. The ones whose spirits can never leave this earth, the ones tied here by a sorrow, a longing stronger than life and deeper than death. When drinking wouldn't drive them away and the haunting got too much to handle, I walked into detox one day and quit drinking. Just quit. Suddenly, I was forty-four. I looked eighty. I felt older than a thousand years.

Hospital was best, they said. I was there a month drying out and learning to eat again. From there I went to a women's program where I could have stayed as long as I wanted, but there was no one there I could really talk to. They were either really young and cocky or older and playing at being sophisticated. Those ones called their drinks "highballs," "cocktails," or other long names a galaxy away from the "rubby," "crock," or "juice" that I knew. And the walls drove me crazy. I felt penned up, frozen to the spot, and even though I knew they would have tried to help me, the street was in my bones and I went back to the only world I knew and understood. They were waiting for me—the shadowed ones. I'd have been about four months' sober by then, so I knew that it wasn't the booze or DT's making me see them. No, death has a presence—thick and black and cold—and when you live so close to it for so long you get so you can see it. Feel it. Accept it and not be afraid. Everyone has a mourning ground, a place where the course of a life turned, changed, altered, or disappeared forever. It could be a house, a park, or just a place on the pavement where the wrong words were said, the worst choice made, or fateful action taken. Our spirits are linked to these places forever and when our sorrow's deep enough we return to them again and again to stand in our pain, reliving the memory, mumbling clumsy prayers that we might be offered a chance to change what happened, bend time so we could choose again. But it never happens. The shadowed ones just keep on doing that after death, returning to those places where their wounds are buried, hoping against hope that something in the walls or ground might emerge to save them. Mourning grounds. We all have them and it's only in learning how to live with our hurts while we're here that we're set free of them. When I came to understand that at age forty-four, I knew where I had to be. Where I needed to be. For them, the shadowed ones on the street that no one ever sees, the living dead. The homeless.

So I went back and lived as one of them. But I never drank again. Instead, I'd make runs for them when they were sick, nurse them when they needed it, or just be around—a voice, an ear, a shoulder—and by doing that I eased my own pain. When a fresh bottle arrived I always asked to open it. See, there's an old rounder ritual you hardly see anymore. When a bottle's opened you pour a small bit on the ground and say "there's one for the dead." That's what I would always do and that's where I got my name. One For The Dead One Sky. I've been here for twenty years and Amelia, little Amelia, resides in a place of memory, standing at all her places of mourning, shedding tears that salve her bruises, offering prayers that set her free. And the river is just a river after all, neither tepid nor cold, with a long log on the other side where the sun shines down like a spotlight from heaven, enveloping my family, my Ben, keeping them warm for me.

Digger

DYING COLD SUCKS. Trust me. I know. I've come close enough to know. Stumbled out of more than a few alleys in my time shivering and shaking like a fucking booze seizure with the cold so deep in the bones your heart feels like it's pumping ice. It takes a shitload more than a few slops of sherry to get the feeling back. Most times you spend the whole fucking day trying to shake it off: coffee at the Mission, hanging out in the doorways of malls until the rental bulls chase you off, knocking back some hard stuff. It's a tough business.

So when they told me that they found three of us dead on the first night of the cold snap I almost felt sorry. Almost. See, there's only two ways you die on the street. One is by being stupid. The other's called unlucky. Ducky Dent was stupid. He was a binge drinker. One of those guys who'd pull it together long enough to score a job, grab a flop, and run the straight and narrow for a time. Then, boom. Goes off like a fucking cannon, loses it all, hits the bricks again, sucking back everything from Jim Beam at the high end to shaving lotion and Listerine at the bottom end. There's a lot like Ducky Dent. But they never last. The street's got an edge to it that'll slice you like a fucking razor if you're not tough enough. Besides, we all knew the cold was coming. The cops and the street patrols and the rest of the Square John do-gooders told us all about this arctic front—a killer cold, they said—and made all the usual moves to get us to move inside at night. Most did. But hard-core guys like me know how to cope. Ducky wasn't hard-core. He wasn't even what you'd call a rounder. Just a stupid fuck who couldn't drink. He scored two bottles of sherry and a blanket, camped out in the doorway of some hair joint, and died. When they found him there was only one empty bottle beside him and the full one was curled against his chest. Passed out and froze. Sad? Sort of. Stupid? Big time.

Big Wolf McKay was unlucky. She'd been street for years and knew the ropes. Called her Big Wolf because she'd be in DT's and running around babbling that there was a big wolf tracking her down. She'd been drinking with one of her pals on the east side and was trying to make it back to the shelter for the night. Thin summer coat, too much booze, and real fucking cold was too much. She sat down to rest in a bus shelter, nodded off, and froze stiff as a board. A bus driver shook her shoulder to wake her up and she fell right over. We'll miss her. She was one of the solid ones, always willing to share, always ready to do a run when you were sick, and never ever went south with your money. Unlucky.

It was the same with East Coast Willy. His dream was always to go home to the sea. He said that for years and for a while he'd even lived in a packing crate labelled *Newfoundland*. Willy was a rounder. Been around since anyone can remember but never got his dream. See, the street's got claws, big, tough fucking claws that grip you once you been on it long enough, and shit like dreams stay dreams, coming and going like handfuls of change. Willy knew how to cope. He took his wraps and laid up on a warm air grate in an alley. But he lay down the wrong way. A delivery truck backed up that alley first thing in the morning and ran right over his head. Squashed his fucking melon flat. Turned the other way, he'd have been crippled at most but now he was dead. They say his body was warm when the cops and ambulance got there, so I knew he'd have made it through the cold except for being unlucky.

Three in one night. The Square Johns all tish-tosh over the stories in the news, say how sad and pitiful it is, how something should be done—but five minutes later they forget. Because they don't really give a fuck, and they don't have to. Shit, to tell the truth, a lot of us out here couldn't give a fuck either. Because we don't have to. Out here you got yourself and that's that. You stretch out and start to give a part of yourself away to others and you set yourself up. Set yourself up to be used, drained, tossed away. Me, I keep to myself. That's why I say I almost felt sorry about the three dead ones. I'll never be one of those street people all weepy and crying over shit. You live on concrete long enough, you pick up the nature of it: cold, hard, and predictable. It's called survival and every rounder knows it. Me, I'm a rounder. I'm concrete. Poured, formed, and set.

Being a rounder's just what it sounds like. You go around and around the same old vicious fucking circle until you've seen and done and survived everything. At first, it's just life screwing with you. Nobody comes here by choice. Life just fucks with you and you land here and once you do you find out real fast whether you have the stones to deal with it or not. Most don't. Because it's a hard go. I mean, you take anybody, plunk them down on the bricks with a handful of nothing but the clothes on their back and say "go." The majority'll run back to wherever it is they came from lickety-fucking-split. The stubborn ones, the ones with rebel bones, will try to hack it but it takes a shitload more than a handful of attitude to learn to live out here. So the rebels and the weepers disappear real quick. But a rounder, well, a rounder is a special fucking breed. See, the street wears people, breaks them down, but a rounder wears the street.

I choose to live how I live and I don't need any Square John pity or do-gooder helping hands. Even in a bitter fucking cold like that I need nothing but my balls and my brains to see me through. That's what makes me a rounder—balls and brains in equal measure. Any other balance, one way or the other, and you're dead. Stone cold, stiff as a frozen fucking board dead. Just like them three.

I know what it takes to stay alive out here. Me, I'm a digger, and that's what they call me. Digger. Dig for cans, bottles, metal, anything I can turn for cash. There's a route I walked for years and I do it every day. Even in that cold. Takes me four hours and by ten in the morning I've always got enough cash for the day. Always got enough for me and the three out of all of them that I allow myself to be with. They pitch in, sure, and it's pitiful even by our standards, but at least they always make the fucking reach and that's what counts. They're all rounders, too. That's the other thing. No one but a rounder gets squat from me, and those three have proven themselves over time and that's the fucking acid test. Time.

There's no leader. Doesn't need to be. A good fucking idea is a good fucking idea no matter who comes up with it. Now, granted

I ain't what you'd call the best at follow-the-fuckin'-leader but I know that out here, one decision, one choice, one move is all it takes to change things for a fucking hour or a fucking day and this one, well, this one fucking changed everything. I remember. We hook up at the soup kitchen around noon like we always do and I can tell right off that I'm not the only one feeling the bite of this bastard. The three of them in their handout coats still bundled up while sittin' at the table, wrapped around their coffee cups like they were pot-bellied stoves. The old lady just winks at me. Her face is all red and raw from wind.

"In-fucking-credible," I go, plopping down beside her. "So damn cold out guys are smoking just so they can get their face close to the lit end."

No one says word one, so I can tell they're worried.

"What're we gonna do?" Double Dick goes.

You gotta get a load of this guy. Double Dick Dumont. Gotta be one of the most all-time fucked-up street names I ever heard. Not because he has this huge dick or anything. No. It couldn't be that simple. You see, Dick's parents argued over his name when he was born. They both liked the name Richard. But it turns out his father, who was French, wanted his kid called in the French fashion. You know: *Ree-shard*. His mother, who was not French, wanted him called in the English way. So they fought tooth and nail. Not so much about the name itself but over how it sounded. There'd be a bottle over the head for *Richard* followed by a slap in the yap for *Ree-shard*. Well, I guess the neighbours were less than impressed and an old woman was called in to settle the issue. Her call, and this was one for the fucking ages, was to have him baptized Richard Richard Dumont. That way everyone could walk away happy. Well, everyone but Richard Richard, who, when he got to the street, was hung with the handle Double Dick. Unfortunately, so the word goes, that's about all he was hung with.

So, anyway, no one answers his question right away. Instead, we settle for looking into our coffee cups like we're expecting the solution to bob to the fucking surface and stun us with its brilliance. Turns out, it did.

"Well, you know," the old lady goes, looking at us in turn, "there's a place we could go where we could stay warm, sleep if we like, have a drink, and no one would bother us."

"Indoors?" Timber, the other one, goes. They call him Timber because you never knew when the fucking curtain's coming down on this guy. He'd drink all day and carry on like normal, give no sign of even being drunk, then stand up, take a few steps, and pass right the fuck out. Never a warning. The regulars in the old-man bar he hung out in would call out to each other every time he stood up: "Timber!" And everyone would grab their glasses and their jugs so they wouldn't lose them when he knocked their table over on his way down. He was a street drinker by now but the name followed along.

"Yes. Indoors," she goes.

"What is this place?" Dick goes, all worried-looking like he gets.

"The movies," she goes.

"The movies? They're not going to let us into the movies," Timber goes.

"No shit," I go. "Square Johns are pretty protective about their Square John hangouts and I doubt they'd let a herd of rounders into the flicks. At least not without a hassle."

"There's really no telling how long this cold is going to last, and while it does we need someplace to go where we'll be out of it," she goes. "We can't go to a mall. We can't stay here all day, and knowing how all of you need to be private, away from people, I figure there's no better place than the movies."

"Why's that?" Dick goes.

"Well, at the movies you get to sit in the dark. No one can see you. It's private that way. It's warm there and if we behave ourselves and don't get too carried away, a drink or two in a warm place like that would feel pretty good, I figure." She looks around at us and somehow I feel myself nodding in agreement. I can tell Timber's considering it too and Dick, well, Dick just eyeballs all of us waiting for someone to tell him what to do.

"Plus, you could nap there if you wanted. Or we might find that we really like watching the movie. They're not that expensive and we can all gather up enough to get ourselves in, probably enough in the mornings for two afternoon movies and a jug."

"For as long as the cold spell lasts?" I go.

"Yes."

"I haven't been to the movies in years," Timber goes. "I can't remember what the last one I saw was."

"Me neither," Dick goes.

"Well, you know, I figure if we keep our eyes peeled, we can slop back a little sauce while we're there. Hell, if we ain't loaded they can't kick us out if we're payin' and the idea of a warm, dark place to lay up for a few hours sounds damn good to me. Dark, I can't see them and they can't see me, I gotta like the sound of that," I go.

"Then it's a plan?" she goes.

"Lady," I go, "it is the plan of all fucking plans."

Timber

I ONLY EVER SEEN one cold like this one. It came on straight across snow—the wind so tight and hard it blew along parallel to the ground. You could hear it. It didn't so much scream across the flatlands as it whispered. *Pssst.* Sharp, slicing like a fingernail across silk. Many a man would tear up in the face of it. That's what I remember. Big red-faced men, their eyes glistening wetly through the slits between their scarves and toques, their breath hanging like curly white beards in the fabric. They would huff and puff for air because that cold was so deep and dense it would suck the air right out of your lungs. It was a huge, everywhere kind of cold. They called it a "monster" cold. Monster because it was huge. Monster because it was unknown and fearful. Monster because it came in at night and monster because it killed things.

The cows. That was the first sign that things weren't right. In that kind of cold you expect the stock to find shelter. Even a cow knows when the weather's gonna turn, and even a cow would get itself to the barn. But I guess that wind blew it in so quick it fooled everything. We found the first one about a half-mile out. I'll never forget it. She was standing there leaned up against a rail fence looking like an old woman waiting for a bus. She stared at everything unblinking, her eyes red, the irises dulled with death, frozen open in surprise. The others were the same. Thirty of them. Not huddled together like you'd expect but spread about all loosey-goosey, frozen into place like statues with that dull look of wonder on their iced-over faces. That was one son of a bitch of a cold.

Just like this one. I thought about that as we made our way along the street. You could feel your nostrils start to freeze. Everywhere there were people hunched over against the cold, moving in a crazy armless trot, peering through slits in scarf and hat and hood. I could hear Digger mutter a curse and Dick ahead of me huffing away in short, sharp gasps. Amelia took it all in silence.

"Shoot me your cash and I'll pick up," Digger says when we reach the liquor store.

"Vodka," I say.

"Yeah," he says, "so what else is new?"

So we get to the theatre and pause on the sidewalk. All of us feeling out of place, out of sorts, out of the predictable patterns we live. We spend a few moments eyeballing each other. Waiting, I guess. Waiting for the brave one to pull the plug on this trip and send us all back to the alleyways, lanes, and doorways that we understand. But no one says a word.

Finally, Amelia nods at us. Just nods, and we head up the steps to the big glass doors. Digger shoots me a look that says, *Keep your eyes peeled,* and Dick moves a step closer to us all. Only Amelia seems certain, unafraid. She walks to the ticket window and says, "Four for *Wings of Desire,* please." Just like that. Just like this was the kind of thing she did every day. Casual. She sounded casual, asking.

"Pardon?" the young guy in the booth asks, and I know we're scuttled.

"Four for *Wings of Desire,*" she says again.

"Are you sure?" he asks, looking the three of us over.

"Yes, I'm sure," Amelia says, still soft, still under control even though I know she knows the guy's ready to call the cops. "Four. *Wings of Desire.* I hear it's very good."

"Ah, yes it is," the young guy says, waving out the back of the booth. "I've seen it three times myself."

"Three? Well, it must be good."

"May I help you?" a briskly walking man in a red blazer asks twenty feet before he gets to us.

"Yes. Four for *Wings of Desire,* please," she says again with a little wink at Red Blazer that surprises me.

"*Wings of Desire.* Yes. It's in German, you know? You have to read the little sentences under the picture while you watch," he says, coming to a stop five feet from us, giving us the once-over.

"I'm sure we'll love it," she says, reaching into her pocket and surprising the hell out of the three of us with a roll of bills the size of a good potato. Red Blazer's eyes widen, too.

"Ah, yes, well, I'm sure you will, ma'am," he says waving at the young man in the booth to do business with us. "However, I'm not going to have any trouble from you, am I?"

"Trouble?" Amelia says with an arch of one eyebrow. "Trouble? Feel much like trouble, boys?"

We shake our heads. Wordless.

"See? Way too cold out there for any of us to want any trouble in here."

"Yes. Yes. Good. That's good. Well, I hope you enjoy the film," Red Blazer says and waves us past.

It's like a scene from a movie itself. The four of us, clearly rough and tattered, walking slowly along this dimly lit corridor, our feet kinda scuffing over the carpet that sinks beneath us. No one says nothing. I don't know about the rest but me, I'm shocked. Shocked by the sudden way the world you think you know can disappear on you. We move along this corridor where they got little signs telling you which picture's playing in which room until we get to the next to last one that reads *Wings of Desire.* Can't tell much from the sign, just a man's face on a big blue background and some kind of wings behind him. Me, I figure a good old-time war movie or even a romance about pilots. But we walk in and we just stand there looking. It's a lot smaller than the movie rooms I remember. Kinda like a big living room with a dozen rows of seats and maybe a twenty-foot screen at the front. There's no one there. Well, there's us and one other old guy, looks about sixty, sixty-five. He's all slicked up with a topcoat, hat, and a long looks-like-silk scarf. He one-times us from the corner of his eye but other than that there's no reaction.

The three of us take to eyeballing each other, waiting on Amelia to tell us where to go. My choice would be one of the back rows nearest the far wall so we can see the usher coming. Kinda hunker down over there and fade into the background. That'd be my choice. But Amelia starts down the aisle and heads right into the same row as the old guy. Me 'n Digger give each other the look and follow right after. I figure it's close enough to be in the same row as the only other guy in the theatre but Amelia slides right along and plops down two seats away from him.

"Hey, mister," she says, "cold enough for ya?"

Well, I gotta give the guy credit. He was cool. Real cool. He just sits there, gives her a small grin, goes "Ahem," and moves on over one seat. No drama, no over-the-top freak-out or nothing, just goes "Ahem" and slides over. Cool.

That would have been the end of it and harmless enough, I guess, until Amelia looks at him for a few seconds, goes "Ahem" herself, and slides over one seat too. Well, I about fell over. I figure now the heat's gonna be on us for sure. This old guy's gonna scurry off after Red Blazer himself and we'll be back in the deep freeze again lickety-split. But the guy's cool. He sits there, looks over at Amelia, looks over at the three of us standing there in the row like storefront dummies, nods once, looks at the screen, and starts playing with the buttons on his topcoat. That's it. Just fiddles with his buttons.

Amelia nods at us and we kinda fall into our seats—Dick right beside her, me in the middle, and Digger at the end closest to the aisle.

"What the fuck?" Digger whispers to me.

"I don't know," I say.

And I sit back and look around and I can feel that feeling again. I feel dreamlike. But there's no panic in it. No need to run away from this. Instead, it's like that last light over the fields on the farm. The dividing line between day and night. That time when every sound you hear, from the cows mooing in the fields to the clink of the sink through the window to the creak of the porch chair you sit in, becomes another colour in the deep blue bowl of evening. Everything, even you, all huddled up against itself like you gotta hold yourself in or you'll explode. That's how it feels and for the first time in a long time, thinking of that, I don't feel no big rush of sorrow, no big unstoppable wetness in the middle of my chest. Just okay. Just calm. And when those lights start to fade, slow and almost unnoticeable like falling into a dream, I let go, I allow myself to fall, sliding, sliding away from the monster cold beyond this place and into the soft, warm arms of the darkness.

Granite

THERE'S A SONG in every board and nail. That is what he told me, my father. On those nights of my youth when the north wind would rise off the lake behind our house to rattle bony knuckled fingers along the eaves and shutters, I would cry. And he'd come to me. He would emerge from the darkness, silently, this monolith of a man that was my father. Listen, he'd say. Listen. The wind is coaxing them free again. They live in every timber, every stone, and every nail. Your people. Your ancestors. They're with you, around you, watching over you all the time. That's what you hear, son. Lullabies. Not ghosts or goblins or witches. Just songs. The wind sets them free to sing them to you. There's a song in every board and nail in this old house and if you listen you can hear them. And he would stretch out his great length beside me trailing the faint aura of granite dust that always clung to him, and we would open ourselves up to the chorus.

In my child's mind I imagined a fabulous music that would become the lullabies and hymns that eased me into sleep. When I woke he would be gone, off well before dawn to the granite quarry where he, like my grandfather and great-grandfather, had built the life that gave me mine. And my name: Granite Harvey.

The house itself was built of the selfsame rock they quarried. Large slabs laboriously placed three storeys high. The ashen face of granite was augmented by lively rows of chert, feldspar, and gneiss, their minerals adding an unencumbered glee to the austerity of pale stone. Each piece had been carried by wagon from neighbouring fields and shoreline. Even the roof timbers, eaves, and shutters were fitted and sawn from the felled trees of the ten acres it sat upon. In this way it seemed not so much to dominate the land as become a natural part of it. For years, I truly believed it had spoken. I believed that the rocks and timbers and nails whispered to me constantly. So that nights alone, reading in front of that huge fireplace, ancestors I had never met kept me company. Now, I shake my head and stare around the empty room.

Above me I hear Mac prowling. He was always a good prowler. It was what made him a good reporter and eventually a great editor. Always able to spot the hidden detail that turned a good story into an outstanding one. Now he was likely inspecting the house in the same way.

I was busy with the fireplace flues when I heard him heading down the stairs. "Fine wood," he said, entering the room. "This whole place is built of really fine wood. Maple, oak, and just the right touches of pine and cedar in the baths. Someone really knew what they were doing, Gran. They don't build them like this anymore."

"No," I said. "Great-grandfather built things to last."

"Still, you know, there's a great place for a sauna up there and a skylight or two would brighten it. Right now, it's almost Gothic—all that *Wuthering* gloom and cold."

"Are you kidding? You should have heard the fight I had just to get the old man to put in the furnace system. He said the house would never be the same again. Said he wanted it kept the way it was."

"Nice sentiment," Mac said. "There's some people who believe that heritage should remain heritage and to alter it forces it to lose its value, its place in time. That's important to a lot of people, Gran—that one place in time that anchors them. You sure you want to sell it?"

I moved to pull across the louvred shutters that covered the twin windows on either side of the fireplace, sending the house into a final gloaming. "Let's smoke," I said. "By the lake, one last time."

He followed me out the back door and across the wide stone terrace I'd helped build as a teenager. At its far end a short set of steps led down to the scraggly patch of grass my father had steadfastly referred to as lawn. Beyond that, a pair of rough timbers and carefully placed stones became the stairs that led to the small dock at their bottom. Neither of us spoke. Mac content to gaze about at the snow-covered rocks and trees, and me lost in the dullness I'd carried for some time now.

"It's a hell of a lake, Gran," Mac said. "Great house, a dock, two hours out of the city, quiet. You ask me, at your age you couldn't swing a better deal. Most of us slave for years to get hold of half of what you have here. It's what everyone wants nearing retirement age."

"Everyone but me," I said flatly.

He turned to face me. I'd inherited the height of my father and Mac was a hand span shorter, but in all the years we'd known each other he'd had a razor in his brown eyes that cut down the difference. He honed it now as he smoked and regarded me. "All right," he said. "I know that burying your father has you feeling all morbid and lost. But death is death. It's a hard fact, sure, but you move on. You move on. Why? Because you're not the one in the ground. Talk to me! Let me in for fuck sake, Gran."

He turned, tossed his cigarette into the lake, and stared across the water. Birds. Water. Wind. Silence.

It had been thirty years. From the very beginning, on our first day of journalism school, he'd recognized me for what I was—the vague face at the edge of the crowd. One of those people who get so used to a life at the edges that they remain stranded on the limits forever. On our third day he'd sat beside me, winked, and slowly began to bring me off the sidelines. It was the inherent goodness in Mac Maude that brought him to my side, and it was the same virtue that kept him there all this time. We'd graduated together, got our first reporter's jobs together, and worked our way up on the same newspaper for twenty-six years. When he left the beat for an editor's post and I moved to writing national columns, he became my editor. Before all the awards and accolades that came my way in those next years, he had prowled my copy relentlessly, many times finding the turn of detail that altered strong phrases into memorable ones. I had trusted him. Not simply in the professional sense but as a friend as well.

"There's a song in every board and nail," I said quietly.

"What's that, Gran?" he asked, turning.

"Oh, just something my father said a long time ago."

"What's it mean?"

I looked back at the house and began to explain. Our secrets are our greatest possessions. We store them like pocket treasures, reassured by their weight, their heft, and the knowledge that though they may be smoothed by time, they bear the same stories, the same unrelenting hold, the timeless chiaroscuro they were born in. I had no knowledge of how they might alter with exposure to light.

"My father was never much of a poet. That whole boards-and-nails riff was the most poetic thing I ever heard him say. So in my childish hope, I believed him. All my life I held on to the idea that my ancestors spoke to me through everything. I never knew them, you know. When I was born I was the only son of an only son. No cousins, nieces, nephews, aunts, uncles, or even grandparents—they'd both died before I can remember them. And I wanted them. Just like every other kid at school that was surrounded by family. So the idea that mine were speaking to me became the link I needed.

"When I held my high school diploma I swear I heard them praising me. When I got accepted to J-school it was like I heard chuckles of pleasure. And when my mother died the year we graduated it was consolation pouring from the timbers. When Jenny and I spent the night together for the first time as man and wife I heard songs of celebration. And I believed, Mac, that when Caitlin was an infant and she'd cry at night, that those same voices gave her the comfort I used to get.

"That crazy childish hope held me up through everything, and if the job got to be too much I'd come here and I'd hear them tell me that I could always cope, overcome, prevail. And I always did. But when Jen and Caitlin were killed in that crash, I came home absolutely needing those voices—and I got nothing. Nothing. It was just a big empty house—and I hated it.

"When Dad died—same thing. Nada. Zippo. Zilch. So why don't I want it? Because it's still just a big, empty house."

He watched me with those deep brown eyes through the entire length of my outpouring. Smoking. He looked up at the house and studied its roofline. "And let me guess—you're leaving the paper too?" he growled.

He could always read me well. This astuteness did not surprise me. Instead, it was comforting. There's a risk that comes with being known, and its most marked form is the loss of subterfuge.

"Yes," was all I could say.

"Why?"

"Because I'm tired. I feel like the story of my life is finished."

"So what will you do?"

I turned. I'd never really had a plan, just a wish to be away. The geography of this lake was suddenly foreign. "Oh, I don't know. Inhabit someone else's stories, I suppose."

Double Dick

AT FIRST, the dyin' of the lights scared me. They went down real slow an' it was like that feelin' just before a seizure when you can feel yourself slippin' away into the darkness. I was gonna run but I'da had to climb over Digger an' he wouldn't like me much for doin' that. So I just sat there waitin' for the big black that comes, knowin' I'd end up on the floor buckin' an' sawin' away like mad an' we'd all get kicked out into the cold again. But it didn't come for me. Instead, the screen lit up in a big flash of colour an' light. Big blindin' kind of light. Then, some music. Sittin' there washed in that light an' music was amazin'. There's a word I heard one time—glorious, it was. I had to ask One For The Dead what it meant on accounta she always tells me about words an' things I can't figure out on my own, an' she said that it meant that somethin' was "jam-packed full of wonder." When she told me that I kinda knew what it meant but I never felt what it meant until right then in that theatre. Jam-packed full of wonder. Timber sat straight up in his seat starin' at the screen with his mouth hung open a little. Digger kinda scrunched down in his seat but he was glued to the screen too, squintin' real hard at it with his jaw restin' on his fist. Beside me, One For The Dead sat forward in her seat, leanin' on her elbows, not movin' at all. Wow. Sittin' there in a light that felt like warm butter an' a sound like big giant hands on me was glorious. Plum fuckin' glorious.

It was like someone dreamin' an' throwin' that dream up on the screen. There was little words to read to help you follow the story but I don't read so I just watched. I watched the faces. There was so many amazin' faces. You could see right into them if you stared hard enough. Me, I got right into that on accounta on the street you don't never get to see no faces. Not really. Rounders call people starin' at you bein' "gunned off" an' they don't like it when you do that. An' the Square Johns don't like it much neither when they see you starin' at them. But here you could stare an' stare an' stare. Seemed like there was lots of sad people in this movie an' the looks on their faces made me feel sad too. I took a big knock outta my bottle then 'cause sad always gets me goin'. It felt good. I didn't wanna be drunk, though, and that was kinda strange. I only wanted to be awake to see all this, be warm an' with my friends.

You never know when a dream is gonna end. It just ends an' when all of a sudden this one was over I wanted back in. I'd have paid again but we all trooped out to the front. Timber an' Digger started scannin' the sign an' I knew we were gonna see somethin' else. None of us was drunk. That was weird. Two hours with a bottle an' none of us was even what you'd call tipsy. We was sure warm, though, an' I looked out the front doors to see that wind sending paper an' cups an' stuff flying along. I was glad I was where I was then.

"Did you like that?" One For The Dead asked, givin' my elbow a little squeeze.

"Yeah," I said. "Couldn't read it, but I liked it anyhow."

She grinned. "That's good. Any idea what it was about?"

"You mean you don't know neither?" I asked, surprised 'cause she's so smart most times.

She laughed. "Well, I have an idea but I wondered if you had an idea of your own."

"Well," I said slowly, "it was like someone dreamin' a real sad dream about people who are real sad too."

She looked at me with a twinkle in her eye and said, "Well, that's about the best answer I think I could have ever heard."

"How come people sell their dreams?" I asked, so sudden I wondered where it came from.

She grinned again. "Well, Dick, I guess some people carry their dreams around in their heads so long it gets so they can't stand it any longer and they make it into a story so others can share that dream. In a way it sets them free to dream other dreams. Bigger ones, maybe. Happier ones, too."

"Which one we gonna see next?" I asked.

"Well, Timber and Digger are working that out right now," she said.

Digger didn't look too happy. "Aw, he won the fucking coin toss," he said when we walked over, "no two out of three or nothing. So I guess we're gonna see this one called *Big*."

"Well," Timber said, "it's got a better ring to it than *I'm Gonna Git You Sucka*."

"Least there'd be some action," Digger said, "and a fucking story. What the hell was that we just saw, anyway?"

"Someone sold a dream," I said, "to set them free."

Digger just looked at me hard for a moment. "You ain't getting none of mine, pal," he said finally, pulling his coat tighter around his bottle.

One For The Dead went an' got our tickets an' we headed on into the next movie. There was four people in this one but One For The Dead headed right down the aisle an' into the row right in front of the same guy we saw the last one with. "Hey, mister," she said, "you aren't following me by any chance, are you?"

The guy just goes, "Ahem," an' starts playin' with his buttons. The lights started to go down an' we sat, the three of us takin' big knocks from our bottles an' the guy behind us goes "Ahem" again an' I'm gone into another person's dream.

Granite

My world had become a movie house. The real world had little to offer me anymore. I'd settled into a small condo in a fashionable area, surrounded by books and music and the few things I'd saved from the stone house. I had no need of memorabilia. Home had become a base of operations, somewhere to sleep, to deploy from, and the movies had become my only destination. I saw everything. There wasn't a foot of film that didn't contain the blessing of escape. I looked for films made by those I thought had something meaningful to say as much as I chased down the fantastic, the magical, the melodramatic, and the inane. Love, family, and the warmth of human kindness were all fine to watch, as were deception, wrath, and chicanery. Story, dreams thrown up on beams of light, made it all palatable. Imaginings. A life lived vicariously now far more comprehensible than a real one. I pulled the darkness of the movie house around me and settled into its depth, eager for the light of fiction. My solitude was my defining line and I accepted it as my lot as easily as I accepted the often skewed optimism of the movies.

Wings of Desire was supposed to be a treat. Everything I'd read about it pointed to a brooding tale of redemption. When the four ragged people appeared beside me I was surprised, to say the least. Some lives have borders that we're never meant to touch. When the bent old native woman spoke to me, it was only the rigidity of manners that allowed me to speak. I could have forced myself to move away entirely but I stayed, determined, I suppose, to display class and dignity although we were the only five in the theatre. When the bottles came out, I expected it, just as I expected drunken babble that would force my moving. But they became engrossed and not a word was said between them, and when they walked out into the lobby sober afterwards I was impressed. I silently wished them well and moved on into the next cinema, thinking how unpredictable life can be and how I'd never see anything quite like it again. So when they showed up for the screening of *Big* and assumed the same positions a row in front of me, I was astonished. When the old woman greeted me again I was embarrassed by my failure to form one word. The bottles appeared again and then a silent rapture almost as they all focused on the screen.

They were a strange lot. The short one on the aisle seemed a pugnacious sort in the way he moved; short, fast movements like jabs thrown in your face. The man beside him was almost studious. Despite the toss-offs he wore and the surreptitious bottle beneath his coat, he had the squint-eyed look of J-school interns in their first week in the newsroom, overwhelmed but determined to see the workings beneath the chaotic surface. Medium height, craggy features beneath a long crewcut, he had a yardstick for a spine and a calculated regality that I sensed he struggled to maintain. Beside him, tall, stork-like, gaunt, and sickly looking, was a man impossible to age, his history tattooed on his features in crevices and marks offset by a boyish dependency on the others, told by the way he trailed clumsily behind them and stared around at them for direction. The woman was short, lean, bent a little by years with veritable walnuts for cheekbones. Long black hair framed her face beneath a thick grey wool toque. But it was the eyes that arrested me. Even in the hushed light of the cinema they seemed capable of snaring its ambiance and retransmitting it. Huge eyes, black, deep, pinched at the corners by twin sprays of wrinkles etched by a life I felt challenged to imagine. Eyes you could never slip a lie past. Obsidian, depthless eyes like those of jungle shamans, infused with equivalent degrees of clarity and mystery, shadow and light, religiosity and fervour. When they rose to leave, she turned and those eyes were aglitter with amusement. Pulling on her coat, she looked at me while I scanned the credits.

"You wanna come for a drink?" she asked.

"What?" I replied, stunned at the intrusion.

"A drink. A snort, a shot of something good."

"No," I said firmly.

"Kind of a one-word wonder, aren't you?"

"Not generally."

"Oops, careful, mister, that was two words." She grinned.

"Yes," I said, "well, I'm generally not one to talk after movies. Generally, I like to sit and think about what I've seen."

"Pretty general kind of guy," she said with a smile.

I laughed and it surprised me. "Yes, I suppose it sounds that way."

"We leavin' or what?" the short one growled from the aisle. The three of them were standing there keeping a close eye and ear on the conversation.

"In a moment, Digger," she said quietly. "How about that drink, mister?"

"I don't drink in public," I said. "Generally."

"But you drink?"

"Yes. I have a glass or two at home at night."

"Them too," she said with a nod at her friends. "Only difference is the size of the glass."

"Yes, I suppose."

"Cold out," she said. "A nice shot would warm you up for the trip home."

"No. Thank you, no."

She looked squarely at me. "Okay," she said finally. "Next time, then."

"Yes, next time," I said, standing and shrugging into my coat.

"Promise?"

"Sure," I said, pulling on my gloves and reaching out to shake her hand.

She took it gently in both of hers, looked at me and nodded. "Okay. It's a date."

She turned, walked to the aisle, and led the three men out of the cinema. I shook my head in wonder. Far from a defining encounter, it was more a random act of cosmic interference. I thought about the promise I'd made for a drink the next time. There'd be no next time. They'd likely never afford another film and the sheer number of movie houses in the city precluded another random meeting even if they could. I pulled my hat and scarf snug and headed out to flag a taxi home. In the distance, shuffling quickly around a corner, the four street people headed in the direction of whatever situation they called home. Odd, I thought, and forgot them.

One For The Dead

WE ARE PEOPLE of the dream, Grandma One Sky said. I remember that even though I was only five when she told me this, in the same year she passed on. Grandma was a storyteller and she would take me with her as she gathered roots and herbs or worked hide behind the little house on the furthest edge of Big River. She knew all the stories of our people, every legend, tale, and anecdote that made up our history. My afternoons were filled by Nanabush the trickster, Weendigo the cannibal, water people, rock people, tree people, flying skeletons, and eerie tales brought back from the solitary trips of hunters and trappers. All of them came from dreams, she'd tell me. Dream life was just as important as earth life, and if I paid attention to what I lived in dreams I could learn more about my earth walk—real life. Visions were dream life. So too were pictographs—the rock paintings on the cliffs just above the waterline up north on the river—and the design work on ceremonial wear. Once I sobered up I remembered her words, and they are where the idea about movies came from.

My boys—Digger, Timber, and Dick—were pointed out to me by dreams. Dick was the first one. I saw him running. Crashing down the street on those big feet of his with fear all over his face, and the farther he got from me the more he shrank and shrank until he became a little boy surrounded by bush and trees and rock. When I saw him at the Mission weeks later, I knew who he was. He was shy at first, more than he usually is, and sick. Trembling and nervous, he took the bottle I brought him in the park across the street gratefully, eagerly, even though I had to help him hold it to his mouth when he drank at first. It calmed him. When he lay down on the grass and slept, I watched over him, hiding the bottle in my coat. Later, I let him have the rest and made a run to the Mission for a cup of soup and a sandwich. He was really just a little boy, worn and tired and far from home. We spent that first night together by a fire in a hobo jungle in the woods beside an expressway and I told him stories till he slept. We've been together ever since.

Timber was next. In my dream I saw him at a desk in a library in a kind of light that reminded me of a chapel. He was bent over, reading something that he held in trembling hands before laying it on the desk and walking out the door. In the dream I walked over to the desk and found a photograph of him and a woman and then I was behind him on the street where he walked and walked and walked. While Dick would always attach himself to the edge of a crowd, Timber stayed away from groups, and when I first saw him he sat in a corner of the park drinking alone, tossing pieces of bread to pigeons and squirrels. Dick and I sat a few yards away and watched him. He felt so heavy even across that space. When we walked over to share Dick's bottle it was the need of liquor that kept him there more than the welcome of company. We met like that for a week before he'd tell us his name or say much of anything at all. Once he realized we were not intent on dragging him out of himself and that I could be trusted for bottle runs, he started to talk to us. Not much at first, a few words here and there, but eventually he spoke. He told Dick about pigeons and squirrels and I knew that he'd spent a lot of time with books, and when I shared a few stories from Ojibway culture about birds and animals he listened with half a grin, nodding and flipping bread at the creatures around us. And we were three.

The toughest was Digger. He'd been around as long as me so we knew each other by reputation. Digger was a fighter, strong and mean with drink. A rounder's rounder, Digger stood by the code of the street through anything. Everyone was afraid of him and his unpredictable turns of anger. But in my dream I saw him building something upward into the sky. Something huge and metallic, something he handled with love, gently, with an assurance that spoke of a long familiarity. He was a dumpster diver, a digger for cans, bottles, and toss-offs, and he acted like it made him an aristocrat among the beggars and panhandlers. He bought a lot of company with the money his scavenging provided and he revelled in the control that the fear he created allowed him. When the three of us first approached him he chased us off with drunken rage, calling Dick an idiot, Timber a pussy, and me a nosy whore. The boys wanted to leave him alone but I knew the strength of dreams and was determined to pay attention to mine. He was tough. When we shared a bottle with him he'd guzzle his share and stomp off with a muttered "thanks" and that would be it. I bought him a new coat when winter came and he just looked at me hard for a moment or two.

"What do ya want for it?" he growled at me.

"Nothing," I said.

"Nothing?"

"No. Not a thing."

He took it. "Nothin's always something," he said and walked away.

It took us all that winter to get him to join us. By spring I knew that he'd been testing us, giving us every rounder ritual to prove we were worth his time. Just when we reached that point, we never knew. He was just suddenly there and never left. Surly, growly, raging, he became our protector, masking the concern he had for all of us behind the staunch front he held against the world. I knew, and I believe that he knew that I knew, but nothing was ever said between us. He appreciated that just as he appreciated the way we let him be the way he was. Timber and Dick grew used to his ways and a quiet, risk-free humour grew among them. We were four, as close to a definition of family as any of us had ever reached. The street prevents that mostly, but we were bonded by the power of dreams and the shadowed ones all about us. And it was the shadowed ones who bought us Granite. They surrounded him too that day in the movie house, and it was like they waved to me.

Timber

THAT BLOW SETTLED IN for a week. It was like it lay over top of the city and dug its fingers in all around it. Didn't move. Lay there blowing its deep-freeze breath over everything, and I guess people learned how to cope. Least ways, most of them did. There were more deaths, more street people who made the wrong choice at the wrong time and paid the price for it, but mostly people coped. We never missed a day at the movies. Dick and me worked a corner for change every day and it seemed like those people knew we were as cold as them and it wasn't hard to get a pocketful of dollars by the time we all got together at the Mission each day. When we didn't have enough, Amelia always threw in from the bundle we had seen that first day.

"So that's a healthy little roll you carry around," I said. "How did you manage to get hold of that? Been sneaking off to pull a few robberies, have ya?"

She grinned. "No, these are my tips."

"Tips?"

"Yes. Over the years I've been tipped for the runs I made for people. Nickel here, a dime there. It adds up."

"You mean to say you saved that money?"

"Well, yes. I had nothing to spend it on and I knew there'd come a day when it was gonna come in handy."

"You never spent any of it?"

"Oh, sure," she said. "Every now and then there'd be an emergency. Someone'd need socks or shoes, someone'd be really sick and need a bottle. Those kinds of things. But mostly I just held on to it."

"Let me get this straight," I said. "All these years, all the winos you ever made a run for tipped you for the run and you just put it in your pocket for a rainy day?"

"Yes," she said. "That's the big secret."

"Why?"

"Why?"

"Yes."

"Well," she said, "I guess there was a part of me that knew that somewhere, sometime this money would come in more handy than it would have if I was going to spend it on something at the time. And there was nothing that I needed."

"Nothing that you needed? Look around you. There had to have been something?" I asked.

"No," she said slowly and looked at me kindly. "There wasn't."

She was always a straight shooter, and hard as it might be for me to believe that any one of us with a mittful of loot wasn't going to spend it on whatever, wherever, I gave her the benefit of my doubt. Still, it bugged the bejesus out of me.

"Not even the smallest kinda thing?" I asked finally.

She laughed then—a laugh like the tinkle of wind chimes. "Well, sometimes I'd think of something, a scarf maybe, some kind of thing that a girl would like and maybe I'd let myself think about how nice that might be. But I got over it."

"Got over it?"

"Yes. See, Timber, money's got nothing to do with my life one way or the other. I choose to be here. I choose to live the way I live. I don't know how to be any other way than street. Tried it years ago but it just didn't take. I guess it's how it's supposed to go for me and I don't have an argument with it. This is my life—and money, well, money won't make any difference. Ever."

"No room even, get off the bricks?"

"No. Me 'n walls parted company a long time ago. You know how that is."

"Yeah. I know. But wouldn't it have made things easier for you?"

"Easier how?" she asked. "I don't smoke. I don't drink anymore. I don't need to ride the buses because there's no place for me to be at any particular time. And besides, it's not enough. It's a few dollars, that's all."

"But it's a roll!"

She laughed again. "Yes, it's a roll. But it's a roll of ones. I think there's a twenty or two in there somewhere, maybe three."

"Still."

"Still, what?"

"Still . . . I don't know."

So we settled into the movies. It was the feel of the place that got to me. Sure, the lights and the sound and the story were amazing after so long in a life where there ain't no light and it's just one long bleak tale, but the feel of it always made me wanna get back. Expectation. That's the word I'm looking for. It's all about expectation. From the time we picked which show we'd see during the walk in the cold to the paying for tickets, which got easier once we'd been a few times, to the stroll through the lobby, into the theatre, into our seats, to the settling in before the lights began to fade, I don't think I even really breathed. Only then, only when those lights slid off did I allow myself to exhale. Only then. Then it was like the sound and light filled me, like I was hollow up till then—and I guess I was. Junkies know that feeling real good. Junkies know the rush, the flow of juice to the brain and then the smooth roll of comfort through the body that tells them that for this one moment in time, this one instant, everything's got a chance to be okay, even for a little while. And they roll with it. So did I.

But what goes up must come down. Junkies know that, too. When the movie ended and the lights came back up and the sound was just a fading tremor against my skin, I always crashed, always fell back to earth again and always found it the same as I had left it. Grey. Cold. Hollow. Now though, for the first time in longer than I can remember, there was a chance for something different in my days. Not enough to make it all go away. Not enough to change everything. But enough to make it seem like I could take it one more time. Like I could carry on. Like a dodge. Like escape. Like a drug. The movies became my fix, my need, and I couldn't fucking wait for another one.

Granite

THE ONLY HEIRLOOM I kept was the story chair. My dad's chair. The one he read from when I was still small enough to fit in his lap and later the one we fought over to read in front of that huge old fireplace each evening. A big overstuffed leather chair with a welcoming depth that seemed to draw stories out and pull you in at the same time. I don't know why it mattered that I keep it, only that it seemed right, only that it felt right to sit in it. Now it was the viewing chair. I invested in the biggest television I could find, a video player and home theatre system to enjoy the movies I began collecting. Browsing through the video collector books I'd purchased led me to fantastic films I'd never heard of and to slick and memorable Hollywood movies I'd either bypassed or ignored. It hadn't taken long to fill a few shelves with titles I would watch over and over. I would gather the night around me and disappear into the chair and the world of the movies.

I'd missed the education that film provides. For the three decades I'd been a journalist, film had been something you fled to on those evenings when the pace of work required escape. It hadn't been elevated to a haven, as it was now, and I wondered how I'd managed to miss the point of it all. The point being, of course, that film is rapture. Film is romantic education. The romance of the senses. It could sweep me away, and I let it.

Cinema Paradiso appeared to be one of those films. Based on what I had read, it pointed to a tale about denizens of a film house who retreated into the romantic whirl of story to elude the mundane, banal, and humdrum course of ordinary existence. The decades it revealed were the war years in Italy, a time of great tumult when loss was the common currency of being. That, I believed, was something I would have no trouble relating to.

The evening promised to be a fine one. The arctic front that had made news across the continent had dissipated and been replaced by an ironic belt of warm southern air that melted the snow and ice, driving the city into an artificial springtime glee. I'd seldom taken the time to actually view my neighbourhood, and on this night it seemed inordinately alive.

The theatre was called The Plaza and it was famed for its eclectic choice of fare. A heritage building, its owners had been careful to preserve the ornate fixtures of its 1920s decor. I had been there often and loved the charming ambience of its subtle art nouveau interior. Movies at The Plaza were a reconnection to the febrile heart of filmdom, and in its air was the very breath of DeMille, Capra, Fellini, and Truffault.

There was a considerable line when I walked up. I stood there in the hushed light of evening and began the lifelong habit of observing the people I shared space with. They were, for the most part, a typical upscale neighbourhood collection of sorts: old-money college students, artistes, former radicals turned realtors, and moneyed elitists bent on maintaining a fey proletarian contact.

The first indication that things were out of kilter was a heightened buzz in the conversation around me. I'd busied myself studying the architecture of the nearby buildings but brought my gaze to earth at the sudden tone of apprehension. The focus of attention was the four street people I'd met a few weeks prior. They were approaching slowly, heads down, eyes cast warily about. They seemed the epitome of the street urchin to such a degree that standing there I imagined myself in a scene from Dickens. All of them, with the exception of the old native woman, seemed perched on the edge of fight or flight. She was merely curious, looking about her and taking in the sights of this neighbourhood in much the same way I had on my stroll to the theatre. The closer they got to the lineup in front of The Plaza the more audible became the confusion of my compatriots.

"Goodness," exclaimed a pert young woman in a fur coat behind me, "they must be lost. We don't get them in this area, especially at night."

"Well, we've got them now," her companion said. "Hopefully they don't put the touch on any of us. I'll be damned if I'm being hit up for change tonight."

"Poor woman," a rail-thin, hawk-nosed woman said. "I hope she's safe with those three."

"You don't think they could be heading over here do you?" asked a pretty young red-headed woman.

"Here? This is The Plaza, not the Union Mission. What would they want here?" her bespectacled friend replied, slipping a protective arm around her waist.

"Coming to the movies, I suspect," I said, surprised at the blurt as much as those close to me who heard it.

There were polite guffaws and chuckles that melted away into stunned silence as the four of them approached the line and surreptitiously joined it.

"Hey, mister! Hey, hey, mister!" I heard suddenly.

Everyone began looking about in something close to panic as the old native woman pleaded for attention from the back of the line. I could feel people pulling themselves inward, downshifting from judgment into a pretended ignorance and sudden deafness.

"Hey, I thought it was you," she said, approaching me and extending a hand rough and raw from wind and chill. "You remember me, don't you?"

I glanced about in embarrassment and then reached out to shake her hand. "Yes," I said, "I remember. How have you been?"

"Good. Me 'n the boys, we've been good. Been to quite a few movies since that cold spell," she said and smiled.

"Yes, it would seem a good place to go for warmth, I suppose."

"Well, it kinda started out that way but the more we went the more the boys seemed to enjoy it. Now, I guess, we're hooked," she said with a wink.

"It's a good thing to be hooked on," I replied, scanning the crowd.

"Better'n some things."

"Yes. Yes."

"So will you save us some seats?"

"Pardon me?"

She grinned. "Could you save us some seats? Something near the middle? We'd appreciate it."

Faces were turned toward us all along the line. I could feel myself getting warmer. "Yes. I'd be happy to. Something near the middle."

"With you," she said.

"With me?"

"Well, yes. We got a date, remember?"

I heard a few guffaws.

"Surely you don't think . . ." I began.

"Wait a minute now," she replied, with one hand held up palm forward. "A promise is a promise. You said the next time we met at the movies we were gonna go for a drink. Right?"

Snickers now. I could see grins on people's faces. "Yes, well, I never meant it seriously."

"How'd you mean it then? As a joke? You were joking with me? Playing with my affections?"

I could see that people were really beginning to enjoy this.

"No. I was not playing with your affections. I was merely being polite."

"Oh, yeah? Polite in your world means lying to people?" She winked at me again.

"Look here," I said sternly, "I was not lying, I was merely applying a deflection, an off-the-cuff, inconsequential politeness. I didn't mean anything by it."

"In the habit of not meaning what you say to women. Bit of a player, are you?" I could hear open laughter around us now. "I've been around, mister, so this isn't what you might call an out-of-the-world experience for me. I've been dumped by pros."

It was my turn to laugh.

"You're right, of course," I said. "Only, let's talk about this later."

"Later?"

"Well, after the film."

"So you'll save us seats?"

"Yes. I'll save you seats."

"With you?"

"Ahem," I said, scratching at my lapel and glancing around. "Yes. Of course."

"Good. Well, we'll see ya in there."

"Fine." I watched her walk back to her friends. Digger leaned out from the pack and glared at me.

One For The Dead

SOME STORIES become your blood. They move beyond the telling or the showing and come to rest inside you. Invade you. Inhabit you. Like there was a secret crevice in your being that it took the tale to fill. That's what that movie was like. *Cinema Paradiso.* I liked how it sounded. A movie about heaven. Or, at least, that's how it sounded to me. And there's always a part of you that knows about the big somethings long before they happen in your world. Always. For me, that night, it was the colour of the night itself. The cold had cleared and left behind it a freshness like the kind we'd get in Big River after a good, hard, cleansing rain. Like the earth was declaring itself one more time, saying, *I am. I am. I am.* I always liked that feeling, and that night while walking to the theatre there was a feeling to the air that made it seem like a colour: a blue kind of colour, all steel and shadow, water and woe, all at the same time. Walking through it, I could tell that this was a night to remember.

The boys couldn't feel it. Each of them was having a hard enough time keeping their feet moving in the direction we were heading. This was a difficult neighbourhood. This was a far step beyond where we normally went. This was one of those areas of the city that shone and glittered everywhere. For those boys it was stepping out of shadow and being seen, and none of them liked it much. But for me it was following a beacon. It was the pull of some strange magnetic force like yearning or coming home or love even, and while that scared me some, it thrilled me too and I walked lighter than I had for years. There were no shadowed ones here, or at least they had no need to tell me of their presence that night.

Seeing the Square John in that line made it perfect. I'd wondered when we'd be thrown together again. Talking with him, teasing a little, joking was easy, and I liked his discomfort. It made him more real.

"Friggin' can't get away from that guy," Digger said on our way into the theatre.

"Well, since we'll be sitting with him, I guess we shouldn't try to get away," I replied.

"You have got to be fucking kidding. Sitting with him. Us?"

"Yes. He's saving us seats."

"Jesus."

I grinned. Timber and Dick just watched me, waiting for their cue to move, eager to be out of the hustle of the lobby and into the dim security of the theatre. We'd made it just in time. There were no seats remaining, or at least not four together. I picked out Granite's triangular hat easily enough and we moved down the aisle toward his row. The boys followed close behind me, none of them looking up at all, and if they could have run to their seats I believe they would have. This was the biggest crowd any of us had been in by choice for years, and all of us wanted the shelter that a seat provides.

"Ah," I said, easing into the seat beside Granite, who nodded at our arrival, "this is the life, eh, mister? Long night at the movies, in the company of your peers."

"Ahem," he said, one hand edging toward his buttons. "Yes. It's fine to be with others who appreciate fine film."

"Like us." I nudged his elbow. "Me and the boys."

"Yes. The boys."

The boys were all taking huge nervous gulps from the bottles in their pockets at that moment, and he watched them from the corner of his eye. Then the lights began to fade and everyone settled deeper into their seats.

As I said, some stories become your blood. As I watched this movie about a man who comes home for the first time in thirty years and finds an incredible gift from an old man he left behind, I felt it enter me with each frame. Here, in one place, was a story about falling in love with the movies, about shelter, about friendship, loss, and love itself. Here was a film about crying in the darkness. About seeing what you crave the most sometimes thrown up on the screen in front of you and recognizing it for the hole within you that it is. About faces, characters, and time—time passing, time stopping, and time reclaimed. It was wondrous. I couldn't stop staring. I couldn't sit back in my seat at all. Throughout the entire spectacle I sat leaning forward, elbows on my knees, chin cupped in my palms, crying sometimes, sighing, watching, feeling the blood moving in my veins, drinking it in, becoming it, feeling it becoming me. Invaded. Inhabited. Known.

When it ended in a long series of captured kisses and the bright flare of romance, I felt alive. None of us moved. The five of us sat there in our seats staring at the screen and watching the Italian credits roll, lost in our thoughts. When the screen went blank I still could not move. Only Digger got us into motion again with a "Fuck" that was one part whisper, one part sigh, and one part the need for a drink.

We walked out in silence.

Double Dick

ME, I WANTED TO CRY. Just wanted to run off into an alley somewhere an' ball my eyes out. Don't know why on accounta sometimes what's going on inside me gets past my head. But I wanted to cry. I couldn't follow the story on accounta you had to read again but I knew what was goin' on. It was about bein' in love with the movies. At least that's how it started. Then it kinda got to be about rooms. Rooms you live in an' learn inside out. Rooms you sit in all alone an' quiet. Rooms you leave, all sad an' alone an' hurtin'. An' in the end it was about rooms you come back to sometimes if you're lucky, an' I guess that's what made me so sad on accounta I can't never go back no matter how lucky I ever get. Me'n rooms is done. That's how come I live outside. On accounta one room always looks the same as that one room I can't never go back to. The one room I carry around inside me. The one room where my heart made big moves one time—big, sad moves. That Cinema Paradise movie reminded me of everythin' an' I wanted to cry about it all for the first time in a long time. Cry an' cry an' cry. But I didn't.

"Drink, pal?" Digger asked, like he knew what I was feelin'. The others were using the washrooms an' we stood outside waitin'.

"Yeah," I said, tryin' hard not to look at him.

"S'matter?" he asked, starin' hard at me.

"Tired, I guess. Too much work tryin' to read what was goin' on."

"Yeah. I know. Friggin' good story, though."

"You think so?" I was glad he was gettin' me away from my feelings an' glad that he was sharin' his rum with me.

"Yeah. Little on the weird side, but it was okay."

"Digger? You ever think maybe someone else knows what's goin' on inside your head sometimes. Someone you never met?"

He squinted at me while he took a big knock. Then he wiped his mouth with the back of one hand an' rooted around in his pockets for a smoke. "My head? Nah. I can't figure out what the fuck's going on there most of the time. Why?"

"Guess that movie made me wonder if other people know stuff. Like where you been. What you done. What you was feelin' sometimes. Stuff like that?"

"This movie got you all rattled up inside, eh?"

"Yeah. Made me think about what I don't wanna be thinkin' about no more."

"Me too, I guess," he said.

It felt good knowin' that someone like Digger could feel like I did. I was thinkin' about that when One For The Dead an' Timber walked out of the washroom doors.

"Well, that was certainly a good one, wasn't it?" she asked, squeezin' my elbow when she reached me.

"Yeah," I said, lookin' at Digger. "What are we gonna do now?"

"Well, I think we have an agreement with our seat-saver," she said.

"Agreement?" I asked.

"Fuck sakes," Digger said. "You're kidding, right?"

"No," she said an' nodded toward the doors where the man was just comin' out.

He was bigger than I thought. Sittin' in the movies he looked like Digger's size, but he was a big guy. Tall as me but bigger: wider, thicker. Like a worker kind of guy, an' when he reached out to shake One For The Dead's hand, his was so big it made hers almost disappear. Big guy.

"Well," he said, kinda lookin' around at us, the street, everythin' all at one time.

"Well," she said back. "How'd you like that, mister?"

"The movie?"

"Yes."

"The movie was fine," he said. "Very, very fine."

"Fine?" She looked at him an' then at the three of us with that arched eyebrow that always told me she was gonna have some fun with one of us. "Fine like what?"

"Well," he said kinda slow, playin' with the buttons on his coat. "Fine like . . . like, like . . . you know, I don't know."

He laughed then. Shy kinda laugh like how I laugh sometimes on accounta I kinda know where I wanna go in my head but I can't get there. The four of us all look at each other an' I felt funny.

"Well, why don't you think about it while we're walkin'," One For The Dead tells him.

"Fer fuck sake," Digger said. "We ain't gonna go through with this shit, are we? Where the fuck am I gonna go with some Square John? Tell me that, will you?"

The guy just looks at him like I look at people now an' again on accounta I'm mystified. I asked Digger one time what that word meant an' he told me it meant "buggered all to hell," so I figure he was mystified.

"I think we should go somewhere where we can all be comfortable," One For The Dead said.

"The Palace," Digger said.

"The Palace? Downtown?"

"Well, where the fuck else do you think I'd go? This frickin' neck of the woods?" Digger asked all hard.

"I know where the Palace is," the guy said. "It's a little out of my comfort zone, though."

"Well, no shit, Sherlock," Digger said, lightin' a smoke.

"It seems like a good idea," One For The Dead said. "You know, mister, we're not exactly the indoor type of people. Going to the movies is something we started to do because of the cold. We like it out where there aren't any walls, so I guess that would be a little out of our comfort zone too."

"Well, let's just do it then," he said. "So I can get on with my evening."

"Yeah," Digger said, "wouldn't want to hold you back."

They looked at each other for a moment an' I felt that funny feelin' in my belly. I gotta give the guy credit, though. I ain't seen many people get away with gunnin' Digger off an' he held that look for a good long time.

Timber

"Fine like rain sometimes," he said.

We were all seated around a table at the Palace, something I found to be unbe-fucking-lievable in the first place, and then this guy, this Square John guy, comes out with an unbelievable description that I could see in my head as soon as he said it. Fine like rain sometimes. When we all just stared at him, he went on.

"There's days when the colour and the light of things are perfect for how you feel," he said. "Or at least you think so. Grey days. You look out your window and you stand there feeling like there's no separation between how you feel between the ribs and the shade of the day in front of you."

"Monochrome," I said.

He looked at me for a moment and I saw his puzzlement. "Yes. One cold, flat, ache of colour that's not really sadness, not really regret, not really sorrow but maybe a shade or two of them all."

"Yearning," I said quietly, and he nodded.

"Yes. All you know is that the day, the day that's all around you, is inside you too, and you think that it's a perfect fit. But you go outside and you walk in your woe. You take it to the streets or the fields or wherever and you walk in it. And then it rains. Not a real rain. Not a downpour or even a shower. A mist. A thin sheen of rain that doesn't really hit your skin so much as it passes over it."

Like a hand, he said, and I knew what he meant.

"That's how that movie felt," he said. "Fine. Fine like the rain sometimes."

I don't know about the rest but I just sat there looking at my hands. Feeling those words and feeling like that movie had moved me beyond where I was too.

Amelia raised her head and looked around the table at each of us. Then, she reached over and patted the guy's hands that were folded on the table just like mine. "That's a beautiful description," she said. "I guess I know what fine is now."

The guy took a sip from the whisky he'd ordered.

"I know what that means too," I said.

Everyone looked at me, as surprised at my willingness to talk as much as I was. I swallowed some beer and went on.

"When I was a boy I used to stand at a window just like you were saying," I said. "It was a farmhouse and the window looked over the forty acres that kinda flowed down to where a railway track ran across at the bottom of the hill. I used to wait for the morning train and try 'n guess where it was going, who was on it, all those kinda kid games you play.

"And something about the train moving through the fog and the mist at the end of those forty acres used to really get me somehow. Made me want to cry. I don't know why. It just did. So when you talk about the rain like that, I know how that feels."

He nodded.

"The movie took you back to that window, Timber?" Amelia asked.

"Yeah, I guess it did."

"How about you, Digger? Did it make you feel fine?" she asked.

Digger swallowed all of his draft in one long gulp.

"Look," he said, wiping at the corner of his mouth with the back of his hand, "what I think is what I fucking think, and I don't share that with anybody. Ever."

"Come on, Digger," she said, "all I want to know is if you can tell me what fine means to you."

"That's it?"

"That's all."

"No scooting around in my head, trying to get me to talk about shit I don't wanna talk about?"

"No."

He waved for another beer. "Okay. Okay. Well, here then. Fine is like that half-empty bottle of brandy I found that time. Remember, Timber?"

"Yeah," I said. "I remember."

"Fucking thing had a name we couldn't even pronounce. Got a couple bucks for the empty, too. Anyway, strangely enough it was raining that day and we were all cold and wet and miserable. We were in the alley back of the fucking Mission and man, that fucking stuff slid down my throat and into my belly like fucking sunshine. Now that was fine. And after a few swallows it changed the fucking colour and the light of things for me too, guy," he said, staring at the Square John and swallowing the new draft as soon as it landed.

"Fine's like Sunday brunch at the Sally Ann," Dick said suddenly.

We all looked at him and he took a nervous gulp of his draft.

"Like you gotta go to chapel first 'fore they'll feed you. Most people don't like that an' kinda sit there all pissed off, but me, I like it on accounta it's different. I like the songs. Especially the one about gatherin' at the river. I like that one. But after, when you all move downstairs an' line up for food an' you gotta wait even though you're hungry as hell an' everyone's bitchy, it gets all antsy for me. Then, I get my tray an' pick up my food an' find a seat an' take that first mouthful. Man, that's fine. All that waitin' just to get to that first mouthful."

He finished his beer off and stared at his feet.

"That sounds pretty fine to me," Amelia said.

"Me too," the Square John said. "What about you?"

She looked at him squarely. "This."

"Pardon?"

"This. This is fine," she said.

"What?"

"This. Us. All of us, sitting here together talking. It's fine. Very fine," she said. "Except that we don't know who we're talking to. We don't even know your name."

"That's right. Well, excuse me," he said, sitting straighter. "My name is Granite. Granite Harvey."

He reached out and shook her hand.

"Granite?" Digger asked, squinting. "Like the frickin' rock granite?"

He grinned. "Yes. Like the frickin' rock granite."

"Well, fuck me," Digger said and reached over to finish off my draft.

"Odd name," I said, nodding at Digger.

"I suppose it is," he said. "My father named me after the rock. My family has been stonemasons for generations. Quarrymen. And granite is how they made their living."

"It's a good name. A strong name," Amelia said. "I'm pleased to meet you, Granite Harvey."

"Pleased to meet you, too, whoever you are," Granite said.

Amelia chuckled. "Let's start with the boys and then we'll get to me," she said. "This is Timber. That's what he's called at least and that's how we know him. The tall one beside him is Dick and, of course, you know that this is Digger."

The three of us sat there not knowing how to move. Granite stood up slowly, reached over the table to Dick, and shook his hand solemnly.

"Dick," he said. "A pleasure."

"Sure," Dick said shyly.

"Timber," Granite said, "glad to meet you."

I shook his hand. It was a warm, soft hand. "Granite," I said.

When he reached over, Digger just stared at the outstretched hand. Then he raised his head and looked squarely at Granite for a moment. "So what're you gonna say to me? Great to meet you? Glad to make your fucking acquaintance? Let's buddy up? I'm your wingman, pal? Fuck."

To his credit, Granite stood there with his hand held out toward Digger. He never moved and never stopped looking right at him while he spoke. Digger stood up and looked across the table at him, finally. The two of them matched looks for what seemed like forever.

"Digger," Granite said finally, "meeting you is like trying to pet a cornered tomcat."

"Fuck's that mean?"

The two sat slowly at the same time. Granite took a sip of his whisky but never took his eyes off Digger, who stared hard across the table.

"Well, when I was kid, our neighbours had a barn and there was always a whole slew of kittens around each spring. But every now and then there'd be a tomcat on the prowl that'd come along and kill the kittens. Trying to protect his territory, I suppose. Anyway, everyone wanted to kill him. But me, well, somehow I got it into my head that all that was really needed was for someone to show that cat some attention and maybe he'd quit killing kittens.

"So I waited. One day, I walked into the barn and that cat was sitting on a beam looking down at me, just like you are now, all far away and cold. When I saw that look I thought, Maybe I'm wrong. Maybe this cat really is a mean son of a bitch and I should stay away. Maybe he is a killer at heart.

"But you know, Digger, something in me understood that there was something in this that I didn't understand, the learning of which could change everything. Now, I can't explain that. I just knew. So, inch by inch, as slowly as possible, I moved toward that cat. He just watched me. Just sat looking at me in that cold, scrutinizing way. Finally, I got close enough to touch him."

Granite waved at the waiter and signalled for another round.

"So? What happened?" Digger asked, frowning.

"Well, the son of a bitch scratched me. Leaped onto my chest and tore the bloody hell out of my jacket and scratched my hands and neck. Then he jumped off and ran away. Never saw him again."

"And?" Digger asked, moving slightly so a fresh draft could be dropped in front of him.

"And? And what?"

"And . . . what was it you learned that could change everything? And, by the way, change what everything?"

Granite chuckled and sipped the last of his first whisky. "Well, I learned that life is risk. I learned that the only way I was ever going to know, discover, find out, learn, was to reach out—especially to the scary things. And what it changed was how I approached my life."

"How fucking fascinating," Digger said and swallowed half his drink. "But what in the name of fuck does that have to do with meeting me?"

"Well," Granite said, looking right into Digger's eyes, "I also learned that life is full of mean sons of bitches, and you can reach out all you want but the bastards will still try to scratch the hell out of you. Meeting you has been a reminder of that."

Digger just looked at him. Then, slowly, he nodded and a grin appeared on his face. "I like that," he said and reached his hand across the table. "Just so long as you know."

Granite shook his hand firmly. "Long as I know."

"Well," Amelia said. "That was fun. Anyway, Granite, my name is Amelia One Sky and I am happy to meet you."

They shook hands wordlessly. We all sat there silently, looking at each other, and if they were like me right then, they were all shopping for something to say to lead us somewhere, anywhere but the deep silence we found ourselves in. The four of us men took turns sipping or gulping from our drinks while Amelia sat there with a small smile on her face, watching us watch each other.

"So what're we gonna see next?" Dick said, and we all laughed like hell.

Digger

So we're sitting there, me and the Square John, after everyone else had split, not really saying much, just eyeballing the bar and drinking. Me, I'm there because I wanna drink and him, well, I kinda think there was something in the way that old-man bar felt that he liked. You can pull aloneness around you like an old coat sometimes and the Palace was full of coat-wearing motherfuckers. Looking at him that night I got the feeling that Mr. Granite Harvey wasn't exactly having your typical urban pleasure trip through life and living. I liked that, really. Made him seem more real, more like me than I ever mighta figured.

"So Timber's kind of an odd name," he goes after a while.

"Yeah," I go. "It kinda is."

"That's not his real name, is it?" he goes.

"No. It's not. It's a street name. We all got 'em. At least those of us that've been around long enough, anyways."

"So what does Timber mean?"

"Means look the fuck out." I swallow my draft and give him the short version of the story.

"And Dick? That's obviously his real name."

"There ain't nothing fucking obvious on the street," I go, and tell him about Double Dick Dumont and how he got his handle. Granite sat there looking at me wide-eyed, smiling and laughing finally.

"Wow," he goes. "That's a story all right. What about Amelia?"

"One For The Dead," I go and wave at the bar.

"What do you mean?"

"Probably the most well-known street name out there. Everybody knows the old lady."

"Where did it come from?"

The fresh brew arrived and I looked at it. "From this," I go, and pour a little slop of beer on the carpet. For a minute or so I explain about the old rounders and their rituals and how the old lady came to get her handle. All through it Granite squints at me, taking it all in and still not touching the drink at his elbow. That bothered the hell out of me.

"Are you gonna drink that fucking thing or not?"

"Oh, yes," he goes, and swallows half of it. "What about you?"

"Me? Well, I'm a digger so that's what they call me."

"What do you mean?"

"I mean," I go, feeling the numb, no-fucking-forehead feeling of a good drunk coming on, "that I dig around for stuff. Dumpsters, alleys, anywhere people toss shit off, and I sell what I can. Metal, cans, old magazines, curtains, fucking toys, it's amazing what Square Johns'll throw away. S'okay though. Makes me money. S'all I care."

He nods.

"So you don't panhandle?"

"Fuck no. I don't ask nobody for nothin'."

"That's good," he goes.

"Fucking rights that's good," I go. "Out there you got your word and you got your fuckin' pride and thass all yuh really got."

"I suppose."

I look at him, half closing one eye so I can focus better. "Fuck you doin' here, man?" I go finally.

"I don't know," he goes. "I really don't know, except maybe being polite."

"P'lite? You be p'lite in Roxborough, wherever the fuck yuh live. We doan need yer p'liteness down here. Fact, yuh can shove it."

"Sorry," he goes, finishing his drink. "I only meant that I wanted to be polite to Amelia. I guess, in a way, I promised her I'd come along."

"She doan need yer p'liteness either."

"No. I suppose not. Well, I should be going."

"Go, then."

"Yes," he goes, standing and reaching a hand out to me.

I shake it limply, not looking at him at all, and he turns and starts walking away.

"Hey, Granite," I go suddenly.

"Yes?"

"If we see yuh at the flicks, s'okay if you sit with us."

He grins. "Okay. It's okay if you sit with me too."

"But don't go thinkin' we're fuckin' wingers all of a sudden."

And he's gone. I sit there a while longer feeling myself pull that coat of aloneness snug around my shoulders, finger the twenty Granite left sitting on the table, pocket it, and head off to my digs.

One For The Dead

THE SHADOWED ONES brought us *Rain Man*. I remember it well. It was a drizzly day as we sat in the Mission going through the newspaper ads while outside the first early thaw was on in full force. The boys were all in a fine mood, mostly because the nights were becoming easier to bear, and even though all of us had places where we were warm enough, sheltered enough, and tucked away enough to be comfortable, the suggestion of an end to winter was welcome. We'd been to movies every day since that cold snap and we'd grown to know what we liked. Digger would always choose the noisy, busy kind of films, especially if they involved some degree of mayhem. Timber seemed drawn to the reflective, people-driven sorts of movies that allowed you a peek at the motions of someone's life. Dick, well, Dick loved everything.

He was enthralled by every film we saw and never failed to display a spirited, childlike anticipation when it came to choosing a movie. And me, well, I have to confess that I liked them all too, but maybe leaned more in favour of those types of stories that reached inside of you, touched something that you hadn't touched for a long time, and reminded you of the soft moments where you really came to be who you are. We'd seen comedies, westerns, horror, fantasy, science fiction, romance, family dramas, and hero-driven action movies. By the time that day rolled around, we had become what Digger called "movie junkies."

"Could we see this one?" Dick asked.

"What one?" Digger replied, looking worried.

"This one here," Dick said, laying the paper on the table and pointing a finger at an ad in the bottom corner of the page.

"*Rain Man?*" Digger said. "It's fucking pouring outside and you wanna see something about rain? Don't you wanna see something that makes you forget that it's raining?"

"But it's not about rain," Dick said.

"The name says *Rain Man*. How the frig could it be about anything else but fucking rain?" Digger asked.

"It's about the man," Dick said.

"What friggin' man?"

"The man who lives in the rain."

"Geez, will one of you help me with this guy?" Digger asked, looking at Timber and me for help.

"What do you mean about the man who lives in the rain, honey?" I asked Dick.

He looked at me with confusion in his eyes. Scared. Frightened at the prospect of chasing the thought until he caught it. "I don't know. But you know sometimes how walkin' all by yourself in the rain kinda makes you feel better sometimes, like Granite said?"

"Yes."

"Well, I kinda think this movie's about a guy like that on accounta everybody feels like that sometimes an' so they'd wanna make a story about it."

"Fer fuck sake!" Digger said. "Now we're gonna go to a flick because the loogan here thinks we all wanna be all fucked up and blue?"

"I don't think that's what Dick's saying, Digger," Timber said quietly. "I think he's saying that this movie might be good to see because it has something to say that all of us can connect with. Right, Dick?"

"I guess so," Dick said. "I don't really know. All I know is that I gotta see this one on accounta my belly tell me it's right. Does that make any sense?"

"It makes a lot of sense to me," I said.

"Sounds like horseshit to me," Digger said.

There was silence for a moment.

"*Rain Man?*" Digger says, looking around at the three of us.

We nodded.

"Un-be-fucking-lievable," he said. "Now I'm going to a flick because of the belly of Double Dick Dumont."

It made perfect sense to me. Grandma One Sky used to tell me a lot about the invisible. We're surrounded by invisible friends all of the time, she would say, and even though the idea of ghosts frightened me a bit, Grandma One Sky's casual acceptance of it made me more comfortable with the notion. She went on to say that our invisible friends sometimes whisper to us and tell us what we should do or choose. We call these whispers intuition, sixth sense, or ESP. Dick's idea that he had to see this particular movie because of a feeling in his belly told me that the shadowed ones were indicating through him that this was the movie we were meant to see. I'd wondered what had happened to them since the first meeting with Granite, but I'd known they'd be back. We'd been tied to each other for far too long for them to desert me just like that.

"*Rain Man* it is, then," I said.

During the walk to the theatre there were shadowed ones everywhere. I was glad to see them. It had become a comfort to me to know that even in the most desperately lonely times, I had never been truly alone, that there had always been an invisible friend or two watching over me, keeping vigil through my pain. Or that in those moments when joy was the gift, they were there too, seeing and remembering the great wide energy of life. I saw them outside the theatre when we arrived and I saw them in the aisles when we walked in. And I saw them standing around Granite.

"Well whatta ya know?" Digger said. "It's the rock man."

He seemed surprised and pleased to see us, and as we made our way toward him I could see the invisible ones around him make room for us. I smiled at that.

"How did you manage to pick this movie?" he asked.

"My belly told me," Dick said, smiling at Granite and shaking his hand.

"Yeah," Digger said. "We're here because of gas."

"Actually, Dick just felt that this was the one we had to see on a day like this," Timber said, reaching over to shake Granite's hand too.

"Well, it's literal, that's for sure," Granite said.

"And you?" I asked. "How did you manage to pick this movie?"

He creased his brow in thought. "You know, I don't really know either. Maybe it was because the director is one whose work I appreciate, or the actor. Dustin Hoffman is an immaculate performer. Or maybe it was the review material I'd read that indicated a good story. I don't know. My plan was to see *Another Woman* with Gena Rowlands but somehow I wound up here. I was actually on my way to another theatre. I suppose that sounds strange."

"Not to me," I said and patted his shoulder.

Timber

RAY BRINGS US another round and I throw mine back like it's the last one I'm ever going to get. My good god. That movie made me want to run away as much as it pressed me back in my seat and forced my eyes to watch it all unfold before me.

"Amazing," was all I said.

"Amazing?" Digger asked. "What was so amazing about that?"

"Just the story," I said.

"The story? The story was about a loogan. Fucking guy couldn't even tie his shoes without help. You call that amazing?"

"No," I said. "What I call amazing is that he was able to teach everyone around him."

"Teach them what?" Granite asked, sipping on his whisky.

I sat back. Sometimes the thoughts just tumbled out of my head and it made me uneasy to try to stretch them out for someone.

"Well, I kinda think that he taught them about life, I guess." I looked at my shoes.

"That's an interesting observation," Granite said. "Taught them what about life?"

Amelia grinned at me and I felt better, more at ease with coaxing the words out. "I don't know," I said. "I guess it just seemed to me that he taught everyone that life is never clear for any of us. Any of us. Not just the ones that didn't get dealt a better hand. Fuck, the truth of it is that life scares the hell out of all of us sometimes. Especially when we think we need to see it better, clearer, more in focus. The Rain Man was able to remind people that it's part of all of us—and that it's okay because we survive."

They all just looked at me.

"You're right," Digger said. "That *is* amazing."

"Thank you," I said, surprised.

"Amazing that you got all that out of a movie about a loser who's gotta live locked up all his friggin' life."

He looked at me hard and swallowed his draft.

"Didn't you like any of it, Digger?" Amelia asked.

"Fuck no. Well, I kinda got into the gambling riff and he shoulda got with the hooker. The fucking guy's sitting on eighty grand and he's not gonna get laid? He doesn't go for that, he is a fucking loogan. I mean, really. What guy's not gonna go for that?"

"Not me," Dick said.

"Says the other fucking loogan," Digger said, and waved at Ray.

"It made me sad," Dick mumbled.

"Sad? Why did it make you sad, honey?" Amelia asked.

"On accounta I'm the Rain Man," Dick said.

"Oh, Jesus," Digger groaned. "Better make that two, Ray. I'm gonna need it."

Dick sat forward in his chair and drank slowly from his beer. Then he looked around the table at all of us and smiled weakly. "I guess he taught me 'bout life, too."

"How, Dick?" Granite asked.

"I ain't never been able to see it clear like Timber said. I always gotta ask on accounta I can't see it at all sometimes. It's like it's all too fast, too noisy, too bright, too dark. Too everythin' sometimes. Like the Rain Man."

"An' sometimes I think I gotta have someone look after me all the time too. To make things clear so I can get by. But I can't do none of the things the Rain Man could do. I can't count or read or nothin'."

"You've never been able to read or write or count?" Granite asked.

Dick shook his head.

"But how can that be?" Granite asked. "Your parents didn't send you to school? Even the first few grades?"

Dick looked at him and swallowed the rest of his beer. His chin shook with emotion and I could sense his desire to run away as fast as he could. He heaved a huge sigh and fired up a smoke with trembling hands.

"I don't wanna talk about that," he said.

"Okay, Dick, okay," Amelia said, taking one of his hands in hers. "You don't have to."

"You know, Dick," Granite said. "The Rain Man had a condition."

"Condition?" Dick asked.

"Yes. A condition. It means a way of being. His way of being was called 'autism.' That's why he couldn't figure things out. That's why the world scared him. You're not like him because you don't have a condition."

"I don't?" Dick asked, brightening somewhat.

"No. At least, not that I can see. You just never got taught how to interpret the world."

"Interpret?"

"Yes. Interpret means to see and understand. There are skills you get taught to help you do that. You learn to read and write and count and it makes it easier to interpret what's going on around you. Apparently you were never given those skills. But it's never too late to learn," Granite said.

"I can learn?"

"Sure. Anyone can."

"Even me?"

"Especially you. Because you know what?"

"What?"

"You're way ahead of most people already."

"I am?"

"Yes. You are."

"How?"

"Because you can imagine." Granite grinned.

"Imagine?"

"Yes. Imagine. See, Dick, stories reach us through our imagination. It's our imagination that makes them seem real to us, real enough to believe in them, real enough to be affected by them, and real enough to learn from them sometimes. And you, because you like the movies so much, have a very good imagination."

"I do?" Dick asked.

"Yes. You do. Can you imagine yourself being able to read?"

Dick screwed up his brow in thought and stared off across the room for a long while. Then he looked right at Granite and smiled. "Yeah," he said. "Yeah. I can. I can imagine that."

"Then that's all you need to get started. You can learn."

"Did you hear that, Digger?" Dick asked excitedly. "I can learn."

"Yeah, well learn to get us another fucking beer then, Rain Man," Digger growled, then rabbit punched him lightly on the leg.

"How do you know so much about stories, Granite?" I asked.

He looked at me. He held the look for a good moment or two and the only word that I can use to describe what I saw in his face is *control.* He was very controlled. Hanging on with everything he had.

"Well, Timber," he said, "I worked with stories for a long time.

Real stories. Not imagined ones like I was talking to Dick about. News stories. I worked for a newspaper. I was a journalist."

"Wow," I said. "So you do know a thing or two about how stories are built."

"Too much," he said.

"And you're retired now? It's over?"

He looked at Dick and said, "I don't want to talk about that."

I nodded. All of us understood that completely.

Granite

TWO WEEKS WENT BY and I found myself wondering when the next encounter would be. They puzzled me. It seemed to me that they were as different from each other as I was to all of them. Yet they hung together. I'd never been hungry. I'd never been dirty, ragged, or penniless. If I had been, I believed that I would have struck out alone and made whatever needed to happen in my life happen in order to get up and away from the sordid confines of the street. I wouldn't have looked for partners to keep me there. Loyalty meant you banded together for a cause, an uplifting, or at the very least, the staunch maintenance of a position. It didn't mean, in my experience, group immobilization. One of them needed to be a driver, the one who impelled the others to reach for something beyond what they'd grown used to. Or maybe, familiarity itself imprisoned them, as if the street had a grip on them that was relentless because of whatever their initial surrender had been. In my mind, you surrendered yourself to those circumstances. No right-minded person went there on purpose and no right-minded person looked for support to enable them to stay there. Still, they were loyal to each other and that impressed me and puzzled me in equal proportion. I wanted to learn more about them if I could.

I settled on a movie called *Stealing Home.* It was showing at a small repertory theatre and even though the review I had read pointed to a romance and a memory-land sort of film, I was drawn to it. Driving there, I noticed the first signs of imminent spring. There was no crowd outside the theatre and few in the lobby or at the confection stand. I amused myself awhile admiring the artistic nature of the movie posters announcing upcoming films, and once it was close enough to showing time I walked into the theatre. And there they were.

I found myself smiling a little despite myself. Both at the coincidence of another meeting and at the sight of them in the row they occupied. They sat like children, awed, eager, staring at the empty screen. I marvelled at how well behaved they were. Even though Digger snuck a surreptitious swallow from the bottle in his coat pocket, it was done as easily as a regular patron sucks the straw of his soda pop—they sat there silent, respectful, and patient, waiting for the adventure to begin again. I moved slowly toward them.

There were others in the theatre and they looked up as I passed, nodded in recognition of another aficionado and watched where I might sit so that they could speculate idly about the type of viewer I was, as if theatre geography could imply great things about me. I heard muffled surprise when I stepped up to the row where the ragged people sat and greeted them.

"Well, well," I said, "this is a surprise."

"Hello, Granite," Amelia said with a big smile for me.

"Granite," Timber said with a two-finger salute.

"Hi, Granite," Dick intoned, big-eyed and grinning.

"Rock," Digger growled.

"Rock?" I asked.

"Well, yeah. Granite's a friggin' stretch but Rock's something I can handle calling somebody," he said and nodded.

"Rock it is, then," I said. "You have room for me here?"

Amelia waved me over to the seat beside her and as I squeezed past the three men we grinned at each other.

"It's nice to see you," I said as I seated myself.

"And you, too," she said and gave my knee a small squeeze. I was embarrassed and looked about to see if any of the other patrons had caught the motion.

"So whose choice was it this time?" I asked no one in particular but leaned forward in my seat and looked down the row.

"Mine," Timber said.

"Why this one, Timber?"

"Blue," he said, and looked at his feet.

"Blue?"

"Yes. Blue." He looked up at me. "The poster. It had a very calm, very light, very peaceful blue in the background."

"An' it's got baseball in it," Dick said. "I like baseball."

"That's because you're out in left field all the friggin' time," Digger said, punching Dick's knee lightly.

"And you?" Amelia asked. "Why are you here?"

"I liked the commentary I read," I said. "And it's not my usual thing. I felt like a change."

"What's not your usual thing?" she asked as the lights began to fade.

"Romance."

"Oh, you're a dedicated bachelor, are you?"

"No. Well, yes. But it's not about that."

"What's it about, then?"

I looked at her. In the fading light her eyes glowed almost eerily, but there was kindness in her face. "Losses," I said. "For me, romance is about losses. I guess I don't really want to be reminded of that."

She nodded and squeezed my knee again.

It turned out to be a story about returning. It was about how the spirit of people can sometimes reach across time and space and call you back to those places and those moments that defined you, even though you wrestle with that definition. It was about reclaiming the past and getting a foothold on the present and a step up into the future. It was about death. It was about departures, sudden and cold, and about families bound together in the eternal weft and weave of time, circumstance and love. It was about home, and I wanted to run away. But I stayed to the end.

We sat there, all of us, staring at the screen while the credits rolled, voiceless and unmoving, until finally Digger cleared his throat and stood, breaking the spell.

"I gotta smoke," he said and headed out.

The rest of us gathered ourselves wordlessly and filed out. There was a weight to it all and I wondered what reactions they would have to what we'd just seen. We moved outside where Digger waited, puffing away and looking around at the rooftops nearby.

"Drink?" he asked.

"Yes," Timber said.

"Sure," Dick said.

"Yes," I found myself saying. "My treat."

"It's getting to always be your treat," Amelia said.

"That's okay," I said. "I like the company."

"This ragged company?" she asked.

"Yes," I said, smiling. "This ragged company."

> *Time is a peculiar thing, isn't it?*
>
> *Yes.*
>
> *For me, it's as hard to capture as light.*
>
> *How so?*
>
> *Well, when you think about time you can't think about it all at once. It's too big. But what you can think about is particular parts of it. The time I went here, the time I went there. That sort of thing.*
>
> *Okay. I follow.*
>
> *So time isn't what we think. Not really. It's fragments, shards, pieces, and when we think back it's the pieces we pick up, not the whole.*
>
> *Yes. Go on.*
>
> *It's the same thing with light. It's too big to think about all at once. But we always remember pieces of it. Like the light of evening in the summer when it stretches out forever, it seems, and then goes out as easily as the lights in a movie theatre when it's time for the show. Slow. So slow you think there's something wrong with your eyes. Everyone remembers that. Or sometimes you recollect how the light was when you sat with friends somewhere special. Or how it shone one time when you were sad and lonely and afraid. We all remember light like that.*

You're right, of course. My memories are all about the light.
But you can't capture it in its entirety.
No. Would you want to, though?
I don't think we would. It's too big. Too elusive. Just like time.
So we have to settle for holding it in pieces?
Yes. Like going back to this story. It's the pieces that make it so good to travel back to.
We were all pieces of the same story.
Yes, we were. We always will be. That's the nice thing.
Because we can always sit and reassemble the pieces?
Yes. We can finger the beans.
Clever. I like the way you led me back to that.
It's just thinking.
I like the way you think. It's magical.
Thank you. Do you ever think about that cold?
Sometimes. Winters mostly, of course, but I go back there sometimes.
It's what made us warm.
In the end, yes, it did.
Funny, isn't it?
Funny and sad and joyous. All at the same time.
Magical.
Yes. Magical.

BOOK TWO fortune

Digger

THERE'S A FAN blows warm air out the back of a building into a rectangle of space with walls on three sides about the size of a jail cell. It stays warm there all year and there's an overhang to keep the rain and snow off. The open end faces a hill at the back of a park and I can see the lights of the city at night when I curl up there. I've been staying there for years and it's gotten so no one says nothing no more. I'm always careful to stash my cart in the bushes on the hill and I fold my blankets up neat and keep 'em in one small pile so no one's really got nothing to complain about. They're used to me. Frig, I even shovel snow off the sidewalks for a little cash now and then. It's at the back so no one even has to see me and I like the privacy. It took me a long time to find it and the original manager was an okay guy named Gus who left me food now and then and even a bottle of whisky one Christmas. Gus was okay. He made it okay for me to be there and every manager since has been okay with it. I don't fuck with that. I don't make noise or get all pissed up and rowdy. It's my space and I protect it that way.

I like the city in the early hours. I don't fucking tell anybody that. A little too friggin' soft and mushy for a guy like me, but the lights remind me of stars or the crazy lights on the water the moon makes sometimes. I sit there and look out at it, maybe slurp a little hooch to get the blood going, and then get up and get on my way. Getting up and doing my thing has been my routine for a long time. I like to get it out of the way so I can get me out of the friggin' way too. Way too much bullshit going on later in the day and way too easy to get caught up in a whole pile of crap you don't really wanna. So I oil the wheels on my cart and head off on my back alley tour of town. It's amazing the shit people throw away. I have found lamps, televisions, radios, small appliances, clothes, books, tools, luggage, and even a guitar one time along with the cans and bottles and metal I generally gather for cash at the second-hand and pawn shops. Every day is different. Every day there's something else to blow my mind. Fucking Square Johns got no idea what things are worth, got no sense of the usefulness of a thing. All they know is it's out of fashion, not new enough, not shiny anymore, or not the latest fucking thing. So they do the toss and get a new whatever. Guys like me know what things bring. Guys like me love the fact that the fucking Square John world is a throwaway fucking world. Guys like me live off that. Takes me four or five hours, and my route takes me through the alleys of the rich part of town. That's why I oil the wheels. The cops have gotten okay with me over the years, used to me being around at that time, but there's no sense fucking with the Square Johns in any way at all. So I oil the wheels so I don't disturb anyone. Most days I end up with thirty bucks or more. I ain't no fucking junkie or no pillhead, so thirty fish is a lot of fish. Keeps me in hooch, scores me a hot meal, pays for the smokes, and gets me a wash. It's lots. And it's always enough to get me into the flicks.

By the time noon comes I'm done, all cashed up and funky. I've seen the fucking desperate way the loogans and losers dash around trying to pull something together to feed their habit, their belly, or their head. Craziness. Like a fucking smash 'n grab, it's a heat score too. No better way to attract the heat of a cop's attention than to be scootin' around trying to get hooked up. But that's what they do and then they force you to listen to them bitch and moan about the hard fucking life they lead. Fuck 'em, I say. You wanna survive out here, you wanna be a rounder, you grit your teeth and do whatever the fuck you gotta do to get things done. And you keep your mouth shut about it. No one wants to hear the whine. No one wants to hear the snivel. But the beat goes on anyway and the faces change and people die and the street stays the same. Bitching and moaning don't change nothing, it just pisses people off. So there I am every day, done and ready to hang while the majority of 'em are still bug-eyed with desperation.

Been like that every day. Every day but the one day. The day that changed everything.

There I am cashed up, heading toward the Mission to meet the others, feeling the glow of a job well done and a drink well taken. I got a mitt full of moolah, a pocket full of smokes, a belly full of booze, and life is on the fucking rails again.

You kick things when you been on the bricks enough. You kick bags to see if there's anything in them. You kick boxes to hear the thunk that'll tell you if something's inside. You kick beer cans and bottles. You kick cast-off clothing. Mostly you kick so you don't have to bend. You still got pride when you're a rounder and you don't want people to see you bending over in the street checking out the empties. So you learn to kick things. It's a habit after a while. So I see this cigarette pack on the sidewalk and I give it a boot. Instead of flipping end over end like an empty does, this fucker slides along the concrete. Slides. Heavy. Full, maybe. So I do the once over the shoulder thing to see if anyone's checking me out, bend over, scoop it up, and tuck it in my pocket. Once I'm around the corner I pull it out and cop a boo inside.

There's three-quarters of a pack of tailor-mades in there. I feel luckier than shit. Then I notice a little green behind the foil on one side. When I pull the edge of it I see a twenty-dollar bill. Scoring a double sawbuck is a mighty big thing and I'm feeling even luckier. When I unfold the bill it turns out to be sixty and I'm about to go through the roof. There's a yellow piece of paper in there too, so I tuck it in my pocket, fire up one of the smokes, and sashay on down the fucking avenue. A glorious day to be alive.

The others are sitting around checking out the movie listings. I must have been grinning like the cat that ate the fucking mouse or something 'cause the old lady flashes a big beamer at me.

"Digger," she goes, "you look mighty happy with yourself today."

"Yeah," I go, "well, some days it's just a friggin' joy to be me."

"Little early to be that loaded, ain't it?" Timber goes.

"Hey, even if I was pissed up and rowdy it'd be okay today, Timber," I go, slapping him on the back and pulling up a chair. "Thing is, I could afford it today."

"Did you have a good day on your route?" Dick goes. He's always interested in hearing about the shit I discover out there. Interested but never enough to grab a fucking cart himself and do the work.

"Dick," I go. "I had the day of days."

The old lady's still grinning away at me. "Sounds like you found something exciting out there."

"If free money and a pack of smokes is exciting then, yeah, I guess I did find something rather cool," I go, tossing the doubles on the table along with the tailor-mades. "The flicks are on me today."

"Wow," Dick goes. "Can I have one?"

"A smoke, yeah, but mitts off the loot."

"Cadillacs," Timber goes, reaching out and taking a tailor-made. "Been a while. Roll-your-owns and butts have been all I smoked for a long time."

"Well, fill yer boots, pal," I go.

We sit there, the three of us, smoking, one leg thrown over the other, leaning back in our chairs, faces pointed at the ceiling, smoke rings drifting through and past each other, and we're like lords of the fucking manor. Some days a little thing like a tailor-made cigarette can be the biggest thing in the world, and right then, it was.

"Ahh," I go. "Nothing like a good friggin' smoke. Got any hooch?"

"I got a mickey," Dick goes.

"Cool. Hand 'er over here, guv'ner."

I take a quick swig and pass the rum back to Dick under the table. The Mission people know we drink but they pretend to not notice as long as you behave yourself and don't get all fucked up and make trouble. Still, it's good practice to play the fucking game.

"Well then," I go. "What's it gonna be today?"

"*Field of Dreams,*" the old lady goes.

"*Field of Dreams?*"

"Yes. It sounds quite nice."

"Nice? Ah, never mind. I could probably do with nice today for a change. *Field of Dreams* it is, then."

"So that's pretty lucky, Digger," Timber goes.

"Yeah," I go. "There's this other thing, too."

"What thing?"

"This thing," I go, reaching into my pocket and pulling out the yellow piece of paper.

"What is it?" Dick goes, leaning across and looking at the paper in my hand.

"I don't know. Probably nothing."

"It's a lottery ticket," Timber goes.

"A lottery ticket?"

"Yeah. It's a big thing now. You pay your money, they give you a bunch of numbers, and if they draw yours you win."

"Sounds kosher," I go. "Kinda like the old numbers game."

"Yes," Timber goes. "Just like that. Only legal."

"How do you work it?"

"I think you just take it to a store and they check the numbers for you," Timber goes.

"That's it?"

"I guess."

"Fuck, might as well check on our way to the flick."

"Might as well," Timber goes. "But luck's been pretty good to you already."

"Can't never get enough of that sweet woman's way."

"What woman?" Dick goes, all worried-looking.

"Lady luck, Double D," I go. "Sweet old lady luck. Once she

calls your number, you better be home because that baby's mighty picky whom she favours."

"Well, Digger," the old lady goes, "I don't think I've ever seen you in such a poetic mood before."

"Dig it while you can, mama. Dig it while you can."

So we lumber on out of the Mission and head down the street. It's a bright, almost spring day and there's people everywhere. Dick's going on to the old lady about the birds and the squirrels and the other things that loogans always seem to notice, and me 'n Timber are just moseying along in silence. We swing into a liquor store and I grab a mickey for each of us.

"You sure?" Timber goes when I hand him his.

"Sure I'm sure," I go. "Let's stop over in that park for a minute."

We head into the park and stop by a big tree. I pull out my mickey and hand it over to the old lady without even thinking about it. She nods her head at me, unscrews the cap, pours a little splash on the ground, and goes, "There's one for the dead." She does the same thing with the other guys' bottles and we all take a drink.

"Ah," I go. "Now then, let's hit the flick."

"Why don't you check the ticket at that store over there, Digger? You never know, you know," Timber goes.

"Fuck," I go. "The chances of us winning anything is a million to one at least. Me, I figure I scored enough already."

"But you never know," he goes.

"Right. You never know. Fuck it. Let's go."

It's just a regular corner store. Garden Grocery, it's called. I walk in and the others wait outside. It's kind of dark in there and when the old Chinese guy behind the counter sees me he gets all nervous.

"Y-y-yes?" he goes.

"Yeah," I go. "How do I check this out?" I show him the ticket.

"Oh, very easy. You no play before?"

"No. No play."

"I check," he goes, and I hand him the ticket.

I stand around pretending to look at the shelves, eager to be out of there. He pushes a couple numbers on the machine behind the till and waits for something to happen. Silence. Then all of a sudden there's music. Not riotous fucking music but just tinkly little music like you'd hear from a doorbell or something. He looks at the ticket, looks at me all wide-eyed, and then starts yelling something crazy in Chinese. He's standing there all excited, yelling his head off, and I can't figure out what the fuck is going on. The door at the back opens and this big, young Chinese guy comes into the store on the run. They gibber away at each other all in a panic and I figure it's time to hotfoot it out of there. The fucking thing probably came up stolen and I'm off to the hoosegow.

"Winnipeg!" the old guy goes, pointing at me.

"What?"

"Winnipeg!" he goes again.

The young guy looks at me and starts around the counter. I'm no track star but I figure my fear can outrun this guy's anger, so I book it on out of there. The fucking ticket was a heat score and I was about to take the pinch, so I was gonna make it at least hard for them to take me in.

The old man's still yelling about Winnipeg when I hit the door and shoot past the other three. I sprint across the street and into the park, figuring on heading over to the alleys where I have a chance of losing them. I hear Timber yelling. I hear the old lady scream but I'm making tracks as fast as I can, thinking they won't have to take any part of the pinch if I pretend I don't know them. The mickey falls out of my pocket and breaks on the sidewalk so I cut to the grass but it's slippery as fuck. I wipe out and take a fucking header into some bushes. As I scramble to get out of there, the young Chinese guy catches up and reaches out to grab me. I swat his hand away and try 'n make another break for it but I lose traction and land on my ass again.

"Wi-wi-win-winni-winnipeg," the old guy goes as he chugs up to us, still holding the ticket.

"I never been in fucking Winnipeg," I go.

"Winnipeg?" the young guy goes, pulling me up.

"Yeah," I go. "What he said."

The other three arrive just then and Timber gives me "the look" to see if I wanna clock this guy and make a run for it. I shake my head.

They jabber away in Chinese again and I hear Winnipeg and figure that this ticket belongs to someone in Winnipeg and I'm the fucking stooge who tried to cash it. I'm thinking that I'd probably only pull a month or so in the joint for fraud, and that'd give me a nice little rest, when they stop jabbering and look at me.

"What?" I go.

"Not Winnipeg," the young guy goes.

"Not Winnipeg?"

"No, not Winnipeg. *Winna big.* My father says you 'winna BIG.'"

"Yes," the old guy goes. "Winna BIG! Winna BIG!"

"Winna big? How fucking big?" I go.

"Pretty fucking big," the young guy goes, smiling.

"Well, exactly how big is pretty fucking big?"

"Thirteen-and-a-half-million-dollars big," he goes.

"Thirteen and a half . . ."

"Million," he goes.

"Thirteen and a half million dollars?" I go, and I hear the old lady gasp behind me.

"Yes. Yes. You just won thirteen and a half million dollars!"

I fall flat on my ass on the wet grass.

Wind on stone.

Pardon me?

Oh. Sorry. Just musing a little there. But I was thinking about something I heard somewhere in my travels about change. Someone told me that sometimes it happens like wind on stone—invisibly, secretly, mysteriously—but it happens nonetheless. Change is like that sometimes.

And other times?

Sudden as a panther from the trees.

Yes. Like then. Like on that day.

Yes. The panther dropped right in among us and we were all suddenly different. Except we really didn't know it. We thought it was the world that had altered. We couldn't see the wind performing its sorcery.

No. You really can't remember where you heard that?

No. It's funny but I've been so many places, seen and done so many things, that it makes it hard to recollect simple detail. But that's okay, because detail obfuscates. I just recall the teachings now. It's wonderful. Memory is like sorcery, too, sometimes.

Yes. It transports us.

Lets us transcend time and distance, longing even.

True. Do you remember everything that happened after?

Like a great dream.

Like a vision.

Like a life.

Yes. Yes.

Yes.

Timber

"I DON'T BELIEVE IT," I said, more to hear myself speak, to feel real, than for anything else.

"It's impossible," Amelia said.

"I don't understand," Dick said, looking back and forth at Amelia and me for guidance.

"None of us do," I said to him.

Digger was sitting on the ground staring at his shoes and shaking his head. The two Chinese guys were all smiles and talking to each other in Chinese. The young guy finally reached down and handed Digger the ticket.

"You got to keep this safe," he said. "Better that you go down now and take care of it."

"What?" Digger said, reaching up to take the ticket. "Go down where?"

"Lottery office. Downtown," the young guy said.

"Downtown?"

"Yes. I write down address for you."

"Go down and cash this in?"

"Yes."

"For thirteen and a half million dollars?"

"Yes."

"Fuck me."

The young guy smiled. "For thirteen and a half million dollar, lots of people want to fuck you now."

Digger laughed. "I fucking guess," he said and stood up. "This is for real?"

"Yes. For real," the young guy said.

"Jesus. Jesus. I need a smoke. I need a friggin' drink. I need to sit down."

We moved to a bench under a tree and sat there, smoking and drinking, not saying a word but looking around at each other like you do when no one really knows what to do or say next. The two Chinese guys walked away but the young guy came back a few minutes later and handed Digger a slip of paper.

"Address," he said. "You lucky. You very lucky."

"Yeah," Digger said. "Winnipeg."

The young guy smiled. "Yes. Winnipeg. You go now or you lose it. You go there now."

We looked at each other again. Amelia moved over and sat beside Digger and put an arm around his shoulder. To my surprise, Digger slipped an arm around her waist and squeezed her gently. "Jesus," he said again. "Jesus."

"What do you want to do, Digger?" she asked.

He looked at her. "I don't know. What's a guy supposed to do at a time like this?"

"Cash it in," I said.

"Cash it in?" Digger repeated, looking at me and reaching for my mickey.

"I guess," I said. "What else?"

He drank. "I don't fucking know. I just do not fucking know. Whatta you figure there, loogan?" He looked at Dick, who stood there scratching at the dirt with the toe of one shoe, trying to make sense of it all.

"You're asking me?" he said.

"Yeah," Digger said. "I'm asking you."

"How come?"

"How come? On accounta you ain't so busy in the brain as me and maybe you got a way to figure this I don't."

"Oh," Dick said. "I don't, though. It's like a movie."

"No shit," Digger said. "It's like a movie. Only what do you think happens in this movie?"

Dick looked at him. "I think the friends all go down there together."

"And?"

"And, I don't know."

"Me neither. I don't even know where to start. I never figured this, you know," Digger said and squeezed Amelia again.

"No one could have," she said. "But I know one thing for sure."

"What's that?"

"I know that someone wants you to have that money. Or else it wouldn't have happened."

"Wait a minute. Wait a friggin' minute. You don't think I'm going through this all alone, do you?"

"What do you mean?" she asked.

"I mean, we're all wingers, right?"

"Yes."

"Then if we're wingers, then what comes to me comes to you."

"What are you saying?" I asked.

"I'm saying that one-fourth of thirteen and a half is four point three or something like that, if I figure right."

"One-fourth?" I asked.

"Yeah. Each of us. Together. Think about it. A guy like me don't have clue number one about what to do with a fucking chunk of change like this, but four of us, well, we might just be able to figure out what to do."

"What's he saying, Timber?" Dick asked.

"I'm saying that you're rich, buddy boy," Digger said.

"Rich?"

"Yeah. Filthy, lousy, stinking, way-more-fucking-money-than-brains rich. Just like the rest of us."

"Wow," Dick said. "We can go to way more movies then, huh?"

"Way more," I said.

"Then I guess we'd better get down there, claim our loot, and then head off to, what was it again?" Digger asked.

"*Field of Dreams,*" Amelia said.

"*Field of Dreams,*" I replied, and felt the world I thought I knew slipping away.

Double Dick

I WANTED TO RUN AWAY AGAIN. I don't like it when things happen fast on accounta I fall behind an' it takes me forever to catch up an' when I do it's movin' away even more. Rich. Digger said we was rich. I didn't know what that meant but I hoped it didn't mean that we was gonna get away from each other, that rich would mean we couldn't be friends no more. I didn't want that. All I wanted was to go to the movies with my friends like we was doin'. I didn't wanna try 'n handle no more than that.

"How come this happened?" I asked One For The Dead while we was walking toward downtown.

"I don't know, Dick," she said. "But maybe you can keep thinking about it like you were."

"How's that?" I asked.

"Well, you said that it was like a movie, right?"

"Yeah," I said. "It is like that on accounta in the movies there's always things going on that you never know about until they happen."

"And what do you do in the movies at times like that?"

"Well, mostly I just wait an' things move ahead on their own an' everything comes out the way it's s'posed to in the end."

"Can you do that with this?"

"I guess. But this scares me."

"What scares you about this?" she asked, and took my arm in hers.

"Well, in the movies when I don't know what's gonna happen I'm excited. Now I'm just scared."

"Scared of what?"

"Scared that everything's gonna be different on accounta we're rich. I don't know how to be rich. An' I'm scared that on accounta everything bein' different that we're not gonna be together no more."

She squeezed my arm. "Dick, I will never, ever leave you. No matter what. You and I are always going to be together."

"Even though we're rich?"

She smiled. "Even though we're rich."

"What's that mean, anyhow?" I asked.

She laughed. It felt good to hear someone laugh. "I don't really know. I've never been there in my life. But I think it means that you don't have to struggle anymore."

"Struggle?"

"Yes. Fight. Tussle. Strain. Struggle to get enough to do what you want to do. Struggle to make it through your day or even plan your life. For you, it means you don't have to panhandle anymore because you have enough."

"Wow. What'll I do if I don't gotta be out there for hours at a time?"

"You can do whatever you want."

"But I don't know how to do anything else."

"Well, I think rich means that you can learn how to do things different."

"But that's what scares me. I don't wanna do things different. I like how it is. Like how we're always together. Like how we always go to the movies an' talk an' stuff," I said, getting more scared by the minute.

"I guess we can always do that too," she said.

"Hope so," I said. "I really hope so."

One For The Dead

GRANDMA ONE SKY used to tell me about the Trickster when we picked berries. They were very funny stories. Sometimes the Trickster was a raven, sometimes it was a coyote, other times a man named Nanabush. The Trickster travelled around the world getting into all kinds of adventures with animals and people. I remember laughing lots. But Grandma One Sky said that the stories were very serious and that one day when I was older and had seen more of the world myself, I would recall those tales and go back into them and learn from them. The Trickster was a teacher, and the lessons the People needed to learn were buried within its adventures. The thing was that you didn't need to be afraid when the Trickster appeared if you believed that it was only around to help you learn what you really needed to learn. In its way, booze was a Trickster. Only when I went back and looked did I see what it had to teach me. This money was a Trickster. I saw that right away. The things about these teachers is that they can appear on the sly so you never know they're among you, or they can make a big entrance that stuns you and catches you unaware. This second way is the Trickster's best way. The big entrance. Digger blasting past us with two guys from the store in hot pursuit reminded me of an old Nanabush story about a footrace, and I knew the Trickster was among us. Finding out about the money was the next clue.

All the way down to the office where we needed I go, I looked around us. The city seemed suddenly more real. There was a speed to it that I hadn't seen before, an energy, a frenzy, an antsy, frantic kind of motion. It was like the edge of a hangover. A paranoid, scared, but not yet terrified way of seeing what used to be normal. The Trickster weaving a spell.

The boys could feel it too, in their own way. None of them was comfortable and I worried for them.

"That looks like the place," Digger said after blocks and blocks of silence. He pulled out a cigarette, lit it, then passed the pack around to Timber and Dick. He pointed to a small green space between buildings and we moved to it. The boys took a few drinks and we studied the office we needed to go to.

"Looks pretty shiny over there," Dick said.

"Looks like money," Timber replied. "All shiny like big loot."

"Wonder why they call it that?" Digger asked.

"What?" I asked.

"Loot. Why do they call money *loot*?"

"It's a pirate word," Timber said. "When pirates used to board another ship and take everything they wanted—the gold, the jewels, hell, even the women sometimes—they called what they did looting. Taking. Pillaging. Getting by overthrow. So they called what they gained loot."

"Well, thanks there, perfesser," Digger said. "I like that. A pirate word. Makes scoring all this loot a bit closer to my heart. So I guess we better do this thing."

The boys looked at each other and then at me. Behind us I could see shadowed ones gathering. There were a lot of them. They filled the empty space leading back to the sidewalk, moved restlessly back and forth, waiting for us to move. "Okay," I said, finally. "Let's get this done. There's a movie I want to see."

"Me too," Dick said. "*Field of Dreams.*"

"Okay, then. Let's do it," Digger said, and crushed out his smoke with the toe of one shoe. "Let's fucking do it."

We moved out to the sidewalk and toward the building. It was a business area and the people were all dressed smartly, so when we walked toward the office there were a lot of stares, whispered comments, and shaking of heads. The boys walked with their heads down, hands stuffed deep into their pockets. We reached the doors and walked through.

The lobby was impressive. All deep red carpet with pictures of smiling people holding cheques with big numbers on them, lots of plants and bright, bright lights. There were a lot of people working there, all seemingly very busy, talking on telephones and moving papers back and forth, but with an atmosphere of cheerfulness that made me feel a little more at ease. We stood there just inside the doors, uncertain where to go or what to do. Finally, a woman behind the counter noticed us and moved across the room.

"May I help you?" she asked. She had one of those open faces that told you that whatever she said you could take for gospel and that her particular gospel was one of kindness and respect.

"Don't know," Digger said. "I got this ticket."

"Oh," she said. "Did you want me to check it for you? Normally you just go to the vendor but I can run it through for you."

"I guess," Digger said. "The guy at the store said it was a winner."

"A winner? Well, that must be very nice for you."

"I guess," Digger said again.

"Come with me and I'll just do a quick check on it, then we'll get you your money." She gestured for us to move up to the counter.

She took the ticket and went back to a machine, typed in the numbers and waited. People began noticing us. Workers looked up from their desks and the ones moving around craned their necks to get a better look. The boys shifted nervously from foot to foot while we stood at the counter. I just looked back at people and gave small nods. It seemed like forever.

The woman gave a small gasp and it seemed like everyone in that office looked over at her. She had her hand up to her mouth and sat there staring at the screen in front of her. Finally, she got up, looked at us, and walked into an office at the back. She was gone a long time.

A man came out with her and began pulling on his suit jacket while he walked. They both seemed very excited. The woman leaned her head toward him, covered her mouth with one hand and pointed at Digger with the other.

"Well, hello there," he said, reaching out a pinkish-looking hand across the counter to Digger.

Digger just stared at it.

"Ahem," the man said. "Margo tells me that you are a winner. A big winner, it seems."

"I guess," Digger said.

"Do you know how much you've won?" he asked.

"Thirteen something?" Digger asked, looking up at the man finally.

"Yes. That's right. Thirteen million, five hundred thousand dollars in fact, Mr. . . . ?" He looked at Digger, his hand still stretched out over the counter.

"Digger."

"Mr. Digger. Well, Mr. Digger, I'm Sol Vance. I'm in charge of prize allocation and if you and your friends will just—"

"Not Mr. Digger. Just Digger. That's my name. Digger."

"Oh, well, er, Digger, will you please come with me?"

"Where?" Digger asked with a nervous look over at me.

"I'd like to take you to our VIP lounge where you can have a coffee or tea, or whatever you like, while we get ready," Vance said.

"Get ready for what? I thought we just pick up the loot and take off."

"The loot?" Vance laughed. "No. No. There's some process involved, Digger. It won't take that long. Please come with me."

Margo stepped around the counter and over to Digger. "It's okay," she said kindly. "It's what everyone has to do when they win. We just want to treat you special, that's all."

"Special?" Digger asked. "Whatta ya mean, special?"

"Well, you're a millionaire now. You're special."

Digger looked at her hard. "Just like that?"

She smiled. "Just like that."

"Well, fuck me," Digger said, looking at us. "Let's go and get treated special."

We walked through the office.

"Tim. Lisa. VIP lounge right now," Vance said as he walked, and two people leaped from their desks and joined the small parade.

The VIP lounge was a huge room with a bar, a couple of leather couches, two armchairs, and a fireplace. Vance gestured to the seats but we were all too nervous to sit. We stood there, waiting.

"Would you like a drink?" Vance asked.

"Does a bear shit in the woods?" Digger said. "Whatta ya got?"

"You can have whatever you like."

"Really?"

"Yes. Our pleasure."

"Oh yeah. You drinkin' too?"

Vance laughed. "Oh no, Digger. I mean it's our pleasure to offer you whatever you'd like."

"Whisky," Digger said. "Boys?"

Timber and Dick kept looking at the floor.

"Them too," Digger said, and the man named Tim went to the bar. He returned with three glasses. The boys all drained them in one gulp. Vance cleared his throat and Margo pursed her lips and looked out the window.

"Tim here is our media guy. All of our winners need to meet the media and he'll make the arrangements. Lisa is our public relations officer and she'll help you make arrangements to get to a bank, make travel arrangements, whatever you need," Vance said. "Now, I'll need to see your identification. All of our winners need to be identified properly."

"Say what?" Digger asked.

"Identification," Vance said. "It's one of the rules. It's spelled out on the back of your ticket."

"Don't have any."

"You don't have any? What happened to your ID?"

"Well, fucked if I know. Guess if I knew that, I'd have it. Never mattered before. I always knew who I was."

Vance, Margo, Tim, and Lisa exchanged puzzled glances. Vance hitched his head to one side and they moved toward the fireplace where they had a short talk, heads close together, gesturing helplessly with their hands. Finally, they came back to us at the bar.

"Digger, are you sure you have nothing? No driver's licence, no card of any sort?" Vance asked.

"Nothin'."

"What about your friends? Maybe one of them can claim the prize for you?"

We looked at each other.

"I don't have any either," Timber said. "Haven't thought about it for years."

"Me neither," Dick said.

"I'm sorry," I said. "We're not your regular kind of people, I guess. None of us has any papers. It's not the kind of thing that usually matters."

Vance looked troubled. "Well, I'm afraid that without proper identification we can't issue you the prize money. It's a rule."

"Let me get this straight there, bud," Digger said. "You're trying to tell me that I got a winning ticket here but that there's nothing I can do about it?"

"Not without identification."

"So I'm standing here with thirteen million nothing?"

"Well, no. The ticket is a winner but unless you can provide me with the necessary information I can't process it."

Digger shook his head. "Fucking Square John bullshit," he said. "A moment ago we were 'special.' Now we're just a buncha fucking loogans with a useless piece of paper."

"What happens if we can't get papers?" I asked.

"Well, you have a year," Vance said. "There's a period of one calendar year from the draw date to process the ticket. After that, the unclaimed money goes back into the prize pool."

"Wait just a freaking fucking minute here, pal," Digger said. "Now you're saying if we don't get our act together somebody else has dibs on our money?"

"If a prize is unclaimed it's available for other winners, yes."

"Jesus. How fucking perfect. Just another set-up for the regulars, eh? Just another Square John waltz around the fucking block."

"Is there anyone you can call? A lawyer, maybe? Someone who works with you? Anybody?"

"Do I look like the kind of guy that's got a, whatta ya call it? A Rolodex? There ain't anybody."

"There's Granite," Dick said softly.

"What's that there, pal?" Digger asked.

Dick looked up. "Granite," he said. "We know Granite. He looks like he'd have the right kind of stuff we need."

"No offence there, D," Digger said. "But tossing another fucking Square John into the mix ain't exactly the kind of solution I'm looking for here. These guys already wanna keep our dough."

"We don't want to keep your money, Digger," Vance said. "We'd like nothing more than to see you walk out of here with the ability to change your life, to make your dreams come true."

"But not enough to just give up the cash."

"Even if we did, how would you cash the cheque? I'm assuming you don't have a bank account?"

"Correct."

"What about this person your friend here mentioned?"

"Fuck. We don't even know how to get hold of this guy. He's just a guy we meet now and then at the movies."

"You have to do something."

"How about you? Why don't I give it to you and you cash it for us and just slip us the bucks? I'll even tip ya."

"Oh, no," Vance said with a chuckle. "That would be totally unethical."

"Unethical?" Digger said. "Thirteen million and change is enough grease to buy a whole lot of unethical, pal. How about you, honey?"

Margo blushed. "I can't."

"There's Granite," Dick said again.

"Yes," I said. "There's Granite."

Digger shook his head. "Even if I did wanna trust that guy, how're we gonna get hold of him?"

I looked at him and there were shadowed ones hovering close by. The room was suddenly filled with them. "We'll just find him," I said. "There's no rush. We've got a year."

"Sitting on a pile of dough for a year will drive me fucking nuts," Digger said.

"Then I guess we'd better get busy," I said.

"Busy doing what?" Vance asked.

"Going to the movies," I said.

"Movies?"

"Yes. That's how we know our friend. That's where we always meet."

"But there's a lot of movie houses in this city," Vance replied.

I smiled. "Yes. Yes, there is. But I have a feeling we won't be looking very long."

"You can't be sure of that."

"What can you be sure of, Mr. Vance? We were sure this morning that this was going to be a day like any other day in our lives and look where we are now."

He smiled. "Yes. That's true. It just seems like a long shot."

I laughed. "A long shot? I think we're getting a handle on the long-shot thing. And besides, it's what we're left with."

"Yes," he said. "Well, good luck."

They ushered us out of the office and walked us to the front of the building. Margo, to her credit, linked an arm through Digger's, and Tim and Lisa tried vainly to make small talk with Timber and Dick. Vance told me brief stories about the winners whose pictures hung around the office. When we got to the sidewalk, they shook our hands warmly.

"I hope you find your friend fairly soon," Vance said.

"Yeah, thanks," Digger said, his arm still hooked in Margo's.

"Is there anything I can do to help? Do you need any cash for now?"

"Cash?" Digger said, finally setting Margo free. "There's always a place for cash."

"Well, here," Vance said, and handed Digger a fifty-dollar bill from his wallet. "I think you'll be good for it."

"Hoo-hoo! It's a day for fucking miracles, boys. First we get into this mess and now I got a Square John handing me a half like it's nothing."

"A half?" Vance asked.

"Yeah," Digger said with a wink at Margo. "Half a yard."

"A yard?"

"A hundred."

"Oh."

"Got a lot to learn about money, mister," Digger said, pocketing the fifty. "Got a lot to learn about money."

We headed off down the street.

Granite

I STOOD ON MY BALCONY in the moist spring air and looked out over the city. I had known this city since I came here after journalism school. I had covered it as a reporter and as a columnist but I had never, in truth, actually lived in it, seen its depths, its reaches. I'd merely been an occupant, inhabiting the spaces that were my reward for, as Digger would say, a Square John life. I had never really known this city, had missed its stories entirely. Beneath the pseudo-rational sheen of a contemporary life are other lives whose existences bear no resemblance to our own. Within that separation is the refraction of light that creates the shadowed ones on the corners and in the alleys or, most invisibly, on the very same streets I walked every day. I'd just never taken the time to see them. Time and money meant I didn't have to. I began to realize that the displaced and dislocated ones are not simply the inhabitants of the shelters and missions, of the cardboard boxes and empty doorways, but condo dwellers like me looking out over the top of the city from a balcony far above it all. The ones who miss the collective heartbeat of the city in favour of the safe, the routine, and the familiar. I had confined myself. I had limited my experience. I had deprived myself of knowledge. I determined to see as much of my new friends' world as they would allow me to. Not to change things for them. That would be far too presumptuous. But merely to see and to know and to understand—to correct my dislocation.

I smiled. I tried to imagine the selection process my new friends underwent in picking a movie. It would be word-driven. The movie would be something that stood out by virtue of the power of its beckoning, something mysterious, something poetic, alluring and indicative of a mystic journey, a story thrown up on beams of light, illuminating the corners of another undiscovered world. According to the ads, it could be *Back to the Future, The Gods Must Be Crazy,* or *Field of Dreams.* I narrowed my search to the movie houses close to the inner city and those with afternoon matinees. Satisfied with my process, I headed out to *Field of Dreams.*

Digger

"So JUST WHAT IN THE FUCK are we gonna do now?" I go.

"Go to the movies, I guess," Timber goes.

"Fuck that," I go. "Let's just head to the liquor store, score a couple of jugs, and head off down to Heave-Ho Charlie's, sit around and suck it up for a change. Far as I'm concerned, we all been too friggin' good for too friggin' long."

Heave-Ho Charlie is an old rounder. He was a stickup man back in the days when you could actually get away with that shit, and he was a good one. Well, good if you mean he always had the balls to do it. Not so good when you figure out the years he spent in the pen and the small amount of cash he got for his trouble. Charlie said it worked out to about a grand for every year he spent inside, and even then I gotta figure he was overpaying himself. But anyway, Heave-Ho was a good old rounder who'd been on the street forever. Fuckin' guy musta been about eighty, maybe even ninety. Tough son of a bitch too, for his age. Charlie had shiftable digs. In other words, he camped out in empty buildings wherever he could find them. Sometimes he would be in a deserted warehouse, sometimes a boarded-up old house, one time he even set up in the basement of a church they were gonna tear down. Old Charlie knew everybody. I mean, every-fucking-body and that's how we knew what he told us about himself was true because anyone who knew that many people had to be straight. One of the people he knew was Fill 'er Up Phil. Phil was a bootlegger and a moonshiner but he was also one of the biggest piss tanks you ever seen. He got his name from the plastic pop bottles he made you drink the booze from. Phil never wanted anyone to get pinched carrying a bottle they scored from him, so he'd sell you a pop bottle full of hooch. You had to bring the bottle, though. Then you'd knock on his door, hand the bottle through the little hole in the door and say, "Fill 'er up, Phil." How much you paid depended on how big the pop bottle was. It was always good moonshine and Phil made a lot of money. But he liked to taste-test the product, too. So he needed a place to keep the hooch safe and Heave-Ho Charlie was the perfect partner since he was moving around all the time. Heave-Ho would set up somewhere and Phil would stash a few crocks there. Then he'd drop by to taste-test and the party would be on. Heave-Ho got his name from the fact that he could drink pretty much anyone under the table, and when they got too loud, obnoxious, or just plain fucking stupid at one of Phil's taste-test parties he'd be the one to give 'em the old heave-ho. Not too gently sometimes, either. Those old pen timers knew how to knuckle, and people pretty much behaved themselves at Heave-Ho's. That's why it was good place to piss 'er up at. Long as you were a rounder and solid, you were gonna be okay. I really needed a night with Heave-Ho and the boys.

"We can go to a movie any time," I go. "Besides, I got the cash for a few bottles, maybe even some pickup food, smokes. Damn. Sounds like a hell of a good idea to me."

"What about Granite?" the old lady goes. "I know you really want to kick up your heels now, Digger, but Granite's the only one we know who can help with the ticket."

"Ticket-schmicket. That's just a fucking pipe dream. Guys like me don't ever get that lucky. It's a piece of paper. That's all. A piece of paper that ain't never gonna get cashed. Because I for one am not going to spend my time searching around the city for some Square John who more'n likely will just laugh anyway. This cash is real. This cash I can spend. This cash I can fucking drink and right now I wanna fucking drink. Screw this *Field of Dreams.*"

They all look at me like they know they're up against the wall. It takes a shitload of will to move me once I get set on something, and the more I think about this the more I feel like cutting out and just getting loaded. We're still heading toward the Marquee and I can feel myself getting antsy.

"Look," I go. "For months now we been doing this movie thing and never once did I try 'n scuttle the fucking ship. I liked it, sure, but I'm a fucking rounder. Always will be. Movies ain't gonna change that, and every once in a while a rounder's gotta act like a rounder and right now, that's what I wanna do. I wanna hang with Fill 'er Up Phil and Heave-Ho and whoever's hanging out there, tell some fucking stories, get pissed and do what I do.

"We never know when we're gonna run into Granite. Could be months. Could be a whole frickin' year and then we're screwed anyhow. Let's just go back and do what we used to do for a day. Remember?"

Timber nods. "Heave-Ho always does have some good get-togethers."

"Damn straight," I go.

"And Phil always talks to me about the old days when he was stickin' up people an' drivin' them big cars. I like them stories," Dick goes.

"See? See?" I go. "You guys been missing the action as much as me."

"Well, I have to confess that Charlie's place does have a charm to it," Timber goes. "And a tad of moonshine'd be nice too."

"But what if?" the old lady goes.

"What if what?" I go.

"What if we go to the movies and we meet Granite and he helps us with the ticket? What if he makes it so we can have that money? What if we don't have to struggle to afford movies? What if we don't have to struggle for anything anymore?"

"Yeah, yeah, yeah," I go. "What if the sky falls? What if the fucking sun don't rise tomorrow? What if, what if, what if. Life ain't about *what if.* It's about *what is.*"

"But what if we just try?" she goes.

"Just try?"

"Yes. What if we just try? We go to the movie and if we don't find Granite we go to Heave-Ho's anyway and you boys can sow your oats."

"Still sounds like a stretch to me. Still sounds like we're buying into a Square John dream that ain't cut out for us. This is what we know. This is what we are. This is what we do."

"I like the what-if game," Dick goes.

"Yeah, you would," I go.

We're standing in front of the Marquee and there's a few people moving up the steps and giving us curious glances.

"What if, Digger?" Dick goes. "What if we go to Charlie's and Granite shows up here and we miss him?"

"Then we miss him."

"But what if he wants to help us and we don't get the chance to ask?"

"Then we don't ask," I go, getting frustrated at Dick's excitement.

"But what if we do what One For The Dead says and go here, then go to Charlie's if nothing happens?"

I look at them and shake my head. We really got a long way from where we used to be, and it kinda makes me sad somehow. In the good old days we never woulda talked about this. We'd have been on our way to Heave-Ho's.

"All right," I go. "I'll play your silly little game. What if the next person out of the next cab that pulls up here is anyone else but Granite? If it's someone else, we go to Charlie's. What if we call it that way?"

I got them and they know it. One thing you can always trust a rounder for is that they know when they're snookered and don't make a big fuss about it.

"Okay," the old lady goes.

"Sure," Timber goes.

"Yeah, then," Dick goes.

I smile and turn to face the traffic, and just about shit my fucking pants when Granite steps out of the next cab.

Double Dick

I KNEW IT WAS GONNA BE HIM. I knew it. I don't know how come I knew it but I knew it anyhow. Much as a big part of me wanted to go to Heave-Ho Charlie's, an even bigger part of me wanted him to come so I wouldn't have to struggle no more. I wasn't even sure of what that meant but it sounded real good to me on accounta sometimes it gets real hard out here an' I don't wanna do what I gotta do sometimes. So when he got out of that cab I was glad to see him.

Granite didn't seem too surprised to see us neither. He just smiled at us as he reached through the window to give the driver his money, then walked over and slapped me on the back. "Dick. Good to see you," he said.

"Digger found some money," I said.

"Well, that's good. Not a bad way to start the day, is it, Digger?"

"Better'n a swat in the balls with a frozen rabbit," Digger said, takin' a swallow from Timber's bottle.

Granite just looked at him for a moment. "Well, I never really thought about it that way but, yes, I guess you're right. It would feel better than that."

"And he found some smokes, too," I said, kinda wantin' Digger to spill the beans about the ticket right away.

"Smokes? Well, it gets better, doesn't it?"

"Tell him, Digger," One For The Dead said.

"Tell me what?" Granite asked.

Digger just looked at him. Not hard or mean or anything like that. Just looked at him like the way he looked at an old bike he seen in an alley one time. Kinda like guessin' about it.

"Well, there was a lottery ticket in the pack of smokes I found," Digger said. "So I figured, what the fuck. Been a pretty lucky day already but I might as well get it looked at. So I went into a little store and, well, it was a winner."

"A winner?" Granite said, smilin'. "Wow. What did you get?"

"Thirteen and a half."

"Well, that's pretty good for nothing. Thirteen dollars will always come in handy, I imagine."

"Try thirteen and a half million, Rock."

"Did you say *million*?"

"Yup."

"Are you sure? Did you check?"

"We checked all right. The ticket's good for thirteen and half mil."

"Jesus," Granite said an' looked at all of us.

Digger told Granite all about us all goin' down to the office where they kept the money. Granite got calmer the longer Digger told his story.

"So there was nothin' left to do but get the fuck out of there," Digger said.

"And look for you," One For The Dead said.

"Me?" Granite asked. "What do you want me to do?"

"Well, none of us have any identification or a bank account and they say that we need that to get the money," she told him.

"No ID?" Granite asked. "None of you have ID? How can that be?"

Digger snorted. "Fer fuck sake, Rock. Nobody gives a shit about that. Keeping a few pieces of paper together's a small friggin' thing to worry about out here. And we ain't exactly regular folks who do the things that need us to be identified. I don't gotta have a driver's licence for my cart. I don't gotta have a social insurance number 'cause I ain't exactly pulling a friggin' wage, and I sure as shit don't need no birth certificate because most people don't give a flying fuck when I was born or if I'm alive."

Granite nodded while Digger spoke. "So what do you think I can do?"

"Help us with the ID thing," Timber said.

"Or you could cash in the friggin' thing and then piece us off," Digger said.

"Piece you off?"

"Yeah. Give us the cash."

"I don't think I'd want to do that."

"You don't want someone giving you a ticket that's worth thirteen and half million bucks? Come on, Rock. Get real."

"Well, I suppose I could have my lawyer draw up some papers to say that you are who you are and he could have bank accounts opened for you. You'd have to pay for that, of course, and it would likely take some time, but I think we could get it done that way. Or there's a trust account arrangement."

"Trust account?" One For The Dead asked. "I like the sound of that."

"Yes. Well, someone has an account opened in your name and then looks out for it. When you want money for something, you have to go through them. It's a way of keeping your money safe."

"No. I like the first way better," Digger said. "Cash is cash. I wanna be able to get it when I want it, not on someone else's time."

"Me too," Timber said. "I guess if it's ours, it should be ours."

"You're all sharing this?" Granite asked.

"Fucking right," Digger said. "That's what ya do fer your wingers when you're solid."

"You piece them off?" Granite asked with a grin.

"You piece 'em off," Digger said, also grinning.

"Well, maybe I should go and look into this right away. There're a few hours left in the business day still and we can get the ball rolling for you. Thirteen and a half million dollars doesn't want to sit unused for very long, does it?"

"What should we do, Granite?" One For The Dead asked.

Granite looked at her an' his eyes were really kind. "Did you know that there are movies that you can take home now?"

"Fuck off," Digger said. "How're ya gonna do that?"

"They're called videos. Once a movie's been through the theatres the company releases it as a video or a taped movie. You can rent the taped movie and watch it at home on a player that hooks up to your television. I watch movies that way all the time."

"That sounds nice for you," One For The Dead said.

"Well, it would be nice for *you* if you want to come to my home and watch one while I take care of this business."

None of us was able to talk for a long time. We all stood there lookin' at Granite like he wasn't even talkin' English no more on accounta this was a big surprise. Us guys. Us guys goin' to someone's house. Granite's house. To watch movies. This was gettin' to be a really amazin' kind of day.

"Us?" Timber asked finally. "You want us to go to your house and watch movies?"

"If you like, yes," Granite said.

"Why?" Timber asked.

"Cuz we're fucking special," Digger said. "Ain't that right, Mr. Square John? Now that we got what other people want we're fucking special just like the tarted-up babe at the lottery office told me."

"Yes," Granite said, lookin' Digger right in the eye. "You *are* special. But not because you have money. Money doesn't make anybody special. You're special because you take care of each other. You're special because you don't desert each other. Ever. You're special because even though this big friggin' thing happened to you all, you're still trying to get into the movies. You're still trying to be who you are. That's what makes you special. To me, anyway."

"You got any hooch?" Digger asked.

"Hooch? Well, I don't know about hooch but I have some things to drink. But if you like, you can stop off and get some hooch. You can't get drunk in my home, though."

"No problem," Timber said. "I just want to get into a movie and not have to think about this any longer."

And so we headed out of the park to get a ride over to Granite's house an' all's I could think about on the way over there was rows and rows of movies all just waitin' to be watched, an' I figured if gettin' a bunch of money could get you to do somethin' like that then it must be okay. I was with my friends. That's all I cared about. Long as we was together I was gonna be okay no matter what on accounta they'd never let nothin' bad happen to me. Granite was my friend now too an' I knew he wasn't gonna let nothin' bad happen to me neither.

One For The Dead

AND THEN WE WERE FIVE. Walking out of that little park that afternoon in the company of friends, I felt almost like being home. They were a strange assortment. They were like little boys in great big bodies, and I felt such a strong tug of motherhood in my chest it almost made me cry. I guess I'd never given myself the time to think about my lack of children, never allowed myself to consider how my life as a woman might have changed with motherhood or even whether the capacity for love within me was ever strong enough to make me fit for it. Right then, I knew. Right then, I knew for absolute certain that I could have loved enough to be a mother and raise happy, contented kids. Those boys walking beside me took me right back to the dusty, bush-lined roads of Big River and I felt like little Amelia again, with a heart full of love and a head full of dreams. Around us I saw the shadowed ones moving about in that moist spring air and I wondered how many lives had turned in that little space of green, how many fortunes had been altered through word or deed on that same bench we'd gathered at. Ours had. In whatever way Creation had desired for us, our lives had become something different with the energy of a simple choice. We would go to Granite's home. We would sit in the space that he created for himself and we would share time. We would watch a movie and we would wait to see what motions we needed to go through to get the money that had been sent our way.

The money didn't matter to me. It was still a dream. It was part of the invisible world and not yet here. What mattered was my boys. What mattered was the fact that we were all learning to be together and that we were willing to risk things we might never have risked before. Us, heading to a Square John's home and a Square John inviting us there. The world widens incredibly sometimes. If you stay wakeful enough you can see it. The sky gets bigger at times like that, the light gets brighter and the wind blows harder, more insistently. Like Creation is heaving a huge breath so the new growing can take place. That's what it felt like walking out of that park that afternoon. Like the world was heaving a big breath for us.

We piled into a cab, the four of us rounders scrunched up in the back while Granite sat in the front to direct the driver. It felt like a hayride or the feeling I used to get on the tail of the wagon with my brothers when we'd go to chop and gather wood on Big River. The boys elbowed each other for room and there was a lot of good-natured grumbling and jokes about the smell of feet, bad breath, and bony shoulders. Just like in days long gone, and I had to smile at the impact of this sudden gift, this vague returning.

When the cab pulled up in front of the building where Granite lived, I could feel all of us stiffen. It was a huge, pale pink building with lots of trees and bushes out front and a long curved walkway made of cobblestones leading to a set of big glass doors. There was a small room encased in glass before you got to the lobby where some grandfather-looking chairs sat in front of one of those fake fireplaces and a jungle of plants. Just the kind of place you learn to avoid when you live like us. A police call is made before your feet even get to those glass doors, and the boys and me felt nervous and anxious stepping out of the cab.

Granite led the way. I could see Digger looking quickly in each direction and back over his shoulder. Timber and Dick walked with their heads lowered like they wanted to sink into the cracks between the cobblestones. Me, I just walked behind Granite watching the world breathe.

We didn't pass another person on the way into the building and didn't see anyone all the way up in the elevator or in the hallway to Granite's door. The air was different inside there, though. It didn't move. It felt like you were walking through something in order to get anywhere. I could sense the walls around me. The boys were all eyeballs and Adam's apples, their gaits more cautious, and I knew that they could feel the walls around them too. We were actually grateful, I think, when Granite opened his door and gestured us through.

It was marvellous. There were big windows in the ceiling where the light flowed in, and one entire wall was a window too.

He had a fireplace that stood all by itself in the living room and it looked like a smaller version of the old stove in our house on the reserve. There were a lot of big plants around and even a tree in one corner whose branches spread out over a lot of the room. Dick gaped at the biggest television I think I ever saw and Timber was scrutinizing the shelves of books. Digger stood and looked at everything, nodding his head slowly. I liked it. There was so much light it was like being outside. It felt comfortable, but as I looked around I couldn't help but wonder about the fact that there weren't any pictures of people anywhere around. There was art on the walls but no pictures of people, and as I watched Granite move around nervously, showing us where to hang our coats and directing us to the living room, I knew that he wasn't that much different from the four of us. He was part of our ragged company despite the shimmer and glow of this space he lived in.

"I'll pull chairs out of the den and you can all make yourselves comfortable on the couch and the armchair," Granite said. "Digger, there's a bar over there by the fireplace. The bottom doors in the bookcase. Help yourself."

Digger nodded but he and the boys just walked slowly across the room and planted themselves on the couch. Digger dug his mickey out and took a drink before passing it along to Timber and Dick. They all stared around in silence while Granite brought two more velvet-covered armchairs from another room. When he was finished, he stood in the middle of the room looking about like it was the first time he'd seen the place too.

"Um, Dick," he said eventually. "I've got a collection of movies here if you'd like to see them. Maybe you can pick one you want to watch."

He walked over to a closed bookcase and opened the doors.

"Geez," Dick said. "Them are all movies?"

He got up from the couch and walked over with Timber and Digger right behind him. The three of them stood in front of that bookcase just eyeballing the rows and rows of small cases on the shelves.

"The top shelves are drama. Mysteries are on the third shelf, some comedies and westerns on the fourth, and foreign-language films along the bottom," Granite said. "Have a look."

He handed Dick one of the movies and Dick's face was full of amazement and pleasure. Timber and Digger leaned in and looked at it too.

"Geez," Dick said. "It looks just like the movie posters outside the theatre. What does it say, Timber?"

"It says, *The Deer Hunter*," Timber read.

"Wow. That sounds good, huh, Digger?"

"Could be," Digger replied.

"Here's one you might like, Digger," Granite said, handing him a movie case.

"*Requiem for a Heavyweight*," Digger read. "Fights? Boxing?"

"Yes," Granite said. "And a really, really great story."

"What's a wreck-ee-um?" Dick asked.

"Requiem," Timber said. "It's the Catholic service for the dead or a song or poem, I guess, that has the same feeling."

Granite looked at Timber with a puzzled expression. Timber held the movie case in his hand and tapped it on his palm before looking up and catching Granite's gaze. They nodded to each other and there were tiny smiles at the corners of their eyes.

"So these are all flicks like we see downtown, Rock?" Digger asked.

"Yes. I buy the ones I want to keep and watch again sometime. They're like friends, really."

"Friends?"

"Yes. Someone you're always eager to see again."

Digger looked at him steadily and Granite returned the gaze. Then, they nodded at each other, pursing their lips meaningfully.

"Can we try one?" Dick asked.

"Yes. Which one?" Granite asked him.

"Geez. I don't know. I can't read 'em. You pick, Digger."

"Me?"

"Yeah. It's your day. You choose," Dick said, smiling at Digger.

"Let's do the boxing one then."

Granite busied himself getting the movie ready and the boys settled onto the couch. Me, I just sat there and watched them all. They'd settled into a comfortable place with each other and the strangeness seemed to melt away. Movies were our common ground and we all knew how to be when one was playing, we all knew how to feel when the buildup started inside just before the first flicker of light on the screen. It's what made us friends. It's what had brought us all here.

Granite pushed all the buttons and the screen lit up. He had his television connected to a big sound system, and when he adjusted the speaker controls the room was just like a movie house. He crossed the room and drew the drapes across those big windows and the four of us were at home in the movies once again.

"Drinks, guys?" Granite asked.

When he didn't get an answer from the four amazed faces on the couch, he came over to me.

"Can I get you anything, Amelia?"

I smiled at him. "Maybe a little water. Some juice maybe, if you have it."

"Are you hungry?"

"No. I'm fine."

"You're sure?"

"I'm sure. Granite?"

"Yes?"

"Thank you."

"I haven't done anything yet."

"Thank you anyway."

He looked at me kindly and went to fetch my water.

Granite

James Merton was a lawyer I knew well and trusted. He'd handled the sale of the estate and had advised me through the years on everything from potential libel to investment and real estate matters. I called him from the den while the sounds of the movie playing carried in, along with several oohs and aahs. We traded banter awhile and then got down to the business of the call.

"You're kidding me, right?" he asked.

"No. I'm not." I said.

"Thirteen and a half million dollars?"

"Yes."

"Street people?"

"Yes. Well, homeless, really. There's a difference."

"And they want you to look after the transfer of the money?"

"Yes. They trust me."

"Because none of them have identification enough to pick up the cheque or to cash it if they did?"

"Right."

"In-fucking-credible," he said.

"Fucking right," I replied with a grin.

We talked awhile about the most expedient way to handle getting the money for them and how to set up the necessary banking. James was quick and earnest and it wasn't long before we had a viable option to present to my new friends.

"So when will you see them again?" he asked.

"In a few minutes," I said. "They're right here."

"In your home?"

"Yes."

"You've got four street people sitting in your home? Unsupervised?"

"Yes. But they're homeless, James. They're not street people and they're not unsupervised. They're watching a movie."

"A movie? They're watching a movie?"

"Yes," I said. "It's how we met."

"At the movies?"

"Yes."

"In-fucking-credible," he said again.

"Fucking right," I said, grinning even more broadly.

"You know there's going to be one hell of a lot of media on this. Once the press gets wind of it, those people are going to be under all kinds of scrutiny and pressure. It'll make living on the street look like a holiday."

"I know."

"Can they handle that? Well, basically it's not even a question because the lottery rules say that winners need to meet the media when they pick up their prizes. So really it's a matter of minimizing the effect on them, I would guess."

"If they retain you, many of the questions can be handled by you. Money questions and such."

"Yes. I can do that. But they'll still have to face up to some pretty personal, probing questions. Well, you know the drill."

"Yeah, unfortunately I do. I'll tell them what to expect. If they go for this I'll call you back and we can arrange to meet with you before we do the pickup tomorrow."

"Okay. Are you sure you want to do this? You have no obligation here, after all. Me, personally, I think I'd avoid the headache because it'll be a big one, brother."

"No. I'm sure. I don't know why, really, but I'm sure."

"Okay then. I'm with you. Call me and let me know as soon as you can."

"Yes. Later, James."

I sat in the den and listened to the sounds from the other room. James was right. This was the kind of story the media lived for. The impossible, improbable, unbelievable tale of the nobody suddenly undergoing life-altering circumstances. They'd love it, and they'd milk it for everything they could. The four people sitting in my living room watching Anthony Quinn struggle to retain his dignity and find redemption had no idea how close they were to Quinn's Mountain Rivera at this precise moment. I moved to the doorway that led to the viewing room and saw children at a matinee; children swept up in the Lumiere brothers' grand vision and carried forward by every filmmaker and visionary since, children rapt by the fascination born of dreams, effortless and flowing, cast outward onto a screen and captivating in their telling, children transported to a world far beyond the humble borders of their lives, and children ensnared in the hope of imagined worlds made real, worlds that hope itself brought closer and closer to becoming real through the vehicle of imagination. They were all far too engrossed in story to realize I was there, and when I crossed to the empty armchair no one made a move. We sat in the flickering light of a dream made in 1962, breathless and silent as awe can engender, and lost ourselves in story one more time. Only Digger moved. He tapped my knee with a knuckle and handed me the mickey in the darkness. I drank and handed it back to him, our eyes shining in the refracted light of the television like the eyes of miners in the depths, solidarity plumbed from the cracks, fissures, and tunnels of our world.

Timber

"So this guy will be our money manager?" I asked while we were busy eating the pizza Granite ordered once the movie ended.

"Yes," Granite said. "He'll have you sign papers allowing him to take care of your portions of the money. Then, whenever you need to make a purchase or just need some money for anything, he'll get it for you. It works out well because he can arrange all the accounting, taxation, and investing business you want to do or need to do. You don't have to worry about it."

"And this guy's a straight shooter, Rock?" Digger asked.

"As straight as they come, Digger. He handles my business. Has for years. I trust him entirely."

Granite leaned forward in his chair. For the next while he told us about the radio, television, and newspaper people that would be at the lottery office in the morning. He told us about how they'd want to know all kinds of things about us and what we were going to do with the money. He said that they had a right to ask those questions because it was a public lottery. He said that because of where we came from there was going to be a lot more interest in us tomorrow and for a lot of days after. He said there was no way we could avoid it.

"But you know, James can handle as many of the questions as you like. Any time you don't want to answer, just look at him and he can take it," Granite said.

"Take 'em all," Digger said. "I ain't talking to no one about nothing."

"I'm not comfortable with answering questions either," I said.

"I don't think I wanna neither," Dick said.

"Well, let's just wait and not worry about it," Amelia said. "We've got Granite and his lawyer to look after us now. I say we just enjoy each other's company. Shall we watch another movie?"

"Can we, Granite?" Dick asked.

"If you like. Or we still didn't get to see *Field of Dreams*."

"That's right," I said. "All of this got in our way."

"By the time we get there it's gonna be packed. Night movies, ya know?" Digger said. "I kinda hate night movies. Way too many people and the way Rock here tells it there's gonna be way too many people around us tomorrow."

"That's right, too," I said. "It works good here, though. There's just the five of us. Are you sure it's okay, Granite?"

"It's okay," he said.

"Can I pick, then?" Dick asked.

"No," Digger said. "Not this time, pal. I think we should let Amelia choose this one. She's the one got us watching movies in the first place. We wouldn't be here if she hadn't come up with that plan."

"Why, Digger," she said, "that's the first time I ever heard you call me by my real name."

Digger scratched at his collar. "Yeah, well, been the fucking day for surprises. You wanna know what my name is?"

I was shocked and I knew Amelia and Dick were, too. One of the things that a rounder respects about other rounders is the wish to keep the other life away. We all have other lives. We all have lives we lived before we became what we became and it's no one's business to know unless we want to tell them. I never wanted to tell, and I knew that Digger was far more hard-core than me about it. Being called by your real name brings up things you don't necessarily want to remember. Things that make it harder to be what you became. But I still wanted to know what his real name was.

"What is it?" Granite asked.

Digger scratched at his collar again. Then he took a swallow from the mickey. There wasn't much there and he finished it. When he put the empty on the floor in front of him, Granite picked it up, crossed over to the bar, and came back with a half-bottle of vodka. Digger nodded at him and took a healthy gulp before he spoke again.

"Mark," he said. "Go fucking figure. Mark. Me. Fucking Mark. You know what a mark is, Rock?"

"Sort of," Granite said. "But likely not in the way you know."

"A mark is a stooge, a lackey, a loogan, a fall guy, a boob. In the carnival, whenever someone would drop a bunch of cash at a game joint, the tout would slap him on the back before he walked away. There'd be chalk on his hand. So the boob's walking down the midway with a big mark on his back letting the rest of the hucksters know he's a soft touch. A stooge, a boob. And they fucking called me Mark."

"You're no mark, Digger," Granite said.

"Always going to be Digger to me," I said. "But why're you telling us now?"

"Cause there's a shitstorm coming when we cash this ticket. A shitstorm that'll change everything. You know it. I know it. Everyone knows it. So I guess I just wanted you to know about me before it all goes to hell. That and the fucking movie we just seen. Between the two of them they got me to talking or wanting to talk, I guess," Digger said, leaning back in his seat.

"You don't gotta," Dick said.

"I know, pal," Digger said. "But you're the only friends I had for a long friggin' time, and before this cash fucks it all up I want you to know who your friend has been all this time. So before Amelia here picks the next flick, I wanna tell ya."

"Tell us what?" I asked.

"Tell you about Mark Haskett," Digger said. "The other life.

The other life I lived before I was Digger. I wanna tell you that. So you know."

All the time we'd been together on the street he'd never offered word one about the other life, and he was way too mean and hard to risk asking. Even Granite was impressed by this sudden willingness to open up the vault and let that other life see the light of day after who knows how many years. None of us knew what to do so we just sat back in our seats and let Digger tell his tale.

Digger

MOUNTAIN RIVERA was just like me. I only ever knew how to do one thing. I only ever knew how to do one thing better'n anyone else ever done it. I did it for a long time, too. A long time. But that time has been gone for just as many years now, and thinkin' about it makes me sad to realize how long I been without the one thing I loved more'n anything else in this world.

Didn't start out that way. In fact it didn't start out looking like very much was in store for me at all. My folks weren't what you call the industrious sort. We lived on a scrabble-assed patch of farmland we got from this farmer who let us stay there out of pity more'n anything. It wasn't good for nothing. So him letting us squat there meant that he could at least see some use of that low-lying, marshy, mosquito-filled half a fucking bog that it was. Guess the other reason was that my mother was Metis. Or at least her grandparents were. They come out of that Manitoba rebellion when the half-breeds tried to set up their own kind of government, then got their asses handed to them by the military. My mother's mother got tired of the half-breed label and married white. My mother carried that on when she married Clint Haskett, a white guy workin' on the railroad. So somewhere in me is a thinned-out fraction of rebel blood. Don't make me Metis, don't make me half-breed, don't make me Indian. It don't make me nothing but the only son of a lazy son of a bitch who'd sooner pocket the fucking nine ball than pocket a paycheque. That's how I started out.

Didn't help that my mother was a chickenshit. She just let him run all over and never said word one. Oh, she was okay with me if you buy the absence making the heart grow fonder gaff. Guess after she'd gone through all her schemes at getting him to stay home or go to fucking work, she figured her duty was to go party with him. That left me with the farmer. He was okay. Right off, he kinda knew the score and put me to work on the farm in exchange for food and the cast-off clothes his own kids grew outta. I liked it. Least I was eating and staying busy after school was out. I don't even think my parents knew. I think they were thinking they were doing pretty good. The kid was in school. The kid was wearing clean clothes. The kid looked like he was eating. So they musta been doing a good job. Never occurred to them to think about how the fuck all that was getting accomplished. They kept on slogging through on the welfare cheque and dear old dad's pool-hall winnings. Turns out he was good at something after all.

Couple things happened when I was fourteen. First, school got to be just too friggin' much of a bother. I was strong and tough from the farm work and the farmer was starting to hand me wages for the work I done. I dug that, man. Loot. My first loot and I kept it to myself. So working got to be more of a draw than school and I eventually just drifted out. Lots of farm kids wound up doing that and the truant officers didn't really give a flying fuck after a while so there was no hassle over me leaving. Wasn't anyone for them to complain to anyhow, so what the hell.

Second thing that happened was I discovered the barn roof.

After a long day of working I wanted somewhere that I could be alone and kinda gather my thoughts. Didn't want to walk the fields, I was always too tired for that. But one night I climbed up to the top of the haymow and out the gable window onto the roof. It was amazing. I could see everywhere. It was a clear summer night that first time. Clear like how it gets when the air makes everything brighter and closer like looking through a friggin' telescope or something. I sat there and had a smoke, looking at the land. I could see the town where Ma and Pa were hustling pool and drinking. I could see the other farms where we went to lend a hand at harvest time. I could see horizon in all directions. Kinda like being on the fucking ocean, I guess. Nothing but sky 'n horizon all around you.

Anyway, I kept on going up there every night. Even when it rained. I kept telling myself stories about what was over the horizon in each direction and how someday when I saved enough money I'd go there. That's what I wanted. To be away. Gone. But as long as I had the barn roof I was okay. I could handle shit. As long as I could go out there and sit and watch the world, I could deal with it. So I sat on the roof and planned the great escape while I worked and saved and tried to choose a direction to set off for when the time was right.

Turns out that the time was right when I was fifteen. The carnival came to town and I went over with a bunch of other guys to watch them pull in and set up. I liked it. The carnies seemed like good guys, all cussing, joking, and hard-working. That night we were all standing there when this guy comes walking over. Big guy. Tall. Wide. Ugly motherfucker. He's smoking a big stogie and he comes over and stands right in front of us, staring, sizing us up.

"Anybody wanna work?" he goes.

"What kinda work?" I go.

"I need somebody to help me put my wheel up."

"Wheel?"

"Ferris wheel."

"Ferris wheel? I don't know nothin' about no Ferris wheel."

"You don't gotta know nothin'. In fact, it's better if you don't. Long as you listen to what I tell ya, you'll learn and you'll be safe. Figure you can do that?"

"Sure," I go. "How much?"

"Give ya ten."

"Ten? Mister, ya bought yerself a hand."

"Good. I like the short guys. Easier to pull the spokes for the short guys. Name's Dutch," he goes, and sticks out the biggest fucking hand I ever saw.

Ferris wheels were the big draw back then. Every show had a wheel and every wheel had a wheelman, someone whose only job was running that wheel: running it, moving it, setting it up, and tearing it down. Dutch was a wheelman and one of the best. He was carny blood. Sawdust in his shoes, he said that night as we worked. Sawdust from the truckloads they laid down to sop up the wet on the carny grounds in the old days. He had sawdust in his shoes and it kept him on the road year-round taking that wheel from Louisiana to Manitoba, Washington State to Nova Scotia. He was carny blood and all he knew and all he wanted to know was the Ferris wheel and the next stop on the road.

We put up that wheel that night from the ground up. I'll never forget it. There was a huge steel plate that was the base and we had to find a level patch of ground, or as close to level as we could get. Then we evened it with shims. Next came the bottom half of the two towers, and they were bolted onto the plate. Then Dutch and I carried the support beams from the flatbed trailer the wheel was carried on. Everything was forged steel and heavier than a motherfucker. We slid those ground supports into place, bolted them, and then secured the angle irons that held the towers in place from the side. He was gruff, and when he told you to do something he didn't mean right now, he always meant right fucking now, and with a guy that size you did what you were told. When he directed me in the assembly of the A-frame we would use to block and tackle the top half of the towers into place, he smiled at my quickness.

"You're a friggin' natural," he goes.

"Giving you ten bucks worth, that's all," I go.

"I'da give fifteen," he goes and grins.

"I'da worked for five," I go, and we lifted the A-frame into place.

The towers went up without a hitch and Dutch went to find a couple more hands to help us with the spokes. I was all grease and sweat by then and I loved it. The hammering of bolts, the twisting of cables to tighten them, the pulling of the spokes into the hub while standing forty feet off the ground was joy. Pure fucking joy.

The lining up of the wheel was work enough for two, and Dutch pieced off the others and sent them away. We worked on each side of the wheel securing it, him talking loud and pointing what was needed, me concentrating as hard as I could and fighting to keep up. Finally, it was up.

"Get this into ya," Dutch goes and hands me a beer and a smoke.

"We done?" I go.

"There's the seats still, but I do that in the morning. You can come back and help if you like. Don't take long once I get the motor goin'."

"Sure. It always this much fun?"

"Fun? This is ball breakin', boy. You think it's fun?"

"More fun than I had in a long time."

"Damn, son. You might make a wheelman if you chose to stick around."

"Figure?"

"Sure," he goes, taking a big gulp of beer. "Anybody figures this is fun got wheelman in 'em somewhere."

So I went back the next day. I went back the day after that and Dutch showed me how to work the motor, how to run the wheel. I'd been around tractors for a while already and he was using a McCormack tractor motor, so learning was a snap. Finally I just went there in the mornings instead of showing up for the farmer, and spent the day hanging out with Dutch and talking about wheels.

He told me about this guy who made the first one. George Ferris. He talked about how high into the sky that first wheel went. Almost three hundred feet. Dutch's wheel was eighty and I looked up and tried to imagine how fucking high three hundred feet was and how much fun it musta been to put a big son of a bitch like that into the air. He talked about the road and places with names like Wenatchee, Muskegon, and Tupelo. He talked about the carny life and the "white line fever" that kept him on the road. He talked about booze and gambling and the taste of a grab joint breakfast after a boozy night with the town girls. It was the first time in my friggin' life I ever heard anybody speak with fucking passion about something and I wanted to hear more. When he asked me to come on the road with him and be his apprentice wheelman I just walked away. I just walked away without word one to nobody. I climbed up into that semi that hauled the wheel and watched fifteen years of bullshit drop off over the horizon. No one looked for me. If they did I never heard of it, and I never bothered to write back or call or any of that wimpy, pussy, cry-in-your-beer bullshit. Me, I was glad to be gone.

Dutch and I went year-round. We hooked up with Royal American Shows to tour the south in winter and then hooked up with Conklin to do Canada all summer. God. I friggin' loved it. Town to town, show to show, we followed the white line of highway wherever it called us. I was young and strong and cocky and I fit into the carny life like I never fit anywhere again. Jesus. What a fucking life. Camped out behind the trailers, a big circle of us, playing guitars, drinking, smoking a little weed, the stars above us burning holes in my eyes whenever I looked up, and the feel of freedom. You learn that when you spend enough time on the road: that freedom has a feel. Like there's nothing beyond your skin. Like you could vanish like a fucking ghost, lickety-fucking-split up the set of gears and down the fucking road. On the carny was all I wanted. It was all I needed. It was all I knew.

I became the second-best wheelman anywhere. Dutch taught me everything he knew about the wheel and it got so I could feel it just like he could. I'd be putting riders on and off and the wind would get to blow and I'd put my hand on a flange, feel the tremor and just know, just fucking know where a cable had to be tightened or a cotter pin replaced. Just fucking know it. I fell in love with the stuff of it. The smell of the thick purple-black grease, the weight of the pins and bolts sitting like decisions in my hands, the thrum of a taut cable when you plucked it, the thrill of a spoke snapped smartly into the hub, and the anxious feel of the empty seats when you rubbed them down the morning before opening like horses eager for the race. God. I fucking loved it.

But the best part was walking the wheel. Once we got it all set, once there was nothing left but the seats, I'd hop up onto the outside flange and walk from spoke to spoke checking for anything that I mighta missed. Once I got up to about the third spoke I'd tell Dutch to slip the brake and I'd walk the wheel. Slowly, measuring my pace, I'd walk, and as each spoke came around and down I'd look it over until I'd made the whole circle. Then I'd step into the frame of a spoke, put my feet in the corners of the crossbars and lay across the big X the cables made with my arms stretched out and hands holding on to the other crossbrace and tell Dutch to take her up. He'd run me right up to the top that way and stop it. There I was, standing in the crossbrace in the spoke of a wheel eighty feet above the ground, looking out over Kansas, Ontario, Alberta, Wy-fucking-oming, or wherever. Me. Mark Haskett, Wheelman. And I'd stand there and smoke and look across the land imagining what kind of lives the people led out there and what was over the horizon. I'd stand there and look, feel that wheel trembling beneath me and know that I was a part of it. As much as the cables, bolts, nuts, and bars, I was a fucking part of it. I knew that as long as I could do that, as long as I could go up there at the start of every show, I could deal with it, I could handle it, I was home. It was my place. It was the only place in my entire fucking life that was just for me. When I reached the point where I felt filled up with air and space and time I yelled down and Dutch would ease me back to earth.

"I never seen nobody do that before," Dutch goes the first time I pulled it off. "You're a fucking wheelman, son. You're a fucking wheelman."

But Dutch died. He fell off the wheel when some rube's kid got her long hair caught in the joint where the seat fits on. He heard her scream and stopped the wheel in a heartbeat. He knew that he couldn't move it again or her hair would be ripped right off her friggin' scalp, and while the fucking rube is yelling and crying Dutch climbs along the flange and up the wheel like he seen me do, holding a knife in his teeth like friggin' Tarzan. Then, he holds on with one hand while he cuts the kid's hair. He's up there about twenty feet. The rube is so excited his kid is free that he starts to hugging and rocking her in his arms and the seat bashes Dutch hard enough to make him lose his grip. He fell and broke his back.

I never cried for him. He wouldn'ta wanted to know that I bawled like a baby, but I sure felt like it. He was the only one other than that farmer who ever did me good. Dutch put the sawdust in my shoes. He put the road in my blood. He put the wheel in my heart. I took his ashes up to the top of the wheel and scattered them to the wind.

The show hired me as their wheelman after that. I was nineteen. I inherited the rig from Dutch and drove it from show to show. I never found nobody to apprentice with me but I hired help whenever I needed it. My name got known. People talked about the speed of my set-ups and teardowns, about my ability to feel a change in my engine and add or do whatever it needed. They talked about my wheel-walking and how any show I was on was never really ready to open until "Haskett walked the wheel." I got hired in as a specialist for big exhibitions that put up permanent wheels, the gigantic ones like Ferris's original, and once, for a little while, I lived in a city one whole summer running one of them wheels until the road called me so hard I had to sign up with the show again and hit the white line. I was the best fucking wheelman anywhere.

I signed on with an outfit called Woodland Family Shows as their permanent wheelman. It was a big fucking deal because no one ever got signed forever by nobody. But I was the best, and Peter Wood wanted to run an old-time carnival the old-time way. He wanted the wheel to be the centre of the midway and he wanted a wheelman to keep it there. That carny was a good one. Pete had the old sideshows with the barkers pulling people in, clowns roaming the midway, and a big ring right next to the wheel where his daddy showed off the trained ponies he ran. While the world around us was switching to bigger 'n faster 'n more expensive, Pete kept that show original, and I guess we kinda all got to be feeling like a family. A road family, and I fit right in there. We all helped each other with set-up and teardown. We ate together. We sat out under the stars and partied and drank and sang together. We waited on the side of the road for the stragglers to catch up so we could all pull into the next town together like a big fucking parade. Just like it used to be in the good old carny days. Pete made it special. He made us special. He made me special. The money was good. People loved that old-time feel and came to our shows in friggin' herds. The route we travelled took us to all kinds of farm towns and small places where the carny was always an event. Only trouble was they didn't do winter shows and Pete didn't want me signing with the southern circuit in the winter. He didn't want to risk losing me to a bigger show. So he paid me my regular wage all through the winter but it meant I had to get digs somewhere. For anybody else it was a plum fucking deal but for me, an old-time carny with sawdust in his shoes, it was like death. We'd pack it up after Halloween and start doing parking lot shows again in March or April. Five months of sitting around with no road beneath me, no wheel spinning over my head, no world like I knew. It was like dying every fucking year.

Pete got me a room in a rooming house, which he paid for. Every Friday a cheque would come for me and I was supposed to rest and relax and wait out the winter until we could hit the road again. Well, fuck. I was still young enough to get friggin' bored sitting around and I started to look for the bars where other snowbound carnies hung out. I found them. I found the biker bars, too, the cowboy bars, the fistfight bars and the old-man bars where you just sit and nurse your drink and bide your fucking time. Got so I just spent the winters in those bars waiting for the spring that always came but took its own sweet fucking time.

I don't know what happened but something broke inside me. Nothing that you could see, nothing that a guy could point out to someone and say, "Hey, don't this look fucking weird." Nothing like that. Just a break somewhere that made lifting anything a fucking agony. I covered it up for a long time. Just said "fuck it" and worked through it anyhow. But it got so some mornings it was all I could do to get standing up again. People started to notice when the wheel got slower going up and coming down. People started to notice when my face'd be all twisted lifting something I'da thrown around a few years earlier. People started to notice when I started using booze to fight the pain.

But I was still the fucking best and Pete kept me on. I never told nobody how much hurt I was carrying. Never told nobody how the reason I let Pete get me a permanent helper was so I didn't have to get up from my chair more'n a couple times a day. Never told nobody how fucking angry I was getting at my body for letting me down like that. I just stone-faced it. I just gritted my fucking teeth, took a belt of hooch, and let 'er ride just like any good carny would do.

Wasn't long before Pete was keeping me off the shows. Not all of them. Not all at once. Just sometimes when the broke part would be all fucked up and I couldn't do the work, couldn't walk the wheel, couldn't get the set-up or the teardown done. Those times I'd be so pissed I'd get mad and he'd have to send me home in the middle of a show. But I was the best, and when I was fine I was still the best and he kept me on longer'n maybe he meant to. But the broke part inside me was getting worse and it took more to fix it. Took more hooch. One spring he couldn't find me. I hadn't been to the rooming house in about a week, I guess, and the old lady had no idea where I was. It took him a few days but he found me holed up with a few hooch hounds in an old-man bar fighting over a card game. He got me to the show but I was no good. I couldn't fix the broke part and it was hollering like a motherfucker by then. Any kind of lifting at all burned like a flare all down my back and shoulders. I had to drink to handle it. He let me go. Pieced me off with a big bonus and let me go. I tried to sign on with other shows but the word was out that Haskett couldn't walk the wheel no more. Haskett couldn't get the job done, and for a carny that's as low as you can go.

Suddenly I'm like Mountain Rivera in that flick. I'm an old fucking man. I'm an old fucking man who only knows how to do one thing. One thing that I was the fucking best at. So I wander around the city looking for a job but nobody's looking for the best fucking wheelman in the world. Nobody's looking for an old man with no history the real world can use. Long as I kept looking, Pete fronted me the room at the old lady's. But after a while I'd had enough of being turned down at everything I went for. I was the fucking best and no one wanted that. They only saw an old guy trying to score a young man's job, and they always took the young buck. So I quit trying. Pete gave up after that. Once the old lady told him I was spending my days drinking in my room, he let me go completely. The old lady tried putting up with me, gave me a few months on the cuff, but even she got tired and let me go too.

There I was old, drunk, with nothing to put up in the sky no more. But I wasn't going down like that. No fucking way. Maybe I had to sleep outside. Maybe I had to eat at the fucking Mission. Maybe I had to score my clothes at the shelter, but I wasn't gonna be on the fucking mooch like everybody else. I was the best fucking wheelman in the world. I was an old-time carny. So I went to the only work an old guy like me could do without having to ask any-fucking-body. I went and did what I had to do without nobody telling me I was too fucking old or too fucking drunk or too fucking anything. I started to dumpster-dive. I dug for my cash. I worked out my route a long fucking time ago and I stuck to it.

Nowadays, in my little hole in the wall, I'm the king of my world. I'm still the best fucking wheelman. I sit there at night and look out over the city from the hilltop and it feels sometimes kinda like it felt standing in the crossbraces watching the lights of the show beneath me and the lights of the stars above me, the wheel trembling under my feet like a horse ready to race. Except I don't wonder what's on the other side of the horizon no more. I don't wonder what kind of lives the people are living there. I know that there's just another city just like this one. I know there's a million or so other people just like these ones, and I know who they are. I walk the alleys behind their houses. I pick up their toss-offs. I see what they waste and I know. So I only think about me. Me. The best fucking wheelman in the world. Long as I feel that, I know I can deal with it. I know I can handle it.

So many worlds in one.

There you go again.

Oh. Sorry. Sometimes the thoughts just tumble out into air on their own. What I meant was, we look around us and we think we see the world, we think we know it. But in truth, we only see the surface of things. That story was about a whole other world existing side by side with the one I thought I knew.

Yes. That's true. Stories are a great wheel, always turning, always coming back in line with each other.

They make the world go round.

Indeed they do. Indeed they do.

Double Dick

NO ONE SAID NOTHIN' after Digger finished tellin' his story. I liked it but I never said nothin' neither on accounta I didn't know what was right. Digger never told nothing about himself before so I kinda knew it was big. Big enough that nobody said nothin'. We just sat there all quiet until Granite asked us where we wanted to go. Timber told him we'd all go where we went most nights an' he just nodded. He drove us down near the Mission in his nice car an' still nobody was hardly talkin' at all.

"I can meet you all here in the morning," Granite said as we was gettin' out of his car. "We'll need to be at Merton's early to get things rolling, though."

"What's early?" Digger asked.

"Nine?" Granite asked back.

"That's not early but yeah, I guess," Digger said.

"Digger, thanks for telling us that story. For telling me," Granite said.

They just looked at each other then an' it was diff'rent from how they looked at each other before. I can't explain it except that it was different an' it made me feel funny inside. Good, but funny, inside.

"Are you sure you want to go wherever it is you go?" Granite asked us. "I mean, you have money now. You could get a room. You don't have to be outside."

"We haven't any money," One For The Dead said.

"No, well, not now. But you have the ticket and tomorrow you'll have a lot of money. Tonight, I mean, I could spot you the cost of rooms."

"It's a nice night," Timber said. "And I just want to be by myself."

"Me too," I said.

"Same," Digger said.

"But you could think, you could be alone, in a room with a bed and sheets and a television," Granite said.

"And walls," I said.

Everyone looked at me. There was another one of them moments when nobody said nothin' again. The words just slid outta me an' even I was surprised to hear them. But I knew what they meant, though, on accounta rooms made me nervous at night an' I know they made the others nervous too. I didn't know how money was gonna fix that. Granite just nodded finally like he got what I said, waved, an' drove off slowly. I watched his car all the way up the street until he turned at the lights an' disappeared. Digger handed out smokes an' we smoked and had a gulp from Timber's mickey. Nobody still knew what to say. Me, I wished we could go to a movie. Me, I wished I had a story I could tell. Me, I wished we could just stay together that night but I knew it wasn't gonna happen on accounta even though we was hangin' on an' not headin' off on our own we all still wanted to be doin' that an' I could feel that. I felt my insides wantin' that, anyhow.

"Well, fuck," Digger said, crushin' out his smoke with his foot. "I'm gone. Been too weird a fucking day for me and I gotta cash it in."

"It feels like the tracks," I said so fast it scared me.

"What tracks?" Timber asked.

I gulped all nervous and looked around at them hopin' maybe they'd just nod an' pretend they never heard. But they did. "Railroad tracks," I said.

"Okay," Digger said. "What railroad tracks?"

I gulped again. I didn't like goin' where the words was gonna take me on accounta I try'n never go there with people around. I told them, though.

"There was some railroad tracks near where I lived when I was small. We wasn't supposed to go there on accounta there was a big turn an' the driver of the train couldn't see us when it was coming around. But we usedta go anyhow. We usedta go an' kneel down beside them tracks an' put our ears on the rail on accounta someone said you could tell if the train was comin' on accounta it made them rails hum. So we'd kneel down an' try'n guess how big the train was. I never could. The other kids got good at it an' always said before it got there how big it was an' even sometimes what kind it was. Like a grain train or a cow train or just boxcars. I could hear the hum an' all but I never knew how big the train was. Never. This kinda feels like that. Like I know there's a train comin' but I don't know how big."

They all just nodded an' we went our separate ways.

"All aboard," Digger said as he walked away, one hand reachin' up and pullin' a invisible bell. "All board."

One For The Dead

James Merton was good man. I could tell by his face when I met him. He didn't half look away like most people when they meet us for the first time. No. James Merton came around from behind his desk, greeted us, shook our hands, and looked each of us square in the eye. It wasn't because of the ticket. It wasn't because of the money. It was because he was a good man. Pure and simple. His hand was warm and strong and when he asked me how I was I knew that he wanted to know, not giving me that pinched look at the corner of the eyes that people do to fake concern.

"I'm feeling like a fish out of water," I said. "This is all pretty new."

"Yes. It would be. And it will get a lot stranger as we go," he said. "The media will badger you pretty good today."

"They know?" Granite asked.

"They know that the winners of the draw will be there at eleven to claim the prize. They don't know anything other than that."

"So what's the deal here?" Digger said.

"Well, the deal is that you don't have what it takes to get this done, Digger. But I do. You pay me a fee to represent you, to act as your power of attorney, and I set everything up that you need. That's the deal."

"How much?" Digger asked.

James gave Digger a look that said, *I see you*. Digger gave the same one back. "Ordinarily, a percentage. For you, because you're friends of Mr. Harvey, you cover my costs, buy me a dinner with a nice bottle of champagne to celebrate your win, and I'm all yours."

"That's it?"

"For now. If you want to keep me on to help you with this, I'll charge you what I'd charge anyone else for the same services." James went back to sit in his chair. "Coffee, anyone?"

I liked him. Straightforward, strong, and he smelled nice. I could tell that the boys were impressed, and despite their discomfort at the strange surroundings they settled into the chairs James had arranged around his desk and listened. There were papers to sign that he said would let him set up bank accounts for each of us, and other papers that said he had the power of attorney over the money for now so he could do that. Granite explained whatever we needed to understand. He told us that the papers were only temporary and that once we had the accounts set up for ourselves, James would step aside and we'd be on our own. James was only getting us started. We filled out the papers. It felt odd printing my name, and the boys seemed awkward with it too. We handed the papers to James when we were finished so he could sign them.

"Ms. One Sky," he said, handing me a copy of mine.

"Mr. Dumont," he said to Dick, who just blinked and blinked, trying to keep up with the happenings around him, and tucked his papers in his pocket.

"Mr. Haskett."

"And finally, Mr. Hohnstein."

"Hohnstein?" Digger said to Timber. "Your name is Hohnstein?"

"Yeah," Timber said, folding his papers and putting them in a pocket. "Jonas Hohnstein."

"Jonas," Digger said. "After all this time. Jonas. Fuck me."

Timber looked at me and I just smiled. He looked at the floor.

"Nice to meet you, Jonas," I said quietly.

He just kept looking at the floor.

"That's all we need at this end," James said. "But we need to discuss how we're going to deal with the media. There will be television cameras there and news photographers, so you'll have to be okay with having your pictures taken."

"We gotta?" Timber asked.

"Unfortunately, yes," James said. "The government wants everyone to see how good they make things for people by allowing them a chance to win a lottery. In order to do that, they ask that winners have their pictures taken and their stories told in the media. The rules state that you have to agree to go along with it."

"Train a'comin'," I said quietly.

"What's that, Amelia?" Granite asked.

"Nothing. Just something Dick told us last night."

"Nervous?" James asked.

"Yes," I said.

"Well, try to relax. I will handle anything that comes up that any of you don't want to deal with. The news people only want to sell papers, get viewers, get listeners. They only really want you for a few minutes and then they'll go away and write their stories. For those few minutes, I'll be right there. And so will Granite."

We all stood up. None of us seemed too eager to walk out the door, though. I guess somehow we knew that as soon as we did, our feet would be touching a new kind of ground, a ground none of us had ever walked on before. Even James and Granite would be on different footing today. I felt like the old people must have felt when they struck their lodges at the end of a hunting season and headed for a new territory, each step bringing them closer and closer to a different landscape, each step coaxing their feet onto a new moss, a new ground where every skill they'd learned would be called into play and all the teachings would have to come into practice if they were to survive. As I looked at the faces of my boys, I could see the desire to run from this etched in their faces. I could see the uncertainty. I could see their hunger for the feel of the familiar—the streets, the alleys, the shelters and drop-ins they were used to—for the city, alive as an animal and all of us grown used to it, needing the reassurance of its presence, the feel of its wildness at our backs.

"Let's fucking do 'er, then," Digger said.

"Yes," Timber said quietly.

"Okay, then," Dick said.

And we stepped forward onto different ground.

Granite

WE PULLED UP in front of the lottery offices and the limo driver opened the door. Along the block I could see media vans parked already. We walked into the building and as we entered the reception area I could see a large crowd waiting in the main lounge. A nattily attired man and woman moved forward eagerly when they saw us. They were Sol Vance and Margo Keane, and as introductions were made I felt myself growing as nervous as my four friends appeared to be. Vance took control effortlessly and guided us to a small, comfortable anteroom. Timber, Dick, and Digger all asked for drinks and then gulped them down hurriedly. Amelia watched over them and murmured quietly to them while they drank. Merton busied himself making arrangements with Vance.

"You're Granite Harvey. The journalist. How are you connected to this, Mr. Harvey?" Margo asked me.

"I'm a friend," I said. "I arranged the lawyer for them."

"You came to my school to speak when I was trying to decide between journalism and public relations. I loved your work."

"Thank you. What did you decide?"

"After hearing you speak, I chose PR."

"That compelling about journalism as a life, was I?"

She laughed and reached out to touch my forearm. "No, no. I just decided that I wasn't cut from a responsible enough cloth to cover events. I was better at planning them. I was better at people than stories about people. But you were compelling. Maybe we can talk more later?"

"Sure," I said. "This is going to get crazy once we're in there."

"Got that right, bucko," she said and touched my arm again.

Vance and Merton had finished making their agenda arrangements and were ready to meet the press. The boys asked for another round of drinks, and gulped them down as quickly as they had the first.

"Vance and I will go in, make a general statement, and then Granite, maybe you could bring them out," Merton said.

"Sure," I said. "No need to cue me. I'll listen for it."

"Okay, then we're a go."

When they made their entrance, the babble of voices died down slowly. Vance introduced himself and announced that the winners of the thirteen and a half million–dollar prize were there to pick up their winnings, then introduced Merton.

"I have been instructed to speak on behalf of my clients today," he said confidently. "They are not like previous winners you've seen. They are not like people you may have met before. They're unique. They're special, and today they are exceptional.

"My clients are not working-class people trying to make ends meet. They are not single mothers struggling to maintain a life for their children. They are not students toughing it out for tuition and rent. Nor are they settled families content in their financial security and amazed at their luck. They are none of these. My clients are homeless people."

There was an instantaneous babble again throughout the room.

"My clients are chronically homeless. I am here because they are so indigent that they had no identification. No way to identify themselves and so pick up the prize being awarded this morning. I am here to act as power of attorney, establish bank accounts for them, and instruct them in money management. I'm also here to help them through this process with you, because as I'm sure you can glean from what I have just told you, this will not be a standard grip-and-grin photo op. I will answer on their behalf when required, and I ask you to consider for a moment the tremendous sweep of emotion that must be present in my clients this morning. I ask you to consider their unfamiliarity with this process and the fact that you will be addressing persons from a socio-economic background totally displaced from any you have encountered in this room before. I ask you to be humane and gentle.

"With that, may I introduce to you Ms. Amelia One Sky, Mr. Richard Dumont, Mr. Mark Haskett, and Mr. Jonas Hohnstein, our newest millionaires."

I led them from the anteroom and the pop and flash began long before we reached the table where six chairs and six microphones awaited us. Once there, I stepped back and motioned for them to move ahead of me. Their heads were down and they all stared at the floor as they took their seats.

Margo Keane and an assistant entered the room carrying a large cardboard facsimile of a cheque and made their way to the front of the room where Vance stood waiting.

"You never really get used to this," Vance said. "You never get used to the idea that you change peoples' lives when you make these presentations. But today feels even more powerful because of the lives of the people to whom we make this presentation. I can honestly say, in my ten years here, that I have never made so special a presentation. Thirteen and a half million dollars may not be the biggest prize in our history, but today it is certainly the most life-changing.

"It gives me great, great pleasure to present this cheque in the sum of thirteen-point-five million dollars to Ms. One Sky and Messrs. Hohnstein, Haskett, and Dumont."

I motioned for the four of them to rise and make their way over to Vance. They crowded around the large cardboard cheque and looked sheepishly at the throng. None of them was able to look at the cameras. Timber winced at each flare of light. Amelia simply nodded at Vance and looked down. Digger shook hands limply without raising his head and Dick looked ready to bolt at any minute, his eyes darting back and forth across the ceiling. Margo Keane came over and stood beside me.

"They're like frightened children," she whispered.

"They *are* frightened children," I said. "I hate this."

"It's good you're here for them."

"I hope so."

Vance placed the cheque on an easel behind the table and my friends returned to their chairs.

"Questions, please," Merton said.

"Mr. Haskett," a red-headed woman said, standing to ask her question. "Mr. Haskett, how do you feel right now?"

"Digger," was all he said, staring hard at the microphone when his voice boomed out over the speakers.

"Pardon?" the woman asked.

"Digger. My name is Digger. There ain't no Mr. Haskett here."

"Oh," she said, scribbling a note in her pad. "Well, Digger, how do you feel?"

"Like I could use a fucking drink."

There was laughter all around the room and Digger raised his head to glower at them all.

"Mr. Dumont. What will you do with your share of the money?" a well-built man with a crewcut asked Dick.

Dick gulped and looked at Amelia.

"Do you people have names?" she asked. "Dick likes to know who he's talking to. He's very polite that way."

"Oh, quite right, I apologize," the reporter said. "Mike Phillips, *The Telegraph*."

"That man's name is Mike, Dick," she said, and he nodded. "He wants to know what you want to do with your money."

Dick kept his head down. "I wanna see *Field of Dreams*," he said. "With my friends. We didn't get to see it yesterday."

"You want to go to a movie?" Phillips asked. "That's all?"

"I like movies," Dick said. "All of us do."

"Do you go to a lot of movies?" Phillips asked.

"Every day," Dick said. "Sometimes twice."

There was a lot of note scribbling over that, and a large round man in a brown suit near the back of the room stood.

"I don't mean to take attention away from the winners, but I have to ask," he said. "Mr. Harvey, sir, why are you here? Are you returning to journalism and doing a column or a story on the winners?"

I grimaced. I had guessed that my presence would not go unnoticed but had hoped that the focus would remain on the winners. Margo Keane squeezed my hand and gestured with her chin for me to approach the table.

"No. I am not coming back. I'm here to support these people, that's all," I said.

"How are you connected, sir?" the round man asked.

"He's our friend," Dick said proudly. "We go to the movies together an' he even showed us a boxin' movie at his house while he was fixin' up things with the lawyer guy."

There was even more babble and a lot more note scribbling. Vance's assistant brought another chair and I was squeezed in between Dick and Amelia. Margo gave me a thumbs-up from the corner.

"Hello, Granite," said a tall thin woman standing near the middle of the room. "It's good to see you again."

"Jilly," I replied in recognition.

"My name is Jill Squires," she said to my friends. "I write for the same newspaper Granite worked for. So you are all movie buddies, is that it, Granite?"

"Jilly," I said. "It's not about me. It's about these people here. The winners. I would be happy to speak with you after this is over, but right now it's for them."

"Fine," she said. "I'd like that opportunity. Ms. One Sky, then."

"Amelia," she replied. "My name is Amelia."

"One For The Dead," Dick blurted.

"One For The Dead?" Jilly asked.

"Yeah," Dick went on. "It's her rounder name. We're all rounders an' we all got rounder names."

"Well, that's interesting. What are your rounder names, Mr. Dumont?"

Dick looked at his friends and then looked at me. I nodded.

"That there's Timber," he said pointing at Timber, who nodded with his head down. "Next to him is Digger. This is One For The Dead an' I'm Double Dick."

"Pardon me?"

"Double Dick." He seemed pleased with the attention. "I'm Double Dick Dumont."

"What an interesting name," Jilly said, a little red in the cheeks. "How, ah, how does someone get a name like that, I wonder?"

Merton spoke up suddenly. "Well, you know, Ms. Squires, that's a good question. But my clients are all a little anxious and I'd like to move things along. I would like to propose that Mr. Harvey and myself, through Ms. Keane from the Lottery Corporation, make ourselves available for background questions at a later time. Right now, I'm going to have to ask that you keep your questions specific to the matter of the prize. Next?"

"Gordon Petrovicky, All News Radio," an older gentleman said. "Amelia, what do you think you will do with the money?"

Amelia took her time, and when she was ready she looked directly at Petrovicky as she spoke. "I guess it's more important what we won't do," she said. "All the time we've known each other we have looked out for each other. We've shared everything. We've been there for each other. This money is a big thing but it can't be bigger than that. It can't be so big that we forget that we're together, that we're friends. That we take care of each other.

"I guess we could spend it on anything. But I know that none of us knows what that anything might be. Not right now, anyway. We have James and Granite to help us and that's enough. Today, like Dick said, we'd just like to go to a movie. Do what we know and try to stay as we are."

"So you have no plans? I mean, you have enough money now to set yourselves up for life. You don't have to be street people anymore," Petrovicky continued.

"It's happened too fast. We haven't had time to sit and talk about it. Our lives have been about getting enough every day, not about having enough."

"Mr. Hohnstein? Or Timber, is it?" an older, greying woman asked. "My name is Susan Howell. I work for the Life Network. I'm doing a series on lottery winners and I wonder how you see this affecting your life?"

"Can't," Timber replied.

"Digger? How do you see it affecting your life?" the woman asked.

"Right now it's keeping me from getting another friggin' drink," Digger growled. "So far it's mighty fucking inconvenient."

"Do you drink a lot, Digger?" she asked.

"Now wait a minute," Merton said.

"No," Digger said. "It's okay. I can handle this."

He reached into his coat pocket, pulled out his cigarettes, and lit one, exhaling dramatically. Then he reached in again, pulled out a bottle, and took a huge swallow before putting it back in his coat.

"There. It ain't so fucking inconvenient no more. Do I drink lots? I don't know, lady. I don't know what lots is. I drink enough. That's all I know. Enough to handle this shit. Enough to handle your phony Square John concern and your friggin' poking around where you ain't been invited to poke. I drink enough for that."

"I didn't mean—" she began.

"Hey, we all know what you meant, lady. We're fucking rounders. We ain't idiots. We coulda come in here all dressed to the tits and not said word one about our friggin' life. Rock or Jimbo here would have fronted us the cash to score some duds. Hey, Rock even offered to get us a room last night. Did we take it? No. Did we get all gussied up for your benefit and try 'n hide who the fuck we are? No. We're rounders. We live on the street. We got plumb fucking lucky and won a big chunk of change that we got no friggin' idea what to do with except go see Field of fucking Dreams like we were gonna do before all this shit started. Sure, you got questions. Sure, you're curious. Sure, you wanna sell whatever you're sellin' and you wanna use us to do it for today. But you know what, lady?"

"What?" she asked quietly.

"You don't give a fuck where we been or what we done to get by. You don't give a fuck about that and you really don't give two shits about what we're gonna do with the money except that you wish it was you and you wanna tell this story to a whole bunch of other Square John fucks who will wish it was them too. You wanna know how all this feels? Imagine. Just imagine if it was all the other way around. Imagine if you landed on the bricks and you had nothin'. Then you had to start to live your life that way. How the fuck would that feel, lady? What would you have to say if someone stuck a camera in your mug and asked you what the fuck you were gonna do now? Would you have an answer? No. You wouldn't know whether to shit, do a handstand, or go blind."

"You're supposed to provide us with an interview," the woman said.

"The friggin' interview's over," Digger said. "Jimbo over there said he'll give you whatever you think you need. Rock'll help him. Us? We just want out of here. Now."

Merton stood. "That's it. I'm sorry, but at my client's request I'm ending this now. Mr. Vance and Ms. Keane can provide you with sufficient information for your stories and, as I said, Mr. Harvey, myself, and Ms. Keane will ensure you get all the relevant details. My clients' wish is to retire and reflect on their futures."

There was a crescendo of complaint as reporters threw questions at the table. But my friends busied themselves with getting back through the door that led to the anteroom. Vance and Margo moved to the front of the room with Merton to make arrangements for further contact with and information about the winners.

"Jesus, Rock," Digger said. "That's what you did for a living?"

"Well, not really," I said. "I was more of a political writer."

"Fuck," he said. "That was weird."

Margo entered the room. "Okay. That was maybe a little less graceful than I'd hoped, but they can work with it. What we need to do now is make sure that they get enough later to file good stories. They'll want to do follows, though."

"Follows?" Timber asked her.

"Yes. They'll want to follow this story with stories about how you deal with the money. Where you go, what you do."

"Do we have to talk to them?" Timber asked.

"No," she said. "You're no longer obliged to talk to them."

"Good."

"Still, Granite and I should talk and provide them with more background. Granite, you know the drill. You know what they'll want. Will you work with me?"

"I guess I have to. In order for them not to hound everybody, we'll have to give them what they want. When? Where?"

"Anywhere," she said. "But I think we should get everybody settled somewhere and then we can get to it. Can you give them a quick interview now?"

"Alone?"

"No. Mr. Merton said he'd help. Good old legal obliqueness always makes good copy. Remember?" She laughed.

"I remember. Okay."

I turned to my friends.

"I'll do this thing with them," I said. "I'll make it fast. Then we'll go with James. I don't know what his plan is but we'll get this out of the way first and then we're gone."

"Fast, eh, Rock?" Digger said.

"Yes."

I followed Margo to the door. Before I entered the media room I looked back. They sat there close together with Amelia in the middle, passing the bottle back and forth and smoking. It hadn't been a stellar meet-the-press situation but it was over now. They no longer had to perform for anyone. They no longer had to speak unless they chose to, and I was strangely ready to act as a buffer on their behalf. I wouldn't let them be insulted or belittled. They had become elite. They had become the envied minority. They'd become visible, and I wouldn't desert them now. I couldn't desert them now. Amelia looked at me and grinned. I gave a small wave and stepped through the door.

"Ready?" Margo asked.

"No," I said. "But let's fucking do 'er."

She laughed and squeezed my arm.

Timber

I DIDN'T KNOW what the Christ to do. It'd been some long time since I was in a place where I didn't know the next move. You live that way. You have to know the next move or you're hamstrung and lost, and out on the street you can't ever afford to be lost. But there I was sitting in that small room waiting for Granite and James to finish with the media and I was plum lost. And it scared me. None of us were comfortable. The free liquor helped but it didn't do the whole deal, and I found myself wishing that it would. Liquor usually shut the lights out and deafened me, and I coulda used that right then. But all it did was stop me from shaking. I guess that was enough.

It didn't take long, like Granite said, and we were gone, back in the car, and headed for the bank in the same building as James's office. He had the cheque in his briefcase. It felt better then. Better because of the feel of the four of us together and on the street. No one said very much. Everyone was out of sorts after the prize ceremony, and even Granite and James, who'd done this sorta thing before, were winded and spent and looking like they should dive into the bar too. We got to the bank and followed James inside, where we were directed to the manager's office. The sign on the door said HARRIET PETERS and she turned out to be a friendly looking woman in a pearl grey suit and high heels.

"Welcome," she said and shook all our hands.

We sat in leather chairs while James signed papers and chatted with Harriet. We rounders just looked around. No one spoke. I could feel myself getting edgier and edgier. Finally, they finished their business and the papers were arranged on a table at the side of Harriet's desk.

"Well," she said in voice that reminded me of a schoolteacher I once had. "You're all likely very anxious to get this fussing over with. Mr. Merton and I have papers for you to sign along with some papers that the bank needs in order to activate your accounts. Once that's done, it's official. You are millionaires."

We all worked our way through the forms, just scribbling our names where the Xs were, wanting to get the fuss over with like she said. Granite helped Dick, who gripped the pen in his fist and scrawled letters like a child across the narrow space provided for signatures. When we were finished and the papers were in a pile on Harriet's desk, she smiled.

"I'm your bank manager now," she said. "Any time you need help with anything you ask for me and I'll gladly sort it out for you. I've pre-approved credit cards for you. You signed for those already and Mr. Merton will advise you when they are ready. Likely in about two weeks."

"Credit cards?" Dick asked.

"Yes," Harriet said. "They're what you use instead of cash."

"Like empties?"

Harriet looked perplexed.

"No, Dick," James said, reaching into his wallet and pulling out a gold plastic card. "You get one of these and whenever you want to buy something you give the people this and you just sign for whatever you want."

"Free?"

James laughed. "No. It only feels like it."

"Wow," Dick said. "Now I don't gotta mooch for money when I got none."

"Not only that, Mr. Dumont, but the bank provides you with other cards that allow you to buy things without having money on you at all," Harriet said, gleaning the necessity for explanations. "You just present the card, punch in your secret code numbers, and the money is automatically taken out of your account."

"Secret code numbers? Wow," Dick said. "Let's go do that."

"Okay," Harriet said and led the way to the main banking room. "This area is called private banking and it's for our larger account holders. Any time you come in, you just come here and we'll take really good care of you. This way, please."

For the next while we were busy getting the bank cards sorted out and punching our numbers into a small machine to activate them. Harriet told us that we had no pre-set limit, meaning we could take out and spend as much as we wanted every day. Digger and I just looked at each other blankly when she said that. We were introduced to the four tellers who worked in our area and though they had a moment or two of shock at seeing us there, they relaxed and became quite charming once they heard we'd won the lottery. It wasn't long before we were finished.

"So how much would you like today?" Harriet asked.

"What?" Digger replied.

"How much of your money would you like? What do you think you need for today?"

We all looked at each other, not knowing what to say.

"Lemme get this straight, lady," Digger said. "Now that we're all set up here we can just ask for however much we want and we can have it right away?"

"Yes, Mr. Haskett. It's your money. You can have as much as you want."

"Jesus. I like that. How about a hundred?"

"A hundred is fine, sir," she said.

"Sir? I get a yard just like that and a 'sir'? I like this already," Digger said, and headed for a teller.

"I could have a hundred, too?" Dick asked.

"Yes," Harriet said, and Dick dashed off after Digger.

Amelia and I just stood there.

"You can have what you want. You know that, don't you?" Granite asked.

"I know," she said. "I just don't know what that is right now."

"Me neither," I said. "I just want to get out of here."

Granite nodded. "Yes. Well, we need to stop at James's office first. He wants to make sure you're taken care of and then we can head out. It won't be long. Are you sure you don't want to go over and get some of your money?"

"Not right now," Amelia said.

Digger meandered over with a big grin on his face and we headed up to James's office. When we got there, Margo Keane was waiting for us. She was all smiles and made sure she talked to each of us for a moment while we sat down.

"Margo's here to help Amelia," James explained. "Hanging around with you three guys must be tough on a girl, and Margo's taking some time off to travel around with her to help her get settled."

"Well, thank you," Amelia said. "It will be good to have a woman to talk to."

"I'm glad to help," Margo said. "What Digger said at the media scrum really touched me. I can imagine how I would feel if I was suddenly thrust into a world I had no idea how to negotiate. We'll get you settled in no time."

"Granite, since you know the boys already, I want to ask you if you'd mind travelling around with them a while longer and making sure they adjust smoothly?" James asked.

"I don't mind at all," Granite said. "In fact, I was just starting to think that I'd like to spend more time with them now. What Digger said was important. It's a whole new world and everybody needs a guide now and then."

"Well, we're agreed then. Margo and Granite will be your chaperones, for lack of a better word, and I will manage the accounts and finances. I'll only ask that if there are going to be major purchases that you talk to me first. Investments we can discuss with people I know. That's a good idea to look at, but I think we'd best look at getting the basics covered first."

"The basics?" I asked.

"Yes," James said, leaning back in his big leather chair and lacing his fingers behind his head. "I don't mean to scare you or to make you feel demeaned at all. But your life is different now. It's just different. It's as big a change as any human being can make. Bigger than any other lottery winner has had to make, because up to now everyone who's won has had an established life before they won. They've had things. They've owned things. They've belonged somewhere. They've had homes. But you're all starting from less than zero and it means that everything, everything that happens from now on, is going to be absolutely new territory, and I don't want to see you swamped by all of that. That's why Margo's here and that's why Granite's agreed to help too.

"When I say the basics I mean you all could use a good wash. Then you could use a good selection of clothes. You need a place to operate from, a place to settle for now, a place to live until we can find you the kind of accommodations you'd like. A good friend of mine is the manager of the Sutton Plaza. I apprised him of your situation and he's agreed to give you suites there. The bills will come to me. I want you to go there. I want you to get settled. Then I want you and your chaperones to go shopping. Get whatever you want. Whatever makes you feel good.

"Please don't think I'm telling you what to do or that I'm trying to control your lives. I'm not. It's just that Digger told the truth over there this morning. You're being thrust into a strange new world and someone needs to help you make decisions. Good decisions. Good choices, because there are a lot of wolves in the woods, my friends, and they're all going to be after you now. I'm just making sure they don't get you."

"How much?" Digger asked. "You one of the friggin' wolves there, James?"

James stood up and looked Digger square in the face. "No. I'm not. I'm a Square John, Digger. A friggin' Square John. But I'm a Square John that had to work his ass off to get here. I didn't have my fucking ticket punched for me. I worked my way up here from a start that's not all that far from yours. I've been poor. I know what money can do. Am I one of the wolves? Fuck, no. I'm just someone trying to get by the best he can. It won't cost you an arm and a leg for me to help you. But it will cost you. That's how the world works."

"Okay," Digger said. "Works for me."

"This is nice," Amelia said quietly.

"What's nice?" Granite asked.

"This. All of this. There used to be one lonely rounder walking around out there. Then, one by one we came together. We were two, then we were three, then we were four. Making it while we were on the street was easier because there were more of us. I thought that four was a magic number. It felt right. Then last winter we found the movies and we found Granite and we were five. It got easier. Five felt right. Now, because of that ticket we have James and Margo and we're seven. Seven. It's quite a little company we've become, don't you think?"

I thought about that on the way down in the elevator. My life had become bigger than I'd intended. Back a few years, I'd convinced myself that alone was better, that I deserved that. There wasn't anyone left for me. Then Amelia came up to me in the park and offered me a drink when I really needed one and the world became bigger. Not bigger in any major kind of way, just more to think about. For years it felt good moving around the city as one of four. Being known in a small way. Being recognized when I appeared somewhere. Then the movies happened and Granite happened and the horizon flattened out and spread wide. The movies brought me the world. A big, bright, shining world that felt good as long as it stayed on the screen where it belonged. Now this. This.

We stepped into the flow of the street and I really just wanted to walk away. Just hightail it around the corner, down the alley, and back to the small, shrunken world where everything was known, where there was nothing new to wonder about and fear. But I was still one of four and I thought they'd need me. Funny. I hadn't been needed in a long time and it was that more than the money that got me into that car.

Double Dick

I HAD ME a good drink from the bottle in the car while we drove through the city. Geez. It felt nice an' warm an' thick. Different than I drunk before. I figured the hundred in my pocket could buy me some of that 'cept I didn't know what it was called. Timber would know. He always knew stuff like that an' I'd just ask him later on accounta he never minded at all whatever kinda questions I'd ask him. It felt good in there. There was six of us now an' the lady Margo was pretty an' nice an' she smelled like a big bunch of flowers when she leaned in to talk to me. I didn't mind bein' in the car. Long as my friends was around I didn't mind doing nothin'. All the talk about livin' in a whole new world didn't bother me so much on accounta when we went to the movies we was in a whole new world an' it kinda turned out okay. So I just sat back an' let myself be with my friends.

We pulled up in front of a big hotel. There was a long red carpet leading up the stairs to some big double doors an' two guys in uniforms an' real shiny shoes waiting outside. They moved over real quick when the car stopped. Granite got out first when they opened the door an' Margo went out next.

"Good afternoon, sir. Ma'am," the younger guy said, an' for a minute I thought he was gonna salute like in the movies when they say *sir.* "Welcome to the Sutton."

He was all smiles when he turned to the door again, an' then Digger stepped out. The guy blinked real hard an' moved his head back a few inches. Then Timber stepped out an' the guy moved back a step. When One For The Dead got out, he almost fell over an' then I climbed out an' I thought he was gonna faint.

Margo put an arm on the guy's shoulder. "These people have just won the lottery. They'll be staying in suites while they're here and they'll really be needing your help from time to time," she said. "What was your name?"

He shrugged his shoulders around a bit an' tugged at his sleeves. "Greg," he said. "Ma'am. Greg."

"Ah, you're here," said a tall, skinny kind of guy with big feet and a nice-lookin' dark blue suit. I wondered how I'd look in one of those an' if all of us tall, skinny guys with big feet could wear those kinda clothes. "Pierre Lajeunesse. I'm the manager and I'll be taking care of you personally while you're here."

He shook hands all around an' was real friendly. Then he walked us into the hotel. I felt my mouth open up real wide but there wasn't nothin' I could do to stop it. It was like the movies in there. Like a castle with all kinds of people movin' around lookin' real busy an' happy. Me 'n Timber stood side by side not movin' an' Digger came over too once he got over his jaw droppin'.

"Fuck me," was all he said.

"We won't register you right now," Mr. Pierre said. "We'll get you settled upstairs and I'll take care of that later."

"I'll do that," Margo said. "No need to bother them with it."

The elevator was like a tiny lobby. There was thick carpet on the floor that my feet kinda sunk down into, mirrors on the ceiling, an' corduroy stuff on the walls. I put my hand on it an' it was like the pants I got one time from the shelter.

"Timber," I said. "They took someone's pants and put 'em on the walls. Corduroys."

He reached out, touched it, an' smiled at me. "Yeah," he said. "Funny, eh?"

We got to where we was supposed to go an' Mr. Pierre led us down a real long hallway with arches every now an' then. It felt more like a castle all the time. While we was walkin' he told everybody all about the hotel but I missed it on accounta it was so amazin'. I never seen so many mirrors. Every couple feet it seemed like there was another one an' I figured castle people must like to look at themselves a lot. I wasn't gonna like that part so much. I never did like lookin' at myself. Never. Finally, Mr. Pierre stopped at a door an' slid a little white card into a slot an' there was a click an' he pushed the door open. Me 'n Digger looked at each other in surprise again an' followed the others into the room.

"Mr. Haskett, this will be yours," Mr. Pierre said. "I hope it meets with your approval."

He walked over to the far side of the room an' pulled some curtains apart that was coverin' the windows. When the sun poured into that room I thought for sure we was in a castle. It was all red like valentines. Everything was all puffy. The chairs looked like if you sat in 'em too fast you'd just keep on goin' down an' down an' down. There was big mirrors in there too, an' when Mr. Pierre led us to the bedroom I couldn't believe it. The bed was bigger'n the whole doorway I slept in. It looked like a big lake on accounta the covers was so thick an' puffy they looked like waves. Big waves. There was mirrors again on the dresser and on the walls an' when we walked into the bathroom you couldn't look nowhere without seein' yourself. Digger walked over to one of the two toilets an' waved me over. We stood there lookin' at the pair of johns.

"Howda ya figure this, pal?" he asked me.

"Geez," I said. "Guess castle people poo together, maybe."

"Ya figure?"

"I guess. Flush one."

Digger pressed down the handle an' instead of swirlin' around an' down like toilets do, this one sprayed water up at us an' we both jumped back.

"Fuck off," Digger said. "You ain't getting me on that thing."

Margo came over an' whispered in Digger's ear for a moment. As she spoke he got redder 'n redder an' I wondered what she was tellin' him.

"You got to be fucking kiddin' me, lady," he said, an' when Margo shook her head he looked at me an' shook his head too. "Don't ask, pal. Don't friggin' ask and just don't sit on it."

We walked back out to the main room an' Mr. Pierre showed us where all the stuff was. Digger walked right over to the bar an' poured us a glass each an' one for Granite too. The four of us stood there looking around an' watchin' while Mr. Pierre finished showin' things to One For The Dead and Margo. I was amazed at it all. Then he walked over to a big tall cabinet, opened the doors an' there was huge television sittin' in there. Huger even than Granite's an' I couldn't stop my feet from takin' me right over there.

"Wow," I said. "Do I get one too?"

"Yes," Mr. Pierre said. "Every suite has one. There's even one in your bedroom."

"Can it do movies like Granite's?"

"Yes. You call down to the switchboard and ask to see the one you want from the menu and it starts within minutes. Or we have VCRs if you should want to rent or buy your own."

"I could watch one any time?"

"Any time," he said. "It's yours to use."

"Can I go see mine now?"

Mr. Pierre laughed. "Yes. You're right next door. We can go through the hallway or if you'll look over here there's a door connecting your suite to Mr. Haskett's."

He walked over an' opened the door an' I walked right through. I got confused right away on accounta it felt like I walked into the same room 'cept no one was there. Everythin' was in exactly the same place. My head kinda spun over that.

"Hey, Digger," I said. "I'm right beside you an' my room's just like yours."

I found the TV by the bed. Mr. Pierre showed me how to turn it on an' change the channels with a little black box you held in your hand an' I switched it on. Both TVs worked the same way, he said, an' went on tryin' to tell me more about it but I was too lost. I never had a TV of my own before an' even when I watched at the Mission they never let any of us change the channels on accounta we couldn't 'cause there was a big plastic window in front of it to stop guys from throwin' bottles at it. There wasn't no such window in front of mine. I never even heard the rest of them leave.

One For The Dead

THE BATH FELT GOOD. Mr. Pierre had called downstairs for someone to bring us a big selection of soaps, shampoos, deodorants, toothpastes, razors, and bath oils. While we waited, a man from a shop near the hotel came and measured all of us for clothes. Then, once the bath stuff arrived, they left us alone in our rooms to wash up. Margo stayed with me and helped me as much as she could and I liked that. It felt like having a sister. Together we filled the tub with nice warm water, measuring enough bath oil and bubble bath to make a really nice foamy-looking tub for me to step into. I couldn't remember the last time I took a bath. We could always find a place to shower on the street. There were shelters that let us go in there every day if we wanted, but you couldn't lounge around because there was always someone waiting behind you. But that bath at the hotel was amazing.

I used to float on my back in a shallow place in Big River. There wasn't much of a current and the river bent around in a sweeping curve, making a kind of a bowl against the riverbank. The sun shone down there really nice, and floating in that warm, shallow water with the bright light of the sun against my eyelids was how I imagined it must have felt inside my mother's belly. I loved it. Only when my dangling feet touched the sandy bottom would I open my eyes and return to the world. That bath was like that.

There was a big white fluffy robe waiting for me, and wrapping myself in that after a spray of perfume made me feel as special as everyone was saying we were now. When I saw myself in the mirror I wasn't looking at the same woman. I smiled. Margo knocked lightly on the door and told me that my new clothes were ready. I looked in the mirror one more time and studied my face. I was an old woman. Old, but not ancient. There were more lines than I recalled, more grey in my hair, and a looser face. But clean felt good and I liked the way the expensive-smelling soaps and things made my skin feel.

Margo helped me pick out an outfit from the selection the store had delivered.

"We can go out together and pick out the things that you'd really like," she said. "But these are nice for now."

"Where are my old things?" I asked.

She looked at me with the kindest eyes I'd seen in a long time. "It's a whole new world, Amelia," she said. "You won't be needing the clothes from your old one. I took care of them for you."

We picked out a pale blue shirt with a nice pleated pair of black slacks, black loafers, and black silky-feeling socks.

"What would you like to do with your hair?" she asked. "There's a stylist waiting if you want to cut it or change it."

I looked in another mirror. My hair was long and loose and wavy. It had always reminded me of the way the old women from Big River looked and I had kept it long all through the years despite the difficulty. Somehow, keeping the look of the old ladies from the reservation had been important to me and I didn't want to change it.

"Maybe just a braid," I said.

The stylist was braiding my hair when there was a knock on the door. Margo got up to answer. I couldn't believe my eyes when Dick walked into that room.

"Look at me," he said rather proudly. He was beautiful. He was clean and shaved and someone had cut his hair. His skin was a little pink from the scrubbing and he wore pale brown pants, a white shirt under a dark brown patterned sweater, and brown shoes that sort of looked like moccasins except with regular laces. He stood there in the middle of that room with his arms spread wide, turning slowly around and around.

"How come you're cryin'?" he asked, worried and walking over to where I sat. "Don't you like it?"

"I love it," I said when I could. "It's just that I always imagined that you shone, Dick. Whenever I saw you, you shone like an angel for me and now, now you really do. You really do and I am so happy."

He put a hand on my shoulder and I saw clean nails and knuckles and lines free of the charcoal grit of the street.

"A lady came an' took care of my hands," he said. "It was nice. Kinda funny feelin' on accounta she cut my nails an' all but it was nice. She said she could come back an' do my feet if I wanted."

I patted his hand and we smiled at each other.

"Timber 'n Digger are ready too," Dick said. "Wanna see them?"

"Yes," I said. "Yes, I do."

He trotted across the room and out the door. Margo sat down beside me and met my eyes in the mirror. "You okay?" she asked.

"Yes," I said. "He looks so beautiful, that's all."

"Are you ready?" Dick asked, peeking around the open door.

"Okay," Margo said. "Let the gentlemen enter."

I gasped. It's all I could do. There was no place for language at all as Digger and then Timber walked kind of shyly through the door. I had spent years with those boys and never really saw them like I did right then. Rounder clothes are bulky clothes. We dress in layers out there so we don't have to carry big bags around all day and so no one can steal the clothes we've got. Coats are oversized with as many pockets as we can get, and the people we see are baggier, bigger, and their bodies aren't defined at all. You get an idea of height and weight most times, but you never see the lines of anybody. Ever. Now I saw my two boys for the first time.

Digger wore a pair of black slacks and a deep blue shirt with buttons at the collar. He had on a pair of black boots with heels, so he was taller. But his face amazed me. He'd shaved off the scruffy beard he always wore and his hair had been cut back from its curly length to a short wavy style. When he looked at me I saw the blue of his eyes clearly, because the beard was gone and someone had trimmed his bushy eyebrows. Those eyes were filled with humour and I sensed that he was enjoying this.

"Digger," I said. "You're handsome."

"Ah frig," he said and headed toward the bar. "Bubble baths, shaves, haircuts, someone trimming away at your hands, a guy'd have to get better looking after all that fuss and stuff."

"Hello, Amelia," Timber said, and I turned.

I put my hand to my mouth and felt tears building in my eyes. This wasn't the same hunched, lonely, and ragged man I had approached in the park so long ago. This wasn't the shadowed, weighted man who seemed to slog down the street. This was a tall, slender, quiet-looking man in brown pants, pale purple sweater, and tan oxford shoes. There was a crewcut where there had been a tangle of brown hair beyond his collar before. This was a clean-shaven man with soft brown eyes and long graceful lines around the corners of his mouth and eyes.

"Timber," I said. "You look like a gentleman."

He grinned shyly. "Thanks."

The stylist finished with my hair and began packing her things. "You'll need to have some deep conditioning work done, Ms. One Sky. And there should be some thinning and trimming done. You can call me when you want that done."

When she left I stood and smoothed my new clothes before turning and walking toward the boys, who were seated around the dining table.

"Wow," Digger said. "Who'da figured you for a cutie?"

"Geez," Dick said. "You look nice."

"Amelia," Timber said. "You make those clothes look pretty darn good."

"Thank you, boys," I said. "I feel very fine, too."

Granite came in and stood looking at us.

"Oh my god," he said.

"Pretty impressive cleanup, wouldn't you say?" Margo asked.

"Pretty impressive is right."

"Well, I don't know abut anyone else around here," Digger said, "but I need me some friggin' street."

"Street?" Granite asked.

"Yeah. Real life, ya know? This shit is all fun and games and while it's entertaining as all fuck it's like being plunked down on someone else's friggin' planet and I ain't liking it all that much. I ain't used to it."

"So what do you plan to do?" Granite asked.

"I don't know, Rock. I just need some space."

"Alone?"

"Fuck yeah, alone," Digger said. "I spent years out there, pal. Years. It's what I know. Money ain't about to change that. It ain't about to change me. I just wanna go wander around like I'm used to."

"You'll be okay?" Margo asked.

"Lady, I'll be fine. I got this little plastic card that lets me back into some swanky digs. I got this other plastic card that lets me have as much friggin' money as I want. I got smokes. I got drinks. And now I got good looks. What the frig else does a guy need?"

He stood up and looked at the three of us. "You guys know what I'm talking about here, right?"

We nodded.

"Okay. Explain it to them, maybe, but I gotta go."

And then he walked out.

"I don't know," Granite said.

"I don't know, either," Margo agreed.

"Digger just needs to be Digger," Timber explained. "I know how he feels. I wanna get out of here too. I wanna do something normal."

"Normal like what?" Granite asked.

"Normal like walking down the street with nowhere in particular to go," Timber said. "Just walking. Just looking. Maybe having a drink somewhere. Just out. There's too many walls."

"I wanna go to the movies," Dick said. "That's normal, huh?"

"That's normal," I said. "I need to get out for awhile too."

We talked for a long while about the best plan. Granite and Margo worried about us. They wanted to make sure that whatever we chose would be safe for us. Timber finally put on his coat and moved toward the door. He turned when he got there and I saw the ragged, lonely man from the park in his eyes.

"I just have to go," he said. "This is nice, but it's all too much. I need to walk. I need to be away right now."

"Be safe," Granite said.

"I will," Timber said. "I'll be back. I will. Don't worry. I need some street too."

"Should we go see *Field of Dreams*?" I asked when he was gone.

"Not without them guys," Dick said. "We all picked that one together."

Granite had a paper sent up from the lobby and we scanned the movie ads and Granite read a few reviews out loud. We settled on *Three Fugitives* because it sounded funny. I needed to laugh. I needed to not have to think. I needed to do something normal like Timber and Digger had said, and the movies felt normal. Every step we took on our way out of the hotel felt lighter. The closer and closer we got to the open space of the street, the looser I felt in those new clothes. Finally, when we stepped outside and my feet touched pavement again, I breathed a full breath. This wasn't a neighbourhood I knew. It wasn't somewhere I had travelled before but just the feel of concrete on my shoes made me more comfortable, and as the four of us walked down the street toward the theatre I found myself wondering how money might change that if it could at all. Around us, the shadowed ones moved in their relentless search for peace, and seeing them again I knew that the part of me that was born and the part of me that died on those streets would be joined with it always; my spine concrete, my blood rain, my heart unrestrained by walls.

Timber

IT FELT GOOD to walk. It felt good to be away from the walls and the air that felt like it didn't move. I didn't know where I wanted to go. I didn't know what I wanted to see. I only knew that being outside was the only thing that made sense. So I wandered. I found myself miles away from downtown eventually. Miles away in a neighbourhood of small stores, coffee joints, and tree-lined side streets. The people I passed nodded at me. They were dressed neatly and comfortably and my new clothes seemed to fit into the surroundings even though I didn't feel like I did. There was a liquor store on a corner near a park so I stopped there and used the plastic card from the bank to pay for a mickey of Scotch. I never drank Scotch but somehow it felt like a good thing to say when the man asked me what I wanted. I got some tailor-mades too, and a lighter. The man called me *sir* when I'd finished paying with the card and I could only look at him. Three letters, one little word that had been missing from my life forever, it seemed, and it only took a leather blazer and clean clothes to earn it. I found that curious. I thanked him and crossed over to the park.

The Scotch tasted good. Smoky. Rich. Fine. I sat on a bench close to where people were playing with their dogs and watched for a while. It was like a little social club for Benji, Spot, and Rover and I found myself smiling at the play.

A Frisbee sailed over the head of a black mixed-breed pooch and landed at my feet. The dog trotted up, looked at me with big brown eyes, sat on its haunches, and thumped its tail on the ground.

"Go ahead, sir!" his owner yelled. She was a young blond woman in running shoes and a track suit. I picked up the Frisbee and flung it over the dog's head. It tore off after it, kicking up a spray of dirt with its back feet. "Thanks, sir!" she called to me.

"You're welcome," I called back and waved.

I took another pull on the mickey and fired up one of the tailor-mades. It was a warm late afternoon and the park was busy. Around its edges were fine older houses. Three-storied with hedges, garages at the side, and walkways that curved slightly, meandering their way toward steps that led to big doors with brass fittings and stained glass windows. People emerged from them and crossed over to the park with children, dogs, and playthings.

"Afternoon, sir," a young couple said as they passed arm in arm.

"Sir," an older gentleman in hiking boots and a sweater said.

It amazed me. One day earlier, sitting in the same park with the same mickey in my pocket would have earned me a phone call to the police in this neighbourhood. But today, showered, shaved, and dressed expensively, I had become a *sir*. What had the soap washed off, I wondered? What did the clothes cover? What did the plastic bank card in my pocket buy me that I didn't know I'd purchased? It felt strange. Despite the six hundred dollars on my body, the twenty-dollar Scotch in my pocket, the tailor-made cigarettes, and the key to a suite in a fancy hotel, I was still the same man. Nothing had changed but my appearance. I sat and laughed at the joke. All the *sirs* and all the politeness, all the nods, small salutes, and other signs of inclusion couldn't hide the fact that I was still a ragged man inside, still a rounder, still more street than neighbourhood, still on a park bench alone while the world happened around me.

I sat there and watched. I drank. I smoked. And when the light had faded from the sky, the streetlights and the house lights had flicked on around that neighbourhood, and all the little worlds around that park had settled inside the comfort of their walls, I got up and began walking back toward the hotel. Toward downtown. Toward the streets I knew. Toward a predictable place with the people I'd inhabited it with. Toward Dick and Digger and One For The Dead. Toward shelter.

Double Dick

THE MOVIE WAS FUNNY. Some people was on the run from pullin' a robbery an' there was lots of action an' funny stuff goin' on an' I kinda forgot all about being rich on accounta the movie was so good. We all talked about it after on the way back to the hotel an' I was happy that everyone had liked it too. But it felt funny without Timber an' Digger. Granite an' Margo were nice an' I liked them, but it wasn't the same. I even missed Digger bein' grumpy an' I wondered what Timber would have thought about the movie. When we got back to the hotel, Granite and Margo were gonna head off to where they lived.

"Do you want to come to my room and watch TV, Dick?" One For The Dead asked me.

"No," I said, feelin' kinda sad an' missin' my two pals but not wantin' to worry her any. "I think I wanna be alone."

"Well, if you change your mind you just come and knock on my door. It might feel strange being here the first night."

"Okay," I said.

Granite an' Margo each wrote their telephone numbers down for us an' told us to call if there was anythin' we needed. They'd come back in the mornin' to see us again an' help us make plans. Once they left I gave One For The Dead a hug an' headed for my room. It felt strange in there. But I had a few drinks from my bar an' switched through all the channels on my TV until I found somethin' I liked. It was a western movie an' I always like western movies so I sat on my bed an' watched.

I fell asleep an' started to dream. I didn't have enough to drink before I fell asleep on accounta the dream came back. Most times, if I drink enough I don't have no dreams. I don't like dreams. Dreams scare me on accounta mine are all bright an' shiny like movies an' they feel real. Everythin' in my dreams is like life an' the one dream I hate the most takes a lot of drinkin' to keep away. But that night it came for me. It came for me like it always does. Like the night it happened. Just like that. Just like I remember. Everythin', right down to the strange kinda white light from the TV set that night, flashin' an' blinkin' an' makin' weird shadows across the room so that I screamed on accounta when I opened my eyes that same light was in my room an' I thought I was back there. In the room I never wanna go back into again. The room where everythin' went bad. So I screamed.

The next thing I knew, Timber was there an' he was shakin' me. I kinda came back to the real world then an' sat up higher in the bed.

"Are you okay, pal?" he asked.

"Yeah," I said, rubbin' my head to make the dream go away. "Get me a drink, would you?"

I flicked off the TV an' turned on the lamp beside my bed to chase those weird shadows away. Timber handed me a glass an' I swallowed all of it. He got me another one an' we sat there smoking for a bit.

"Nightmare?" he asked.

"Yeah," I said. "Bad."

"Not surprising. This place is strange."

"You don't like it neither?"

"No. Not much. It's too different. Too new. I'm too used to being outside. Too used to the street."

"Me too. Did you just get here?"

"I was just getting in when I heard you scream. Glad I left that door between our rooms unlocked. Is Digger here?"

"You haven't seen him?" I asked, feeling kinda worried all of a sudden.

"No."

"Geez."

"Well, I know he was thinking of going to the Palace. Maybe he's still there? You want another drink?"

"I better."

"I think we'd better go look for him."

"Go look for him? How come? Nobody I know can look after himself better'n Digger."

"I know. But this is different. We've never been in this kind of spot before. Digger hasn't either."

"Kinda spot?"

"The money. It makes my head spin just thinking about it."

"Me too," I said. "Scares me on accounta nothin's the same no more. All of a sudden. Too fast, kinda."

"I imagine it's the same for Digger. We better go look."

"Should we tell One For The Dead we're goin'?"

"No. No sense bothering her. We won't be gone that long. We could even take a cab if we wanted."

"Okay. That's faster. I wouldn't want her to worry."

We put on our coats an' headed out. Timber stopped at the front desk to get some money with his new plastic bank card an' we got the men at the door to get us a cab. We told the driver that we wanted to go to the Palace an' he gave us a real funny look but pulled out anyway. All the way down there I watched the street go by. It was different in a car. It felt different. I couldn't get no feel for where we was. I couldn't really tell what corner was what an' I felt kinda lost riding in the back of that cab. But the driver knew where he was goin' an' we was there pretty quick.

"You guys be careful," he said. "This isn't the kind of neighbourhood you want to be out in at night."

"I think we'll be okay," Timber said an' grinned at me.

I grinned back an' we got out.

Granite

THE TELEPHONE RANG at 3 a.m.

"Granite?"

"Yes."

"It's Amelia."

"Amelia? What's wrong?" I asked sitting up in bed and switching on the light.

"I'm worried about the boys," she said. "None of them are in their rooms."

"They're not? Are you sure?"

"Yes. I checked all three. I thought maybe they were together in one room or another watching a movie. But they're not."

"I guess I can't really ask you if they've ever done this before, can I?"

"No."

"Okay, look," I said, fumbling for my wallet. "I'll call Margo and James and we'll come down there. She can sit with you while James and I try to figure out what to do. They might show up before we get there, though."

"I hope so. Thank you, Granite."

"No problem. Are you okay until we get there?"

"I think so. Just worried. We've never been in this situation before."

"I know. We'll be as quick as we can."

Both James and Margo were waiting in the lobby when I pulled up. They looked surprisingly fresh after the day we'd had and I was impressed at their ability to pull themselves together in such a hurry. My own scratchy chin and hastily thrown-together attire seemed boorish in comparison. We discussed the possible whereabouts of our friends in the elevator. We agreed that the available money meant they could be anywhere.

Amelia sat with her coat on at the edge of her bed. Margo went and sat with her, throwing an arm around her shoulder and talking softly in her ear. I made a pot of coffee while James called the concierge.

"Well, apparently Timber and Dick left here in a cab about four hours ago and Digger hasn't been seen all evening," James said when he joined us.

"They'll be together," Amelia said.

"How do you know that?" James asked.

"They're rounders. They'd stick with each other."

"Stick with each other where, though?" Margo asked.

"I don't know," Amelia said. "I wondered if they'd go to one of their digs."

"Digs?" James asked.

"Where they stayed before," I explained.

Amelia nodded and gave me a small grin. "Yes."

"Do we know where that is?" Margo asked.

"I only know where Dick stayed. It's an empty warehouse in the industrial area on the north side of downtown," Amelia said.

"We need to check there," James said. "Would they go there, though? I mean, they have money. They don't need to go there now."

"They need to go there," Amelia said quietly. "More than anything, right now they'd need to go there. Or somewhere like it."

"What about the Palace?" I asked. "Digger mentioned that he wanted to go and shoot the breeze with Ray."

"It's almost four in the morning," James said.

"Well, maybe Ray or someone is still there closing up or cleaning. Maybe they might know where Digger went. And apparently where we find Digger is where we find the other two," Margo said.

James and I headed out. We drove through the dark streets slowly, both of us keeping an eye on the sidewalks as we passed. I'd never had to look for anyone on the street at night and it amazed me how different it looked when you really pushed to see it. There was a depth of shadow there that was spectral. There were holes. Impossible holes that streetlights couldn't penetrate, and if someone were in there they couldn't be seen. I'd always wondered how the homeless became so invisible to the rest of us, and I realized that night that we never really know the geography of our city. We know buildings, streets, intersections, and neighbourhoods but we never know the holes. Not until we're forced to look. Not until someone close to us is out there in the night. Then we discover them. Then we learn to see them. The holes. They're everywhere: behind a stairway, in a doorway halfway down an alley, beneath the lower branches of a pine tree, behind a wall. Holes in the city. The holes where the lonely go, the lost, the displaced, the forgotten. The holes that lives disappear into. The holes that daylight's legerdemain makes vanish so that we come to think of the geography of the city as seamless, predictable, equal. It's not. The holes in the streets told me that as we drove.

"There it is," James said, pulling me back from my thoughts.

We pulled up in front of the Palace and could hear music. A man stumbled out the door with a bottle in his hand, lurching down the sidewalk and disappearing down an alley. A couple followed right after and wobbled crazily to a car parked a few yards from the door.

"Wild freakin' bash," the man said. "Wild."

James and I walked quickly to the door and pulled on it. It was locked. James rapped loudly with a gloved hand and we waited. He rapped again. Finally, the door opened a crack and Ray's face was there.

"We're closed," he said. "Private party."

"Ray? I'm a friend of Digger's. Granite. Remember?"

"Granite? Oh, yeah, the Square John from the movies. They ain't here. They *were* here but they left."

"Where did they go?" James asked.

"Fucked if I know. Nobody bails on a bash like this, man. Especially if you paid for it. We got strippers, man, some good smoke, tunes, and an open friggin' bar. But they walked."

"They paid for this?" I asked.

"Well, Digger did. Did you know the son of a bitch won the lottery?"

"Yes. We did. That's why we're here," James said.

"You a cop?" Ray asked. "We got a permit for this. Private party, not sellin' booze, we're good, officer."

"I'm Digger's lawyer," James said.

"Oh," Ray slurred. "The money guy."

"Yeah. The money guy. Now where did Digger say he was going?"

"He didn't. They didn't. Just kinda got up an' walked out about an hour ago. Hey, listen, man. You're gonna have to slip me a few more bucks here 'cause it costs more the longer it goes, ya know what I'm sayin'?" Ray grinned drunkenly.

"Yes. Well. Send me an invoice and I'll see what I can do. Here's my card."

"No, no, no," Ray said. "See, I need cash now, man. Gotta have it. Gotta pay the band, piece off the peelers, pay for the booze."

"I thought Digger did that?" James said.

"Yeah, well, he did, man. But I need more."

"More?"

"Yeah. Come on, man. He's got it. I figure a couple grand would pretty much cover it."

"Send me an invoice. Make it itemized. I'll run it by my friends at the liquor board, make sure it checks out, and we'll see what we can do," James said.

"Itemized? Fuck. Come on, man. Granite? Hey, man. How about a little for old Ray? Digger would."

I shook my head. "Sorry, Ray."

"I'll throw in a peeler," he said. "You ever had a peeler, Granite? Good friggin' toss. Best rattle you'll ever have, I guarantee it."

"I don't think so, Ray. I'll see you later."

We walked back toward the car. Ray stepped out onto the sidewalk and yelled after us.

"You can't change 'em, ya know. You can't. Rounder's a rounder. Always will be. That fucking money'll be gone, Granite. Gone. You'll see."

"Jesus," James said when we got into the car. "With friends like that, who needs enemas?"

I smirked. "Right. Now what?"

"Back to the ladies, I suppose. You have any ideas?"

"None. It's a big town. That's a lot of money. If they can do this, they're starting to get an idea of what they have in their hands now. That scares me."

"Yes," James said. "There're an awful lot of Rays out there."

"And a hell of a lot of holes."

"What?"

"Nothing," I said, and drove hard across the city.

One For The Dead

MY LITTLE BROTHER Harley. While I sat there in that strange hotel room waiting to hear from Granite and James, it was my little brother Harley who came to me. Oh, I didn't see him. At least, not really. He came as a shadow person, hovering behind me when I looked in the mirror. Just a wave, a motion, a wrinkle in the light, but I knew it was him. I felt him. And I knew where the boys were. Just like that.

"They walked home," I said to Margo.

"Pardon me?" she replied.

"The boys," I said with a small smile. "They walked home. They walked back to what they knew."

"And that would be where, exactly?"

"Dick's digs," I said. "They'll be at the warehouse where Dick sleeps."

"Slept," she said.

"Yes. Slept. But they're there."

"You're sure?"

"Yes. They'll want a fire. They'll want that shelter."

When Granite and James returned, Margo told them what I knew. They actually didn't seem surprised, and since I was so convinced they settled into chairs to rest and have a coffee before we went to pick the boys up.

"So if Dick stayed in a deserted warehouse prior to this, where did you stay?" James asked.

"Oh, never in one place. Not like the boys. They found one

place where they felt comfortable at night and went there for years. I moved around a lot."

"Like where, Amelia?" Margo asked.

"Well, you have to be safe and you have to be warm. Especially if you're a woman. There's air grates all over downtown behind office buildings and such and there's back doorways in alleys away from the wind. But I always tried to stay near the people. One winter, a big bunch of us slept together under a bridge. Kept each other safe. Made runs for food for each other, runs for booze if someone was real sick. Another time we found a boarded-up house and stayed there for a year and a half until the city finally got around to tearing it down. There's always places."

"Always holes," Granite said.

"Yes," I said, and patted his arm.

"You never wanted to come inside? Have a room somewhere? A place of your own?" James asked.

He was a good man. Gentle but strong. My people would have called him a warrior. "No," I said. "I tried that. But I never ever found a place that wasn't filled with stories, with history, with voices from the past."

Granite stared at me intently as I spoke.

"I could hear them. The stories of the people that used to live there. The stories of the lives that were created there, and they always kinda conjured up the voices from my own life and I couldn't bear to hear them anymore. At least, then I couldn't."

"Ghosts?" James asked.

"Not really. Just shadowed voices, shadowed memory, shadowed people."

"Do you still hear them?" Granite asked.

"Sometimes. When I'm someplace strong. Someplace where someone's life changed too quickly, where something was lost. I can hear them then, but most times I just get a sense of them being around us."

"Psychic," James said.

"No. Just aware," Margo said.

"Yes," I said. "*Aware* is a good word."

Granite nodded solemnly. "I believe you," he said. "I used to have the same sort of experience."

"Used to?" I asked.

"Yes." He looked at me with a weary, looking-back-too-long-and-too-far kind of look. "Used to."

"And this is how you know where the boys are?" James asked.

"Yes."

"That's good enough for me," Margo said. "We should go, then."

Margo and I drove with Granite while James followed in his car. I watched as the city changed block by block. We moved from the neat, wide avenues, through the glass and gloss of the office district, and on into the darkness of the warehouse area. It took me a while to get my bearings because I'd only ever walked to Dick's digs, but I sorted it out eventually. We turned the corner onto the road we were looking for and I immediately felt panic. It got even more severe when we pulled in behind the warehouse. There were three other cars parked back there. Three cars at a deserted building wasn't a good sign, and as we walked toward the boarded-up door we could hear laughter and see the flicker of fire high against the roof.

I pushed the door open and began to lead the others through the rabbit warren of things that Dick had piled up to make the place secure, to keep the light hidden. As we got closer to the centre where he had his fire, I could hear rowdy, drunken laughter, the clink of glass, and women's voices.

"Yeah, baby," Digger was saying. "That's right, that's right."

When we stepped into the lighted area I couldn't believe my eyes. Digger sat on a pile of pallets with a crock of whisky in one hand while three women danced and moved around him, reaching out to touch and grab and rub him. They were naked or close to it. He was flipping money in the air while they bumped and grinded around him. He wore headphones that were connected to some kind of music player that sat on the pallet beside him. The box it came in had been tossed on the ground at his feet.

On the other side of the fire, Timber was laid out on another pile of pallets where another barely dressed young woman massaged his temples and rubbed his chest. An empty whisky bottle lolled on the ground beside him.

Dick sat a few feet away with a stunned look on his face while two more women danced around him. He was on the ground and his head was rolling from side to side, spit showing at the corners of his mouth. As we watched, he leaned slowly to one side and passed out on the women's feet. They just laughed, picked up a handful of money off the ground, and moved toward the fire.

Three men sat there drinking and smoking cigars. There was a case of whisky and empty pizza boxes on the ground with loose bills everywhere.

Digger leaned his head back to take a swallow from his bottle and saw us at the edge of the light. His eyes popped open in surprise and he tugged the headphones from his head and scrambled to stand up. But he lost his balance and sprawled in the dirt. The women laughed.

"Shit," he grumbled and stood up. The whisky had spilled and drenched his new pants and he stood there muddy and confused. "How'd joo know we's here?" he asked, swaying.

"Digger," I said softly and moved toward him.

Margo crossed over to where Dick lay and tucked his coat under his head.

"Fuckin' party's goan good," he said to me with a lopsided grin. "More the merrier, ya know?"

Granite had moved to Timber. "He's out," he said, looking over at the two of us.

"Friggin' wusses," Digger said. "Fin'lly can party like we mean it and they pass the fuck out. Hey, Rock! Lookit all the tits!"

The women had gathered around the men at the fire, who stood to face us. They were big and mean-looking.

"Friends of yours, Digger?" one asked.

"Huh?" Digger said and reeled around to look at him.

"Thought we were partyin' in private here? Reason we left the bar so we could come here and have our own gig. What's *this?*"

"Friends," Digger said. "Friends. Little friggin' straight, maybe, but they're okay."

"We have to go, Digger," I said.

"Hey, hey, he's not goin' nowhere," one of the other men said, and the three of them separated to stand a few feet apart facing us. "This is our party. We say what goes. We say who comes and we say who goes."

"And we're sayin' that you're goin'," the third man said, putting a hand inside his jacket as a warning.

The women moved behind the men and stood there nervously, looking like they'd want to be anywhere in the world right now other than where they were. Dick groaned and Margo tucked the coat under his head a little snugger.

"No," Granite said, stepping away from Timber and closer to the men by the fire. "I think we'll be leaving. All of us."

"I think not, pal," the first man said. "We're owed a little scratch here and I don't figure anyone's making a move until we get it."

"How much are you owed?" James asked, taking a step closer too. "Margo, Dick's fine for now. Come over here behind me."

Margo moved to stand with me behind James.

"My name's James Merton. I'm a lawyer. These people you're partying with are my clients and I think it's time we left."

"I don't give a flying fuck who you are, pal," number two said. "There's a bill here needs payin'. You make one move at takin' these guys out of here, well, it ain't gonna be the prettiest sight those ladies have seen."

Digger shook his head to clear it and moved to stand beside James.

"Fuck you sayin'?" he asked the men.

"We're sayin' you owe us for the girls, for the dancing. You owe us for our time too," the first man said.

"Owe?" Digger asked. "Owe? Who friggin' owes? We're partyin' here." He shook his head again and cricked his neck a few times.

"You're the one doin' all the fucking partyin'," number three said. "We're sitting around waiting for you to get your stones off so we can get the fuck out. Party? With you? Here? You're just a buncha fucking stumblebums who got a lucky break. Sure, you're dressed up and cleaned up but you're still a buncha fucking losers. Losers who owe us. Owe us big."

"We get what we're owed or we bust heads," number one said.

"Stumblebums?" Digger asked. "*Stumblebums?*"

"How much are we talking about here?" James asked.

"Well, two hours of the girls' time, times six, two hours of our time, times three. Let's call it even at five," number two said.

"Five hunnerd? What about all this?" Digger asked, pointing at the money on the ground.

"That's tips. And it ain't five hundred, stumblebum. It's five thousand," number three said.

"There's that fuckin' word again," Digger said. "I didn't much like it the first time, pal. Jimbo, we gotta pay these fuckin' guys?"

"No," James said flatly. "No, we don't."

"You better," number one said.

"Or?" Digger asked.

"Or you'll be in a shitstorm like you never seen."

Digger looked at me and grinned. I could see the rounder in him then, see it through the booze, and I knew he'd stepped beyond the drunkenness. "Gee," he said playfully. "I'm not sure I like your tone, pal."

"What?" the third man said.

"You heard me. You want five grand from me, you gotta ask nice."

"Fuck you."

"That's not asking nice." Digger stepped toward him. James and Granite moved with him, keeping their eyes on the other two men. "Come here, man. I got it in my pocket."

The man stepped over to Digger, who reached into the pocket of his wet pants. He was taller than Digger by three or four inches and a lot heavier, and he sneered at him. He crossed his arms and rocked a little on the balls of his feet, which he spread while he waited. I knew what was coming. Digger rummaged around in his pocket, stepping closer to the big man while he did so. Then, when he'd gotten close enough, he dropped quickly to one knee and drove a fist straight into the man's crotch. Hard. Hard enough to lift him an inch or so off his feet. It was called the Mashed Potato on the street. The man screamed and dropped to his knees in front of Digger, who slapped his hands over the man's ears and then pulled the man's head hard into his bent knee. After that, the man lay on the ground unmoving.

"Next?" Digger said.

The other two men suddenly realized they were outnumbered. "Hey, hey, Digger. No need to get nasty. We were just joking around. It's a party, right?" number one said.

Digger shook his head slowly. Then, as he moved closer to them, he tilted his head back and sniffed the air. "Smell that?" he asked.

"Smell what?" the second man replied.

"Smells kinda like a shitstorm to me. Or maybe that's just you."

"Digger, that's enough," James said. "Now I think you guys should take your women friends, drag your buddy out of here, and get lost. Or my associate Ms. Keane will call 911 on her cellular phone and you can maybe explain the pimping, the assault, and the threats to the police."

"Okay, okay, we're out of here. But he still owes us," number one said.

"Pick it up," Digger said.

"What?" the man asked.

"Pick it up. The loot. On the ground. All of you. Get down on your fucking knees and pick it up. Take it with you. It's yours, but you gotta pick it up."

They scrambled about for a minute or two grabbing handfuls of bills off the ground. When they'd gotten all of it they picked up the third man, who was conscious but groaning, and headed out of the warehouse. Digger collapsed onto the pile of pallets.

"Fuck me," was all he said before passing out.

Digger

DICK WOULDN'T WAKE UP. He just wouldn't fucking come out of it. The four of them that wasn't into the party thing that night got us back to the hotel. Me, I got it together after a few minutes. Drunker'n a bastard, but I walked out. Timber came to enough to make it to the car if he leaned on Granite. But they had to carry Dick out. Toted him out and propped him in the back of Granite's car between Margo and the old lady. He never friggin' moved all the way back. When we got to the hotel the guys at the door helped get Dick to his room, and even when Margo wiped his face with a cold cloth he never friggin' moved. It was like he was dead. Dead. That sobered me up fast.

He never came out of it that night. We took him to the hospital in the morning and he never came out of it most of the next day. The doctor told us he was in some kind of coma from drinking too much too fast. We belted 'em back pretty good at the Palace. All the music and the excitement, the girls, made it easy to just roar into partying, and I never seen how much anyone was drinking. Never watched before. Never mattered. Then when we got to the warehouse with those three goons who offered us the girls and the private party, I knew we was drinking it up real good but it never mattered to me then. Fuck. The three of us have been on some wild friggin' binges in our time and Dick could always keep it up for a good while just like us. He was a rounder, for Christ's sake. He wasn't no stumblebum drunk like the fucking goon called us. We drank, sure, but we knew when was enough, we knew when we needed to lay out, get off the street, sleep it off, just like we knew that we was gonna need a slurp or two when we woke up to take the shakes and the sick away. We knew all that and we took care of it. We took care of each other. When one of us didn't have it in the morning and we was sick, the other'd give us what we needed to keep on going. But this? This was something fucking weird. Far as I could see we didn't have more'n we had other times when we was partying with Fill 'er Up Phil.

Dick poisoned himself. He wasn't used to drinking so much anymore, and when we partied like we used to he drank too much too fast and his brain and his body couldn't hold up. *I* did that to him. Me. If I hadn't gone all fucking crazy and got the party going at the Palace he wouldn't have been laid up in that hospital bed with tubes in his mouth and some fucking machine beep-beeping away with green lights showing his fucking heart-beats. If I had just walked out and away like they wanted me to when they showed up at the Palace, we'da been okay. But no. Me, I hadta make them stay. Me, I hadta challenge 'em. Call 'em pussies, Square Johns in training, loogans. Me. Fuck.

All that night he was out. No one could tell us when he'd wake up, if ever. Alcoholic coma, they said. No way to tell. If ever. Fuck me. If ever. Two little words but they were huge motherfuckers. Huge. I stood around his bed with the rest of them, looking at him and feeling helpless. Helpless and guilty. I felt like they could see it on my face. Like they could feel it coming off my friggin' body and I hadta get out of there. Couldn't stand looking at the people I called my friends. Couldn't stand looking at Dick. My winger. My backup. My pal.

I wound up sitting in the chapel all alone. Well, except for the bottle in my pocket. I sat there drinking, looking up at the little cross on the front wall, wondering how the fuck any kind of God could let this happen to a guy like Dick. He was slow, and that bugged me at times, but he never had a hard word for anyone. Never did nothing to me but be there. Always. Tall, skinny fucker with the biggest friggin' feet I ever seen. Fuck. I sat there a long time, thinking about all the days and nights we prowled the street together. There was some hard times. Tough times. Times that no one but a rounder coulda seen his way through, and Dick seen 'em through. Seen 'em through and never once whined or snivelled like a lot of them do. He was a rounder. A good rounder.

I never heard Rock until he slid into the pew beside me.

"That holy water looks a little brown there, Digger," he goes.

"Yeah," I go. "Diff'rent kinda religion."

"I suppose," he goes. "Got a little?"

"Yeah." I hand him the bottle. He takes a little sip and hands it back.

"He okay?" I go.

"He's stable."

I nod. "Nothing new, then?"

"No."

"I gotta smoke."

"Okay. I'll go with you."

We go downstairs and find a small patio with benches. It's mid-afternoon by then and people are moving around all over. I fire up a tailor-made with my new lighter and stand there looking at it. Rock eyeballs me all the while.

"I feel fucking bad," I go. "Real bad."

"Like it's your fault?" he goes. "Like you did this to him?"

"Yeah," I go, glad for the understanding.

"Good," he goes.

"Good? Fuck me, Rock. If this is some kind of a pep talk, you're really fucking it up, man."

"It's not a pep talk," he goes. "You need to hear the truth."

"Jesus," I go. "I don't need this."

"Yeah, you do."

"I do? Why?"

"Because you're fucking everything up. Or, at least, you will."

"I will? How?"

"You don't realize what you have here."

"I fucking know what I have."

"Yeah? What do you have?"

"I got four and a half friggin' million dollars. That what's I got."

"No. That's not what you have. That's only part of it."

"Part of it? That's fucking all of it, Rock."

He moves right in front of me and looks me in the eye. We stand there for a moment gunning each other off and I'm thinking that this Square John's gotta lotta friggin' balls. I like that about him. So I listen.

"You have what millions of other people don't have, Digger. You have what every one of us carries around inside ourselves all our lives but hardly any of us ever get to see. You have the power to change your life. You can become anything you want to become now. Anything. You can choose.

"But if you keep on doing what you're doing, if you keep on partying and throwing money on the ground for all the stooges, loogans, boobs, losers, and stumblebums to pick up just because you can, you'll throw all of it away. You'll piss it all away, and when you do there won't be anyone in this world that will feel sorry for you, because you squandered the chance that everyone wants. To just *be.*

"Dick's lying up there because of choice. You chose to party. He chose to join you. He chose to drink like he used to drink. You didn't cause that. You might feel like you did, but you didn't do this to him. You're not that friggin' big and powerful, Digger. Dick chose. He made a choice. You're guilty only of setting a bad example, of making your own choice—and I have to say it was a pretty piss-poor one. But you can end all that right here. You can choose to make that money work for you and go out there and be. Be whomever you want.

"And the others will follow you. They'll follow you because you're their protector. They'll follow you because you're the rounder's rounder. So this money gives you two big friggin' gifts, Digger. It gives you the power to choose to be whomever the fuck you want to be, and it gives you the power to help the others become whomever they want to be. But if you keep on going the way you're going, you're only going to be one thing in the end."

"What's that?" I go.

He looked at me as hard as I let anyone look at me for as long as I can remember. "You'll be a loser—a boob, a stooge, a loogan, a stumblebum. And if you take the others with you, you won't even be a rounder anymore because rounders don't do that to each other. Rounders watch each other's back, and it's time, Digger. It's time for you to watch their backs like they've been watching yours all this time. Especially Double Dick Dumont."

"Why him especially?" I go.

"On accounta he doesn't have a filter," he goes. "Not like you and me. You do things out of anger—rage, really. Rage that your body failed you, rage that time went by too fast, and rage that there's no place left for the best friggin' wheelman in the world. You filter the world and your choices through that rage, that anger."

"And you?" I go.

"I filter it through anger too," he goes, and we look at each other for a moment or two. "But Dick doesn't filter it through anything. He just respects you. He just believes in you. He just follows you—and he just watches your back in his own small way. He's pure that way, Double Dick is. He's innocent."

I nod. "Lot to think about."

"I hope so," Rock goes.

I reach out and shake his hand. Just as we're doing that I catch a glimpse of the old lady hotfooting it across the patio. Something in my heart pauses.

"He's awake," she goes. "And he's asking for Digger."

One For The Dead

THEY PUT THEIR HEADS TOGETHER like little boys trading secrets. I don't know what they said to each other, but as we stood at the far end of the room and watched Digger and Dick talk, I looked at the rest of us and saw how tied together we had become. There couldn't be anything wrong with that. No matter how scary this had been, no matter how close we might have come to losing Dick to drink, it brought us even closer—all of us, not just us rounders, but the whole lot of us. I knew he wasn't going anywhere. You been around death as long as me, you get to know its feel, its weight, even before it gets here, and I knew it wasn't time for Dick. There wasn't anything I could say, though. There's times when you have to keep a deep knowing to yourself so others around you can find the teachings in a thing. Those of us who can see know that, but the hard part is letting others go through it. While it hurts to watch them deal with hurt, you know that you still have to let them, that it's a gift, that it's a teaching way. So I bided my time until Dick came out of the deep darkness that the booze had put him in and tried to offer the comfort that I could. I was glad to see that Granite and Digger had talked. I wouldn't have changed that for anything.

Dick waved his hand to invite us to his bedside.

"Me 'n Digger got a plan," he said.

"That's good," I said. "What's your plan?"

"Well, first we're gonna get me the frig out of here, then we're gonna go see *Field of Dreams* like we meant to all along, then we're buyin' everybody dinner."

"Sounds like a really good plan to me," Margo said. "I'd like to go to the movies with you, Dick."

"Yeah, an' you could sit with Granite on accounta I think he kinda likes you, Miss Margo," Dick said with a grin.

"Well, that sounds like a nice plan too," she said.

"The doctor says you need to rest another couple of days, Dick. To get the alcohol out of your system," James said. "But we can get you a TV in your room and a VCR hooked up to it so you can watch movies."

"Yeah?" Dick asked. "They let you?"

"They let you, all right. Especially a wealthy man like you. I'll get them to move you to a private room as soon as the doctor thinks you're ready."

"Okay. Digger?"

"Yeah, pal?" Digger asked.

"You wanna watch movies with me in my room?"

"Yeah. I'd like that."

"Okay. You choose then. You go get us some from a movie store an' we'll watch until they let me out of here."

We spent an hour or so talking around that bed. It felt good. Granite, James, and Margo joined right in, and as I stood there and watched these friends standing knee deep in relief together I felt mighty grateful. There was no way in the world that seven people like us could have ever found each other. There was no way that the lives we lived before could have ever brought us together across so much time and distance, sorrow and longing, living and dying. Well, there *was* a way, in fact. It was a magic way. A mystery way. A great mystery way like Grandma One Sky had talked about a long time ago. The hand of Creation moving in mystery, bringing teachings to us in the smallest things. I looked around me. In that hospital where so many lives had turned, where so many sorrows were born and losses taken, there were no shadowed ones around us. I expected them. But in that room right then the light of friendship, alive and powerful, burned away all shadow and there was no room for them to stand. I smiled at that.

The nurses came and told us that Dick needed to rest. They were giving him medicine to help him with the hangover. He'd had so much that they were afraid he might have a seizure, so keeping him calm was important.

"Amelia? Can I talk to you in private?" Dick asked.

"Yes," I said.

The others said their goodbyes and left the room. I took Dick's hand in mine.

"What is it, Dick?"

"You know how I don't like dreamin'? How it scares me?"

"Yes."

"An' you know how I drink so I don't have 'em an' how that always helps me get through the night most times?"

"Yes."

"Well, I didn't have no dreams. I was asleep a long time there an' I didn't have no dreams."

"That's good. You needed to rest."

"Do you think the money made 'em go away? Could it do that?"

"I don't know. Maybe. What do you think?"

He turned his head and looked out the window, lay there quietly for a minute or so. "It was quiet where I was. I don't know where that was but I know it was real quiet on accounta nothing woke me up. I just kinda opened my eyes when I was ready. So I think maybe I wanna buy some quiet with my money. Maybe if

I buy enough quiet then the dreams'll go away. Can you do that? Can you have enough money to buy quiet?"

"Yes," I said. "I think you can do that. It sounds like what I'd want to spend my money on too, Dick. Quiet. It's nice to think about."

"Okay," he said. "I need to sit with Digger now. I don't want him to feel bad no more about what happened."

"Okay," I said. "You're a good man, Dick."

He grinned at me and I walked into the hall to join the others.

Digger

I SAT WITH HIM for five days while he got better. They got him a good room that next morning and we had us a TV and a movie player right off the bat. The others came and stood around for a while but I kinda figured they figured that me 'n Dick was having some time together and left us alone to do that. We musta watched a hundred movies in that room. Me 'n Dick were friggin' amazed at how many you could get to watch on your television set. It was kinda like heaven. We never said word one about the party or about him slipping away like he did. Instead, we just watched movies and we laughed. Fuck. I didn't even hardly drink. When I did I'd slip into Dick's bathroom and have a little swallow but not enough to bug him by getting tight or nothing. After five days he was ready to leave and we made it back to the hotel finally. I was actually glad to be there, and that friggin' amazed me. I never stopped to think that for five nights me 'n Dick was inside. Inside. In between walls. Off the street. It just kinda happened and when I finally realized it, I was in my room, towelling off after a good hot shower, trying to find a movie to watch on the television. There I was in between walls. I walked over to the big windows in my room and hauled open the thick heavy drapes. There it was. The city. The streets. It all kinda lay below me like something you forgot you had. Seeing it again surprises the shit out of you and you want to pick it up again and feel it, remember, recollect, remind yourself of somewhere you mighta travelled once or somewhere you mighta been. Then you just put it back on the shelf or in the corner where it sat and keep on moving wherever you happen to be moving at the time. That's what I did. I kept right on moving.

We made it to *Field of Dreams* the night Dick came out of the hospital. All of us. All seven of us. And when we walked into that movie house there wasn't any fuss at all about us being there. We were dressed good. We were clean. We were seven regular movie-loving people out to catch another flick and the forgotten thing—the street—was just something we were walking on to get there.

The movie was about baseball. Or at least it started out that way. It was about a guy having to make a baseball field out of his farmland so some dead ballplayer could get to play again. Not really my kind of thing. Not enough action and lights for me. But it got to me. Everyone had a reason for being where they were in that movie. Everyone had something important to do so the story could move where it was supposed to move, and as I looked along that row of people I was a part of that night, I wondered what I was supposed to do. I wondered why I was there.

Rock said that the others would follow me. Follow me where, I wondered. They followed me to a drinking party and it almost cost us big time. Then near the end of that movie the big black guy gets invited to go where the dead players go every night. He gets invited into the mystery and he says something like "if I have the courage to do this, what a story it'll make." *What a story it'll make.* That's what I heard. I figured if I had the courage to go where this money could take me, into this mystery place, maybe it'd make a pretty good story too. I didn't know what was out there. I didn't know what would happen when we got there. I didn't know nothin' about nothin'. But I knew that I had to go there. For them. For my friends.

If you build it, they will come. That was the other thing I heard. I remembered me 'n Dutch standing at the back of the big semi looking at the wheel all piled on the flatbed, all pulled apart and empty laying there. When I put my hands on those pieces of steel there wasn't nothing in them. No energy. No motion. But as we raised the wheel to the sky it got to be something. Bolt by bolt we put something magic together, and when we were done it wasn't empty no more and neither was I. I'd stand in the crossbrace and look across the midway, across this field that held the dreams of all those people that would come because they saw the lights of the wheel spinning around and around against the sky, and I'd hold my hands a little tighter on the cables and struts of that wheel and feel it thrumming and pulsing and I felt like a magician. I felt alive. Alive as the wheel.

There were four and a half million pieces to put together here. And later, as I stood at the window in that hotel room far above the city watching them lights twinkle and dance and shine like tiny eyes looking up at me, I felt like I stood in the crossbraces of another great wheel in the sky. A wheelman. Someone who could build it from the ground up. It didn't scare me like it shoulda then. It didn't make me wanna bolt and run back to what I knew. It didn't even make me wanna drink it all away. No. Instead, it made me wanna finally get over that far horizon, my horizon, our horizon, and see the life I could live on the other side.

Were you ever on a Ferris wheel?
Only once, when I was small.
Did you like it?
It scared me at first but after a few trips around it got to be exciting.
What was the most exciting part for you?
I suppose that moment when the wheel's turning and you're sitting in your seat looking across it, seeing the backs of the other seats, the spokes, off into the fairgrounds to all the lights and then you get raised to the sky. You come over the top and there's nothing but sky and you feel like you're being lifted up into the stars. That was the most exciting part.
Why?
Hmm. Because you can feel the world disappear.
You like that?

I did then. Actually, there were a lot of times I wished for that particular magic.

Never happens, though, does it?

No. You always come down the other side, back into it.

Except when they stop you right at the top. Then you can see the whole world. Or at least, it feels like it.

Yes. I liked that feeling too. Seeing the whole world.

Ferris wheels are like life then, aren't they?

Yes. I suppose they are.

What a ride.

What a ride, indeed.

BOOK THREE dreams

Timber

I WALKED. I still walked. Every morning I'd get up before sunrise and wander the streets. The others would all be asleep, even Digger, and I'd move through the house we bought on Indian Road and get ready for the street. Digger had discovered coffee makers that turned on automatically like alarm clocks and he set it for me so there'd be a hot cup when I woke. He'd discovered a lot of gadgets in those months since we won the lottery. There were gizmos that turned the outside lights on and off at a certain time each night and morning, gadgets that let you tape a TV show or movie while you watched another one, and even one that turned our bedside lamps on when we clapped our hands. It never failed to surprise me when Digger came home trundling another box of something. The world was filled with thingamajigs, doohickeys, and doodads, and Digger seemed to be able to find all of them. I liked it. It made the house a curious place. It made it irregular, and irregular suited me fine in a neighbourhood of sameness and predictability.

We bought a big three-storey house with an attic. We decided that if money meant we had to live inside, we might as well live inside together. So James Merton, Granite, and Margo had found a real estate guy and we'd toodled around the city looking for some digs that would be big enough for us to have our private spaces. We found this place after about a month. Indian Road was close to one of the biggest parks in the city and known as a quiet, stable area filled with hard-working people with families who'd been in the same house for years and years. I actually liked it. It took a few weeks to get used to it, and I didn't sleep much, but just knowing that there was someone down the hall to talk to if I woke up feeling heebie-jeebied made it easier. My room was in the attic. We fixed it up and made it into a living area with skylights and big triangle windows at each end so I could look out across the skyline at night. It was like street digs almost, all tucked away and quiet.

But I still needed to walk. I don't know why really, only that something inside me was tied to the concrete and straight lines of curb and gutter, something that needed to know that it was all still there, that it hadn't been a dream, that I had been a rounder and the street had framed my life for years.

The others understood and they let me do my thing without comment or question. I'd get up and move quietly through the house gathering my coat and shoes, hat and gloves, moving through the darkness easily like I had through the boarded-up buildings I used to squat in once upon a time. I'd coffee up, sitting on the back porch with a cigarette, and then I'd step out the door, down the steps, and onto the sidewalk that led around the house to the front where it bordered the driveway and tumbled down a slight incline to the street. I'd stand there at the end of the driveway and look back at the house. It stood against the morning sky like a living thing, all hushed up and quiet, its lines and edges sharp as solitary decisions made in darkness. It sat there heavy and solid. A place to come back to. A place to remain. I'd look and see it, follow its lines from the roof to the bottom step leading from the front veranda and down to where I stood anchoring it in my head.

Then I'd do what I started doing the very first time I took a morning walk. I knelt in the street. Knelt down and put my hand on the curb and felt the pocked surface of the concrete. It felt like it always had: rough, cold, unyielding; but I felt it every morning anyway. Felt it on the palm of my hand, rubbed it, anchored it in my soul. Then I followed it with my eyes as it flowed down Indian Road, past the grand old houses, the manicured yards, the shiny cars, the kids' bicycles, the discarded toys, and onward to the corner, where it split like choice. I imagined it from there, snaking through the city leading a wanderer through neighbourhoods, areas, zones, and boroughs, linking everything it passed, tying it all together in a long, flowing vein until it reached the inner city. It always led back there. Always. So I'd kneel in the street and feel the concrete, follow it in my mind to its inescapable returning, and then I'd stand, heave a breath, and start to walk.

I walked down Indian Road. I walked through the park. I walked through adjoining neighbourhoods. I walked in a haphazard loop that led me back to the house after a couple of hours. I never measured it. I never wondered how far I'd gone. I just walked, feeling the street moving beneath my feet like it had for years. I liked the feel of the city waking up around me. It was a strange comfort for me to hear the hum of wheels growing louder and louder, punctuated by slamming doors, the whoosh of bus doors, the clank of garbage cans, the cawing of crows, the twitter of songbirds, the chatter of squirrels, and eventually, the voices of the people starting their days. Walking that way that early made me feel a part of it at the same time that I felt detached, removed, isolated from it, and it took me a few weeks to realize that I was recreating the feeling I'd had as a rounder. Part of the flow but removed from it all, like an island in a stream. I guess that's why I liked it. Why I needed it. To remind me that I was still a rounder despite the money, despite the house, despite the fact that I slept indoors and my life was contained. Still a rounder, still what I knew.

And in the evenings, when the light was seeping away, I'd walk again. I'd watch the city curl up and prepare for sleep. Watch the energy recede. Watch it tuck itself away in private places until the streets emptied, became quiet and hushed, and echoed the deliberate footsteps of walkers alone in the gloaming. I'd walk and watch the lights come on in living rooms, the hard click that captured the disembodied heads of families engaged in dinners, chats, and connection. I'd walk and look at the walls of all the houses on Indian Road, captivated and mesmerized by them, by all the possibility that lived there until sometimes, standing at the end of our driveway looking at those homes, it seemed they were enchanted places, filled with the magic light of permanence, elegant with the sound of returning, made divine almost by belonging.

I'd heave a huge breath then. Breathe deep and long, turn my head toward the sky, close my eyes and prepare myself to turn inward again, to enter my own enchanted world, to settle, to rest until the concrete called me forward into another day.

Double Dick

I CHOSE INDIAN ROAD. It sounded right to me on accounta One For The Dead is an Indian an' she was the one what got us all together. She's the one made us all feel like we was supposed to be together. When I seen it, I knew. Like when you know what someone's gonna say before they say it or how you know the next car comin' around the corner's gonna be blue an' gonna almost hit the guy just startin' to walk across the street. That's kinda how I knew, I guess. It was a nice house. It had big windows all over so you kinda felt like you was outside when you was inside, no matter where you were. The veranda went most of the way around an' I liked when we all sat out there at night. It was like when East Coast Willie an' Hand Jive Pete had their oil drum down in the hollow by the expressway. Big buncha us sat around passin' a jug back an' forth an' tellin' stories around the fire in that drum. It felt like that. 'Cept we didn't have no fire. We sat there most nights on accounta none of us wanted to be inside too early. Me, anyhow. Even when it got cold that first winter, Granite got us a heater so we could sit out back on the closed-in porch. Anyhow, it was a big old house kinda looked like it'd been around an' I picked it out of all of the ones we seen.

Fourteen-oh-four Indian Road. It sounded like one of them poems. We all chose where we was gonna sleep and me 'n One

For The Dead got rooms on the second floor. I liked that. Knowin' she was nearby was nice. We spent lots of time with Miss Margo an' Granite goin' around gettin' things for our house. I never knew there was so much stuff. We'd wander around for hours in some big stores an' they had everythin' you could want long as you could afford it. Us, we could afford lots an' I had fun buyin' stuff for my room.

I liked my room. I slept right close to the window on accounta I could open it an' hear the outside an' feel the air on my face. It was big an' I got a real big chair that was stuffed real good so I could watch movies an' feel like I was sittin' in a movie house. Me 'n Granite found a really big TV an' then we got a movie player an' hooked it up to a sound system so that it would sound like in the movies too. But what I liked best about it was my shelves, on accounta I got to buy whatever kindsa movies I wanted to watch. I bought all the ones we first seen together right off the bat. Then I got the ones that Granite and Miss Margo told me about. I musta had a couple hunnerd pretty quick an' the guy down the street at the swap place was always glad to see me come in to talk movies an' swap some of mine for some of his. He said I had a great collection. I thought so too. My shelves was lined with movies an' I liked to sit there an' look at all of them. All them imagined lives. All them stories. All them dreams.

Digger got me a popcorn machine that made it with hot air. Mr. James brought me a drink machine that kept sodas an' had them little paddles that you push in with your cup to fill it like at the movies. So I could sit there an' watch movies an' have drinks an' popcorn. I liked that.

But I couldn't tell nobody that watchin' movies was how I got through the nights most times. I'd pour a big bottle of vodka into one of my pop machines an' sit there alone after everyone had gone to bed. I'd put a movie on an' then put on the headphones Granite got me so no one could hear an' I sat there watchin' movies an' drinkin' until finally I fell asleep. Most of the time I heard Timber goin' out for his walk before I slept an' that was good on accounta it meant the night was over. I was scared of the night. I was scared to wake up in the flickerin' light of the TV screen on accounta it was like the room I never wanted to see again an' I was scared to dream. Dreamin' always took me back to that room an' I needed to have some booze an' I needed to know the night was over so's I could sleep without dreams. I never told nobody that. I'd get up around noon or so an' they'd all be busy doin' what they liked to do an' wouldn't ask me nothin' except how I slept an' stuff. I just lied and said "good." They never knew. I wished I could tell 'em but I couldn't. Everything was going so good for us in our new house, I didn't want to spoil it by worryin' anybody. Me, I figured maybe I'd be able to sleep okay after a while an' it wouldn't be no problem no more. But if that was what was supposed to happen, it was awful slow about it.

One For The Dead

I LIKED THE WAY THE HOUSE SAT. Right away, when I first saw it, I liked the way it sat on the ground. Kind of like an old sow bear. She's big with her age and proud and she sits on her haunches watching her cubs in the meadow chasing mice. With the sun on her face and the warm earth beneath her, she is firm, planted, a part of it all. That's how that old house looked to me, and walking through it I felt no sense of loss here, no shadowed ones lurking in the corners, no weight of history. Instead, the house felt blessed with stories. As if the family that had lived here had been a happy one and their moving on from here had been as natural as an old sow bear lumbering off to hibernate or to find a new hunting ground. History and lives flowing forward, unbroken, unbent, and unbowed. I knew it was our home as soon as I saw it.

There was a big yard in back and I got the boys to clear me a good patch of ground for a garden. I remembered Grandma One Sky and me weeding her small patch of ground and talking when I was a young girl, and I wanted a growing place for our new home. Sometimes one or another of the boys would wander out when I was fussing around back there and sit on the ground like I used to, idly plucking small weeds and talking. It was a good garden that first year: lots of cucumbers, tomatoes, and peas, a few potatoes, and some corn. Gathering it all with one of the boys helping was a small joy.

Margo and Granite took me to a play just after we moved in and I loved it. It was like one of our stories, one of our Ojibway stories come alive in front of me. When I was a girl and Grandma One Sky told one of her stories, I would close my eyes and see the Animal People or the Ojibway people moving around just like the actors moved around on that stage. I loved it. It became one of the things that the three of us did together regularly.

We still went to movies. None of us could quit doing that. We'd scan the papers or watch the ads on TV and choose the ones we wanted to see. Most days, we went. None of us liked the feel of a crowd and we chose to go to afternoon showings to avoid the crush and push of lots of people, and because in the beginning that's how it had been—our little ragged company seeking the shelter of the movies. Granite showed up now and then and it was always a joy to see him there. We'd sit in our row together, talk quietly for a minute or so and wait, almost holding our breaths until that first dimming of the lights that you felt before you actually saw it. Then we'd breathe, sit back in our seats, and disappear into the magic of story one more time. It was always like that, and all of us loved it as much as we had that first time. Always.

But I knew there were changes, and I knew that those changes were hard for us. Only Digger seemed to settle, and I think the scare of almost losing Dick made it easier for him to make choices in his new life. The other two boys worried me. Timber couldn't shake the concrete from his soul. His walks told me that. He couldn't see himself, couldn't envision himself, couldn't imagine himself away from the street. It was like he'd convinced himself in the most desperate way that it was all he deserved. When he walked I'd stand back from my window so he couldn't see me and watch his ritual touching of the concrete, see him looking down the road where it led, and know inside myself that he was seeing himself walking there, now and always. There were always shadowed ones there, just behind his shoulder, and I worried that he might never find a way to rid himself of the weight of their presence.

Dick thought I didn't know about his nighttime habit. I knew he wasn't sleeping. That only the promise of morning made it possible for him to drift off into troubled, tossing sleep. He thought I didn't know that the pop machine was never just soda. I could sit in my room and see the flickering light from his television against the big oak tree that stood outside our windows, or see it living in the crack under his door against the floorboards. I gave him his space. I left him alone. I would only embarrass him by entering his room late at night and asking about him. He was still a rounder and rounders needed the privacy of the night, needed the ritual of alone time, needed to pull the night around them like a blanket and huddle in it, planning what they planned, thinking what they thought, and preparing themselves for the battle of the next day. When the time was right for him, he'd let us know.

Digger carried the street in his chest. Timber and Dick carried the street on their shoulders. They carried the story of their street life, the story of how they got there, the story of how they had survived. Even though that splendid old bear of a house we lived in bore no weight of loss, no burden of sorrow, no hauntings, it didn't need to. Some of us brought our own.

Digger

THE FRIGGIN' GARAGE was mine. I claimed it right off the hop. I seen it sitting back there and I claimed the fucker. I had a room in the house but I wanted to sleep out back. So me 'n Rock and Merton got together and fixed it up. We put in insulation, changed the windows, put a real floor down over the concrete, carpeted it, put in heat, a shower, and lickety-fucking-split I had me some digs I could handle. After the talk died down on the veranda or the porch at night, I'd mosey on back and settle in. It was like digs. It was like being in my little alcove looking out over the hill except there weren't no view there. But it was tucked away and quiet and I liked it fine.

And I bought a friggin' truck. Me. Digger. I had me a fucking old Mercury some Square John had fixed up and couldn't afford to keep. Fucking old Mercury with headlights like cat's eyes. I'd head out early in the morning on my new route. I'd drive about three hours along the alleys of the new neighbourhood, listening to music on my CD player and slurping coffee, looking for interesting castoffs. I didn't grab bottles or cans no more. Didn't need to. But I loved it when I found some Square John toss-off that could be fixed up. I found bicycles, lamps, radios, televisions, toasters, stoves, all kinds of shit left for dead that still had life in them if a guy wanted to spend some time coaxing the breath back. I did.

I found out I had a talent for it. Don't know why but I could eyeball a thing for a while, kinda follow its line and wires and shit and figure out how it was supposed to run. Then I'd tinker around. That's all. That's how I explain it. I'd just tinker around and feel the way it was supposed to be, like feeling the wheel, like knowing from the sound of that old MacCormack engine what was right and what was not. So I fixed things. Made 'em work. Made 'em live again.

Merton found me an old store in an area filled with antique joints. It had a fair-sized front end to show off stuff and a big friggin' work area in back. We got me all kinds of tools and I sat back there fixing up the toss-offs, painting them, making them breathe again, listening to music on an old stereo I fixed. Now people brought me stuff to sell for cash. Except I didn't do no buying. I didn't even try too hard to sell anything but people always wanted to buy it. Couldn't get my head around that Square John kinda thinking that says something's useless and tossable until someone makes it all new and shiny again and then spend way too much friggin' money on it to let folks know they got a soft spot in their hearts for old and fucking charming. Only a Square John thinks like that. So I sold some shit but I was always more interested in getting something back into the sky again, so to speak, and I hired a young rounder named Gene to work the front. It was a good go. Damn good go, really, and I slipped into it without even thinking much about it. We called it Digger's. There wasn't much of a choice to be made about that even though we toyed around with calling it The Wheelman's, Rounders, or even From the Street, but Digger's had a nice ring to it. So there it was, a tiny store with a wooden sign painted bright orange like a carnival sign that said DIGGER'S. And it was mine.

Joined the AAs too. Well, not friggin' really. I went to a meeting now and then to keep my head straight, but I still liked my hooch on the veranda at night and I liked to lay in my garage digs, slurp from a bottle late at night, and listen to music. But I went. Rock made sense when he told me I could piss it all away, and once I got going with the fix-up thing, the store and the house—well, it was too much to risk pissing away. Plus, almost getting Dick killed scared me. I wouldn't tell nobody that. But it scared me and I wanted to make sure I didn't get close to that again. So I went to the odd meeting. Couldn't buy the whole psyche but I liked hearing the old guys that'd been around tell their stories. Kinda like rounder stories and I got a kick out of hearing them. Never told mine, though. None of their friggin' business. I just listened. I'd say something about looking for a fix-up project and take off from the house every once in a while. None of them said nothing and I sure as fuck wasn't going to volunteer any information but they could tell I wasn't as drunk or drinking anything like I used to.

So there I was living on Indian Road, working for myself, driving a charming old fucking truck, staying more or less sober with a pocketful of loot, and hitting the flicks like regular. Life was good, and if I missed the rounder life at all I didn't notice.

Granite

I RENTED *An Affair to Remember* for Amelia and Margo, really. There was a charm to the saccharine sweetness of old romance movies that Amelia had come to love, and Margo was easily swept away by the tug on the heartstrings that Old Hollywood seemed to specialize in. I much preferred the classic dramas or film noir, and they got a much better reception from the guys, but on that night, browsing the aisles for a quality rental, I was drawn to the Cary Grant–Deborah Kerr love story.

We'd generally sit on the veranda on those nights we rented films and wait for the night to fall, and either Margo or I would tell them what we were going to see. It had become a habit after Digger and I had shopped around for the best and latest viewing equipment and installed it in their living room. They were the proud owners of the biggest domestic television, which was hooked up to a top-of-the-line home theatre system. The sound was magnificent. The image was dumbfounding. We'd sit in the plump and spacious chairs bought especially for their viewing potential and get as lost in story in that house as we did in the movie theatres. Then, after the viewing, we'd assemble ourselves on the veranda again and talk. They had become astute aficionados of film. Even Digger, in his gruff appraisals, made astounding critical sense.

"No fuckin' way someone'd say that in that situation," he'd say, and go on to explain the reality of life's little moments. It was always enlightening, always engaging.

I enjoyed the film. There was a part of me that still clung to the necessity of admiring the technical handiwork of emotional films rather than comment on their content. Still, a part of me had pulled away from all that. I'd try to concentrate on the lighting, the sound, or the camera angle. But in those moments when the crucible of human feeling is laid bare upon the screen and there's the warmth of a woman's hand on your arm in the darkness, like Margo's on mine that night, it's difficult to focus on workmanship. Despite myself, I was drawn to the poignant drama of love's great endurance, its tragic loyalty, its resilience that lay at the heart of that great old tale. Drawn to it as much I was drawn to enclosing my hand about the hand that lay on my arm in the darkness. When it was finished we gathered on the veranda.

"Ah," Amelia said settling into the rocker we'd found for her at an antique store near Digger's new shop. "That was very nice. I liked that."

"Me too," Dick said. "I thought that the lady was gonna stand up at the end, though."

"Now why the hell would you think that?" Digger asked.

"I dunno," Dick said. "I guess I thought that maybe the love would make her strong enough once she seen the guy again."

"Jesus," Digger muttered.

"I guess everybody hoped that some miracle would take place," Margo said. "When you're in love you always believe the miraculous can occur."

"That'd be pretty fucking miraculous there, lady," Digger said. "Shit like that don't happen to people, though."

"No?" Margo said archly.

"No."

"And you live where nowadays, sir? You have how much money?"

Digger grinned. "Touché. But still."

"Still nothing, you old grump," Margo continued. "Love can't truly be defined and neither can its properties."

"Where'd you hear that?" Digger asked. "Some old movie?"

"No. Just my observation."

"You been in love, Miss Margo?" Dick asked.

"Yes," she said. "It was some time ago now but yes, Dick, I was."

"What was it like?" he asked.

She smiled wistfully and looked off down the street. Then she crossed over to the railing, leaned on it, and looked up into the sky. "It was like blue," she said finally. "Like that blue you see when the light changes from day into night. A deep, eternal blue that gets put in your heart and then, when it's gone, for whatever reasons, you discover that it lives in the sky, right there where you can see it every night. An eternal, haunting blue. That's what it was like."

"Wow," Dick said. "Is it always like that?"

She turned, leaned on the railing, and said, "I don't know. But that's how it was for me."

"Me too," Timber said.

He crossed the veranda as well, looked up at the sky, and then turned and leaned on the railing beside Margo. His hands trembled while he lit a cigarette and all of us, hushed by the deep quiet we felt in him, waited. He exhaled a thin stream of smoke, pressed his eyelids tightly together, and rubbed the tight space between his eyebrows with the first two fingers of his hand. Digger got up and brought him a glass. He drank all of it in a long, slow drain, then wiped his mouth with the back of a hand.

"It was a long time ago for me, too," he said. "Sometimes I think that it was so long ago that maybe I could forget, that maybe time could take care of it, that maybe enough years can go by after something that you walk through it eventually. But you don't. You can't. Because there's always sky, there's always that blue up there to take you back to it. Always."

"Take you back to what, Timber?" Amelia asked.

"To the city by the sea," he said quietly.

"Where's that?" Dick asked.

"It's far away from here, Dick," he said. "Back a long ways and back a lot of years now."

"You ain't never gone back there?" Dick asked.

"No. Not until tonight. Not until that movie. Not until Margo mentioned the sky."

"I'm sorry," she said.

He smiled sadly at her. "It's okay. It's been coming anyway. I guess it's been coming since we first walked into the movies that day and the screen lit up in front of me. The light reminded me."

"Do you want to tell us about it?" Amelia asked.

"No," he said. "No, I really don't. But I think I need to."

Digger filled Timber's glass again and we all settled into our chairs and watched and waited for Timber to tell his tale. And as we sat there in the hushed light of that summer evening, I looked up at the endless blue that hung above our heads and recognized something of my own there, something I'd tried to insulate with the years. Timber's story took me back to it again.

Timber

I USED TO WALK through the bush at the back of our farm when I was a kid. The others would get together for kid games but I learned real early to enjoy my own company better. I liked walking through the trees. I liked how the shadows played in there. I liked how the wind sounded moving through those big old branches like it had a lotta songs it needed to sing. And me, back then—well, I wanted to hear all of them. The Hohnsteins were farmers for as long back as anyone could remember, even back to Germany before they crossed the ocean. Seemed like the natural thing for a Hohnstein to do was take to the farm. But me, well, I felt something different inside me and it was only when I walked through the bush that I got a sense of what that might be. It was like they called to me. The trees. I used to put my hand on the trunk of one sometimes and I could feel the vibration moving through it. I could feel its life. I could feel its spirit. I could feel its hunger for the sky.

One night after chores I sat with our hired hand out on the back stoop. I must have been fourteen. He was a whittler. He'd sit back there and smoke and think and whittle on wood. That night he pulled out his jackknife and a four-inch block of pine and started in on it. I watched as stroke after stroke of that blade slimmed and reduced that wood. Watched as he mindlessly shaped it, fluted it, edged it, scraped it, and rounded it until finally there was the vague shape of a cow in his hands. He smiled and handed it to me.

I'll never forget that. When I held that imperfect little cow in my hand I felt the same thrum of vibration that I felt in the trunk of a swaying, bending, living tree. The same spirit lived there. The same energy. I rubbed that little cow. Rubbed it and felt its lines, its curves, its clefts and hollows, and I felt in my fingers, in my palms, in the inside lines of my thumb a hunger for the blade, the wood calling itself to shape, to form, to life again. I asked him if I could borrow his knife and when he handed it to me I ran off to my room.

The next night I walked out to the stoop and handed him the knife.

"What'd you do with it?" he asked. "Did you work on that cow?"

I handed him the little cow in my pocket and he looked at it wordlessly for a long time. "Jesus," he said finally. "Lordy, Jesus. You're a carver, boy. You're a carver."

I can't explain what I did or how I did it. I only know that the energy that I felt in that piece of wood hummed against my skin and called to me, told me how it wanted to live, the shape it hungered for. And I made it happen. That little cow became a miniature of the cows in our field, alive with the same placid laziness, the same fat roll of contentment.

He gave me the knife and I began to work wood. It seemed like I had a second kind of vision, a whole other way of seeing so that pieces of wood became something else to my eyes. I saw the bear that lived there. I saw the caribou. I saw the eagle. Then I put a blade to it and coaxed them forward into shape and substance. My parents were amazed, and in a show of staunch German pride they bought me a carver's kit and put a workbench in the garage for me. School became less important suddenly and I spent most days and nights in my little shop working the wood. I got better. I got faster. I got more and more sure-handed. I sold some pieces at the fall fair. I was happy. We turned the garage into a full workshop for me and I fell into project after project. People came from miles around to commission pieces for their homes and I was always busy. When I was sixteen I bought a truck and had money in the bank. I never worked the fields again. I was a woodsmith and I loved it.

I wanted to make pieces that would live and breathe with the spirit of the trees they came from. I wanted to honour them. For a while it was enough to take the small commissions from those neighbouring counties, but I wanted to do more. I wanted to learn more and when I heard about an apprenticeship available in the city, I applied for it. When the man saw pictures of my work he offered me the position right away.

Marek Milosz was a Czech, and a distant cousin of a poet of the same name. You could tell. There was poetry in his work. In his blood was the blood of intricate Czech carvers who'd fashioned great moving clocks, and in his shop was a clock fashioned like a whole town with wheels and tracks that moved miniature men, women, and children through the motions of townsfolk. It was amazing. It took up a whole table. I could have watched it for hours. I wanted to create the same life out of wood.

Milosz taught me very deliberately. Where my self-taught hands had blazed away at wood, he brought them patience. Where my mind's eye had told me how to bring a piece to life, he brought me spontaneity, the ability to fashion wood as it presented itself, to use the whorls, knots, and imperfections to highlight and augment a piece. Where I had taught myself through large scale, he brought me the intrigue and magic of the miniature, the fine, the subtle, the detailed sculpture of wood. It was all I cared for. It was my world and I tucked myself into a small room near his shop where I slept. All of my awake time was spent in the shop.

Then she came. I remember that day in its smallest details. It was one of those sunny spring days when the sudden absence of rain makes it wonderful and light explodes over everything. The light in the studio was perfect for the small moves I was making on a clock in the shape of an old gypsy fiddler. I was adding small filigrees to the surface of the fiddle's neck when the door opened and the smell of spring wafted in. I looked up and there she was.

She was small. Short and as perfect as a carving. She wore hiking boots and jeans, a long duster coat with a scarf thrown loosely about her neck and a brown wool sweater underneath. When she shook her hair she closed her eyes to do it, and I remember thinking, *Freedom*; she looked like freedom when she did that. Then she opened her eyes. They were the sharpest blue I'd ever seen.

Set against her thick black hair and angular face they were startling, and when she looked at me she squinted and I felt seen. She walked about the shop for a while, trailing her hands across the surface of the things Milosz had finished enough to consider selling, and she stopped now and then to inspect some work up close. A tiny fragment of a smile stayed on her face the whole time. My work had stopped. I just watched her.

Finally, she turned and walked toward me. I felt my heart beating strongly in my chest and I swallowed hard. I felt awkward and clumsy, far too big for my clothes suddenly. She looked past me at the fiddler and wordlessly reached out to touch it.

"Romany," she said quietly.

"What?" I said.

"It's a Romany fiddler. You can almost hear the sweet ache of Hungary falling off the neck of that fiddle. Are you Romany?" she asked, looking at me.

I swallowed, my Adam's apple feeling like a huge, dry thing in my neck. "No," I said.

"Could have fooled me. It takes a gypsy to carve a gypsy. The face, the expression, the hands, the fiddle, they're all perfect. Alive, almost."

"Thank you."

"Not a big talker, are you?" she asked with a smile. "That's okay, though. Your work speaks for you. This is amazing. This piece is amazing. Is all of this yours?"

I cleared my throat. "No. It's my teacher's. This piece is mine, as is the bear and cubs over there and that chair."

She walked over to inspect the two pieces of mine that Milosz had deemed worthy to sell.

"They're better than his," she said. "Anyone could see that. This chair is awesome. Such brittle-feeling wood but so strong, and the scrollwork up the legs and along the backrest, very, very fine."

"Thank you."

She smiled. "You're welcome. I'm Sylvan. Sylvan Parrish."

I introduced myself. She was a librarian. She'd come to the city from the East a few months before, where her father was a poet and teacher and her mother a basket weaver. Art and creativity had never come to her, she said, but the love of it had always been with her, as had the love of books.

"When I'm in the library, surrounded by all those volumes, all the stacks, I feel like I'm in the company of a great many friends. Friends who never leave and friends who are always there when you need them to offer comfort and warmth. I feel anchored there," she said.

She'd read about the Romany gypsies. Her mother had suggested that somewhere along her lineage there had been a gypsy and the culture had always attracted her. "But this fiddler is the most alive gypsy I've ever seen," she said. "Is he for sale?"

"Well, it's not finished."

"When it is, will you sell it to me?"

"Yes. Certainly."

"How long?"

"Tomorrow. Tomorrow afternoon."

"Fine. I'll come back then. Say, five?"

"Yes. Five is good. But don't you want to know the price?"

She looked at me and I felt myself falling into those deep blue eyes. "No," she said quietly. "No. See the way you've done the hands? See how they caress the bow and the neck? That's love, my friend. That's love. There's no room in love for cost. I'll be back tomorrow at five. I'll buy you dinner."

And she was gone.

All that day and all through the next I laboured on that gypsy fiddler. I put everything I had into it. Milosz just nodded his head and left me alone. I didn't tell him it was sold. I just bent to my work, coaxing life into that wood and thinking of the smile it would bring to that beautiful face and the sparkle it would bring to those magnificent eyes. When I applied the thin lacquer at noon the next day, it seemed to glow on its stand like it was waiting too.

She was right on time. When she saw it she put both hands to her face and breathed deeply though her fingers. Then she cried. Thick beautiful tears slid from the corners of her eyes and I could feel my heart breaking in my chest as I watched her. She bent forward at the waist and looked closely at the face of that old fiddler.

"The eyes," she said. "What you did with his eyes since yesterday is amazing. You put love there, love and agony and joy, like the music itself. It's like you can hear it now. It's an evocative piece."

"Evocative?" I asked.

"Yes," she said. "It means to call forth, to summon, to bring out. You've called forth the spirit of Romany. The spirit of the gypsies. I love it."

We walked to a tiny restaurant near the shop. She ordered for us because I was simply too lost to make a decision. She laughed at that and her laughter was like spring rain: quiet, regal almost. We drank some red wine while we waited for our food and she talked about her work and the world of books. I spoke about the farm, about how I felt among the trees, their vibration, their energy, their life, and how I came to be a carver and a furniture maker. I talked about my family and the generations of farmers that I came from. When the food came I was amazed that I had talked for so long.

"Do you hear that?" she asked halfway through our meal.

"What?"

"The music. Listen."

A song was playing over the sound system in the restaurant. It was a music I had never heard before played on instrument foreign to my ears. But the sound it made wasn't strange to me. It rubbed against something I'd carried in me for a long time, and that something recognized itself in the music.

"Dvořák," she said quietly. "*The Cello Concerto.*"

"Dvořák?"

"A Czech," she said. "A Romany too, I think. At least his music sounds that way to me. I have this at home."

"It reminds me of Milosz," I said. "He's a Czech."

She placed her fork on the table and looked at me with those wonderful eyes. I looked back, unafraid and open. "You are a wonder," she said. "Milosz. A Czech. And you've been around him and picked up the influences he carries without even knowing it.

Picking them up and turning them into something magical through wood. Do you know how special that is?"

She spoke for a long time about the people she'd read about. Writers, painters, musicians, architects, all of the great builders of the world, and as I listened I felt my world getting larger through her words. I found myself wanting to meet these people too. The meal passed almost without my knowing.

"May I see you again?" I asked as we stood outside the restaurant.

"Yes," she said. "I'd like that, Jonas. I'd really like that."

And my world became more. Every night we met at the shop and she'd look at what I was working on, then we'd head off into that great city by the sea and she showed me the world. I discovered Gustav Klimt, Ella Fitzgerald, and Zora Neale Hurston all in one splendid evening of browsing. I found Winslow Homer, Jelly Roll Morton, and Auguste Rodin one Saturday afternoon. I heard Dvořák's *Slavonic Dances* while learning to cook machanka, a tangy mushroom soup from Czechoslovakia. It was a drizzly, foggy evening and I thought it the most sublime moment I'd ever had. Together we visited restaurants, galleries, nightclubs for jazz and blues, museums, and the great stretches of oceanside where she'd tell me invented histories about the people we passed. She brought me forward into a shining new world.

Some evenings we'd read aloud to each other and I learned the why and how of words and books and fell in love with them too. Or if there was a project I was working on, she'd sit quietly in the shop and watch me as I shaped the wood, remaining motionless for hours while the slim shavings fell and the form of the piece emerged. Other nights, we'd walk. Just walk and feel the city breathe around us, down the length of bright avenues into the gloom of rundown neighbourhoods and shadowed parks, watching the changing face of the city until each of those nights became another kind of entrance we made together, another move deeper into the world we discovered together.

When I fell in love, I don't know. Only that when she kissed me one night in my small, shabby room with Chopin's *Études* playing in the background, I felt the rarefied air of heights I'd never imagined. In candlelight, we loved each other. She showed my rough, worn fingers how to trace the clefts and canyons of her, to follow the grain and texture of her skin, to carve her in long flowing lines with my palms. When I entered her it was like the vibrato of a great orchestra emitting a long, tremulous note into the void of the universe, a music unheard and spontaneous that changed the fabric of everything. We lay there, drenched in our passions, watching the candles melt away to nothingness while the light of another morning broke over the bare sill of my window.

We were married a month later. She wanted a small, elegant ceremony without family or fanfare and we spent a glorious week in a cabin in the mountains of the interior before coming back to our work. With her urging and direction I sold more and more work and earned more commissions, so that within a year we'd moved into a small house with a garage in the back that became my private workshop. She'd come home at night and find me there and we'd walk together into the house that was our home.

We had a cat named Cheever and a jade plant called Eudora, after the great comic writer of the American South. She spent a lot of time and love on the interior of our home and it was, in the end, a shelter, a haven, an eclectic, subtle extension of her, and I loved it. There was a veranda at its front and we sat there deep into the night, drinking tea and talking, listening to the great music of the ages pouring through the open window. She had sculpted my world so effortlessly that it became the line of her back in the morning light, the shine of her eyes in moonlight, and the swish of sunflower stalks against the veranda rails. We were happy.

Then came Cameron Gracey.

Cam Gracey was a railroad engineer. Or at least he had been for thirty years. He'd been pensioned off after one too many bouts with liquor on the job and he lived a block away from us. He was one of those drinkers everyone knows about, and he was avoided as much as possible. Cam spent most of his time watching soccer and rugby matches at the Beachcomber bar, where he'd parlay his pension cheques into wagers that surprisingly kept him in liquor and escort agency girls the neighbours reported seeing arrive at all hours of the night.

He won big on a soccer match one afternoon and was headed home in his old red truck to celebrate his victory. He was drunk enough to overshoot his block and the neighbours who saw it say the turn he made onto our street was fast enough to take the truck onto two wheels before it levelled out and struck my Sylvan, who was crossing the street with a bag of groceries in her arms. The impact threw her fifty feet. When our next-door neighbour came to get me and I walked out of my workshop and into the hard glint of sun, I felt that great and glorious world closing in on itself. When I knelt beside her broken body, the only music I heard was a drone—heavy, onerous, and flat—from somewhere in the middle of my chest.

She went into a coma. The doctors were able to mend her bones but they couldn't coax her back to the light. I sat there by her bedside waiting. I read to her. I played her favourite music for her. I told her about our home and the woman I'd hired to care for it while she got better. For weeks on end I sat there, only leaving long enough to shower, shave, and return. I carved nothing. She didn't wake.

After four months they moved her to a private unit. The medical costs were high and I sold all of my work to maintain her care. I sold my car and began taking the bus to the hospital each day. The longer she stayed under, the more difficult it got to keep things going. Eventually I had to sell the things she'd decorated our home with, and as I stood there and watched the things she had loved so dearly being toted out to another home somewhere, I felt like the greatest traitor in the world. Pieces of her, leaving. After two months, the house was empty except for Eudora, the jade plant I slept beside on the pale wooden floors under the window facing the veranda where the music had once flowed.

And then she woke up. I was shaving in her small washroom with the door to her room open.

"What day is it?" she said in a small, dry voice I barely heard.

I almost fell getting to the door. I towelled the shaving cream from my face and walked toward her bed with huge silent tears rolling down my face. I could hardly breathe. She lay there small and scared under the sheets, and she turned her head and looked at me. Those magnificent blue eyes were still the clearest blue I'd ever seen, and when she looked at me I felt the wellspring of hope rise in my chest like a crescendo.

"Why are you crying?" she asked.

"Because you came back," I said.

Then I heard the words that took all remaining light from my world.

"Do I know you?"

Amygdala. That's the word. *Amygdala.* It sounded like the name of a great and final battle, and for me it was. The accident had damaged the amygdala in her brain—the area responsible for emotional memory. Along with other significant memory loss, Sylvan could not remember who I was or the tremendous love we had shared. To her I became a kind stranger who entered her room each day and told her stories about a life she had lost all touch with. She just sat there while I told her how we met, how we fell in love, and about the home we'd built together. Just sat there looking at me with those beautiful eyes that no longer held the gloss of love within them. Merely confusion. Blankness, like a slab of wood.

Her brain damage was such that she could not retain memory of anything. The doctors had to tell her every day who they were, who she was, where she was, and who I was. But I went there every day. Went there with the hope that this day would be the day that the sun broke through the clouds and she'd turn to me with the squinting look that always said she saw me and be my girl again. But it never happened. Each night I'd ride the bus back across the city, saddened and empty, until I couldn't afford the cost of the extended care facility she was moved to and had to sell the house in order to keep her there.

I moved to a small room in the Astoria Hotel. A welfare room where my veranda was the fire escape. I'd sit there long into those empty nights watching the grey and drizzled streets, smoking and drinking until I was dull enough to sleep. My bus trips to the facility became less and less frequent. I couldn't bear seeing the face that had once looked into mine so lovingly now so empty of emotion, so closed to possibility and so lost to experience. I couldn't stand being so close to the heart that had beat against my chest, filling me with the warm, languid flow of belonging, and feel its hopeless distance, its oceanic impossibility. It haunted me. Her face haunted me and I couldn't stand having the depth of my love go unanswered, be so unrecognized, so unremembered.

Drinking helped. The booze cut through everything and made it go away. I'd sit in my room and drink and drink until I would lean out into the darkness and emptiness of the night, vomiting and sick, yelling, cursing Cameron Gracey, amygdala, and Jonas Hohnstein, the great carver, the artist who could not create a bridge to close the gap between us. I drank. Eventually, it's all I did. It's all I could do because I didn't want to surface to the blankness, the emptiness of my life. I drank until, finally, even the Astoria kicked me out and I landed on the street.

I left then. I took what money I had, caught a bus, and landed here so many years ago I can't recall. I became a rounder, and until Amelia approached me in the park that day I didn't want another person near me. Near enough to know how much I hated myself for not being able to save her and, in the end, for deserting her, leaving her behind like she'd never mattered, like she'd never existed, like she'd never given me the world.

Fucking movies. Who'd have guessed? It was the first time in forever that I'd seen light, and it touched me, filled the empty, filled the coldness. This one. This *Affair to Remember*? I wanted her to stand up too. I wanted her to toss that blanket covering her legs into the corner and stand up strongly, walk over to that man and kiss him with all the passion in her. I wanted her to do that. Not because it would make the story better. Not because it would be more romantic. But for me. For me. Just for me. So I could see that sometimes stories end the way they should and love remains as it should: undefined, unrestricted, and open like a pair of arms.

It *is* like blue, you know. The blue of that evening sky and the blue of the eyes I haven't seen in forever. Haunting. Eternal. Blue.

Do you remember love?
Most certainly.
How do you remember it?
Hmm. Like light, I suppose.
What kind of light?
Like the light that comes first thing in the morning. You know, on those nights when sleep eludes you and you find yourself sitting alone watching the sky, waiting, the hours slipping by you unnoticed, and suddenly there's a change to it all. Nothing you could ever pin down with language, no name for it, just a subtle shift in the colour and the nature of the sky.
Yes. I've had nights like that.
That's how I remember love. Arriving without fanfare. Just a subtle shift in the sky and when it happens it's like watching morning light arrive—everything around you takes on different shape and form and texture, the world becomes new.
Yes. That's the magic, isn't it?
Magic? Maybe. I like to think that we attract it, that somehow we are the creators of it, that our lives allow us to build a little chamber inside of us that calls to it, beckons, lures it like a lightning rod calls the bolt from the sky. We create love with longing. Longing is the lightning rod and it sits within us all.
I know longing. And you're right, it makes us ready, eager, anxious.
You've learned a lot.
I suppose. Strange how that happens too.
What do you mean?
I think I mean that becoming, changing, evolving is like the light you describe as love. You move around the world and suddenly there's a shift and you realize that you understand, comprehend, know, and it changes everything. Changes you.
You've changed.

Can't help it.
No, I suppose you can't.
Do you remember the next part of the journey?
Like it was yesterday.
It was yesterday.

One For The Dead

MANITOU NODIN. The Spirit Wind. That's what the Old Ones say blows across Creation when a great truth is revealed. Maybe not so much the big mystical kind of truths, because they are only shown once in a great long while, but the simple heart truths of simple men and women leading simple lives, the kind of truths that are told in darkness, in quiet rooms, or on verandas in the dusk. That's when Manitou Nodin comes. That's when the energy of life is released and the breath of Creation blows across the face of everything. It's a giving-back wind. Giving back the breath of life to chests tightened through the years. Giving back the flow, the spiral of energy that connects everything, to a life lived in slow motion or none at all. Giving back relief, salvation, some say. Grace, the Ojibway call it. You can hear it if you listen hard enough. It starts with the heaving of a sigh, the push that delivers truth to the world, and continues through the rattle of speech along the vocal cords—moving the air, pushing it, becoming the breeze—and changes suddenly, becoming the wind in the branches, the soft swish of clothes on a line, a sound carried from miles away. It becomes alive in the world.

When Timber finished his story, I heard it. More a hint than anything, but I heard it. Manitou Nodin. The Spirit Wind delivered in the voice of this great, sad, haunted man. This friend I had been with for years but never really known until now.

"Thank you," was all I said.

He turned and looked to the sky again, toward that impossible blue that hung there like a promise. None of us knew what to say. I didn't. We sat there in a silence that was like that summer night itself, all fat and self-contained, waiting for Timber to tell us how to breathe again. He just looked at that sky, his hands gripping and releasing the railing, gripping and releasing, gripping and releasing. Finally, he turned and looked at us, filled his cheeks with air and released it slowly.

"She should have stood up," he said, and then he turned and walked down the steps toward the street.

"Where are you going?" I asked.

He stopped. Without turning around he sighed and said, "I don't know. Walking, I suppose. Just walking."

And he walked along the front of our house and disappeared.

Manitou Nodin. The Spirit Wind. It doesn't always blow from the direction you'd choose.

Granite

HE DIDN'T MAKE IT BACK that night. He didn't make it back the next day. Digger and Dick went to the downtown core twice to look around but didn't see him anywhere. James filed a missing-person notice with the police and we waited for word. The house was quiet. The silence was pervasive, sepulchral, unnerving. As evening approached again, we made a small supper together, listened to some music, and bided our time, hoping that we'd hear his step on the veranda and he'd return in good form, tired but safe. Sunset called us out to the veranda again and we sat, each of us looking down the stretch of Indian Road, waiting for the familiar shape of our friend to emerge from the depths of the city.

"The hard part is that he could go anywhere now," James said. "With the money at his disposal, he doesn't need to stick to the usual places. He could be anywhere."

"That's true," Margo said. "He's hurting and he's somewhere trying to take care of his wounds."

"Damn," I said. "I never thought. I never considered. I thought I was renting a charming romance. A tearjerker, yes, but not one that held such a trigger."

"You didn't know," Margo said. "You couldn't have known. Amelia didn't know and she's been with Jonas for years."

"Me neither, Rock," Digger said. "It ain't your doing."

"I suppose that's true. A part of me accepts that, but there's another part that knows how movies approximate life and how those approximations sometimes ignite things in you, make what you'd prefer not to recall suddenly real again, illuminated, cast in front of you on the screen. It's rough when that happens unbeknownst to you. That unexpected confrontation with self is dramatic when your whole intention is escape."

"That sounds awfully autobiographical, Granite," James said.

"Yes," Margo said. "Does it happen a lot for you, Granite?"

I looked at all the houses down Indian Road. I could have told them the names of each of the stones used in their masonry, could have spoken of their qualities, their essential perfection for the task or the enhancement at hand, could have talked of the quarrying necessary to make them available. It was all background information in a larger, more complicated story, the flotsam and jetsam of a life, the details of the construction and demolition of the structure that contained them, the truth of me.

"It happens a lot," I said, finally. "And the truth is, I don't know why I go back. The movies were supposed to be escape. They were supposed to be a seat in the darkness, a darkness I pulled around me like a cloak to keep the world away. The trouble is that they are the stuff of the world, the stuff of life, all the great internal stuff, all the hurt, grief, joy, turbulence, pathos, tragedy, displacement, rage, tenderness, and love. They are all of that. At least, the good ones are. The sum of our experience. The only escape is to avoid them and I can't do that. I can't do that because I love them too much. Love them because they do remind me, love them because they do take me back, love them because they do allow me to relive, to touch again, to hold again all the things I thought I didn't need anymore."

And we sat on the veranda and I told them my story. I told them everything. I spoke across all the years and all the hurt, all the departures, all of the dying and all of the living, the fading of the light, the drawing of the shades, the closing of the doors to that great stone house and the silence it fell into, total and complete, like it had become to me. I told them of my own leaving, the coda, the great thematic echo, the dwindling note of Granite Harvey in all he had been.

"Wow," Digger said when I finished. "You're as friggin' homeless as I was."

One For The Dead

WE TALKED all through that night. When it got too chilly on the veranda we went inside, lit a nice fire, and sat around it on pillows. Six of us brought together by worry and joined by words from another great, sad, haunted man. As that fire burned, I told them my story and I told them about the shadowed ones who had brought me each of my boys and, in the end, Granite himself.

"So they're not ghosts?" Margo asked.

"No. Not really," I said. "I think when some great sad thing happens in some place with some people, we leave a part of ourselves there, a part that wanted or needed things to come out different, a part that got separated from itself, a shadow of ourselves. If we never get right with it and we're asked to move to the Spirit World, that shadow stays here, revisiting those places and those people, hoping maybe that it can reclaim the part that got lost."

"Can it?" James asked.

"Yes."

"How?" Margo asked.

"By watching us," I said. "By watching the living ones. By watching us learn to deal with our hurt, our losses, and reach out to life again. It tells them that we're okay. That they don't need to patrol, revisit, or haunt those places anymore. That they can take their place in the Spirit World and prepare for the other part of the journey."

"What other part?" Granite asked.

"Returning."

"Returning? Coming back?"

"Yes. Returning."

"You mean we all come back here? We all get a chance to live again?"

"No," I said softly. "That's not the returning I'm speaking of."

"Well, what then?"

"The other part of the journey is a returning to yourself. Reconnecting. Getting whole again. That's what the Spirit World is for. Getting whole again and preparing to continue the journey."

"There's more?" Dick asked. "After? There's more?"

"Always," I said.

"Geez," he said and looked into the fire. "Do you think Timber's gettin' whole?"

None of us had anything to say.

Digger

GOT KNIFED one time. Knifed pretty good in the friggin' leg. Hurt like a son of a bitch and I knew going to the hospital was only gonna bring me heat. They'd wanna know who shivved me and there was no way I wanted any friggin' interference on me handling the outcome. So I laid up. Got me a few crocks, some rubbing alcohol, some bandages, and a lay-up away from my usual and waited until the leg was good enough to walk on again. Days. I spent days there waiting to heal. But I still had to make a move or two. Still had to hobble down for a fresh crock, score some smokes, or grab a bite to eat somewhere. Had to. Had to because it wasn't about the dying, it was about the getting it together one more time. I could only hope Timber was getting it together. I didn't want to think about the other possibility.

If he was using the money to hole up somewhere different I was fucked. Man, I had no idea how a guy'd use all that cash to put himself away from people. But he was still a friggin' rounder and I depended on that when I sent the boys out to look for him.

Cost me a few bucks over the next three days, but I figured it was worth it.

Nothing. No sight of him. No word. No hint of where he might be. When the cops had nothing to say to us, I had to kinda let go a little. I guess if the friggin' bulls can't figure out where the hell you went there was no one gonna know. I only hoped they wouldn't bring a body back. That was my big fear. That he'd bought it. That the movie touched something in him that wasn't supposed to be touched again and he took the desperate route. But I still drove around and around and a-friggin'-round. I saw more of them streets than I wanted to over those three days. Saw more of the way people lived, how they stumbled, lurched, fell, puked, and hunted for the next whatever that'd make their blood move again. Saw them lined up for the handout food. Saw them laid out in parks or leaning out the windows of welfare digs, looking out over the street like they're waiting for something to move along it that'll change everything. There ain't nothing that big. I coulda told them that. Nothing that big that'd change everything. Even money. All the loot we had still couldn't make it any easier to live. Not for Timber. Not for the ones with woe. The shadowed ones. Haunting the world while they're still in it. What a fucking bummer.

One For The Dead

I SAW THEM from the living room. I watched them talk. Watched them move closer together as they spoke, leaning inward, hoarding each sound like a private treasure. I watched them watch each other and I watched them kiss. They held it. Held it like a cup to parched lips, and I smiled. I remembered. Remembered my Ben's kisses in the soft orange glow of neon so long ago and how they soothed me, how they made me feel alive on the inside of my skin, how they lifted me up and made me more, how they filled me. I was happy to see it. Happy that Granite had found a light beyond the movies, found a story that was real, found a heartbeat to echo against his own. I didn't let them know that I was there. I crossed to the other side of the room and sat in my favourite chair to drink tea and send my thoughts to Timber, alone in his pain.

The telephone rang. I stared at it, didn't want to answer. All I could do was stand up and stare at it. Granite and Margo hurried into the room followed by Digger and Dick, who ran down the stairs from watching a movie in Dick's room. No one moved to the phone. It rang and rang before Margo finally reached over and picked it up.

"It's James," she said.

We waited while she listened. We could hear his voice from where we stood: excited, fast, hurried. Margo pursed her lips into a tight line while she listened, nodding her head and tapping at her belt with the fingers of her free hand. "Okay," she said finally, "I'll tell everyone. Is that it? There's no more?"

There was a final burst of reply.

"Okay. We'll wait here for you."

She hung up the telephone and plopped down into an armchair. We all moved a little closer.

"What?" Digger said. "Fer fuck sakes, what?"

"They've been able to track his movements through his bank card withdrawals," she said. "They have a rough idea of where he's been but nothing concrete. For the first three days, he withdrew a few hundred from bank machines in different parts of the city."

"Walking," I said.

"Yes. It appears so. The bank machines are pretty far apart and it doesn't appear he was taking a particular direction. He was just walking, apparently. Because it's cash, they don't know where he spent the money, only that he got it."

Margo looked at us with tears building in her eyes. "Two days ago it stopped. No more withdrawals. Just one big one for eight hundred and no more. That was early in the morning two days ago."

"Jesus," Digger said.

"The police are looking for him but I think we all know that if he really wants to disappear in the city, there's places where no one could find him."

"Yes," I said, quietly. "There are places like that."

"James has contacted the media. I'm sorry, but he had to. He had to put Jonas's picture out on the off chance that someone somewhere has seen him. Maybe they sold him something, maybe they rented him a room—anything that might lead us to where he is."

"God," Granite said. "Here we go again."

"What?" I asked.

"Well, they'll make a big thing of it. Homeless lottery winner disappears. Millionaire street person vanishes. All of that. And they'll be after all of you, too."

"We don't gotta say nothing, though, right?" Digger asked.

"No. James and I and Margo can handle the dodge for you. But there'll be cameras and reporters outside the door, you can bet on that."

"Will it help get Timber back?" Dick asked.

"Yes. Well, it might," Granite said. "More people knowing his face. You never know. Someone might see him or have seen him already."

"Should we put up a reward?" I asked.

"No," Margo said. "Not right away. Let the media machine do its work. People generally want to help, and if someone's seen him they'll let us know because they've seen it on television. James will be here shortly to fill us in on exactly what to do when reporters arrive."

"What do we do until then? Until something happens?" I asked her.

She came and stood beside me, put an arm around my shoulder and bent her forehead to mine. "Pray, I suppose," she said. "That seems like a good thing to do."

"Yes," I said. "It's a good thing."

They all came then, my boys, and stood around us, arms encircling us, heads bent close together, eyes closed, and joined in silent prayer for a lost one.

Double Dick

We never went to the movie store for a coupla days an' there wasn't nothin' new for me to watch. So I started lookin' through my collection for somethin' kinda happy on accounta I needed that right then. Granite an' Miss Margo had got me all kinds of movies they said I'd like an' I never got all the way through them. There was a pile on my table waitin' for me to watch. I thought about *Back to the Future* and *The Color Purple* on accounta they sounded nice, but the one I decided to watch was one called *E.T.* There was a picture of a boy on a bicycle ridin' across the front of the moon way up high in the air an' I figured that would be good on accounta I remembered always wantin' to fly when I was a kid. So I put it in an' started to watch.

At first I was scared on accounta this little guy gets left behind by a spaceship an' has to find a place to hide. But then he gets helped out by a buncha kids an' everythin' was kinda happy for a while. Then some bad men come an' try an' take him away, so he's gotta run away an' that's when he flies the boy on the bike across the front of the moon.

Then, it got to me. They sent a message into space an' the spaceship came back for the little guy. But he was friends now with one boy an' they was both sad on accounta nobody likes to lose a friend. I was thinkin' of Timber right then an' it kinda made me cry. Then the little guy points his finger at the boy's heart an' says, "I'll be right here."

Well, I set right to bawling on accounta I missed my friend. I cried hard. It scared me to cry so hard, so I had to have another coupla drinks to settle down. The movie was over, so I went over an' sat on my windowsill an' looked up at the moon that was full that night too.

E.T. went home an' left his friend behind. He had to on accounta that's where he lived. That's where he belonged. And that's when I knew. That's when it come to me. That's when I knew how come we couldn't find Timber, an' I ran down the hall to tell everyone.

Timber

I WATCHED CLOUDS. That's all I did that first night on the bus. I sat in my seat, leaned my head against the glass and watched clouds sail by. There's a funny thing that happens when you do that. When you look at something long enough and hard enough when you're moving, it gets to looking like whatever you're looking at is sailing alongside you. That's how those clouds looked after a while. Like they were sailing beside the bus. It's called parallax or the Doppler effect or some such thing she put in my head a long time ago. She called it ordinary magic. She said that kind of magic was everywhere all the time, and that we only ever have to open our eyes to see it. She said it was our minds, our brains, our rigid thinking that discounted it, made it a kid's trick, a conversation starter and not the magic that it was. Relative motion. That's what made it work. You both needed to be in relative motion to each other in order for clouds to chase a bus down the highway. In order for the magic to happen. I thought about that. Thought about how it works that way with people, too, how it works that way with lives, with histories. You can't get away from ordinary magic. It's always there. Waiting. Waiting for you to believe again, to open your eyes and look for it. That scared me. Being on this bus, crossing the country to get back to a city, a history, a life, a person I'd abandoned so many years ago, was the first time in all those years that I allowed myself to look for it, to open my eyes, to believe.

I never labelled anything that happened to us since we started going to the movies as magic. I couldn't. I couldn't open up hope like that. To me, it was all distraction, something to take us away from the lives we were living—entertainment, escape, disarray almost. Even the money. That wasn't magic. It was a fluke, a jest, a cosmic joke. I always told myself that it hadn't happened to me. It had happened to Digger. The magic was that he had shared it. To ascribe it to magic was to ascribe it to hope, and hope was something I had walked away from too. I had left a lot of things in that city by the sea and I had left hope in a chair beside a hospital bed. You can only carry so much with you when you're a rounder on the street and hope is a weight you can't afford.

It wasn't an easy choice to get on that bus. Walking around the city for three days, I wanted to die. I couldn't drink enough, it seemed, and when I holed up in some shitty-assed hotel each of those nights, I hoped I wouldn't wake up. But I did. And the thought came to me that death wasn't going to come along and claim me. No, I was going to have to do something to force its arrival. I just couldn't make that choice even though I felt like it. I walked. Walked and walked and walked and looked around for an appropriate height to jump from, an appropriate depth to dive into, or a sharp enough point to slip against. I didn't find it. All I found was Sylvan. All I found was guilt. All I found was a jettisoned life I hadn't had the courage to see through. Courage. That was the word. It wasn't hope I'd abandoned in that chair at all. It was courage.

She told me once that courage was a French word originally. It came from *coeur*—the heart. *Coeur*-age then meant *from the heart.* To live with courage was to live from the heart, that involuntary muscle that drives a life, that beats in the darkness despite itself and propels us onward to become ourselves. Her words, not mine.

I loved Sylvan Parrish. My heart was filled with love, then and now, and if I was to have courage then I needed to return, to go back to that sad chair in that sad room and look into those eyes again and reclaim my heart. It was courage I needed to return to, and if hope came along for the ride, so much the better.

Digger

MOST TIMES a loogan's a loogan. But when Dick come running downstairs to tell us E.T told him that Timber wasn't in the city no more, well, it made sense. I'll be frigged if I could figure out where he went in this town. Merton was there by then and he got right on the blower to the bulls. He was telling them to start running Timber's picture to the airlines to see if any clerks recognized him. I stopped him.

"He ain't on no friggin' plane," I go. "He got here by bus and that's the way he'll go back."

You wanna find a rounder, you gotta think like a rounder. Sure enough, a clerk at the bus station recognized Timber right away. Way Merton figured it, it took four days to get to the west coast. The two days he wasn't taking no cash from the machine meant he'd been on the bus them two days and he'd be arriving there in another couple days.

"There's really nothing we can do, legally," he goes. "He can go anywhere he wants. He doesn't need to tell anyone where he's going. Not even us."

"He's not missin' no more?" Dick goes.

"Technically, no," Merton goes. "I'm still worried about his state of mind, though."

"Aw fuck, Jimbo," I go. "If he was gonna do himself he'da done it by now."

"Maybe so," he goes. "But what about what happens when he gets back there? What about if he manages to find her and it's the same situation that he left originally? What if she still doesn't recognize him?"

"That's not why he's going back," the old lady goes.

"Pardon me?" Merton goes.

"He's going back to sit in the chair again."

"You lost me, Amelia."

"The chair beside the bed. That's where his life turned. When he got up from that chair and walked away from her, he left himself behind. He's gotta go back and sit in it again. No matter what."

"You're saying he's got no expectation? That he doesn't carry the hope that she'll look at him and all the years will vanish in a heartbeat and she'll be his one true love again? He's not going back for that?"

"Are you asking me if he's crazy?"

"No. Well, yes. I mean, I guess so. It sounds crazy to me."

"It's not crazy. Even if he *is* hoping that. It's love, and I don't think love is crazy."

"Me neither," Margo goes.

"But he's setting himself up for some major hurt," Merton goes. "Just walking back into that situation after all this time, he's setting himself up for pain. What will he do then?"

"James is right," Rock goes. "I couldn't imagine it, myself."

"That's why I'm going to the fucking coast," I go.

"What?" Merton goes.

"I'm going out there. What do you expect me to do? Let my winger walk into a set-up? I don't fucking think so, pal."

"I'm goin' too, then," Dick goes.

"Me too," Amelia goes.

"Not without me, you're not," Margo goes.

"Or me," Rock goes. "He's my friend. I can't see him setting himself up for pain. Or at least, not alone."

"Well, I guess we're all going then," Merton goes. "I have some contacts out there who can do the legwork before we get there, and maybe we can shorten the time he's alone with it."

"It's perfect," the old lady goes.

"Perfect?" I go. "How you figure?"

"Well," she goes, "in the old stories I was told as a girl there would come a time of great trouble for the People. All kinds of things happened to the People then. Just like now. Most times, a hero would come forward and make things happen. But other times, times when great strength was needed, it took the People themselves. Everyone would make a journey, a trek."

"Why?" Rock goes.

"When great strength is needed, great strength is gained."

"Say what?" I go.

"Sometimes it takes a whole community to save itself, and when people come together in strength, on a mission, what they get in the end is what they spent in the struggle."

"Stronger?"

"Yes."

"Who's drivin', then?" Dick goes.

"Driving? We have to fly, Dick," Merton goes.

"Fly?" he goes, all goggle-eyed.

"Yeah," I go. "Fly. You sit on the handlebars, I'll pedal like a bastard, and we're out of here."

He looks at me for like a whole minute, and you can see the light coming real slow like someone carrying a candle down a hallway. "Aw, Digger," he goes finally. "That's just *E.T.* Just the movies. We're gonna take a plane."

Like I said. Most times a loogan's a loogan.

Granite

ICARUS FLEW too close to the sun. I wondered how many times in the history of man's fascination with flight did expectation outweigh outcome. Icarus plunged into the sea to perish while Daedalus flapped onward alone. I wondered where we would seek our friend. I wondered if the cost of this journey would be a long, mournful flight homeward. I wondered if the escape from the Labyrinth of the street was worth a plunge into the sea of despair.

"What are you thinking?" Margo asked.

"Oh, nothing," I said. "Some lines from Ovid."

"Ah, *Metamorphoses.*"

"Yes."

"'Icarus, Icarus. Where shall I seek thee, Icarus?' That riff?"

"Yes."

"I love the myths. So much contemporary wisdom in those ancient stories."

"That's their charm, yes."

"Amazing how much you can learn from a little paraffin problem, isn't it?"

I laughed. "Yes. Yes it is."

The plane began its taxi down the runway and I looked at the rounders across the aisle. This was the stuff of myth itself. Three beggars flying to rescue a fourth in a city by the sea. Amelia closed her eyes and gripped the arms of her seat as the thrust built up. Digger sat stoic, unmoving, and Dick leaned toward the window despite the gravitational force and watched the ground flash by. They'd borne this adventure quite well. Dick had been fascinated by everything at the airport, especially the moving sidewalk, the horizontal escalator that moved travellers and their bags from landing gate to baggage claim. He'd ridden it twice while we waited. Digger, despite his standoffish defiance, was amazed at the conglomeration of people, their types and manner, humanity in its variety rendering him speechless. And Amelia just grinned her small grin and moved slowly, measuredly, through the rush and crush, moving like a matron at the fair, observant and attendant to her brood walking gangly-legged beside her. Perhaps the gravity of the journey held them up or else the enormity of the changes over the last year had granted them immunity from the strange, the fantastic, the world beyond their world. Either way, they were magnificent. Now, as the plane reached takeoff speed and lifted itself from the ground, I heard various muted expressions of awe at the power that caused it. Joy from Dick, discomfited admiration from Digger, and a sigh from Amelia. Rounders in the sky. I was far from inured to the changes around me.

James sat making notes at the window, too used to jets and travel to be impressed. Margo held my hand in hers and leaned her head on my shoulder. She was a surprise. As we rose higher and higher and began a long, slow, angled pass over the city to engage our westward flight path, I marvelled at this wonderful occurrence. Love? I didn't know. I only knew that touch and closeness felt freeing. I only knew that our togetherness had begun at the lottery office with an easy, offhand banter, and progressed casually through shared concern for our friends, joy at their newfound home, to this arena of gentleness we found ourselves in now. Our moves measured, graceful, calm like wings beating currents of air, moving us further from the shore of yearning where we'd stood flightless, alone, hungry for the sky. *Flap, flap, flap.* The sun at an appropriate distance.

One For The Dead

IT WAS A SHINING CITY by the sea. The plane arced out over the ocean and banked back toward land with the sun behind us like it was gently pushing us downward, and beneath us I could see the city shining in the light of sunset. Everything shone in various shades of orange against an approaching purple sky. Those are spirit colours. Orange the colour of old teachings and purple the colour of spirituality, the spirit way, the ancient path, the path of the soul. He was down there. And if he didn't know that those spirit colours shone on him too right then, he would. They were a sign of a great teaching, a great coming together of the energy of Creation, and it didn't scare me so much as it comforted me; a simple knowing that this journey had been the right one. We landed and made our way to the hotel that wasn't all that different from the Sutton where we'd stayed that first night off the street. The boys were anxious, antsy for their friend, worried about his aloneness on streets he no longer knew. The others were quietly firm, making considered moves and gathering themselves for a focused search. Me, I wanted a good meal, tea, and a movie—a story to ease me into the night and prepare me for a fresh start in the morning.

We met in James's room to plan our night.

"According to my sources at the newspaper who've been able to track down information on Sylvan Parrish-Hohnstein, she's still alive. Or at least, there's no record of her death in this city," James said. "People can live with the brain damage Timber said she suffered. There is no record of her at any of the extended care facilities or at the hospitals, so she is out of care if she's alive or in the city."

"Where does that leave us?" Granite asked.

"In the same place as Timber. We don't know where she is. We only know the name of the hospital where she was taken after the accident and the name of the extended care hospital she was moved to."

"So whatta we do, then?" Digger asked.

"We go to the extended care hospital and wait," James said. "That's where Timber will go."

"When?" Dick asked.

"First thing in the morning," James said. "The sooner the better, I'd imagine. We don't know when Timber might make it there and we don't want to miss him."

"That's right," Digger said. "I'm ready to go now."

"Well, they'll be closed now. We'll rest and get a very early start tomorrow."

"Sounds good to me."

"There's just something we need to sort out first."

"What's that?" Margo asked.

"Well, it concerns Granite, actually," James said.

"Me? What is it?" Granite asked.

"It's about the story, Granite. My sources want the story. They saw the television coverage when he went missing and of course they know all about the lottery win and where he came from. So they want the story."

"And that matters to me because why?"

"Because you already have it."

"Have what?"

"The story."

"The story? You want *me* to do the story? You know I'm retired?"

"Yes. But I also know that no one else could give this story the justice it deserves. If you let it go and turn it over to them, we have no idea how it'll spin. At least with you writing it there's some measure of integrity built into how it's handled."

"You've got to be kidding."

"I'm not kidding. Former homeless person now a millionaire comes back to find the wife he deserted twenty years ago. Who's not going to want to do that story?"

"But I'm retired."

"You're never retired, Granite. Not guys like you. Not born-in-the-blood storytellers. Not lifelong journalists. Stories just walk right up and beg you to be told, and when they do there's nothing you can do but tell them."

"I don't feel much like a storyteller anymore."

I moved over to him and took his hand. When he bent his head shyly, I played with his hair. They were like little boys. All of them. I felt grateful that I'd been given the chance to be with them, to watch them come together and begin teaching each other.

"We're all storytellers, Granite," I said. "From the moment we're graced with the beginnings of language, we become storytellers. Kids, the first thing they do when they learn to talk is tell you all about what they're doing, what they're seeing. They tell you stories about their little lives. Us, too. When we get together after not seeing each other for a while, the first thing we do is tell each other a story about what we've been up to. What we've seen, what we did, what we felt and went through. Guess we kinda can't help ourselves that way. It's who we are."

"It doesn't feel too much like who I am anymore."

"That's because you haven't told a story in a while. Not on paper, anyway. With us, you tell lots. Stories don't have to have a formal education, you know. Sometimes they're better when they're simple, a little rough around the edges, kinda tumbling out into the daylight all owl-eyed and talking crazy."

"I got tired of it. I wrote for a long time and it never seemed to change anything. Not in my life. Not in a lot of the lives I saw."

"That's because you made your stories for a reason other than what they were supposed to be made for."

"Pardon?"

"The only reason to tell a story is for the story itself. My people taught that. You got paid money to write stories. Funny thing is, the story's always gonna be what it is anyway, no matter how you try to deal with it. That's how stories work. They're tricksters. They tell you how they wanna be told."

"No spin," he said.

"That's right. It'll be better for us if you write this story because there won't be any spin. It'll just be the story for the story's sake."

"I might not have what it takes anymore."

"You'll find that out."

"What if I don't have it?"

"Then you don't. But at least you'll know. At least you'll have tried. At least you won't have just walked away."

"Like Timber?"

"Yes. Maybe he's teaching you that you don't have to wait twenty years to reclaim yourself. You don't have to make a long journey to continue your story."

"Is that what he's doing?"

"I don't know. I guess we'll have to see how the story turns out before we know," I said, and squeezed his hand.

He looked at me for the longest time. Then he smiled, slow and sweet like a little boy. "Okay," he said. "Okay."

Double Dick

HE DIDN'T EVEN SEEM SURPRISED to see us standin' there when he come out. We got to the hospital place early an' we was all just gettin' ready to move inside to wait for him to show up when he come walkin' out the door. Just like that. Just like he didn't go nowhere. Just like we never seen him for a week. Like it was only a few hours. He just kinda shook his head an' walked over to us. He looked tired an' kinda sad but he didn't look bad, really.

"I'm sorry," was all he said.

"We know," One For The Dead told him.

"I shouldn't have made you worry."

"Price of admission, pal," Digger said.

"Guess it wasn't hard to figure, was it?"

"Well, yes. We thought you were somewhere on the street at home. We thought you were holed up somewhere. We looked everywhere. Dick figured it out," One For The Dead said.

"E.T.," I said.

"What's that, bud?" he asked me.

"E.T.," I said again. "He had to go home an' leave his friends. That's how come I knew where you was goin' on accounta it was like E.T."

"Movie?" he asked.

"Yeah," Digger said. "Don't get him friggin' started."

"You know about all this?"

We all nodded. He pointed to some picnic tables on a patio an' we moved over to them. Digger handed out some smokes an' we sat down. Timber pulled a mickey from his coat an' passed it around after he had a drink. I was surprised on accounta Granite and even Mr. James had a swig too.

"She's alive," he said. "After all this time, she's alive."

"Do you know where?" Mr. James asked.

Timber nodded an' had another drink.

"Here," he said. "In the city."

"What do you want to do, Jonas?" Miss Margo asked him.

"I don't know. I guess a big part of me wanted her to be gone. I guess I wanted to be able to go to her gravesite and say what I had to say and be done with it. But this changes it all. She's alive."

"Can you use the same words?" I asked.

He looked at me an' grinned all sad-looking. "I don't know, bud. I don't know. I'm not sure what I'm supposed to say now."

"But you want to see her?" Granite asked.

"I don't know. I think so. I think I need to. I think I need to get some things said. I just don't know what they are, really, now that she's still here."

"Love will tell you," One For The Dead said.

"What's that, Amelia?" he asked.

"Love. Love will tell you what you need to say. It always does in the end. I think maybe you need to go back, revisit that love in all the places it grew, and let it come back to you. Then you'll know what to say."

"Go back?"

"Yes. To where you met, to the places you went together, to where you lived. All these years you've been haunting those places in your mind anyways, looking for the words to make it all make sense, to make it all come out right for you. Now's your chance to let those places go."

"I'm not sure I can," he said.

"Bull-fucking-shit," Digger said. "You came all the way out here, all alone, leaving your wingers behind because you friggin' wanted to. Because you friggin' needed to. You made that trip and spent all that friggin' time on the way out here thinking and thinking and thinking, hoping that maybe she could free you from it all. That you could stand somewhere and say all the words you been wanting to say all these years. But she can't fucking do that, pal. She can't cut you loose from this. You gotta. Nobody else. So if you gotta cab it around for three fucking days going back to all them places, then you gotta do it. There ain't no fucking *can't* here. *Won't*, maybe. You won't 'cause you're scared. You won't 'cause you don't wanna feel fucking guilty all over again. You won't 'cause you'll remember how much you lost and it'll feel like shit again. Well, we're here now. I'm here now and if you need me to walk you through this motherfucker that's what I'll do. You owe me that. You owe me the ending to this friggin' story because you really pissed me off, Timber. You really pissed me off."

"I did?"

"Oh, yeah. I been pissed before, but this time you really did it."

"I should have talked to you before I made a move. I'm sorry."

"That's not what pissed me off."

"What then?"

"You're a millionaire, for fuck sake. Take the jet, don't ride the fucking bus. It's faster and makes a better fucking story," Digger said with a grin. "What a friggin' loogan."

He slapped Timber between the shoulders an' they grinned at each other.

"Thanks," Timber said.

"Fuck it," Digger said. "Let's get it done."

"Let's get it done," Timber said. "Finally."

We all walked together to the limousine.

Timber

IT WAS A HOUSE. That's all it was. A house. It sat near the curve of a quiet little street in a neighbourhood of trees and lawn, set back thirty feet at the head of a curving cobblestone walk with three steps leading to its door. There were decorative bushes along the front that hadn't been there in our time and a pair of old-fashioned-looking gas light standards at either end of the driveway. It remained pale green. The shadows of the pine and elm trees still played along its roof and eaves and there was a row of cedar shrubs along the edge of the property line. Quiet. Thoughtful, almost. Serene and placid as the face on a cameo, untroubled by the depth of loss that had occurred here, it sat sturdy and plump with years. A house. After all this time, just a house.

I sat in the limo and looked at it. Just looked and tried to remember to breathe.

"Thirty-two steps," I said quietly.

"What's that, pal?" Digger asked.

"Thirty-two steps. That's how many it took to get from the sidewalk to the door. I counted them the first time I got back here after being out on my own one day. Thirty-two steps to home and to her. Funny what you recall."

"I guess," Digger said.

We sat there. It was a late morning like many I had seen on this street. Nothing moved. But there was a vibration everywhere. A quickening, the trembling pulse of lives—mysterious, enchanted, unseen—going on behind the walls of houses. I always imagined the fronts folding down like a doll's house, revealing the lives there in all the busy rooms, the day-to-day motions of home displayed for all to see. She gave me that vision one night on a stroll just after we'd moved here. It never happened, of course, but the street was charmed forever by that imagining. I smiled at the recollection.

I opened the door without thinking. For the first time in twenty years I stood on the street where I had lived as a young man. The memories scampered along the lawns and sidewalks and I felt a lump of compacted time forming in my throat. Air. The air still felt the same here, fresher somehow, cooler by a degree or two, and laden with the promise of the coastal rain to come. Who remembers air? Who, after all the time away, recalls how the air felt in the lungs and against the skin of the face, on the hands? I shook my head and looked at the house again. It was like the very first day when we'd stood near this spot, arms around each other, looking disbelievingly at the structure that would soon enfold us, wrap us in possibility and dreams. Our home.

I walked toward it slowly. I reached the edge of concrete and cobblestone and knelt to touch it, felt the gash of space and recalled the day we'd worked to lay the walkway. Marek, me, and Sylvan on a sunny day, with neighbours gathered around us pitching in when they could, until by evening it lay in a gentle swirl from the steps to the street.

"Can I help you?" a woman's voice called.

She was coming around the corner of the house with a basket of clipped flowers, smiling, and though it wasn't her, I imagined Sylvan as this older woman in a floppy straw hat, duck boots, and a baggy print dress to the ankles.

"I'm not sure," I said, rising. "I used to live here. A long time ago."

"Well, we haven't changed much out here. A few things, but it was so charming the day we saw it, we wanted it kept the way it was. We did some work on the interior, but the yard is pretty much the same."

"I can see that."

"Would you like to look around?"

"I don't mean to bother you."

"Oh, no bother. Walk around and look. I'll be in the kitchen if you'd like to see the inside. You and your friends are just visiting the city now?"

"Yes. Just visiting again."

"That's nice. Must be really nice to ride around in a big fancy car like that."

"Yes."

"You go ahead. Let me know if you want a peek at the inside."

I walked back to the car. I wasn't certain that I wanted to look around and I was even less certain that I wanted to walk back through that door.

"Well, what's the scoop?" Digger asked.

"She says I can look around. If I want, I can look inside."

"And?" Amelia asked.

"And I don't know. I'm scared, really. It all looks so much like it did back then that it's like it never happened. When that woman came around the corner, my heart almost stopped because I thought of Sylvan. How she must be that age now and how she'd look like that."

"Is this where you made the wooden animals?" Dick asked.

"Yes. I used to have my workshop around back."

"Can we look?" he asked.

"Okay," I said, heaving a sigh. "Might be easier if I walked with someone."

"Okay, then," Dick said. "Can anybody else come?"

"Well, I guess it's okay if we all go. She was kind of impressed by the car."

"I'll knock on the door and give her my card," James said. "Always a good move to let them know who's looking at their property."

We crossed to the walk together. I could see the woman peeking at us through the curtains and James spoke to her briefly while we stood and looked at the front yard. She smiled and nodded and we moved to the back. The bushes were taller and fuller but the shadow thrown by the trees and the house itself felt the same depth and colour. Haunting. It was haunting. The garage stood like it had always stood and I felt the odd rush of recollection, of time collapsing on itself, of yesterday reappearing in a heartbeat. Dick and I walked to it and looked in the window.

"This is where?" he asked.

"Yes," I said. "There used to be work tools and benches and moulds and racks of material all over. Now it's just a garage."

"Must have smelled real nice. I like how wood smells when you cut it."

"It *did* smell good. I always liked that smell, too. From the time I was a boy and carved that little cow, I liked how it made my hands smell. Old. Strong. Like the wood itself."

"Geez," Dick said. "You ain't had that smell on your hands for a long time, huh?"

"A long time."

"Maybe you could make me somethin' after? Then you could have that smell back."

"Maybe. I don't know if I'd know how to start now, though."

"Your hands'd remember."

I smiled. "Yes. I suppose they might."

The back door opened and the woman stepped out. I walked toward the patio. "Are you the original owner?" she asked.

"No," I said. "We bought it from the original owner."

"My god," she said, and lifted her hands to her face. "Then you're the man whose wife had the horrible accident here."

"Yes."

"How is she doing these days?"

My friends had moved around me while we talked and I looked at them before I could answer. I filled my cheeks with air and breathed out slowly.

"I don't know," I said. "We haven't spoken for a long time."

"Oh, that's too bad," she said. "It happens in a marriage. She looked fine when she came here, though."

I felt my heart drop out of my chest.

"Sylvan was here?"

"Sylvan. That's right. What a beautiful name. Sylvan, yes."

"When? When was she here?"

"Oh, a long time back now," she said. "Must have been fifteen years, maybe more. She came with a doctor. He told me she needed to look around to help her memory come back. A really nice woman, very quiet. She spent quite a while in the house."

I sat down heavily in a patio chair. I couldn't believe what I was hearing. Sylvan walking through this house like I was, working on memories. Sylvan. Alive and walking and talking and moving through the life we had shared. I could barely breathe.

"Did you not know?" the woman asked. "The doctor said her memory was coming back in flashes and blips and he wanted her to come here to see if being in her old home again might trigger it fully. I guess she had no recall at all after the accident. Horrible. The neighbours told us all about it when we moved in. Horrible."

"Did she say where she was living?" Merton asked.

"Well, no. We hardly spoke. I was rather shy about it. I'm not good around infirm people, I suppose. But the doctor left his card."

"Do you still have it?" James asked.

"Oh, I doubt it after all this time. But my son has a marvellous memory. He can remember the smallest details about things you'd never consider important. He was here then. I'll call him," she said and disappeared into the house.

Granite sat in the chair beside me. "How are you, Timber?"

"I don't know. This is too much. I never thought there was a chance. I never gave it any hope, all this time. Never once considered they might have been wrong about her condition back then."

"They get it wrong all the time."

"She looked so lost. She looked like one of those shells you pick up on the beach, beautiful but empty. You know something lived in there once upon a time but you get no sense of it. But you can still see beauty. That's how she looked and I never thought she'd change. Never thought she'd come back. That's what I couldn't handle. That's why I ran."

"No one could blame you."

"No need. I did a good number on blaming myself."

"If we find her, will you see her?"

"God, Granite. How am I supposed to answer that? Right now I feel like running again. Fuck the whole thing. Go back to what I was."

"What you became. What you were is right here, right around you right now. You don't need to run. You just have to grab this."

"See her?"

"I think so. If you can't, I'll understand. So will the rest. But I think you owe it to yourself. I really do."

"She likely hates me."

"You don't know that."

"Better if she does."

"You don't know that either."

The woman came back out. "The doctor's name was MacBeth," she said. "Like the king. That's how he remembered his name. Scott, my son. He said the doctor's name was Lyndon MacBeth."

I walked to the edge of the patio and stared up at the trees over the garage, my old workshop, my castle. I remembered the play she took me to when we were very young in our togetherness. *Macbeth*. I didn't understand it. The language was thick and hard to follow. But I felt compelled to go back. We went back four times, and when I finally got it I felt the world open up before me. Love brings you that. It opens up the world.

"'Was the hope drunk, wherein you dressed yourself?'" I said.

"What?" Digger asked.

"Oh, nothing. Just a line from a play."

"Oh, good. Thought you were losing it for a minute there, pal."

"So did I," I said. "So did I."

Granite

LYNDON MACBETH'S OFFICE was in an older brick building downtown. Frankly, I was surprised to see the name on the building directory given the amount of time that had passed. Timber looked at it posted there in little white plastic letters and trailed his fingers idly over the glass. I could understand how this was affecting him. In the car on the way downtown, I had thought about how I would react if I were given the opportunity to face the people of the past, to re-enter places, to allow my senses to prowl over remembered territories. It would demand a far greater covenant with courage than I believed I possessed, and I felt proud of Timber for the grit that enabled him to make this journey. We rode the elevator to the fifth floor in silence. The rounders kept a close eye on their friend, slipping surreptitious glances his way, watching him closely for any sign of crumbling or a move for the sidewalk.

It was a cheery-looking place. One of those retro decors augmented by the retention of original wood and sturdy antique furnishings. There was an ebullient feel to it that heartened me. The receptionist was a round-faced woman in her thirties with sparkling eyes and a friendly voice.

"Good morning. Is it still morning? My goodness. Afternoon already. Anyway, good afternoon, then. May I help you?" she said, all in one apparent breath.

"We need to speak with Dr. MacBeth," James said, handing her his card. "It's a personal matter."

"Are you a claims lawyer?" the woman asked.

"No," James said with a grin. "A trust attorney, actually."

"Trust attorney," she said. "Kind of an oxymoron these days, isn't it?"

James smiled. "I suppose. We need to speak with the doctor about an old file."

"Old file? Okay. Why don't you give me the patient's name and I'll dig it out for him and then check if he can see you."

"Certainly. Parrish. Sylvan Parrish-Hohnstein," James said.

"Spell that, please?"

James spelled the name for her and she scribbled it on a small pad.

"Please wait here," she said and walked into a room laden with shelves of files.

We sat on the couches available and waited. Timber's knees were quivering up and down and he breathed through his cheeks nervously. Digger gave him a nudge in the ribs and handed him a mickey. He drank in three small quick gulps. I wouldn't have minded a shot myself right about then.

The receptionist came out of the back room, smiled at us, and entered the doctor's office with a small knock. I noticed she was not carrying a file. James and Margo were looking at me and I knew that they had picked up on this too. I shrugged.

The door opened and a small, slender man dressed in a light tan suit walked out. He was in his forties with a balding head and small wire-rimmed glasses.

"Mr. Merton," he said. "I'm Dr. MacBeth. How may I help you?"

"Doctor," James said, standing and shaking his hand. "My client, Mr. Hohnstein here, is interested in some information about his wife. Sylvan Parrish-Hohnstein."

"Sylvan Parrish? She isn't one of my patients."

"She's not? We were under the impression that she was. Although given your age I would find that difficult to believe."

"She was my father's patient. In fact, he spoke about her all the time. It was quite a case."

"Your father?"

"Yes. He passed away five years ago. I came back for the funeral and stayed to take care of my mother and take over his practice. Never enough good psychiatrists in this town, it seems."

"Lyndon MacBeth, Jr." Margo said.

"Yes. But patients don't seem to trust a 'junior' so I dropped it from my shingle once I went into practice."

"Do you have any idea where we can find her? Or who we can talk to who might know her whereabouts?" I asked.

"Well, there aren't many case files left from dad's time—a few older people still on my list now, but nothing from that far back. I don't even recall what happened in that case now. Once I got into medical school I lost touch with what Dad was doing. I'm sorry."

"Do you remember anything?" Timber asked quietly.

"Only that she was a puzzle to my father. A great, intriguing puzzle. It had to do with memory, didn't it?"

"Yes," Timber replied.

"He kept her on even though she wasn't funded. I remember that. He wouldn't give up on her. He cared for her gratis all that time. He was interested in her and wanted to help, so he worked for free. It was a car accident, wasn't it? A very horrible accident. I remember now."

"She was hit by a drunk driver," Timber said. "She was in a body cast. They moved her to a private place after a while."

"That's right. And the husband disappeared. He just . . . Oh, I'm sorry," the doctor said, looking at Timber.

"It's okay," Timber said. "They all know the story."

"Where have you been all this time, Mr. Hohnstein?"

Timber looked out the window. We all watched him and waited. "Nowhere," he said. "I've been nowhere all this time."

MacBeth studied him briefly. "I understand. She walked again. Did you know that? I remember my father being very happy about her physical recovery. She walked and her general mobility was fine."

"I heard."

"I wish I could tell you more. But like I said, once I got going on my own studies I lost touch with Dad's work. There is one thing that sticks out to me, though. Would you like to hear it? It's kind of odd."

"Yes."

"There was a jade plant in her room. She wouldn't let anyone touch it. Dad was the only one she'd let water it for her until she got mobile enough to do it on her own. She guarded that plant. Screamed at people who went near it. I remember Dad telling me about that because it was the only emotional response he was able to get from her and it was a key for him. It gave him the motivation to keep working with her. Odd. And the plant had an odd name too. What was it?"

"Eudora."

"Yes! Eudora!" MacBeth said, snapping his fingers. "If it wasn't for that plant, my father might well have given up like everyone else did."

"I left it there," Timber said.

"You did?"

"Yes. The last time I went to see her. It was all I had left of our life together. I couldn't just throw it away, so I brought it to the hospital. I don't know why. It just felt like the right thing to do."

"Well, it certainly helped."

"It did?"

"Yes. The day she remembered the plant's name, Dad was ecstatic at dinner. Ecstatic. Eudora. I remember now. After Eudora Welty, the writer."

"Yes. We loved her. Strange now to think that our favourite novel was called *Losing Battles.*"

"But you didn't lose."

"What?"

"You have the memories. No matter what happens, you have the memories. You came back here from the nowhere you've been living in for a reason, Mr. Hohnstein. Whatever those memories are, they're good. Because you came back. Because you returned to reclaim them. Some patients pay me a great deal of money to reclaim their memories. It's a big deal."

"Even if I don't find her?"

"Even if you don't find her."

"That's not much comfort."

"It will be, Mr. Hohnstein. It will be."

"It will?"

"Yes. Eventually, it will be. In fact, do you know what?"

"No."

"I just remembered that my dad kept a personal journal of his work with your wife. That's how much she meant to him. He kept a personal journal of it. Would you like it?"

Timber just stared at him. Stared at him with a face as stunned into immobility as I've ever seen. MacBeth just nodded, clapped him lightly on the shoulder, and crossed the room to a credenza in the corner. He rummaged around the shelves and returned with a worn, leather-bound journal.

"Here it is," he said. "I've never read it. I don't know what it says or whether it can help you much at all. But I do know that my dad would want you to have it. He cared about her. He really cared. It's the best I can do."

Timber held the journal in his hands, turning it over and over, rubbing its surface with his palms. When he looked up, he was crying.

"Thank you," he said.

"You're welcome, Mr. Hohnstein. Welcome back."

Timber

IT'S HARD TO READ the words of a man who loved your wife. Even a wife you dispossessed. Even a woman you deserted. Reading the doctor's journal that afternoon in my room, I knew that he had loved her. Not in any romantic way, not in any needy, weird kind of way, but just loved her for who he saw—a woman struggling through the blackness, a beautiful woman reaching out for vague clues that eluded her as quickly as they appeared, a woman barricaded from herself by the thick bricks of amnesia. An abandoned woman. Even though she did not know that, the doctor did, and it made him even more desperate to see her through to reclaim herself from the darkness. He came to love the way she squinted into the corners of her room when he spoke with her, the pinched look I remembered that had always told me she was seeing everything. He came to love the way she stared into the mirror at her face and traced its outline with the tips of her fingers as if trying to coax recollection from the lines and hollows. He came to love the way she watched people as they spoke, as though the words themselves, the air they moved, had shape and substance and clues for her. He loved the way she grabbed at the world around her.

They found the photo album I had brought while she still lay in her coma. I'd forgotten that. I'd sit there night after night and hold the snapshots up to her face and describe the day, the place, the happenings involved in each of them, hoping against hope that something in that effort would chase away the darkness, encourage the light. It had sat among her belongings until they moved her to a small four-bed care home that Dr. MacBeth used for severe cases. He had absorbed the cost himself. When they began to lay out the things I had brought, they discovered the photo album. Sylvan did not react at first, merely stared at it like she stared at everything, uncomprehending and vacant. Then, as the doctor began the practice of thumbing through the pages with her, she began to show signs of ownership. He found her one day, alone on the veranda, tracing the faces of people in the photographs like she traced her own in the mirror. She was quiet, staring at the snapshots with a calm, assured look, a trusting look, as though she believed her fingers could divine identity, conjure time and place, gather them in her lap like a child's building blocks, allow her to build a simple structure of a life. It made me cry. The vision of her tracing the lines of my face softly, tenderly, like she had on those nights in our bed as I eased into sleep comforted by the delicate buds of her fingers, made me weep, deeply and disconsolately, until only the reading itself could ease my pain. She touched me every day like that, and the doctor wrote about the change in her look from trusting and innocent to frustrated and sad, the snapshots a captured world she could not re-enter.

"Me," she said one day, pointing to herself. "Sylvan."

"Yes," the doctor said. "Yes, yes. Sylvan."

After that, she seemed to progress. She became able to remember from day to day. She became able to recall the names of her caregivers, her address, the date, the times of her favourite television shows and why she enjoyed them, simple day-to-day things that gave the doctor great hope. But she never remembered me. When I read that, I felt the heartbreak I had felt so many years ago all over again, full and thick in my chest, an unbearable weight pulling me to depths I recollected clearly enough. I read on. He would point to me and say, "Jonas." She would repeat it, touching my image, saying, "Jonas. Jonas. Jonas." Over and over again like a spell. Then she would look at him with trembling lips and the deepest, saddest eyes he'd ever seen and slowly shake her head. *Jonas* was just a word, a push of air, a label on an empty package. I drank then. Drank deeply and deliberately, waiting for the burn in the belly to steel me for whatever came next in the doctor's small, neatly formed words.

I read on all through that afternoon. I read about the pulling together of my wife's small world. I read about her growing ability to manage time. Present time. The past a shadow just beyond her optic range, a fleeting thing, tempting in its closeness but elusive, wild, unsnared, uncaptured, and roaming forever beyond her grasp. The doctor gave me her world and I immersed myself in it, grateful for the chance to see her live again, to be vital. And as I worked my sad way through those pages, I relearned love, felt it spill open within me, drenching me in its warmth, a fluid thick, viscous, essential as blood.

Sometime that evening I walked into Granite's room, where everyone had gathered to watch a movie. The journal was tucked beneath my arm. They looked at me warily, concerned, worried. I took a seat on the arm of the sofa.

"Are you okay?" Amelia asked.

"Yes," I said. "I'm fine."

"Did that book give you anything you could use there, pal?" Digger asked.

"Yes. As a matter of fact, it did."

"Like what, Timber?" Granite asked.

"Like an address," I said. "Like an address."

One For The Dead

SHE LIVED in a cottage in a city by the sea. She was an old woman. She had made a long journey through the darkness and memories had been like stones she bumped her foot against, shadowed, hard, unmoving, giving nothing back, not even light. There had been a man to help her travel. A man, gentle and wise, who tried to teach her to gather up the stones in the road, hold them up to the pale glow of the moon and make them known. But she was frail and tired, scared and alone, and the heft of stones became an awkward, uncomfortable act. So he let her be, walking behind her as she travelled that darkened road, always wondering if somehow the stars might lead her to the distant horizon where the light was born. They never did. She was destined to always be a nomad on that road. The stones about her feet, untouched and unclaimed, lay forever dormant and told no stories of their own, sang no histories. So she found her way to a cottage by the sea and there, washed in the sound of waves, the birds, the laughter of other peoples' children in the surf, and wind keening across the sky, she learned to leave the darkened road behind and exist in a new light in a new world. There were no stones on the beaches of her mind. She was an old woman in a cottage by the sea.

Digger

LOVE STORIES should always be told like Cyrano de fucking Bergerac. We seen this flick, this French flick about this big-nosed motherfucker who is the country's greatest swordsman. Tough son of a bitch who tells jokes while he's fighting six or seven guys. My kind of guy. But he falls in love with his friggin' cousin. Head over heels, puppy dog–eyed in love, and he's fucked. Roxanne. Roxie. Great name. Kinda like a stripper's name or maybe a big blond biker broad. But she's his cousin. Anyways, he's an ugly motherfucker and he knows that Roxanne would never have anything to do with him on accounta he's so friggin' ugly with a nose the size of a baked potato. So he gets a big strappin' handsome lad to declare his love for her while Cyrano feeds him lines from the bushes. It all goes to hell. Roxie falls in love with the handsome lad and Cyrano dies after getting wounded in a sword fight. But not until he takes out about eighty guys. Love oughta be told like that. It hurts like a blade under the ribs, I'm told, so I figure if you're gonna tell it, tell it like it is. Who knows? Mighta helped old Cyrano.

I'm thinking this while we're driving out to see Timber's woman. He's sitting there beside me having a good knock out of a bottle and I can tell he's getting ready for anything. Good.

Maybe he won't get a chance to take out eighty guys before he falls but it's good to be prepared. Not that I know he's gonna go down on this, but if love hurts like they all say, don't go in unprepared. If you know you're gonna be shanked before the shanking happens, it helps to be a little pissed off first. Or a little pissed. Either ways, a good way to go.

We swing out of the downtown and move into an area kind of like the one we were in when we found Timber's old house. Nice. Kinda like Indian Road, so I figure good folks gotta live out here. Every now and then I see the ocean through the houses and trees and I feel good because I never saw an ocean before. Big mystery, oceans. Always been a big mystery to me because I never seen one. We start slowing down when we pull into a little curved road that runs along a cliff overlooking the big water. The houses are mostly small with a huge mansion-looking place thrown in now and again. Everyone is eyeballing them, wondering which one is the one we're looking for. Turns out that it's a little place with a wraparound veranda, all lit up in the night, warm-looking and cozy. A nice place. A home.

There's two people sitting out there in rocking chairs with blankets wrapped around their shoulders. I look over at Timber and he's staring at them. Hard. Not moving. Not even blinking. I can tell they seen the car because they put their heads closer together, talking about it and obviously wondering what a big limo's doing pulling up in front of their house. None of us know what to do. We're waiting for Timber to make a move, and just when I'm wondering if he's going to change his mind and tell the driver to take us back to the hotel, he heaves a big breath and turns his head to look at us.

"Now or never," he goes.

"Guess so," I go.

"You ready for this?"

"I'm not the one that's gotta be ready, pal."

"Yeah."

We step out of the car and into the salty air. I can see the two people on the veranda gesturing toward us, and when Timber starts walking to their gate they both look at us with their heads cocked like pointer dogs. He stopped with his hand on the latch. I put a hand on his shoulder and can feel him shaking.

"It's okay, pal," I go. "We're here."

He breathes out loudly, pushes the gate, and steps through into the yard.

"Good evening," the guy calls out. "Can we help you?"

Timber keeps on walking toward the veranda stairs. He's stiff in the back like someone's got a gun to his ribs, his hands dangling at his sides. The rest of us kinda wander after him like kids on a field trip. He climbs the three steps to the veranda and just kinda stands there looking at the two people, a man and a woman, still wrapped in their blankets and drinking coffee from steaming white mugs. The man looks at us evenly, not too worried about these five strangers stepping out of their fancy car to pay a late-night visit. The woman stares too, but she's squinting hard. Even in the dim light of the veranda I can tell she's a babe. An old babe, but still a babe. She stares at us hard but doesn't say a word, nothing moves in her face.

"Hello," Timber goes.

"Good evening," the man goes.

"Hello, Jonas," the woman goes, and I have to catch Timber before he falls off the fucking steps.

Timber

SHE LIVED. She lived and she breathed and she walked and she talked and she spoke my name. She spoke my name. I felt my knees buckle when I heard it and Digger pushed both hands into my back to keep me upright. "Hello, Jonas," she said, like I'd come back from the store with milk or something. Casual. Light. Not cutting through a tangle of years or anything, just "Hello, Jonas," and those two words were enough to tumble me. Two words I thought I would never hear again. Two words that still had the power they had the first time I ever heard them come from that lovely face. I straightened myself on the steps, grabbed ahold of the handrail and pulled myself square again, with Digger pressing from behind. When I stood, my knees were shaking and I didn't know what to do with my hands. They felt like paddles at the end of my arms. I stood there looking at the two of them in their rocking chairs with blankets about their shoulders like the old couple I used to imagine Sylvan and I would become.

"You know who I am?" I asked.

"Oh, yes," she said lightly. "I have your picture in my house."

"You do?"

"Oh, yes. Lyn told me to keep it out."

"You remember me?"

"Yes. You're Jonas."

"Yes."

"Yes. Jonas," she said and smiled.

The smile cut me. It was like the moment when the wick on a candle springs to life, peeling the darkness back to reveal the world to you again. Sylvan's smile. My Sylvan's smile. I grabbed the top of the handrail again because all she did was smile.

"Mr. Hohnstein?" the man asked, standing and reaching out to shake my hand.

I shook my head to stop myself from staring at my wife five feet away from me. "Yes?" I asked.

"Mr. Hohnstein, I'm Phillip Greer. I'm Sylvan's husband." He held his hand out to me, waiting for a reaction. "Maybe you should come into the house and sit down. You and your friends. Sylvan, dear, let's take these people into the living room and have a visit."

"Yes," she said. "A visit. A visit would be nice. Coffee and some cake, maybe."

Greer held the door open and I watched as she rose slowly, small hands clutching the blanket around her. She smiled at my friends gathered behind me and as she passed she looked at me. I saw those incredible blue eyes and I felt something warm and pliant rip smoothly apart again inside my chest. She grinned. She grinned and passed wordlessly, following Greer into the house.

Sylvan. It meant quiet. Peaceful, pastoral, tranquil as a forest glade, an idyll, a calm and undisturbed wood, rife with shadow, light, and mystery. All I felt as she passed was the mystery.

I walked through the door watching her back. She didn't move the same. I saw that right away. The Sylvan I knew moved with an assured step like she was in tune with everything around her. This woman walked carefully, as though she didn't want to disturb anything, as though she needed it all to remain where it was, as if walking a planned route. Greer pointed us to chairs and a sofa and we all sat, my friends staring at me for clues as to how to move or what to say. Greer made Sylvan comfortable in a big easy chair, plumping pillows behind her back, setting her feet on a round cushioned ottoman and covering them with the blanket. He moved like he was used to watching over her, like he cared, like he loved her. I felt a spear of jealousy rack my insides.

The room was lovely. Rustic and charming. There was a fireplace with silk flowers adorning the mantle and a Gainsborough-like painting of countryside under huge billowed clouds. The furniture was all wood and cloth like an old country home, and there were pillows everywhere. Pillows on the sofa, pillows on the chairs, pillows in a pile on the floor, and pillows leaning on shelves.

Greer watched as I looked at them.

"She likes pillows," he said. "I don't know why. It's just one of the things she latched on to right away and it's like she can't ever have enough of them. We have more pillows in this house than air."

"No books," I said.

"What's that?" Greer asked.

"There's no books. She loved books. She was a librarian."

"I didn't know that," he said. "There's a lot I don't know, really. Maybe you can help with that."

I looked at him. He was a soft man. Tall, stocky enough for the height, with a slight bulge of belly, glasses, balding, with wide hands and feet. But soft. He'd have never made it on the street.

"I don't know," I said. "I don't know what I can do."

"Maybe I can clear up some things for you, Mr. Hohnstein. Sylvan functions with a memory that clicks on and off like a broken switch. Some days it works and other days it doesn't. I never know when I wake up in the morning what I'm going to have to tell her, what I'm going to have to introduce her to again. It's like trying to keep something on a slippery surface. You never know if it's going to stick or slide.

"She seems to hold on to activities better. Actions. She can remember how to do things, the repetitive things we all do, but she can't remember why. I have to tell her to wash. I have to tell her to change her clothes. Some days I even have to tell her to dress. Things like that."

"But she remembers me?" I asked.

He sighed. "You," he said. "You are the face of hope. Dr. MacBeth told me when I started to take care of Sylvan to put your picture where she could see it every day. It was his hope that something would click for her. Something that would start all the tumblers rolling back into place. That's why there's a picture of you in every room. In the hope that she would one day remember."

"She doesn't?"

"No. She doesn't. She just knows your face and she knows your name because we told her over and over again in the beginning."

"We?"

"Dr. MacBeth and I. I was Sylvan's physiotherapist after the accident and at the extended care home. When she moved here I came with her to be her live-in care. We were together for such a long time and I watched her fight to get her body back, watched her fight to get the world back in some kind of order she could handle. I fell in love with her. We were married three years ago."

"But I'm her husband," I said dumbly.

"Dr. MacBeth took power of attorney for Sylvan. When you disappeared and didn't return, someone had to take care of her needs and the doctor wanted to do that. He loved her too. When it looked like you'd never resurface, he put the divorce papers through *in absentia.*"

"*In absentia?*"

"Yes. You were nowhere to be found. The court considered the fact that you hadn't been heard from for seven years and made it official. I have the papers somewhere upstairs."

"No need. I understand. Does she understand?"

"She doesn't need to," Greer said. "I've always been here, Mr. Hohnstein. Through everything. Through all that time. All those years. All that struggle. You weren't. You weren't there when she had night terrors and cried and needed to be held, to be told that she was safe, that she was going to be okay. You weren't there for the bedpans, the walkers, the back braces, the massages, the ten-minutes-to-take-three-stairs ordeals, none of it. You weren't there to teach her to wash herself, to potty train her, to teach her about knives and forks and spoons again, to teach her how to cross the street. But I was. I was. And I'm sorry if that sounds like anger and judgment, but I love her. I love her. I loved her through all of that and I didn't disappear. That's all she needs to understand; that I've always been here and that I always will be."

"Yes," I said.

"I knew there was a small chance you'd resurface someday. I don't know why but I just knew. Maybe because I know what love is and I understand how much torture you went through when yours was wiped away. Maybe because I know that once it's planted in your chest and sinks its roots right into your being, it never goes away, never stops trying to find the light again. Maybe because I know that you loved her. Perhaps as much as I do right now. Maybe more."

"What makes you so sure of that? I ran. How much love does that take?"

"Look in the corner."

"What?"

"Look in the corner," he said again, and pointed to the far corner by the sliding glass doors that led to a back patio.

Eudora. The jade plant. She was huge, almost unrecognizable from when I last saw her, but I knew it was her. She was more of a bush than a plant now, round and thick with a gnarled trunk that spoke of years and time. She sat in a large red clay pot, looking content in her spot by the sundeck. I walked over to her and let my fingers trail across the rich buds of leaves, remembering the nights alone on the cold hardwood floor of our home when I'd slept with my arms wrapped around her.

"Eudora," Sylvan said. "That's Eudora."

"Yes," I said, turning to face her. "Eudora. You gave her that name."

"Me?" she asked. "Why?"

"Because there was a great writer named Eudora. A woman. When you read her stories to me, you told me she sounded like mist on the bayou."

"Eudora told stories?"

"Yes. Very well."

She looked at Greer. "You never told me that."

"I didn't know, dear," he said.

"Oh," she said quietly, and looked back at me.

"You left that plant by her bedside, Mr. Hohnstein. Now, I can't tell you what was going through your mind but I do know that it was a loving thing to do. Maybe it was the only loving thing you had left to do. I don't know. But that action told me a lot about how much you loved Sylvan. That you would leave a reminder even though you didn't believe she could ever be reminded. Hope against hope. Against all odds. Love."

"I don't even remember leaving it," I said. "I was drunk when I left. I stayed drunk a long time."

Greer looked at me and nodded. "I guessed. I read the history and I know that you had to sell everything in order to provide for her. I know that you had to sell your home. And I guessed that Eudora was the last thing left and you left it with Sylvan. Where did you go?"

"Down."

"Yes. And why come back now?"

"No choice."

"I see. What did you hope to achieve?"

"I don't know. I guess I just needed to see her. Needed to know that she was all right. Needed to know that what I did wasn't my curse. My failing."

"She doesn't remember. Anything. Nothing of that life before the accident. She doesn't even know there was an accident. She just woke up to a new life that had its starting point in a hospital bed. How you feel about what you did is your business, but I know that she bears no feeling for you. No love, no malice, no need. Nothing. She can't. It's beyond her."

"Can I ask her?"

Greer studied me for a moment. There was nothing in his eyes but concern. I felt like if I made any sort of wrong move, he would plant himself dully in my path. He looked at me and I knew that I was being studied, not as any kind of threat, not as any kind of competition, but as a man looking for a straw, the one that provides just enough buoyancy to keep you from slipping under, away, down, gone. "Go ahead," he said. "For what it's worth. Okay, ask her."

I looked at the others. They sat like stones, watching, listening, waiting for any sign from me that they needed to move in, surround me, plant themselves as obdurately in front of me as Greer was planted in front of Sylvan. Amelia nodded. I moved forward.

The room was like an ocean. The carpet was a placid sea and I was a mariner adrift in the doldrums, seeing the shore in his mind's eye but incapable of getting there. Sylvan sat calmly with her hands folded in her lap, looking at Greer and then at me adrift there on my isotropic sea, the going back and the moving on appearing to be the same direction. When I moved, she grinned at me. A small girl's grin. Each step closer brought a crash of memories like waves on the beach and I felt myself floating among them, bobbing helplessly, flotsam, jetsam, at the whim of the surf.

Sylvan on a Christmas morning waiting in her chair while I carried a present festooned with ribbons toward her. Sylvan in a camp chair high in the mountains beside our tent, her chin pointed upward into the breeze, eyes closed and sighing while I brought her coffee in a steaming mug. Sylvan demurely seated in a concert hall, one leg folded over the other, the trails of her evening dress dropping to the floor, and me standing in the aisle with a program, seeing the symphony of her. Sylvan in her chair at the library, head bent over text, the walls crammed with the spines of books, then seeing me and smiling, her one hand gesturing to the room, to the words, to the stories, to the idea of so many possible worlds. Sylvan sleeping in her armchair, a book slumped against her chest, her fingers entwined around it, Horowitz playing Brahms in the background and me leaning in the doorway watching her, learning how to breathe.

I reached down, put my hands gently under her ankles and lifted them, placing her feet on the floor and hitching the ottoman closer to her before I sat down. She smiled. I felt a large, agonized lump in my throat and the saline wash of tears in my eyes and on my tongue. I took a moment and smoothed the blanket over her knees. She sat there and grinned at me, waiting. Then I took her hands. Took her soft, lined hands in mine and traced their backs with the pads of my thumbs. These were the hands that once gave structure to my world, the hands that taught me how to carve a life out of the shapeless lump that it was, the hands that coaxed emotion and feeling out of skin that had never known the touch of such magic, the hands that cupped the universe and held it out to me like a folded thing, showing me how to open it slowly, easily, outward into its glory like an origami bird. I felt them. Felt their warmth, their satin promise, their stories. One large tear fell from my eye and landed on the back of her wrist. I massaged it dry with my thumb and struggled to hold back the deluge I felt building inside me.

"You're sad," she said.

"Yes," I replied, tight-lipped.

"Why?" she asked quietly.

I looked at her. She sat in the chair, squinting at me like she had always done, the pinched look that brought together all of her focus, all of her attentiveness, all of her energy, so that you knew you existed, really and truly existed, existed to the exclusion of all else in that one glorious moment. I choked back tears and tried to smile bravely.

"Because time has hands," I said.

"Hands? Like a clock?"

"Yes. Like that. You can watch them move but it's only after you've been gone somewhere, after you've left something and come back to it, that you can feel them."

"Are they soft hands?"

"No. Not really. They're heavy."

"You're sad because they're heavy?"

"Yes."

She nodded. "I feel heavy sometimes. Sad. Sad, and I don't know why. Sad for something I can't remember."

"You do?"

"Yes. It's funny. It just comes over me sometimes. Kneeling in the garden or walking on the beach or even watching a show on television. I'll just feel sad. Just for a moment. Just enough to know I'm sad and then it's gone again. Like time put its hands on me."

"Yes. Me too."

"You're a nice man."

"I hope so. I haven't felt like a nice man for a long time."

"Because you left something?"

I looked up expecting to see that focused look, to become captured in it again. But all I saw were the eyes of a child, fascinated, curious, asking questions just to get to another question. And I knew.

"Yes. A long time ago," I said. "I left something beautiful and valuable and precious because I was afraid I couldn't keep it. Because I was afraid that I wasn't strong enough to hold on to it."

"Was it still there? When you came back, was it still there?" she asked.

"Yes. It was."

"Was it still beautiful? After all that time, was it still beautiful?"

I closed my eyes to hold back the rush of tears. I closed my eyes so I could hold on to the world, so I wouldn't collapse in shudders of agony on her lap. I closed my eyes so I could breathe and I held my hand up to my face to cover my mouth and pinch my nose so none of the hurt would erupt in front of her.

"Yes," I said finally. "It was still beautiful."

"Was it still yours?"

"No," I said, looking at Greer, who had tears in his eyes. "No, it wasn't. It had grown into something even more beautiful and valuable than it was before, and someone else was taking care it."

"Like Eudora."

"What?"

"Eudora grew into something more beautiful and valuable too."

"What do you mean?"

"I don't know where she came from. All I know is that she has always been here. Always been with me. Wherever I went, she was always there. She got pretty big for the pot after a while and I didn't know what to do. But Phillip knew. He took part of Eudora and promised to take care of her for me and she got more beautiful. Would you like to see?"

"Yes," I said. "I'd like to see."

"Can we?" she asked Greer.

He wiped the tears from his eyes and stood up. "Yes," he said. "We can do that, dear. I'll get the lights."

He flicked a switch on the wall and the lights on the back deck came on. Sylvan stood up and moved toward the door. Then she stopped. She turned and looked at me. She looked at me with the wide open look of the young woman I met so long ago and then she reached out and took my hand and led me to the door. The others stood and followed us out.

Greer was standing by the steps at the back of the deck and he guided Sylvan to the top riser. "Careful," he said.

We walked down wordlessly, Sylvan still clutching my hand, and stepped onto the lush grass below. "Over there," she said, pointing. "And there, and there."

I was amazed. All along the property line, along both sides and along the back, was one long hedge of Eudora, one long stretch of jade plants, healthy, succulent, and vibrant.

"He took care of it," she said.

"Yes," I said. "He did."

"Isn't she beautiful?"

"She certainly is," I said, looking at her. "She certainly is."

"She got to be more."

"Yes. She got to be more."

"So maybe you don't have to be sad about the thing you left. Maybe whoever's taking care of it now has let it get to be more."

"Yes."

"Can I give you something?"

"Yes."

She walked over to a small structure resembling a greenhouse beside the deck stairs. She bent over and reached inside. I looked at Greer and he closed his eyes and nodded. I waited. She came back holding a potted plant in her hands.

"It's Eudora," she said. "Maybe you can take her with you to where you live and take care of her. Would you like that?"

I smiled. "Yes. I'd like that very much."

"Jonas?"

"Yes?"

"It'll be all right."

We stood there in the amber light and looked at each other. Something in that depth of shadow, in that hushed space just at the edge of darkness, made all the years disappear. We were Jonas Hohnstein and Sylvan Parrish and she had just given me a part of the world. We were young. We were alive. We were lovers. We were on a journey neither of us could describe adequately enough to cover the territories we explored together. I smiled. She smiled back. She reached out and took my free hand and it was like being enfolded in that amber light, sealing us within it forever—intact, whole, memorable, a keepsake.

"It really will be all right," she said.

And I believed her.

Double Dick

He was gone again when we woke up the next mornin'. We was gonna walk around the beach together an' he was gonna help me grab some driftwood on accounta I wanted to get some for One For The Dead's garden. He said we'd do that before we went to our rooms but he wasn't there when I went to get him up. His door was open a crack so I just walked right in. He wasn't there. At first I kinda figured he was downstairs gettin' something so I sat on his bed an' watched some TV. When the show ended an' he wasn't back I started to get worried an' when he didn't come in after another show was over I went an' got Digger. He snooped around in his room an' then we both went to One For The Dead's room. When we told her she just sat in her chair an' nodded her head real slow before she said anythin'.

"The hands of time are heavy," she said.

"What's that?" I asked.

"It's what Timber said last night to Sylvan. That time's hands are heavy. I think that when he got back here he started to realize how heavy they really are and he has to get used to that."

"I still don't understand."

"Timber's been walking a long time, carrying something he thought he could never put down. Now, since he came here and found Sylvan again, saw her, talked to her, he realizes he doesn't have to carry it anymore and he doesn't know how to walk without that weight."

"Oh. You mean he's gotta learn how to walk again?"

"Yes."

"How's he gonna learn how to do that?"

"I don't know."

"Alone, I guess, huh?"

"I think so."

"Are we gonna get the cops to look for him again? Do we gotta fly to some other place now?"

"I don't think so. Not this time. I think that wherever Timber needs to go to settle this with himself is a place we won't find him. He'll make sure of that this time."

"How come?" I asked, worried now.

"Well, Dick, it's like a bear when it's wounded. Instead of being around other bears or around any other animal, that bear will walk far into the bush to be alone. Then it'll find a good place to lay out where it can lick its wounds, maybe roll around in the mud and let the earth work its magic on the hurt, and spend as much time alone as it needs to get better. To heal."

"No other bears know where he went?"

"No. I guess the bear doesn't even know itself, really. Not at first. It just knows it needs to get away. Get away so the other ones close to it don't have to watch it hurt. Don't need to see it learn to walk without the pain."

"Timber's a bear?"

"Yes," she said. "A very old, wounded bear that doesn't want to let the others see its pain."

"It'd be all right," I said. "He could be hurt around me an' I wouldn't bother him."

"I know, Dick. And Timber knows that too. But he's an old rounder bear and rounder bears really only know how to do things the one way."

"Do rounder bears come back when they're better?"

She took my hands in hers. "I hope so," she said. "I really, really hope so."

Granite

WE WAITED FOUR DAYS. We remained in our rooms at the hotel and waited for him. Digger and Dick cruised the streets of the Skid Row area, hung out at the missions and soup kitchens in vague hope that familiarity might bring him to those spots. Margo and I spent time on the beach scanning its length for a tall walking man, perhaps waiting for the sea to carry its balm to him like a message in a bottle. James agreed that it was pointless to involve the police and we resolved to bide an appropriate time and then head home. I understood. Maybe more than all of them, I understood his pain. There had been so many times through the years that I had imagined myself walking into a room and seeing Jenny one more time. She'd be sitting in a chair just like Sylvan had—comfortable, cozy, at ease—and I would cross the room silently, bearing all the years on my shoulders, and slump down in front of her and tell her everything I had never taken the time to say, all the things that time had never allowed me to say, and I would feel the heavy hands of time release me. But dreams are dreams. For most of us, they never materialize in the concrete world and it's best they don't because we'd never say the things we imagine ourselves saying in dream state. Hearts have vocabularies all their own, after all. So I understood that he didn't get to say what he most wanted to say and I understood that he could never go back. You dream hard sometimes, and waking is cruel. So we waited and we walked and we wondered until the night we were supposed to fly out.

"We need to see the house again," Amelia said.

"Why?" I asked, with caution. There were inescapable parallels here that frightened me in their accuracy.

"Because that's his mourning ground. That's where his life changed. That's where the course of things swung in an unbelievable direction and it's where he'd go before he did anything else."

"You're sure?"

"Yes. He knows about mourning grounds. He's heard me talk about the shadowed ones and their need to return to the places where life was altered forever. It's where he'd go. He'd want to heal from it."

So that night, we stood in the twilight and looked at the small pale green house where someone's dreams had fractured. It was a house. Just a house. It stood in the hushed light of that fading evening innocent and calm, waiting like houses do for lives to animate and define it. It was peaceful.

She opened the door before we got there, stepped onto the front step to greet us. "Your friend was here," she said. "Four days ago. We found him standing in the backyard early in the morning. It's lucky I remembered him, because Jack wanted to call the police. He was cold so we gave him coffee."

"Did he say anything about where he might be heading?" I asked.

"No. He just asked if he could leave something here."

"What was that?"

"Over there," she said. "Beside the garage."

I think we all knew it was Eudora. I know I did. I walked over to the garage that used to be a woodcarver's shop and I knew he would have left her here. No one spoke. We all stood and looked at the tiny sprig of jade plant hugging the earth, reaching for the sky. I looked around at the yard, at the verdant green bowl it created, and wondered how lives, cupped in the roundness, the fullness of life itself, can crumble. I wondered where you'd go to heal from that. In my experience, there was nowhere that had made that possible. As I looked at the trio of rounders gazing helplessly at a small fingerling of plant life pressed into the ground, I understood—briefly, fleetingly—that pain, like spirituality, needs community to find its truest expression.

"She got to be more," I said.

Timber

I DIDN'T GO BACK. I wanted to. More than anything, I wanted to go back and sit at her feet and tell her about the life I'd led since I saw her last. But there was nowhere for the words to go. She would just sit and look at me, unknowing and innocent. So I walked away again. I walked away to think. I walked away to figure out the how and why of fate, of hope, of dreams. Dreams. Of all the things we carry, they are the lightest and the heaviest all at the same time. I had dreamed for all those years. Dreamed of Sylvan. Dreamed of us. Dreamed of love. But I always woke up. Always emerged again into the world where dreams are haunting things, because they have no power in the real world. Looking into those beautiful eyes again and seeing nothing reflected back was a dream deferred. I had dreamed that she was still there, and making my way back across the country I had allowed myself to dream that seeing me again might rekindle everything. But there was nothing to rekindle. Not for her. For her, the world was a blank slate every day, and she had a man who helped her fill it. She had no need of me. She had no need of history. She had no need of something tossed away, lost in the *clock, clock, clock* of departing footsteps. I wondered whether I did, though, and that was why I walked.

I walked to a valley far away. I walked to a farmhouse where a young boy carved a small cow out of rough pine. I walked to a family that had lived in wonder almost thirty years and talked to them in halting sentences about where I'd gone, what I'd done, and who I'd been. I talked to them about a woman they had never met who had been the promise of a future generation and who was now far removed from those kinds of dreams. I talked to them about being lost, about the great voids in this world where a man can remove himself from the promise of anything and everything. I talked to them about dreams and dreaming and how dreams are fleeting always, leaving nothing behind in their wake but the vague hope of more dreams, bigger dreams, brighter, bolder, more hopeful dreams that never seem to come once one is dashed. I spent a week with them. I spent seven days walking in the past wondering whether it held enough to call me back to the farm where it had all begun. I laid my hand on that life and felt it, recognizable and foreign at the same time, and walked away again.

I walked to a small town on the opposite coast of the country. I walked to a house I had never visited and introduced myself to people who had lived in wonder almost twenty years and talked to them about a daughter who had been their promise. I talked to them about a love that had been my promise, about how that energy had shaped my world and how the loss of it had left me shapeless, deformed, and crippled. I talked to them about a pale green house on a tree-lined street, about a jade plant, and about a drunken man who had erased it all as casually as a drawing in the sand. I talked to them of booze, how I lived in it, how it made it easier to ignore but not forget the feeling of something inscribed on your skin like an abandoned tattoo: unfinished, undefined, ugly in its lack. I told them of the life she had, the man who cared for her, and where to go to find her. There was no need to say I'm sorry after all that time. Sometimes language is unfulfilling, sometimes words can never lead you where you need to go, sometimes a solemn look is all the phonics time requires. I offered that look and then I walked away.

I walked to the streets of the city. I walked to the haunts I used to frequent like a ragged spectre and asked them for admission. I asked them to allow me to disappear again, to crawl back down into the depths and pull the concrete around me one more time, enshroud myself in it, allow its hardness to infuse my heart, my mind, my spirit, to weigh myself with nothingness. I walked there for days and for the very first time I felt like I did not belong there. I sat under a railroad bridge one rain-filled night, alone except for the whisky in my coat and her, the vestiges of her. She had made me more. She had lifted me beyond this forever. She had rekindled a fire, an ember at first, a struggling cinder beset by the winds and random breezes of doubt and fear, but a fire nonetheless. There was really only one way to honour the love that we once held so sacred, one way to validate it in the face of twenty years of denial and drunken absolution. If I loved her, then I would reclaim the life that she had empowered, reassume the boon she had granted. So I walked to a supply store the next morning and ordered wood and tools and knives. And then I walked back home.

Granite

"YOU'RE NOT GOING TO BELIEVE what he wants me to do," James said over coffee the morning after Timber had returned.

"Likely not. But tell me anyway," I said.

"He wants to sign over everything to her."

"All of it?"

"All of it. Except for what he needs to live."

"What are you going to do?"

"What can I do? It's his wish."

"What about him? What's he going to do?"

"He's going to carve. Digger's going to give him space at the back of his store."

"Jesus."

"Well, I don't know about Jesus but somebody's watching over things. Somebody with a very particular sense of humour."

"Hell of a story."

James smiled. "You're right, Granite. It *is* a hell of a story. How are you doing on that?"

"Well, I'm making notes. That might not seem like much but at least I find myself doing it. And the strange thing is, they were right. I *am* the only one that can tell it properly."

"Not surprising. You've been on the inside all along. There's nothing in any of this that you missed. Except maybe the life, maybe the details of surviving like they did all those years. But you have the feel of it."

"Yes. It bamboozles me sometimes. I mean, just the understanding. I actually understand how something could drive you to the street, how you could survive there, how you could want to survive there."

"Certainly gives an irreverent twist to the old 'all the comforts of home' idea."

"A fire, a crock, and a wrap."

"A few smokes, a laugh."

"It's a whopper of a tale."

"Make a hell of a movie."

"Yes. But you know, James, I'm flummoxed to say why I met these people. I mean, I figured I'd hid out pretty well. Then the cold front comes along, we meet in the theatre, next thing you know these ragged people have become my life. Mystical as all fuck, wouldn't you say there, pal?" I said with an appropriate Digger-like growl.

James laughed. "Yes. Yes. And then there's Margo."

"Margo," I said. "It's amazing really."

"Amazing?"

"Yes. It's like a carving, I suppose. You hold it in your hands at first and you know there's something there. Something calling you to whittle and nick and shape the wood but you're not really certain what it is. But you can't halt the process. So you slice away a little more and a little more and it starts to assume a shape and form almost on its own. Next thing you know, you're seeing something special begin to materialize in your hands. Special because you took the time to discover where it wanted you to go. It's like that."

"You're becoming quite the romantic."

"Hard not to with this crowd."

"I know. But there's a more important question, Granite."

"There is?"

"Yes."

"What is it?"

"Are you getting laid yet?"

I laughed. It felt good, this camaraderie in a café. This banter. This old-boy chuck-on-the-shoulder kind of conversation. "Yes," I said. "Yes."

Digger

WE'RE SITTING at the Palace tossing back a couple pints. Me 'n the boys. Well, the old lady's there too, but she ain't drinking. We never said squat to Timber when he walked back through the door. Didn't need to. You hung through together as long as we hung through, there ain't no need for speeches. The most that happened was the old lady gave him a big hug and they held on to each other for a long time right there in the living room. Dick and Margo and Rock give him a hug too, and Merton just shook his hand and clapped him on the shoulder. Me? Frig. I just grinned at him and nodded. He knocked on my door late that night and we sat there while he told me about it. Brothers. No fuss, no friggin' muss. Just brothers telling tales. He knew. So did I. He made that same knock on each of our doors that night and the next morning we just carried the fuck on like rounders do. Carried the fuck on.

"We need a good movie tonight," Dick goes. "We ain't been out to one for a while now an' I miss goin'."

"Yer right, pal," I go. "We do need a flick."

"*Mountains of the Moon,*" Timber goes.

"What?"

"*Mountains of the Moon,*" he goes again.

"That don't sound too bad," I go. "Adventure?"

"Friendship, really," Timber goes.

"Well, that's a friggin' adventure," I go, and we all laugh like hell.

Rock, Merton, and Margo swing through the doors just then and I figure this is turning into a real party.

"Digger, you're looking particularly fine today," Margo goes.

"Yeah? Well, come here and give me hug and a peck on the cheek there, lady."

"Oh, I don't know," she goes. "I might swoon getting so close to a manly man like yourself."

"Yeah, well. Life is risk," I go, and we all laugh again.

Pretty soon we're all leaning across the bar and telling tales. Rounders. All of us. Rounders. In our own way, every one of us sitting there in that old scrub of a bar had lived a rounder's life, had survived. I was never gonna figure how it all worked out the way it had, so I didn't even friggin' try. Didn't even want to, really, if the truth was told. Didn't even friggin' want to. The thing was, we were solid. Solid. On the street it means you're dependable, trustworthy, strong in the face of bullshit and never tellin' other people's tales, never gonna buckle under questioning. Here it means carrying the fuck on. No fuss, no muss, no worry over choices, just hanging at your winger's shoulder helping with the load. I liked that. Here there were no Square Johns, no us and them, no have and have-nots, no ups no downs, no rich or poor because we had been all of that. All of that. Rounders. So we sat in that bar all through that afternoon, laughing together, telling stories, arguing some like old friends do, and getting kinda looped. Then we went to the movies. *Mountains of the Moon.* An adventure. An adventure about friendship. Now that was something I could believe.

Timber

THEY FOUND THEIR WAY through famine, drought, hunger, attacks by both human and beast, and made their way to the Mountains of the Moon. They fought. They disagreed. They disappeared on each other. But they were friends. I sat in the theatre and watched this incredible story of hardship and friendship, the two forever intertwined in the lives of two explorers, and I was amazed at how easily art copies life. We're all explorers, really. We're all seeking the source of something like Burton and Speke sought the source of the Nile River. We're all of us engaged in the process of finding our way. And it's a hard go. So easy to become lost, confused, befuddled by territories you've never seen before, never expected to find, never knew existed or would become so important to you, so much a part of the tale you'd tell.

I walked again that night. Left the house in the early hours and walked the neighbourhood surrounding Indian Road and looked at the houses that comprised it. There were histories there. Incredible histories framed by the walls containing them, and I thought about the house that had once held mine. It sat on a street of trees in a city by the sea. It occupied space. It occupied time. It contained me. It contained her. In a tiny space at the back of that house, a plant would grow. It would grow and become something more. It would change the space it occupied by virtue of its purpose: to live, to thrive, to be. That was all I needed from that tiny house now. The knowledge that I had left something of myself behind. Something soulful and precious. Something that might sing of history to those who would see it, nurture it, urge it to grow. It was the same with the money. All I needed was the knowledge that I had left something behind that mattered. Not to me. I had no need of it. But it made life easier for Sylvan. I was taking care of her. Finally. After twenty years of famine, drought, and desperation, I'd found my Mountains of the Moon. The source of my magic river. And I gave it all to her. It was the only choice I had. Love told me that just as it told me that I would carve again.

I would carve again. I would bring wood to life. I would make it breathe. I would infuse it with spirit because life had taught me how to do that for myself and for the people I shared my life with. My friends.

When I went and told the story of my wanderings to Amelia, she told me one back. She told me of the Ojibway people and the ceremony they went through to become man and wife.

"They go and sit with the Old Ones," she told me. "They go and sit and listen to the wise old men and women tell them about life and how we gotta live it.

"They do that because the Old Ones have seen it all. They know what these people are going to encounter on their path together. So the young ones sit and listen and get told some very important things. They get told about the need for prudence, acceptance, and honesty. But above all, they get told about the need for loyalty and for kindness. Without them two things there can be no togetherness, loyalty and kindness. It takes a lifetime to really get to know what those two things mean, but it's the willingness to keep on learning to find that out that makes a coming together so sacred.

"The people call that relationship *weedjee-wahgun*. It means companion, fellow traveller. Being a good companion means being willing to always learn more about loyalty and kindness. Your path with Sylvan taught you lots, and if you think about it long enough you'll know what you need to do to learn from it all."

Weedjee-wahgun. A trail blazed in the darkness. Hewn from the stark forest by the axe of principle and marking the pathway to a lifetime of learning. It taught me lots. And as I walked, I considered that ancient word and its meaning. *Weedjee-wahgun*. In those purely tribal times it stood for the relationship between a man and a woman, but as I walked and I looked at the homes around my own, homes guided and made possible by that same set of principles, I understood it to mean any coming together. Any joining of spirit.

For the first time, I didn't hear the concrete call to me that night. Felt no need to reach down and place my palm on its grained surface, to consider its winding progression downward to a place I had lived for far too long. Instead, I felt a need to enter the house I called a home. Felt the need to rest and rise refreshed, take a piece of wood into my hands and open myself to the immense possibility of Creation. Felt the need to honour love with an act of love itself. *Weedjee-wahgun.*

I was no longer a millionaire, but I didn't need to be. I had reached the Mountains of the Moon and found them beautiful.

Those Indians had a great understanding of the universe, didn't they?

They still do.

Yes. They do. I sat with a teacher for a while on my travels.

Really. And how did you find that experience?

Like talking to an old friend. Like talking to you. It felt like she knew everything about me even though I hadn't offered any details. It was like she saw into me and knew exactly what I needed to hear to fill me up.

Yes. It's not nearly as magical and mystical as people like to think. It's just about filling up, like you say. Human things. Spirit things.

I liked the pipe. Smoking the pipe made me feel gigantic. Like all the pieces of me had finally come together at one place and at one time. There's certainly some magic in that ceremony.

Yes. It's where weedjee-wahgun *teachings came from. The joining. The becoming. Two parts in harmony, balance, equality, needing each other, craving each other, calling out to each other across time and space for union. When it happens, when they're joined in that ceremony, the bowl and the stem,*

it's weedjee-wahgun, *two parts creating wholeness.*
And the smoke?
The smoke is the words we say, the thoughts we think, the feelings we project making their way to the ancestors, up and up and away, back to the spirit where the Old Ones can consider them and guide us.
Spirit guides.
Yes.
So we're never alone.
Never.
Good thing to know.
Yes. It's a good thing to know.

BOOK FOUR home

Double Dick

TWO TINY FEET stuck out of a five-gallon lard pail. That's what I see. That's what I see in my dream. Two tiny feet stuck out of a five-gallon lard pail. My nephew. Earl. Three months old. Drowned. Drowned in my vomit. Drowned in my puke. Drowned in the pail I puked into on accounta I was sick from all the drinkin' me 'n Tom Bruce was doin' back then. I can see it all like it was a movie.

I wake up sick. Sick an' shakin' an' tremblin' an' I know there's a seizure comin' on accounta I got that nowhere feelin' in my head that says the big black is gonna fall over me again. Terror. That's what it is. Terror. An' the only thing that makes that big black dog of terror run away is another drink. A big drink. A real big drink. I'm so scared I jump up off that couch an' I don't feel the bump. The bump that's little Earl asleep beside me. Asleep beside me on accounta my brother an' his girl is gone to a country dance down the way an' told me to look after him. I don't feel the bump on accounta I'm so scared the big black's comin' that I run to the kitchen where I know there's a bottle under the sink. Then I throw it down me. Throw it. There's twitchin' going on in my muscles an' nerves an' I just know that if I don't get it into me I'm gone. Down into the hole. I feel the burn in my gut an' I close my eyes an' breathe real hard. Deep. Holdin' it in. Deep again. Then I feel the wash of warm at the sides of my head an' I know I'm not gonna fall over, I'm not gonna lay on the floor all buckin' an' sawin' away. Doing the chicken. That's what Tom Bruce called it. Doing the chicken like when its head's chopped off. I breathe. After a few minutes of leaning on the counter I feel like I can move again. My muscles is still weak an' shaky but I know I'm gonna make it.

I walk back through the door. The door that's a curtain of beads on accounta my brother's girl likes all that kinda stuff. I push the curtain of beads apart. The light from the TV is flickerin' all grey an' white. Snow. There ain't nothin' on that channel an' it's snow. Movin' through that flickering light is like movin' in slow motion an' that's the really scary part. It's all slow motion. I move around the end of the couch an' I got the bottle in my hand. I step around an' I see somethin' in the shadow of the coffee table. It's darker there an' the flashin' light don't help so I gotta lean in toward it. I gotta squint to see. My eyes adjust to the light. The shadows melt an' I see Earl's tiny feet stuck up outta that lard pail. Not movin'.

I wanna scream. But I gotta do somethin' so I pull him out by the ankles. He's so small. Light in my hands like a chicken. The top of him's all covered in my muck. In the snowy flickerin' light I try to wipe it off his face but it's slimy an' slippery an' all I do is mess it up more. I'm shakin' again but it's a different kinda terror now. So I put him on his back on the couch an' I put my mouth to his an' start tryin' to breathe life into him. Fill his air with lungs to make 'em work again. But all I get is a mouthful of puke. Horrible, stinkin', three-days-of-drinking kind of puke. It makes me puke again. I heave it all over the coffee table an' I see the spray in the dream flowin' out across the room, a slow motion cloud of puke. I puke again an' again an' I can't bring myself to put my mouth to his. I can't. So I try to rake it out of him with my fingers but I'm shakin' way too much now an' all I do is wipe it around his tongue, his teeth, his lips. I'm groanin'. Groanin' from somewhere real deep. Somewhere I ain't never groaned from before. It sounds real old an' it scares me. I got him in my hands an' I turn him over and try an' slap his back hard enough to make him cough but it ain't workin'. This is all in that snowy, flickerin', slow-motion light, an' time feels like rubber, every second stretched way, way long an' outta shape. I'm quiverin' like a crazy man an' I put him down an' reach for the bottle. Some of it spills on the way to my mouth an' I get all frantic an' gulp on it real hard an' real deep. Earl's not movin'. He's not movin'. All covered in my puke now an' not movin' at all.

I stand up an' look at him an' there's a buzzin' in my head from the booze an' from knowin' that I killed him. I turn my head one way, then the other, not knowing what to do. Desperate. Desperate an' crazy to run. An' then I feel it. It starts way down by the bottom of my spine but further inside like in the middle of me. A howl. A fuckin' howl, all ragged an' sore an' old. Old. It comes out of me an' all I can do is stand there with my head pointed upward at the ceiling, my eyes closed, the bottle clutched in my hand, an' Earl layin' there all dead. An' I howl.

That's when I wake up, most times. I wake up with my neck stretched back an' if it's dark or if the TV's flickerin' I don't know where I am. Not right away. So I gotta slam back some juice to get me right before I can pull it back together. Before I can feel like I can make it another second without goin' crazy. That's why I don't sleep nights. That's why I gotta wait till there's some kinda light of mornin' or even sometimes just mornin' sounds like when Timber used to head out on his walks. Then I'd know. Then I'd know that dreamtime wasn't gonna send me to that room again. Then I'd sleep. But now that Timber don't walk no more, I go without sleepin' at all sometimes. I just sit in my room on Indian Road an' drink. Drink until I feel myself numb enough to move around. Drink until there's enough pressure in my head to keep the dreams away or even keep thinkin' about the dream.

Two tiny feet stuck out of a five-gallon lard pail. It's what haunts me. It's what won't go away no matter what.

One For The Dead

"HE'S NOT SLEEPING," I said to Margo and Granite.

"Ever?" she asked.

"Maybe a few hours every night, but that's all."

"Have you checked on him?" Granite asked.

"No need. My room's right next to his and I hear him rattling around. Or when I get up to use the bathroom I see the blue light of the TV under his door. He keeps himself awake."

"Keeps himself awake? You mean it's not insomnia? He forces himself to stay awake?" Margo asked.

"I think so."

"Why?"

"I don't know. Nights have always been our territory. When we were on the street we went our separate ways each night because night was the only time we got away, the only time we had to ourselves, really. So we never intruded."

"We need to intrude now," Granite said. "If he's not sleeping, he's not very healthy."

"He drinks all night, too," I said. "He sneaks bottles in."

"Why would he do that? No one ever said anything at all to any of them about their habits. Even after the episode at the hospital, no one said a thing about his drinking again. He knows we know he drinks. Why sneak in bottles?" Granite said.

"He doesn't want to worry us," Margo said. "Dick is so genuine. Everything he feels comes out on his face or in the questions he asks about things. But there are obviously some things he doesn't want to face. He uses drink so he doesn't have to feel them. So he isn't reminded that they're there."

"You sound very familiar with that sort of thing," Granite said.

"I had an uncle like that. He died. A heart attack during an alcoholic seizure."

"Jesus."

"We need to talk to him about it. If he's drinking all the time—and I smell it on him whenever I hug him—he's putting himself at risk. The alcohol poisoning that put him in the coma was a sign of trouble."

"Yes," Granite said. "He knows he can drink enough fast enough to kill himself now."

"It's not the booze that worries me," I said. "It's other things. He won't spend money on himself. I even have to talk him into buying clothes."

"You do?" Margo asked.

"Yes. He won't get himself anything."

"Just movies, apparently," Granite said. "Have you seen his shelves? There're hundreds of titles there, and the majority he hasn't even watched. He just squirrels them away."

"That's because movies are like a drink," Margo said. "They allow him to get away. Escape. Not think."

"A stash," I said.

"Pardon me, Amelia?" Granite asked.

"A stash," I said. "When you get lucky on the street and you can afford more than the jug you're working on, you get a stash bottle. You stash it somewhere you can get to it quick when you need it. He had a lot of stash bottles in his digs. Half a jug here, a quarter jug there, a full one sometimes. Movies are his stash bottles."

"He does love the movies," Granite said. "It's like they wake up the little boy in him."

"The little boy who drinks?" Margo asked.

We looked at each other solemnly.

"Someone has to talk to him," Granite said.

"Who?" Margo asked. "He trusts you the most, Amelia."

"No. He wouldn't think about worrying me with anything. Granite?"

"Me? No. It has to be one of the others."

"Timber, then," Margo said.

"No," I said. "He's always treated Timber more gently than any of us. He wouldn't want to cause him any worry either."

"Digger," Granite said.

"Yes. I think so. He's always looked to Digger for a way through things. He admired him on the street. He listened to him."

"Who's going to talk to Digger?" Granite asked.

Margo and I looked at him and he nodded his head slowly.

Digger

"WHAT THE FUCK are you talking about?" I go, wiping the foam from my mouth with the back of a hand. We're sitting at the Palace. Me 'n Rock.

"Amelia's worried about him," Rock goes. "Me too, when I think about it."

"So you figure he's using the flicks like a fix? That he's staying up all friggin' night, not sleeping, sucking up the sauce and passing out when it's daylight?"

"We think so, yes."

"Fuck. That's normal where we been."

"You're not there now."

"Well, no shit, Sherlock. But what I'm saying is, it comes with the territory. It's a rounder being a friggin' rounder and just because he's living in a Square John situation don't mean he stopped being a rounder."

"I think we know that, Digger, and none of us have said anything to any of you about how you have to be. We just let you be and do what you choose. But this is different."

"How?"

"It's not safe for him."

"Well, pardon me all to fuck. But how are you to know what's safe and what's not? Maybe this is what he needs to do. Maybe fucking with it's the unsafe thing."

"Maybe. But we want to offer him a choice."

"A choice of what?"

"Of dealing with it another way, I suppose."

"Of dealing with what another way?"

"We don't know."

"Egg-fucking-zactly."

Rock grins at me. "Egg-fucking-zactly, what?" he goes.

I suck back a little of my draft. We been together a long time now and I wonder why it takes him so long to catch on sometimes.

"You don't know because he ain't friggin' talking. And the reason he ain't talking is because it's nobody's fucking business. What he's got in his head is what he's got in his head and until he wants to let that go we don't got a say in how he deals with it."

"Not even if it's harmful?"

"You don't know that. Look at Timber. Until he got ready to let the cat out of the bag, none of us knew what he was carrying around. That was a pretty friggin' big weight too, but we didn't know nothing until he copped out."

"Yes. But we had to go find him. If we hadn't, we don't know what he might have done."

"Okay, maybe that's right. But we found him on accounta he copped out first. I'm saying, minding your business means minding your business, and Dick ain't ready to come up with the deal yet."

"He might if you talk to him."

"And say what?"

"That we're worried about him."

I finish off my draft and wave for another. "*We?* Have I ever looked like the kind of guy who lost a lot of sleep over small-time shit like this?"

"Small-time?"

"Yeah. Small-fucking-time. How's that line go? You can take the boy outta the country but you can't take the country outta the boy? Well, same applies to rounders. It's how we deal with shit."

"But maybe it's wrong."

I suck up a little of the new drink Ray drops and look at Rock. Hard.

"Wrong? Me 'n the boys been handling our shit the rounder way for a long friggin' time there, Rock, and we're still kicking. We're still here. Sure, maybe it's not the clean, scientific, Square John way, but it's our way and it works for us. Having a mittful of money don't change that. It don't change us. If I had something that was gnawing at my guts these days, I'd be duking it out my way too. Dick's a rounder. He thinks like a rounder. He deals with shit like a rounder, and all the friggin' money in the world won't change that. Not now, not ever.

"You all think it's wrong. You all think him having a drink or stewing over whatever the fuck he's stewing over is bad, horrible, dangerous. Well, all I know is, forcing somebody to haul out into the daylight what ain't ready for the daylight is a lot more fucking dangerous than leaving it be. Talk to him? Yeah, I'll talk to him. I'll walk up and give him a buddy-buddy shot on the shoulder and tell him it's all good. It's all fucking good. Let him know I'm a winger. That I'm there. I'll always be there. Even though he might not be perfect, even though he ain't sailing a smooth fucking sea, I'm fucking there. That's what I'll tell him and if everyone else would just do the same friggin' thing maybe he'd relax a little. Maybe he'd sleep at night. Maybe he'd ease up on the hooch a little."

We look at each other across the table. Sometimes money can't buy shrinkage. Can't bring worlds any closer than they're meant to come. Rock just stares at me and nods his head. Oceans away.

Can I tell you what the elder told me?

Certainly. I'd like to hear that.

She said Creation gives us three ways to get to the truth of things.

Yes.

She said the first tool we're given is thought. We're able, unlike all other animals, to create thought, an idea, about what it is we're confronting. Then, we're given feeling. Emotion. We get a sense of how something affects us and we feel it. And last, we're given words in order to bring it to life, to express it, to give it to the air.

I follow that. It sounds right.

The shame of it is, we somehow have become convinced that thinking is the most powerful tool, followed closely by words.

I agree.

But the thing is, it's emotion, feeling, that's the most powerful tool in finding the truth of things. It's also the most difficult to employ. You actually have to allow yourself to feel the experience, then explore it with thought, and then express it in words to capture it, own it, learn from it.

You've given it some thought.

Ha ha. That's funny. Did you ever wonder how the story might have gone if we'd have known that then?

Sometimes. But the story is the story, isn't it?

Yes. Yes it is.

More than words can say.

I think you're getting it.

Ha ha. That's funny.

Timber

I FIND HIM sitting on the porch wrapped up in a blanket even though it's a mild afternoon. He's staring at the floor, making small motions in Amelia's rocker, just enough to move it slightly. He doesn't hear me. I'm standing at the living room window looking out, resting my hands from a few hours of whittling and shaping a piece I started. He just sits there looking at the floor, rocking slowly. Alone. Amelia and Margo have gone on a shopping jaunt somewhere, Digger and Granite have disappeared, and I've been in my room for a few hours, so I had no idea of how long he'd been there. I reach into my back pocket and pull out the little notebook I've taken to carrying around with me since I started carving again. I scratch down the outlines of things that catch my eye. Scratch them down to remind myself of how they held the space around them, how they breathed. I look at him and start to trace an outline on the paper. He's like a cloud. The loose wrap of the blanket hides all the angles of his body and it drapes down to the floor, concealing everything but his feet. Those big flat feet. His shoes are worn, deeply sidewalk cut at the back outside edges of the heels, so that they have a skewed placement on the floor. A severe downward slant. Old shoes that look as though they carried the tales and stories of a thousand miles in their scuff and smudge. Old shoes. The ankles that stick out of those shoes are bony, skinny, brittle-looking. The blanket distorts the shape of his legs and trunk and it's only at the upper torso that his body begins to show itself again. A sharp jut at the elbow, a small mountain range of knuckles, and the roll of forearm toward the other side of his chest, his other wrist hidden by the angle. His arms are thin. The blanket sags above the elbow, hung from the poke of his shoulder, the slender blade of bone draping the blanket sharply along its length. And then the neck. Sticking out of the trimmed edge of fabric, it's an old neck, criss-crossed by a ragged tartan of wrinkles on loose, dry skin so that it resembles more a turtle's neck than a man's. It folds beneath the chin that's angled downward toward his chest, a narrow chin, a button of bone that holds the tight angular lines of his face closed. The face. The face that stares at the floor looks as though gravity worked hardest on it, like that magic force gathered itself at that one point on earth, pulling it all downward, the skin sagging, slumped and tired, etched with the crease and cut of wrinkles that aren't so much ancient as earned, culled from a lifetime of stitching days, hours, minutes together with the slender thread of worry, fear perhaps. His nose hooks slightly at the top of the bridge, a small flat plateau between the eyes marking its descent. The eyebrows are bushy. They seem to hold the cliff of skin that is his forehead in place before it can landslide down his face, pushed by the curled black weight of hair that's speckled with a flurry of grey. But it's the eyes that have all the power. The eyes. They bulge somewhat in their sockets, and from the angle I'm standing at, the one I can see perfectly in profile looks full, like a bladder, a filled wet sack of life. Staring at the floor they droop, hanging like tears on the skirt of bone that's the upper edge of his cheekbones, two small fists under the skin. Unblinking. Unmoving. His eyes hold all of him. They stare at the floor with an intensity a saint might have, a martyr perhaps, or a prisoner who can only see freedom in the patterns in the concrete of his cell. They're sad, wistful, lonely, scared, and weary all at the same time, and they pull you, even in profile, to the hint of history, the vague tease of experience and circumstance that shaped this face, this great, sad face hung in solitude over all the ragged miles. I move the nub of pencil slowly as though I could coax the feel of this moment into the paper, not wanting to risk forgetting the texture of the man. He doesn't move in all that time, not even a blink, and as I fold my notebook and step away from the window to leave him in his shadowed glory, I wonder why he wears old shoes, why he sits alone on a perfect afternoon, why the floor is all the vista he requires, and why this world of money can't buy him more than solitary moments in a rocking chair huddled in upon himself like a great sad Buddha. I think about all of this as I walk up the stairs to my room and start to shape the man in the chair.

Granite

"So you're going to tell me that a story walked up and introduced itself, aren't you?" Mac asked.

I grinned. He always came right to the point. When he walked into the Palms to join Margo and me for supper, he moved right past the formalities and started in on the point of the meeting while easing into his chair.

"Hi, Mac. Good to see you too," I said.

"Yeah, yeah, yeah," he said with small waves of a hand. "That's all well and nice, Gran, but when you don't call an old friend for months at a time and then suddenly ask for a meeting, you don't get banter. But before we get to it, there's one thing I want to know."

"What's that?"

"Who's the squeeze?" he asked with a grin.

I introduced him to Margo and she got him back to his charming self in seconds. I knew I wasn't forgiven for my absence; it had just become less important. They chatted briefly and I watched him, amazed at how time has no effect on some people, at how it passes without a wake for some and nothing is left behind.

"So fill me in," he said after the waiter left to get our drinks. "I know you were a big part of the street people winning that lottery, and I got some scuttlebutt from the coast about you getting an exclusive on the update, and I have to say I found that intriguing. But what do you have? What do you want to do with it? And most importantly, do I get it?"

The intuitive sense of the journalist. Mac Maude had always had it and he knew our meeting was about a story, not some small reconnection between friends, not some jovial evening spent recounting memories and tall tales, but about a story, my story, the one that had walked up and introduced itself just like he said it would a few short years ago.

"You get it all right," I began. "I just don't know exactly what it is I have. I mean, I've been there for all of it. I watched it all happen. But we don't have denouement. We have no closure. We have no ending."

"Do you need one?" he asked.

"Don't I?"

"I don't know. Sometimes you don't. Sometimes stories are better when left hanging in the wind. The flapping is what makes them memorable. Why don't you tell me what you have? We'll eat. I'll listen. We'll talk."

So while we ordered and ate, I talked about the journey I'd been on with the ragged people who'd become my friends. Margo held my hand while I talked, squeezing it now and then when I got emotional. Mac sat and listened, scribbling notes to himself, and it felt good to sit in a story with an editor again, to see details punctuated by a raised eyebrow, a nod, a squint of comprehension, a stare. When I finished, we sat in silence, sipping at our drinks.

"Wow," he said finally. "That's a ripping good yarn you've got there, Gran."

"Yes," I said. "But what to do with it?"

"Well, you definitely have to write it. But I can't use it."

"Why the hell not? You just said it's a ripping good yarn."

"Yes, I did. And it is. But it's not for me. Not for the paper."

"Why not?"

"Because you have too much story. We can't contain all that and do it any justice. I mean, sure, you could come back on board and do a serial piece, tell it in segments, but even that's doing an injustice to the story. What you have is a book."

"A book? I don't know how to write a book. I'm an eight-hundred-word guy, tops. Maybe twice that for a feature, but I'm not a book writer."

"Well, pardon me, Gran, but you aren't any kind of writer if you're not writing, and you haven't been for years now."

"Granted. But a book?"

"It's a great idea," Margo said. "I agree with Mac. It's too big for a paper, and you tell it so well."

"It tells itself, really," Mac said.

"Except for the ending," I said.

"No biggie. You wait for it. Write what you have. It's journalism, Gran. You do that better than most people. It's in your blood. You're a natural. Write what you have and chances are, while you're doing that, the ending will present itself."

"It's true," Margo said. "Some stories tell themselves like Mac said. I think you should just write it."

"I don't know if I can. It's been a while. I may even have forgotten how to type."

"Then go longhand," Mac said. "This story is not going to go away, Gran. It chose you. Now, that might sound all metaphysical but I mean it. You spend enough time thinking about it and you'll see what I mean. Just from the elements you gave me I can see how it makes you the only one who could really tell this story."

"How so?"

"Because you're just as homeless as they were," he said.

One For The Dead

DANCES WITH WOLVES. We walked to see that movie, all seven of us, strolling through the late afternoon sunshine in a tangled bunch, talking, giggling like kids and eager for the magic of the movies. Dick didn't say much. He just grinned his grin and poked along like the shy kid in the bunch, the one forever at the edges, and I gave his hand a little squeeze of comfort. He smiled. We'd chosen this movie because the preview we'd seen the last time we were at the movies had been stark and eerie: darkened humps of buffalo charging through the mist and darkness. For me, it had been like water after a long walk. For me, it had been like seeing my own story told on the screen. I had seen the ghosts of a way of life charging across the screen and something in me had connected right away to the sweep of drama that small bit of film contained. I was eager for this one.

I sat between Margo and Dick. She nestled closer to Granite on her right and smiled a small-girl smile at me. Dick sat unmoving, slack-jawed, staring at the screen as usual, and when the movie started he didn't move a muscle. For the three hours it ran, I didn't see him move more than to sneak a drink. It was glorious. This was a movie that shone from start to finish. I saw the People as they had once lived: free, unencumbered, tribal. I saw the land as it had once been: open, free, pure. I saw a vision of myself that I had never seen before: a tribal me, a tribal woman, strong, resilient, proud, and in harmony with her world. It made me cry. I thought of all the ones who had never got a chance to see a magic like this, all the ones who had gone before who had never been introduced to the world in this way; the departed ones, my family, my Ben, friends, native people for whom the world was never the free and open place it was on the screen that night, whose identities were never so focused, so sharp, their history rolled out like the great carpet of the plains. I cried. When the credits rolled at the end and the hint of the death of that way of life was left hanging in the stillness, I saw shadowed ones in the aisles, as unwilling to leave as I was. Moved beyond life itself.

We walked to a small café in silence. Everyone, even Digger, was touched by that film. The waitress did her job quickly and moved away to let us chat, and for the longest time none of us had anything to say.

"I'm in love again," Margo said finally. "I'm in love with the movies."

"Yes," James said. "I feel somewhat swept off my feet too."

"Compelling," Granite said. "A compelling way to tell that story."

"I don't know about compelling," Digger said. "But it rocked, that's for sure."

"Touching," Timber said. "It reached out and touched you."

"Yes," I said. "I feel wrapped in buckskin right now. Old buckskin. It let me see how I might have lived a few hundred years ago."

"I was ashamed," Margo said.

"Ashamed? Of what?" James asked.

"Of history," she said. "Of what happened here. Of what people allowed to happen here. How we let a people die right in front of us. How we let a way of being disappear."

"Progress," Granite said. "The great locomotive of civilization moving forward at all costs. I felt mournful for the land. It looked so wild, so free, so unspoiled."

"I felt sorry for the animals," Dick said, suddenly.

"What's that, pal?" Digger asked.

"The animals. Those men was mean to the animals."

"Yes, they were," I said. "They didn't know how to respect them."

"They didn't know that the animals was always here to help us," he said.

"No, they didn't," I said. "Animals are our teachers."

"Animal People," Dick said.

"What?" Digger asked. "Animal People?"

"Yeah," Dick replied, sneaking a drink from the mickey he held under the table. "Before there was people like us there was just the animals an' they was like people. They could talk to each other an' stuff."

"They could, huh? Is that from one of your movies?"

"No. It's just somethin' I know."

"How do you know that, Dick? That's a very old teaching in the Indian way," I said. "I don't remember telling you about that."

"You didn't," he said, sneaking another drink.

"Then how do you know?" I asked.

"On accounta I'm an Indian too," he said. "I'm an Indian too."

Double Dick

We was poor. We was poor like all the rest around there. They called us sawmill savages. The sawmill was the only place anyone could get a job an' people hung around waitin' for the chance to get in. My dad was one of the ones what hung around waitin'. But he wasn't so good at it like the rest of them on accounta he always had to have somethin' goin' on. Kinda like Digger. So he made up a still in the woods behind our shack. The brew that come out of there was the best anyone had ever had an' people liked my dad's recipe so much they protected him from the cops an' stuff. The sawmill guys came around all the time for jugs. My first drink was dad's moose milk. That's what he called it. Moose milk on accounta he brewed it so it come out kinda foggy lookin' in the glass. White, kinda, a watery lookin' white. Moose milk.

Anyhow, we hadta leave the reserve on accounta there was no work an' there was a big buncha us that set up shacks on land no one wanted near the sawmill. Swampy kinda land. Or land where there was a lotta rocks. No one said nothin' as long as we Indians behaved ourselves, an' when the moose milk got known around no one said nothin' to any of us no more. We didn't go to school on accounta that was somethin' the reserve took care of an' only the white kids got to go for schoolin' around that sawmill town. Me, I worked with my dad. When I was small, I went with him to the still all the time an' he told me stories. Stories about the Animal People. Stories about how we got to be the kinda people we was. My dad wasn't like a real Indian. He wasn't even half, he said. But he looked like it. Me, I don't, but Dad did. Anyhow, he knew all them stories an' he told them to me while I was buildin' a fire or juggin' the brew. That's when I got my first drink. I think I was six, seven maybe, an' Dad told me to test the batch. I didn't know what I was doin' but I took a big belt of that moose milk anyhow. It burned all the way down but when it got there it was real nice. I felt all warm an' I was standing in the snow but I felt all warm anyhow. I liked it. After that, Dad let me drink as much as I wanted on accounta I didn't go all stupid in the head like some other kids.

I was the only one Dad trusted that much. I don't know how come, but it was just me he took with him an' when I got a friend he let me take him too. Tom Bruce. That was my friend's name. Tom Bruce. Me 'n Tom got to haul the sled around when it was winter, an' the wagon around when it wasn't. That was how the moose milk got around. Me 'n Tom Bruce went wherever Dad told us with that wagon. We got a free jug now an' then, too, an' we'd sit up in the woods an' make a fire and drink it. Just me 'n Tom on accounta we didn't wanna have to let other kids in on our deal. We was drinkin' regular by the time we was nine an' when the men would get together to play cards or just visit, we was the only ones allowed to be around on accounta they knew us better. We was like little men. If we got drunk an' started to fall around they'd just laugh like they laughed at the other men who got all fucked up. No one said nothin'.

But we didn't live like in the movie. I guess we wasn't that kind of Indian. We lived on moose milk. There was some who told stories an' stuff. Others went to hunt an' got meat. But it wasn't like them Indians in the movie. We was moose milk Indians. That's all. Moose milk Indians.

Digger

I WATCH TIMBER working on this big piece of wood in the back of my store. It's huge. Like a log that he stands on its end and starts to shaping with all kinds of strange-looking blades. Seems like he's cutting off way too much if he wants to make anything come out of it, but what do I know. To me, it looks like he's lost it. He moves around that wood like a crazy person, whittling, slicing, chopping for a couple of fucking hours until finally he sets the tools down, fires up a smoke, swallows a little beer, looks at the wood and the slivers and chunks laying all over the tarp he's thrown down, smiles at me and goes, "So what do you think?"

Jesus. I look at that log and see a whole bunch of scrapes and cuts. Even when I scrunch my eyes and walk around the friggin' thing I don't see nothing. "What am I supposed to be looking at?" I go.

He smiles and reaches into his pocket. "Sorry," he goes. "I forget that no one knows where it's all going when I start. Must look like a mess, huh?"

"It looks like a pissed-off beaver, that's what it looks like."

"It's supposed to look like this when it's done," he goes, and hands me a small piece of wood that fits in my palm.

I look at it. It don't weigh nothing but it sure does say a whole lot. It's a man. A man sitting in a chair all huddled up in a blanket, looking down like he's studying something near his feet.

"Fuck me," I go. "It's D."

"Yeah," he goes. "I saw him on the porch a couple days ago and he looked like this. I wanted to make it for him."

"This little guy?"

"No. A big one."

"You're gonna make one outta this huge fucking log?"

"Yeah. The small one's the model. If I work small and get it right it's easier to go bigger. It gets my hands ready. Helps them remember."

"Your hands remember?"

"Yeah. You know the feeling, if you think about it."

"I do?"

"Yeah. If you had to put a wheel up right now, this afternoon, even after all this time, your hands would remember what to do even before your head did. Don't you think?"

"I guess. Never thought about it. But you know, Timber, all them friggin' wheels is hydraulic now. Don't matter a fuck if my hands remember or not. They don't need an old-time ground-mounted wheelman no more."

"Still."

"Yeah. You're right. Why is that, I wonder?"

"Because you're an artist."

"I am?"

"Yes. You said so yourself. The best fucking wheelman in the world. It takes an artist to get to that point."

"Yeah, you know, I am. Or I was. You figure that's how I know how to fix up all the shit I find?"

"Yes. You have an artist's hands. They can bring something to life."

"I can't do nothing like this, though," I go, waving the little carving at him. "This is scary. It's so small but you can see him. It's like, whattaya call it? Voodoo."

"Effigy," he goes.

"Hey, no need to be fucking rude."

He grins at me and gives me a shot on the arm. "An effigy. It's a small image of somebody. The old tribal peoples used to make them, some in voodoo like you say. But this is a different kind of magic."

"What kind is that?"

"Representational. Playing it for real."

"How come?" I go, firing up a smoke and staring at the log.

"I don't know the theory. But I do know that when I carve something from life, life goes into it. It comes out like it could breathe. Real. Like it's carrying the spirit of the person in it."

"That is friggin' voodoo."

"In a way. But this is like an honouring. Respect. Giving him dignity. I'm honouring the spirit of our pal."

"He could use it right now."

Timber looks at me and takes a drink. "Yes. I feel like he wants to say a whole lot more but he doesn't know how."

"I kinda know that feeling."

"Me too."

"You know, I heard some pretty incredible shit in my time but I never heard nothing like that. Friggin' kid. He was just a friggin' little kid and his dad had him hauling fucking moonshine around. Pretty harsh friggin' times."

"Pretty harsh."

"That's why you got him like this? So you can see the shit he went through on his body, in his face?"

"Yes. I suppose. Only I did the small one before we went to *Dances with Wolves* and before he told us about being a kid. I only saw him in a private moment when he was lost in it, I guess. I never imagined what the story was like."

"Rock figures there's more."

"What do you mean?"

"I mean, Rock and the old lady and Margo been talking and they figure D's got a whole lot more that he ain't telling. Rock wanted me to talk to him. Try 'n get him to spill the beans."

"And?"

"And nothing. You know the fucking drill. We don't spill. Not ever. Unless we really want to."

"Rounder's code."

"Fucking right."

"Maybe we're not rounders anymore, Digger. Maybe this money changed all that. I mean, if we look around, we're not exactly living a rounder kind of life anymore. You own a store. We own a house. We're not exactly street."

"That's kinda what Rock said and I got pissed. Maybe I'm pissed now too. I don't know. All I know is that there's stuff I gotta hang on to from the life, you know. The friggin' life taught me how to survive. Taught me how to not give a fuck about the irritating stuff that drives everyone batshit. Taught me how to tough through anything. I don't wanna forget that. Ever."

"I guess we don't have to. But maybe there's things we can do different without exactly selling out."

"Like what?"

"I don't know. Like talking to each other. Like this. Like staying on each other's wing. Wingers. Just like the old days but in a different way. Maybe that's what we're supposed to learn how to do now. Be the same solid rounder kind of guys but in a different way now."

"You figure?"

"Guess."

"Still don't gotta spill the fucking beans unless we want to. That'll never fucking change."

"Maybe we're supposed to help him want to."

"How the fuck do we do that?"

"I don't know. I want to figure it out, though."

"Me too. You know he don't sleep nights?"

"No."

"The old lady says he watches friggin' movies all night. Stays up all night, watches flicks, and drinks."

"He's never pissed up. Not bad, anyway."

"Maybe he gets to the line and stays there. He's always got a mickey on him."

"That's not new. Shit, I carry sometimes myself still."

"Yeah, but you 'n me, we got somewhere else now. I figure Dick hasn't moved. He's still where he was when we scored the loot. That's what you seen when you seen him on the porch."

"The movies," he goes.

"What?"

"The movies. In the beginning we went to the movies. All of us. Together. To get out of the cold. Nowadays we don't go as much and Dick, well, he's got his collection in his room and he watches all by himself. I think we need to get back to where it all started again."

"How do we do that exactly?"

"Well, I guess if it means staying up all night and watching movies with him, that's what we'll have to do."

"Do you think he'll go for that?"

"It's Double Dick Dumont we're talking about. No matter how he might be acting or what kind of stuff he has going on inside, he's still Double Dick. Still our winger. Still one of us. He'll be tickled pink to have us sit and watch movies together."

"You're right. We used to go to a flick every day. Be nice to get back to that."

"Yeah," he goes. "The four of us."

"Five."

"Well, six, really."

"Seven if you count Merton."

"Seven if you count Merton."

"Do we count Merton?"

"Fuck yeah," he goes, and we head out for the truck and the drive back home.

One For The Dead

THERE'S FOUR DIRECTIONS in the Great Wheel of Life. The Medicine Wheel. Each has things that make it special, give teachings to the People. The whole point of being is to learn to move through all those directions and pick up the teachings on the way. That's what Grandma One Sky taught me and what I recall thinking about Dick and how our lives have changed so much so fast. Sometimes life gets so busy we forget what we're really supposed to be doing, and I guess that's what happened to us. We're supposed to consider where we've been. The way we came together was like the spirit of the Medicine Wheel. See, there's the east first. The east is where the light comes from and the teaching there is how to be a physical person. That's Digger. He's always been the tough one. Then, the south is where growing takes place and the teaching is how to be an emotional person. That's Dick. He's always the one who feels things the most. The west's teaching is thinking, reflecting, and that's Timber. He was always the one who needed to know, to understand. The north teaches spirituality, because the journey around the great Wheel of Life brings you to that if you look back at where you've been. That's me, I guess, since the shadowed ones let me see them. So we came together for a reason. To be strong together. To be whole. To be a circle. Thinking about it, I could see that the only way to help Dick through this difficulty was to come together again like we did in the beginning. Dick didn't need us poking around his insides. He didn't need us asking questions that required tough answers he wasn't ready to give. He didn't need us worrying about how he was. He needed us to be a circle again. He needed us to be the tiny band of wanderers that we were. Funny, even when you forget, the Wheel is always working in your life. Sitting there in my rocker, alone, while Dick slept upstairs and the other two boys were at work in Digger's store, I was grateful for that invisible energy that moves us. The Wheel, turning and turning, spinning on forever, relentlessly, moving us inch by inch sometimes, always in the direction of home, in the direction we all want to go, regardless.

Timber and Digger pulled up in front of the house in Digger's truck, and as I watched them climb out and walk toward the veranda steps I saw how strong they'd become, how purposefully they walked, and how determined their faces were. I saw how far they'd travelled around the Wheel. North. They stood in the north now. Together. They stood together in the place of spirituality—and therefore, wisdom.

"We know what we gotta do for Dick," Digger said as they entered the room.

"I know you do," I said. "I know you do."

Timber

IT WAS LIKE A CARNIVAL. Every day for a week we went to the movies again, and it was like a carnival. We sat in the kitchen with the newspaper spread across the table and we talked about what we wanted to see that day, just like we used to do at the mission. There were the usual good-natured debates and arguments, generally started by Digger, who although determined to see Dick through whatever torment he was going through, was still gruffly rebellious about anything soft or romantic. Dick responded like he always had: excited, antsy as a kid. He seemed happy to have us all back in the swing of things and he didn't feel as heavy as he had. He still sat all slack-jawed at the movies like he had the very first time, only the rise of a hand with popcorn or a mickey showing he was breathing at all. We saw *Pretty Woman*, *Reversal of Fortune*, *Total Recall*, *Cadillac Man*, *Bird on a Wire*, *The Hunt for Red October*, and *Hamlet* all in a glorious splash of sound and light and colour. It was amazing. Amazing as a carnival for the senses, and even if we didn't see any films that moved us spectacularly, we saw ones that told us again about the particular grace of the movies: to lift you up and away. We were happy.

I carved every morning, and as the man in the chair took shape and form and substance beneath my hands, I saw little of that moment in Dick those days. Little. But now and again, you could see it rise in him. See it in the way his shoulders slumped or in the woebegone way he looked at you. We didn't worry, though. Digger and I took turns sitting up with him. We'd turn the volume down low in his room and watch whatever he wanted to watch, and when he nodded off now and again I made sure to make no sudden moves, no sounds that would disturb the haven of sleep he'd wandered into. When he awoke he would see me in my chair and grin like a kid caught sneaking cookies, and turn to the film again. I saw no ghosts in that room on those nights, and I knew that he was glad for the company. When morning came, I'd cover him with a blanket and leave him snoring gently in his large overstuffed armchair and head off to do my work.

Then came *Ironweed*.

"What do you want to watch tonight?" I asked as we looked through his shelves. We were going to sit in the living room with all our friends and watch movies. Granite, Margo, and James had come over for a supper of Chinese food and we were all looking forward to seeing something on the big screen with the theatre sound.

"Don't matter," he said. "Some I seen, but there's a lot I ain't got around to yet."

His shelves were frightening. There was no order. Movies were stacked on top of each other, leaned crookedly, and piled haphazardly so you had to tilt your head to read the titles. He had everything: westerns, horror, science fiction, comedy, drama, and even some foreign films with undecipherable names.

"Here's one," I said. "*Ironweed*. Have you seen it?"

"Don't think so. Who's in it?"

"Jack Nicholson."

"Which one's he?"

"Hmm. Remember the one about the hitman who falls in love with the lady hitman?"

"Yeah. That was funny."

"That's him."

"Okay, sounds good to me. Let's watch that one."

The others were all settled into their favourite chairs waiting for us when we got back downstairs. Dick settled in next to Amelia and I handed the tape off to Digger, who had assumed the role of machine operator from the very first time we watched movies at home. Then I sat on a large pillow on the floor with my back pressed against the wall.

"What are we watching?" Margo asked, her hand in Granite's.

"*Ironweed*," Dick said. "With Jack Nicholson."

"Oh, that sounds good. I like him," she said and smiled.

"Me too," James said. "Have you seen this one, Granite?"

"Yes. It's quite good."

"What's it about?" Amelia asked.

"Well, it's about—"

"Geez, will you cool it, Rock?" Digger said. "I don't always gotta know the story before I see the flick."

"Okay," Granite said. "But it's good."

"Thank you for the friggin' analysis," Digger said, "but now it's showtime, folks."

He flicked off all the lights and the room fell into the theatre-like ambience we all loved. Digger had set the sound up perfectly and we were all lost with the first flare of light on the screen and the crash of sound. The film was jaw dropping. It told the story of three back-alley drunks in a small city near the end of the Depression, and it told it so accurately that I thought I saw myself there as I had been not so long ago. It was bleak as only a street life can be. It was heavy like the woe we had all carried. It was hard. It was tough. It was gritty and it was as on the nose as anything I'd ever seen except the life itself. When it ended we all sat there, unmoving and silent, until the tape reached its end. Digger got up to shut it off and turn on the lights. We stared at each other. No one said a word.

"I gotta go," Dick said.

"Me too, so hurry up, pal," Digger said.

"No," Dick said, his chin trembling and a frightened look in his eyes. "I mean, I gotta go."

"Where?" Amelia asked.

"Somewhere. Anywhere," Dick said. "I just gotta go."

"A walk, you mean?" Amelia asked.

"Yeah. Yeah, a walk," he said.

"Hang on. I'll go with you," I said.

He looked at me then and I saw the man in the chair.

"No," he said. "I gotta go alone. I don't want no one comin' with me. I don't want no one followin' me neither."

And he got up from his chair, walked out the door, and disappeared into the night.

Double Dick

THE MAN KILLED HIS SON. He was drunk an' dropped him on his head an' killed him. He killed his baby son. Then he tried to go home again an' he couldn't on accounta he couldn't take it back. Ever. He couldn't take it back. He couldn't make nothin' right on accounta that's the biggest thing you can do is make someone die. He was a drunk like me. He was a street guy like me. It's where he was supposed to be on accounta when you make someone go away you gotta go away yourself. You gotta go away yourself. I didn't know where I was gonna go when I walked out the door but I knew I had to go. I had to go away. I walked. I walked a long time an' I didn't worry about nothin', not my friends waitin' for me back at the house, not the time, not nothin' except the fact that my mickey went dry an' I needed another. It was real late so I flagged down a cab an' went on down to Fill 'er Up Phil's. I got a pop from a corner store, poured it out on the street as I walked up to his door, knocked, an' held it through the little slidin' window when it opened and said, "Fill 'er up, Phil," like we gotta.

"That you, Dick?" Phil's voice asked.

"Yeah," I said. "It's me."

"What the fuck are you doing down here?"

"Walkin'," I said. "Thinkin'."

"Jesus, man. You couldn't get a bottle of Scotch or something?"

"Nah, I just run out. You was the first one I thought of."

"Well, thanks. But for fuck sake, you don't need my hooch. Let me give you a nice whisky I been saving."

"Hey, okay. That'd be nice."

"Anything for you, Dickey. Here."

He handed the bottle through the window. "How much?" I asked.

"For you? Nothing. It's on me. But do you think you could lend me something?"

"Sure."

"Fifty?"

"Yeah."

"Cool."

I shoved the money through the window.

"Thanks, Dick. You take care now, man," Phil said.

"I will."

After that I just walked more. I thought about the man in the movie an' how he got where he got. He was a baseball player an' then he dropped his son. I was never no baseball player. I wasn't no nothin'. On accounta my dad was a half-breed we never had no land or nothin'. We just kinda lived on the land that no one else cared for an' we put up the only kinda house we could from scraps offa the sawmill piles. Once the moose milk got goin' we could afford other stuff but mostly we just lived in a shack. A shack. I remember walkin' in there some winter days an' it'd be real cold outside an' steppin' through the door was like bein' burnt in the face on accounta we only had the one big fat stove in the middle an' it was hot. There was seven of us. My mom an' dad an' five kids, an' we all kinda slept together in the same big bed, us kids.

Tom Bruce kinda had the same life. His dad got work more on accounta he knew how to run a chainsaw real good but they still didn't have much neither. When we walked around draggin' that wagon or sled fulla moose milk we talked lots an' we liked each other pretty good. We talked about lotsa things. About what we was gonna do when we got big, where we was gonna go, what kinda adventures we could have. That sorta talk. Tom Bruce was the only friend I had. Least until I met One For The Dead.

Tom Bruce always said, "Us guys always gonna have to hump. No other way."

So humpin' that wagon or sled around was like startin' to make our dreams come true on accounta Tom Bruce said that's how it was always gonna have to be. I believed him. I never seen nobody around there go nowheres. Me 'n Tom dug a hole in our hideout. We put a moose milk jar down there once we'd drunk it empty an' we put coins in it.

"That's yours," he told me. "Next time we got an empty it'll be mine and we'll stash it in the ground side by each."

"How come?" I asked.

"Tucumcary."

"What?"

"Tucumcary," he said again. "It's a place."

"What kinda place?"

"Hell, I don't know. Just a place. Some place that's not here. It sounds like a place I wanna go."

"Tucumcary," I said, an' I liked the sound it made.

So we put them jars side by each in them holes an' we stuck whatever coins come our way in them. We was gonna go to Tucumcary. Me 'n Tom Bruce. We was gonna save our money an' hit the road together. After that, we talked about how we was gonna get there, what kinda girls we might find, what kinda work we might wanna try, an' all sorts of stuff like that. We talked about it all the time when we was drinkin' up in that little hideout. Tucumcary was where everythin' was gonna be all right. Tucumcary was where there weren't no more sawmills an' shacks by the roadside. Tucumcary was where we was gonna lay up in the sunshine an' drink pink drinks an' listen to the wind blowin' through the palm trees. Palm trees. I didn't know what they were back then but I remember I liked how they sounded on accounta they sounded like they was holdin' you all soft an' gentle, rockin' you kinda while you slept in their shade. Palm trees. Me 'n Tom Bruce was gonna go sleep under palm trees in Tucumcary. That was my dream.

It never happened, though. We kept on puttin' them coins in those jars an' haulin' that moose milk up an' down them roads, but Tucumcary never got no closer. We just got bigger an' we drank more moose milk. Got to be we didn't wanna do nothin' but hide out an' suck up that juice. No one said nothin'. Guess even my dad knew, but he didn't wanna queer the deal he had on accounta the cops never once looked at a couple kids with a wagon or a sled, so he pretended like he didn't know we was drinkin'. Or he flat out didn't care. Long as we delivered, we was okay. Once we got too big to be playin' with wagons we got to ride around on a tractor. Big old tractor they used to pull logs outta the bush to cut up for firewood an' stuff. We'd put the moose milk in boxes under a pile of logs an' deliver firewood an' firewater at the same time. We was fourteen. Them mason jars was full by then an' me, I kept switchin' the dimes an' nickels for quarters, half-dollar, an' dollars. It was full up by the time Tom Bruce an' me started gettin' called out to do man's work.

We didn't do much. Mostly I drove, on accounta no one figured I could do nothin' more, or else I chainsawed, an' I got pretty good at that but I didn't like it. But we was young an' the mill guys wanted young insteada old an' we got called out more than my dad an' them. Meant we could go to county dances. We'd head on down there most weekend nights an' stand around the outside talkin', smokin', and passin' a crock back an' forth with the other boys. Didn't bother with no girls. Dances was for drinkin' an' cussin' an' tellin' tales. Only the sissy boys danced with girls, or the older ones who was more lookin' for that sorta thing. Me 'n Tom just settled in at the edges an' watched.

That was my life. Haulin' firewood an' firewater all over the county, doin' whatever man's work come along we figured we could stand, an' drinkin'. By then we was drinkin' with the men, but we still liked goin' to our hideout and talkin' best. We never noticed once we started to get sick. First it was just a little pukin'. A few heaves in the mornin'. Then it got worse an' we'd meet each other up at the hideout all washed-out lookin' and shaky, really kinda needin' what Tom Bruce called a "bracer." Kinda brace us for whatever we had goin' for the day. Them bracers always got us goin' again. We was sixteen.

Then one week them bracers really got us goin'. We didn't even figure on gettin' drunk. We just met up in the morning, sat down in the hideout an' had a few big slops of moose milk, an' the next thing we know we're smokin', talkin', and gettin' pissed-up drunk. We stayed there six days. We only went out to get more or wobble down to someone's kitchen for other company at night. I don't know how much we drank on accounta it all got weird, but we drank lots. Then Tom Bruce had had enough, an' waved me away finally. So we both headed back to our shacks, tired an' sick feelin'.

That's the night my brother asked me to watch Earl. I told him I was sick but he was mad an' he liked to hit things an' people when he was mad an' I was too sick feelin' to put up with that so I waved him off an' they left. Maybe if he'da listened, it never woulda happened. Maybe if I'da said we was drinkin' six days, they wouldn't have got me to look after him. Maybe if I'da just passed out in the hideout. I don't know. I only know what happened. I only know how them feet looked stickin' out of that lard pail.

I ran. I ran through the darkness an' fell down on the ground in the hideout. They found me there the next day an' hauled me off to the county jail. That was the worst on accounta I was dead sick an' they made me shake it off in a cell. Horrible. Nightmares, sweats, puking. I got through, though, an' they brung me up in front of the judge, charged with drownin' Earl. But Tom Bruce told how we drank all them days an' my brother told how I said I was sick an' that judge let me go. He called it an accident. He said it was a horrible accident an' I was free to go. Free to go. When I walked out of that county jail there was nowhere to go. I hitched a ride back to the sawmill town an' walked to the hideout. My jar was still there. I took it an' walked away without saying nothin' to nobody. Took it and headed toward Tucumcary, where them palm trees could hold me soft an' gentle, rockin' me kinda, helpin' me forget the sight of them tiny feet in the flickerin' light of that television. I never made it there an' I never forgot.

Ironweed brung it all back an' I thought about it all while I walked around drinkin'. I walked a long time an' I was gettin' drunk out there on the street so I turned into a motel, got a room, an' settled in. The night man liked me but he liked the roll I showed him better. He got me some more bottles. He got some girls to come over. He got me a player an' some movies. When I called him Tom Bruce, he answered an' laughed. I liked that. Me 'n Tom Bruce. Together again in the Rainbow Motel. Tucumcary. We was finally gonna make it to Tucumcary.

One For The Dead

I SLEPT IN HIS ROOM. I had to. I wanted to be there if he walked back in late at night and needed someone there. I wanted to be the first to let him know that it would be all right. I wanted to see him. So I curled up in his armchair and slept by the light of a single candle I kept burning for him. I placed it on the windowsill and slept by its wavering glow, surrounded by all the movies that Dick had come to love, all the possible worlds he felt attracted to, all the dreams not his own that he watched, hoping a little of that magic might shine for him sometime. I wished I still had the medicines. Wished for the sweetgrass, the sage, the tobacco, and the cedar. The prayer medicines of my people. I hadn't had any for years. If I'd had those medicines, I'd have burned them for Double Dick Dumont, right there in the room that was his home. Burned them so their fragrant smoke could carry my prayers for his safety to the Spirit World—to the Grandmothers and Grandfathers, the Spirit Helpers who watch over us—and ask them to bring him home to me. Burned them so the shadowed ones would know that someone cared for that lost one and maybe whisper something in his ear to remind him of us. Burned them so the spirit of the People from which he came might spark in him again, and he'd find the warrior's strength to travel the dim trail back to his lodge. Burned them so my dreams would be good. Burned them to ask forgiveness for myself.

I should have known. I should have felt the weight he carried more strongly. I should have asked more questions, provided more safety, let him know how much I had seen, survived, and grown up and away from. I should have talked about my Indianness more. Should have told more stories and coaxed his own out of him, allowed him to talk about his father and his father's tribal past. I should have made the path more clear for him because he was incapable of reading signs for himself, unable to follow even the boldest of blazing on the trees, not skilled enough to navigate the way himself. I felt all of that curled up in that armchair, breathing his scent and feeling the hollow where his body rested. I felt his awkwardness cast off and discarded in the nearness of all those stories on the shelves. I felt the unscalable wall of literacy dismantle itself and tumble to the carpet next to the magnificence of time and place and texture presented in those shining tales. I felt loss replaced by dreams of gaining the crown of the world, grief replaced by glorious victory, shame salved by forgiveness, wrath tamed by love, love itself illuminated by a love returned, and homelessness, loneliness, and woe rendered speechless in the face of welcomings radiant and warm. I felt his jubilation in seeing all those things. I felt that just as I felt the chill of departure when the story faded to black again and the man in the chair faced the darkness alone, afraid, ashamed, and not drunk enough to dream a shining dream of his own. I felt all that and I slept there so there would be one place he would not have to feel like he wandered into alone. One place where someone waited, eager to alter the way she had done things, desiring to carry more stories forward and help him blaze a trail through the darkness.

Timber

I CARVED AT NIGHT. While the others slept, I worked on the man in the chair. In the flicker of candlelight I seemed to be able to see him in sharper detail, the shadow moving like a hand telling me where to chip, scrape, slice, and etch. I never knew how much shadow he lived in, how much the darkness haunted him, how twilight never held the romance it sometimes graced other people's lives with, how it only talked to him of another vigil to be maintained, another gathering of hours huddled like bandits waiting to waylay the unprepared. While I worked I thought about the years we'd travelled together, how we had thought we knew each other, how we had called that semblance of knowing friendship, and all the while my grief over Sylvan rested under all that like an uncobbled stone—the pathway to knowing incomplete, the treading difficult, impossible perhaps, impassable. I thought about how I had failed him. How my secret had taught him how to keep his own. My pain granting his permission to fester and growl away at his guts too. I thought about how easy it is to hide in the company of others, allowing the motion of lives to obfuscate your inner workings so that what's presented becomes more a bas-relief than sculpted image. I had failed him then. Failed to let him see me. Failed to let him know me in all the corrugated chips and fracture lines. Failed to let him know that friends are imperfect replicas of the people we think we choose, and that imperfection is the nature of it all. We come together in our brokenness and find that our small acts of being human together mend the breaks, allow us to retool the design and become more. I never taught him that.

So I worked. I let my hands feel our friendship. Those moments when our less-than-perfect selves hold the adze we shape togetherness with. I let my hands trace the face I knew so well. Allowed them to cut and gouge the hollows I had never taken the time to fill with learning, let them trail the fine spray of wrinkles around the eyes that told stories I'd never heard, the dump of mouth above the chin that spoke of disappointments grave and eternal, the angular cut of jaw that spoke of a resolute holding back, a reining in never questioned: the geography of my friend I had never walked. I worked in shadow and allowed shadow to permeate the image, because that is where he was born and lived and dreamed, if he allowed himself to dream at all. I allowed myself conjecture because conjecture was all I had, and I sculpted an idea, made it live and breathe, made it hope, made it dream, made it offer up prayers to a god shunted away perhaps because the crimes of living in the shadow's realm made any other kind of god too difficult to seek out. I carved that. I carved my friend in all his unspoken woe, and I carved my shame over my neglect into the blanket he wore draped around his shoulders.

Digger

I DROVE THE SHIT out of that truck. I stormed around the city going places I'd never gone in twenty years because rounders like Dick and me know how to dis-a-fucking-ppear and recent places ain't the hole-up you head for. No. You head for the private places. The ones you never talk about, like I never told no one about the Palace. Out of all of us, me 'n Double Dick was the most rounder of the bunch and we knew the drill better than the other two on accounta they landed on the street and me 'n Dick was made there. So I drove around like a crazy motherfucker trying to live in his head and figure where he mighta gone those days before we met. Or I tried to think of a new place he'd pick to stash himself and I drove and drove and drove. Gave me time to think. Fucking guy always used to piss me off in the beginning. *How come this* and *how come that*. Loogan talk. Drove me crazy until I started to understand that his wick wasn't completely lit. The light didn't shine into all the corners, and that was okay with me then. The real loogans and loons I never had no time for, but once I realized that Dick was short a few matches I started to lend him some of mine. Goofy motherfucker was always solid, always there, always game even though he'da been as good as a loose fart in tight trousers in a fight. Solid. Stand-up. A fucking rounder. I'da taken him as a winger over a hundred better-spoken, better-thinking assholes who'd crumble under half the shit we seen. I loved that fucking guy. Loved him on accounta he showed me it was okay to not be in fucking control all the time, that sometimes not being fucking clear was good for a guy on accounta the questions got sharper so the answers could come. He taught me that, the flat-footed fuck, and I loved him for it. But I never told him. I never told him. So I drove and I knew that when I found him I was gonna let him know a few things. I was gonna let him know that he taught me something big. I was gonna let him know that he was a solid fucking rounder I was proud to have on my wing. I was gonna tell him that no matter what the fuck was going on I was gonna be on his wing and there wasn't nobody big enough or bad enough to move me from there. Ever. And I was gonna tell him I loved him. On the sly, though. Wasn't no need for anyone else to hear that coming from me.

Double Dick

TOM BRUCE couldn't remember about Tucumcary. When I asked him he just laughed an' told me to have another drink. That was okay. People always forget stuff an' we was just kids. He didn't remember nothin' about me an' little Earl neither an' that was even better on accounta I didn't wanna think about it no more. He made sure I didn't. We got goin' on a really good run. Tom Bruce knew the hooch delivery guy an' we was always workin' on a bottle even when he was supposed to be workin' the desk. Some of the girls he knew brung me movies an' we'd sit in my room an' watch them together an' some of them girls gave me blow jobs an' stuff. I liked that. Made me forget all about *Ironweed* an' Earl an' even bein' afraid of wakin' up at night. Sometimes they stayed with me an' I liked that better on accounta I could roll over an' feel them beside me an' they'd let me fuck them before I gulped down some hooch, rolled over, an' passed out again. I liked that. We never had parties like that with Digger an' Timber. All Tom Bruce needed was some cash every day, so me an' one of the girls would take a cab to a bank machine an' I'd get it for him. He took care of my room an' made sure we kept the party goin'. I was with Tom Bruce again. My first friend an' he made sure I was took care of.

We just partied. It was like it was never gonna stop an' I liked that on accounta finally there wasn't nothin' in my head. I kinda felt bad about not tellin' anyone where I was but when I told Tom Bruce he said that it was better if I let them be an' stuck with him.

"We're old buds," he said. "We're pals. Old times, huh? Old times."

We partied. Night an' day. No one said nothin' when I got sick. No one said nothin' when I couldn't walk to the bathroom an' had to piss in an empty bottle at night. No one said nothin' about nothin'. We just kept right on rollin'. We had movies, music, girls, an' hooch an' a room like the hideout me 'n Tom Bruce used to have in the woods behind the sawmill town.

"Linda needs shoes," Tom Bruce said one day, an' I gave him some money on accounta I liked Linda.

"I gotta get some work done on my car," he said another time, an' I gave him a hundred or so even though he never brung his car around.

"Pearl don't have enough for the dentist," an' I'd shell out on accounta Pearl would strip for me whenever she come around. Real slow an' sexy an' then she'd let me fuck her. I liked her smile.

Every day I went to the cash machine an' that's all I had to do. Tom Bruce took care of the rest. When I started to get sick from the drinkin' he got me some pills that fixed me up real fast. I never had that before. I never knew you could find some pills that'd take the sick away an' let you keep on goin'. Pretty soon I was takin' pills every mornin' or when I woke up at night feelin' all antsy. Tom Bruce called them my "magic pills" an' they sure was. Helped me forget about everythin'. Everythin'. Once I got goin' on those pills we started goin' around to where Tom Bruce's new friends hung out. He knew lots of people an' they was always real glad to see me.

For a while it looked like I found a whole new kinda life. I'da stayed there except for the one night. I was alone. It was rainin'. Everyone had somethin' else to do an' I was sitting there all alone, drinkin' an' starin' at the television. I didn't feel nothin' except a buzzin' in the head that wouldn't go away. There was a man on the TV. He was just sittin' there talkin'. Talkin' to me. Talkin' to me an' tellin' me about my life.

"There's nothing you can do to change things," the man said. "You can run but you can't hide. The facts are the facts and you can't get away. You can't get away."

That's what he was sayin', an' pointin' at me an' lookin' at me all hard an' angry. I didn't like it. I didn't know how the man knew who I was or how he knew about my life. But he did an' he kept right on talkin' to me. I was scared. Scared. So I walked over to the television an' clicked it off. Except it was already off. It was off.

I felt the walls start creepin' in on me. My heart started poundin' in my chest an' I couldn't breathe right. There was crawly things on the floor an' in the walls an' the rain outside was blood. Blood on the sidewalk. The shadows from the streetlights were movin' an' comin' toward me. I saw them through the open door an' I ran over an' slammed it shut. Then I grabbed a bottle an' tilted it back an' gulped an' gulped an' gulped, feelin' the fire in my chest an' closin' my eyes like I could push it into my blood an' make the horrible things go away. I fell on the floor an' felt the crawly things on me. I stuffed a corner of a blanket hard into my mouth so I wouldn't scream an' when I felt the cottony numb feelin' at the sides of my head that told me the whisky was workin' I opened my eyes. The pill bottle was by my head an' I fumbled it open an' swallowed a few before I took another few gulps of hooch. There was still crawly things but they was slower now an' the TV was blank. I got to my feet, grabbed my coat, an' got out of there. Got right out of there an' walked down the road. Walkin'. Walkin'. Walkin' an' tryin' to remember how to breathe.

Granite

A WEEK WENT BY. Two. Then three. The house on Indian Road became a glum place. It sat within the weight of its own shadow. The rounders kept more and more to themselves and the television in the living room was ignored, as though it were to blame for Dick's absence. James had informed us that because Dick was making regular withdrawals from his bank account, he didn't qualify as a missing person to the police and so there was nothing they could do. It was, apparently, his choice to be absent. That news hit them hard. They sat in their chairs dumbfounded;

the idea that one of them would want to be separated for longer than a night was as awkward in their minds as choosing to starve. They tried to stick to their routines. Digger still drove the alleys and back streets in the mornings, but looking more for signs of Dick than for castoffs. Timber carved, but for increasingly shorter durations, returning to sketch in his room for long stretches at a time. Amelia read and sewed and fussed about her garden, but always with an eye to the door or the driveway and always ending on the veranda more content to sit and wait than pass time in activity. They barely spoke to each other. Margo and James and I would arrive each day and need to seek them out in their private spaces rather than be greeted at the door by the gruff boom of Digger's voice or the quiet, almost regal welcome of Amelia. Our discussions centred on word of Dick, and when none was forthcoming they dwindled off into clumsy small talk that itself trailed off to silences huge and rife with unspoken sentiment. When we departed at night it was a sepulchral house we left behind us, shades drawn against secrets or stories unbidden and unwanted, only the glow of the one small candle Amelia kept burning offering any indication that hope nestled beneath the eaves.

"This can't go on like this," Margo said while we were driving over after three weeks had passed with no word or sign of Dick. "They're eating themselves up and it's so sad to see them not even talking to each other."

"I know," I said. "But they've all got that iron-rod spine the street gave them, and when they don't want to speak they certainly don't speak."

"But it's pulling them apart."

"I know. After everything they lived through all those years, hanging together through it all, I didn't think anything was capable of pulling them apart."

"Maybe we should ask them to talk about it. Maybe we should sit them all down together and ask them to tell us how they feel. Get some air moving in there. Get some discussion happening. Anything is better than nothing. Better than this heavy silence."

"Like mourning."

"Yes. It worries me."

James was already there, sitting alone in the living room moving a single checker back and forth between squares. He looked up as we entered—eager, anxious—and then slumped slightly, nodding in recognition. It was mid-afternoon and there was likely a lot of work waiting for him at his office, but he'd taken to spending longer and longer periods at the house. He was a good man.

"Friggin' checkers," he said with a grin. "Digger used to beat me all the time. I didn't pull back. I played to win but the scoundrel did it to me every time. Or at least he did."

"You'll play again," I said, sitting opposite him.

We told him about our wish to get them talking. While he called in an order for Chinese food we moved through the house gathering the rounders together like children. Digger was rewiring a blender in the garage, Timber was scraping away at an oaken cameo, and Amelia knelt in the garden idly plucking at the small heads of weeds barely visible above the soil. Each of them merely nodded and left to wash and get ready for the meal they accepted news of without their usual glee. The three of us shook our heads sadly watching them. Once the food arrived, we gathered in the dining room and arranged ourselves about the table. They busied themselves loading their plates with their favourites and then idly munched on the food. Silence. Margo and I exchanged a glance and she prodded me gently with a toe under the table.

"So, Timber," I began slowly. "How's the work coming along?"

"Good," he said.

"Good?"

"Yeah. Okay. No problems."

"What are you carving?"

"A man."

"What kind of man?" Margo asked.

"A sad man."

"Anyone we know?" she asked.

He looked at her and squinted in concentration. "I don't know," he said. "I thought so in the beginning. Now I'm not so sure."

"Meaning?" James asked.

"Meaning he don't friggin' know," Digger grunted. "Jesus. Questions. Always friggin' questions."

"Sorry, Digger," James said. "It's just that no one's been very talkative lately and we want to know how you're doing."

"How we're doing?" Digger asked. "How we're doing?"

"Yes. It's been hard, I know."

"You know shit," Digger said. "You got no idea about hard. Never will, really."

"We would if you told us," Margo said quietly.

"It's hard to know what to say," Amelia said. "There's so much going on."

"Like what?" I asked.

"Like doubt," she said. "Like fear."

"Never a good combination," James said.

"No," Amelia answered. "Never."

"So, why don't you know about your carving, Jonas?" Margo asked.

"Because it's D," Digger said. "It's a carving of D when he seen him on the porch before this happened. He seen him all fucking worn down and screwed. So he started a carving. Only now it ain't working."

"I don't need you talking for me," Timber said shortly.

"Someone should," Digger replied.

"What's that supposed to mean?"

"It means if you hadda talked insteada whittling this might not have gone down like it has."

"What? What are you talking about?"

"I'm talking about being solid. I'm talking about not letting a pal go down without trying to help. I'm talking about wasting fucking time with a knife in your hands when you could be looking for the fucking guy."

"You're putting this on me?"

"Fucking rights I'm putting this on you. You seen him all fucked up and didn't say word one to him. Didn't ask. Didn't tell nobody. All you did was pick up your little tools and whittle."

"You know the routine," Timber said. "Never ask. Let it ride.

We don't talk unless we want to talk. You know? *Your* religion. The only thing you believe in. The rounder code. The way of the street. The friggin' gospel according to Digger. So if you're going to put this on anyone, put it on yourself."

"On me? How the fuck do you figure that?" Digger asked, putting down his utensils.

Timber gave him a level look. "Because he listened to everything you ever said. He worshipped you. You were his idea of what he was supposed to be, and when you told him to 'never say nothing to nobody' he listened. But the only problem is: we don't live on the street anymore, in case you haven't noticed. Those rules don't apply here. They only work on the street. But you never told him that, did you?"

"Fuck you."

"Oh, thank you for the feedback," Timber sneered.

"I'll feed you back a shot in the fucking head."

"That's your answer to everything. Except maybe driving around in your little truck all day."

"At least I'm doing something."

"In your own words, you're doing shit."

"At least I didn't ignore a pal in pain."

"Actually," I said. "You did."

"Fuck you, Rock."

"But you did. We talked at the Palace and I told you what Amelia had told me about his not sleeping and the nighttime drinking. You said all that needed to happen was a buddy-buddy shot on the shoulder. Remember?"

"You're telling me that I'm not solid because I saw him on the porch and said nothing? Now I find out that they actually asked you to talk to him directly and you said no? Who's not solid now, Digger?" Timber asked.

"Hey, fuck you," Digger said, standing. "I know rounders. I did what a rounder would do for a rounder."

"Oh, yeah," Timber said, standing too now. "Rounders let a friend go down?"

"I didn't let him go down."

"What do you call not offering a hand when a hand was called for?"

"I call it minding my business."

"Your business isn't your pal's safety?"

"My business is my business."

"Now there's a fucking thought," Timber sneered. "Not real deep and not real useful, but it's a thought."

"Hey, listen, Mr. I'm So Sad Cuz I Ditched My Fucking Wife, I wouldn't be talking about turning my back on people if I was you. You're the fucking pro when it comes to that."

"Fuck you."

"Fuck me? Fuck me?"

"Fuck you."

"Stop it!" Amelia said, rapping the butt of her fork on the table. "Stop it. Both of you. This isn't what we need."

"Yeah, and you really know what we need, don't you?" Digger replied.

"Not this," Amelia said.

"Who told you that? Some spook in the corner? The ghost of Humphrey fucking Bogart whispered in your ear, did he? Jesus. Shadowed ones. That's what got us into all this in the first place."

"It's what got us out," Amelia said.

"Got you out," Digger said. "Where the fuck is Dick right now? Huh? Can your fucking shadowed ones tell you that? Huh?"

"Leave her out of this!" Timber said angrily.

"Why? Why? She's so fucking sacred? I'll tell you something, pal. If we're fucking wrong here, she's fucking wrong."

"She's not wrong."

"No? No? Did she say anything? Did she walk up to his door one of them nights she knew he was in there hurting and ask him *what the fuck*? No. No. All she did was walk up to the Square John and say, 'Please, Mister Square John, tell me what to do.' Like a fucking Square John was gonna know."

"She did what she thought was right."

"Bullshit. What was right was coming to us. *Us*. We're the fucking rounders. We're the fucking crew. We're the ones who hung together through a hundred different kinds of bullshit. Not him. Not them. We're still fucking entertainment to them, don't you see that?"

"They're our friends," Timber said.

"Yeah," Digger said, looking at the three of us. "They got a few million reasons for being our friends, don't they?"

"We don't care about your money," James said.

"We care about you," Margo said.

"'*We care about you*,'" Digger echoed in a singsong voice. "Yeah, well I don't see you exactly burning up the sidewalk looking for Dick. I don't see you doing anything except coming around every day looking at us, watching us like we're some fucking movie and then going back to your little Square John love nest and talking about the poor rounders. The poor rounders who can't get a fucking life even with thirteen-million dollars. Fuck you, you care about us."

"Digger," I said sharply. "Watch your mouth."

He turned slowly and stared balefully at me. "Watch my mouth?" he asked. "Watch my mouth? At least I opened mine. At least I had the balls to talk about where I come from. Did you? No. You didn't say shit about how fucked up things got for you, how it made you think it was all for shit. Well, you know what, Mr. Toe-Rubber Square John motherfucker? Maybe if you hadda opened your mouth and talked about yourself, maybe Dick woulda heard some of that and been okay to let the cat outta his bag. But no. You just sat back and listened to our stories and didn't offer up your own. You sat back and let us enter-fucking-tain you. Well, we ain't no movie. We ain't no flick you can walk in and out of whenever you fucking please. So, you can take your fucking Square John friends who don't do nothing for us anyway and get the fuck out of my house."

"It's not your house," Timber said. "It's ours."

"Well, get the fuck out of my part, then."

"Digger," Amelia said. "You're just upset."

"Fucking rights I'm upset! I'm upset that we're the only ones who ever have to spill the beans. We're the only ones on display.

We're the only ones who have to do anything about finding Dick. We're the only ones who ever have to pay the fucking price for anything. These Square Johns just come around for the show."

"Is that how you really feel?" I asked.

"Fucking rights."

"Then I guess we'd better leave."

"I guess," he said.

"No," Amelia said. "Everyone's just hurting. Please don't go."

"We'd better," Margo said.

"Yeah. You'd better or someone *will* be hurting," Digger said.

"Not if I can help it," Timber said.

"Hmmph," Digger snorted. "You ever make a move on me, you better have one of them fucking carving shanks in your hand and you better know how to fucking use it."

"Digger," Amelia said sternly. "I won't have that talk. I won't have it. Not in this house. Not ever."

He looked at her with his head tilted back cockily. Then he looked at each of us in turn, shook his head sadly, and smirked. "Sad fucking bunch," he said. "Sad fucking bunch."

"We'd better go," I said.

"Don't let the door punch you in the pants on the way out," Digger said.

It didn't.

Double Dick

THE LADY in the library said Tucumcary was a place. It was in New Mexico. I told the lady I couldn't read an' she helped me even though I didn't know how to spell it. We found it on a map. Tucumcary. It was real. It was a place. Even though I kinda knew once my head cleared up that the guy at the Rainbow wasn't really Tom Bruce an' I kinda knew that all them people was only after my money, Tucumcary was real an' I still wanted to go. I figured maybe if I slept under them palm trees I could figure out how to deal with my nightmares on accounta Timber went to the city by the sea an' he wasn't so sad no more. Timber. I hoped he was okay. I hoped he wasn't worried on accounta I didn't wanna make no one worried. I walked out on accounta the movie freaked me out an' I thought I hadta get away. I walked out 'cause my nightmare felt real. Like it was right in the room with me. Now it didn't. Now I had them pills an' they was makin' it go away from my mind. I liked that. The Tom Bruce guy got me a big bottle of them an' when one wasn't enough I took another one an' it worked good. So I started to figure that Tucumcary would work for me like the city by the sea worked for Timber. I started making a plan to go there.

After I left the library I went to where the lady said I could get a map. The man at the store was nice an' found me a big book with maps of the whole world an' kinda dog-eared the page I wanted an' put a circle around Tucumcary. I never had no book before. Never. Not my own, least ways. Felt funny in my hands but I liked lookin' at the maps. Then I went to a place that sold tape recorders an' I bought me one of them ones that fit right in your hand. I couldn't write no letter to my friends on accounta I can't write, so I figured to say what I wanted on that tape recorder an' mail it to them. I had to go to Tucumcary alone. I could tell them I was goin' to sort out some stuff. They'd understand that on accounta it's what a rounder does when somethin's got him by the short an' curlies, like Digger says. Digger'd know what I meant an' wouldn't worry. One For The Dead would worry, though, an' I wanted to say somethin' good to her on accounta she always been so good to me. The tape recorder was my best idea in a long time.

Once I got batteries, I bought some clothes an' a bag to tote them in an' a bottle of vodka an' found a nice hotel. The Hilton. They was nice there even though I guess I kinda looked rough after the Rainbow. I paid for three days in cash an' left a few hundred more for room service an' everyone was real nice to me. I got a nice room with a view of the whole city. There was a bar in there too, and a big TV. I planned on stayin' there until I figured out how to get to Tucumcary. Jet, maybe. Even a bus. A train would be nice too on accounta I could relax an' watch the country roll by like in them western movies. I'd figure it out.

I had a shower an' put on some of the new clothes. I was gettin' kinda shaky again so I swallowed some more pills, had a big snort or two of vodka to wash 'em down an' watched some TV while they kicked in. It didn't take long. They made me float. Float so I couldn't really feel my feet. Walkin' on that thick carpet in my room was funny-feelin' an' I kinda giggled when I walked back an' forth to the bar on accounta I felt like I was walkin' in the air. Them pills was good. Later that night I got my book out an' found the dog-eared page of New Mexico. I lay on my bed an' let my fingers trace all around New Mexico, all along the roads that led to Tucumcary, past all the little dots that was towns, past all the country there that I tried to imagine from movies I seen, past the cows in the fields, the rivers, the forests, the mountains, past all the things I ever figured Tucumcary was all about. An' as I let my fingers trace them roads, I had a few more snorts of vodka an' another coupla pills an' remembered my hideout talks with Tom Bruce when we was kids an' Tucumcary was a dream we had, a dream that was comin' true for me now on accounta it was the only place, the only place to be, the only place to be free. The only place where the breeze blew in from Old Mexico across New Mexico an' made little swishin' sounds through the tops of the palm trees I lay under an' found a way to tell little Earl that he could let me go now on accounta I learned everythin' I needed to learn from him an' I needed to be with my friends in our house on Indian Road on accounta that was my life, an' him an' that room with the flickerin' TV an' the shadows an' his tiny little feet an' my puke an' my sick an' moose milk an' wagons an' sleds in the snow an' shacks by sawmill towns wasn't part of nothing no more. So goodbye little Earl. I'm gonna try real hard to forget you now even though I don't wanna on accounta it was you brung me where I went an' without you I couldn'ta met up with my friends an' won all that money for our house on Indian Road an', boy, was they ever gonna be glad to hear from me. So I reached over to that tape recorder an' pushed the red button an' started talkin' about everythin' that come to my mind layin' there on that big bed in that fancy room with that vodka an' them pills. I talked about what I wanted for them an' how I wished sometimes that people like us didn't need to go to places like Tucumcary on accounta sometimes you think that friendship oughta be enough to see a guy through things, an' how even though I was gonna go there alone I was takin' them with me on accounta it was them give me everythin' I got an' I wanted to give back. So I needed to go an' say goodbye to little Earl once an' for all so I could go home on accounta home was the most important thing for all of us an' there wasn't no room no more for little Earl an' nightmares an' not sleepin' on accounta bein' afraid to wake up in your own home wasn't what home was supposed to be. I seen in a movie one time what home was supposed to be an' it wasn't like that an' I was gonna come home soon, soon, soon, once I made the trip that I was gonna go on right after I had this sleep that I could feel behind my eyes an' at the sides of my head. So good night, good night, an' I love you an' I'll sing a song for you all in Tucumcary where the breeze blows across Old Mexico to New Mexico an' carries secrets an' songs an' tales that I'll tell, like One For The Dead tells tales in a voice like the breeze that blows in the top of the palm tree where I'll lay an' learn to say goodbye.

One For The Dead

I HATED what had happened. There had never been one single solitary thing that could get between us in all the years we'd been together until this. It was all about pain. It was all about those things you can't understand in life. The things that should be so simple but never are. Like feelings. Like hope. Like love. I guess love sometimes doesn't have the most gracious vocabulary. It can't. It can't because it comes from the deepest part of us, the part that never sees the light until love itself calls it out of us, and when you live the way we lived for so long your ears aren't attuned to the sound of love so you never learn to talk its language. You learn pain's vocabulary, though. Very well. That was the language spoken in the living room that night. Pain's talk. Love's talk, really, dressed up in anguish clothes. The silence the house fell into was thick like a bush you've never walked through before with no pathway, no blaze on the trees to tell you where to plant your foot, no clear-cut, no way to see direction. All of us without a compass.

Digger

FUCK 'EM ALL but six. All but the six you need, because everybody needs pallbearers. The six I had would be rounders. Screw the Square Johns. The thing about a rounder is he'll wrap himself up in his stuff, his inside stuff, like he wraps himself up in the blankets he sleeps in. Insulated. Guarded. The KEEP OFF sign suggested like a fist in the air. Tell me I'm not solid. Tell me I let Dick down by not talking to him. Tell me that I'm to blame. Fuck. I wasn't never no charity case and I sure as hell ain't one now. I don't need anyone to tell me how to figure out my way around the world. I don't need anyone to tell me what I'm supposed to do. Do for a friend. How to talk. How to behave in my own home. Home. What a friggin' laugh. This isn't a home. It's a flop, just like every other flop in every fleabag joint I ever laid up in. Garbage. There's still fucking garbage everywhere. Only thing is, here the garbage's got a fancier name. I'll find Dick. I'll drive that truck into the friggin' ground until I find him. Then what'll they say? That I don't know how to look after my winger? That I let him down? That I don't take care of my end? Fuck 'em. All but six. I don't need anybody. Never did. Never will.

Timber

I SMOOTHED HIS FACE like the blade was my fingers. I sat there in candlelight and used the very least edge of my knife, nicking the wood, barely touching it with steel, caressing it almost, urging it to talk, to tell me where the man who inhabited this wood was sitting right at that moment so I could go to him. We needed him. *I* needed him. He was as essential as breathing. Without him, we were separated by distances too huge to cross. We had strength and thought and spirit, but we lacked innocence and trust and feeling. Dick was that. All of that. The nexus. The joining. Our bridge to each other. This carving was going to tell him that. It wasn't about sadness now. It wasn't about weight. It was about being there. Inhabiting your place in this world. Regardless. It was about being seen, visible, real. It was about the great fact that some of us get to realize: that home is not about a place, not about a building, not about geography or even a time; home is belonging in someone else's heart. Just the way you are. Warts and all. This carving would say all that because that was Dick's great teaching, the learning hidden in his absence. I would tell him that. I'd tell him that he had a home in my heart now and always. Regardless.

Granite

I SAID IN THE BEGINNING OF IT ALL that some lives are never meant to cross. I told myself that gross circumstances cause disparate meetings and that the only rational reaction is dismissal and moving on. I told myself that those four lives and mine had no common denominator, no edges that overlapped. Except for the movies. I wondered whether that had ever truly been enough. They were right to be offended by my prodding. They were right to be angered by my reluctance to talk about my world. Other than the sketch I'd given that one night, I hadn't said another word about myself. When the hands on the street are held out, it isn't always alms that are beggared; it's life, contact, touch, generosity of spirit—and I'd lost sense of that, if I ever really had it at all. Beggary. It's not the sole property of the street people or the ill defined. It's part of all of us, part of everyone who has ever suffered loss. A handout. It meant something more suddenly. It meant more than the image and the idea of a dirty, wrinkled, weakened hand stretched outward to accept nickels and dimes. It meant every hand extended across the galaxy of separation that exists between all of us. All of us beggars. We are in the end, all of us, beggarly, seeking connection, the redemption of contact. Double Dick Dumont was teaching me that, and I'd tell him and thank him as soon as I saw him.

Time doesn't exist.
Pardon me?
Time. It doesn't exist. Did you know that?
No. Sometimes it seems like it's all that's real. Like time is the only thing we have to keep things together.
Well, it's not. It's not because it was a creation of our imagination when we believed we needed something to pin our lives on, some way to measure progress, some way to try to control change. Funny how we get so big in our britches sometimes, isn't it?
Yes. It is. But tell me more about this idea.
Well, if time was real, it would leave some residue behind. Something tangible, some evidence of its passing. But it's invisible, so there's no residue. All there is, is now, this moment, this instance, this time. Then it's gone. Like a firefly in the night. Winking out, becoming invisible again.
I see that. But where does it go?
Inside us. Time disappears inside us. It becomes real through memory, recollection, and feeling. Then, only then, can it last forever. When it becomes a part of us, a part of our spirit on its never-ending journey.
Journey to where?
To completion.
You're losing me.

Don't worry. You'll come to understand it all too.

When?

In time.

One For The Dead

BEN STARR came to my room. He walked right in through the window and sat at the edge of my bed and started talking as though the years between our last meeting had never happened, as though life had simply carried on and absence and longing were not a part of the language we spoke. He talked about travelling. He talked about poetry and how words on paper were becoming the song he was learning to sing. He talked about love in the blinking orange light of the Regal and how it had put the poetry and the music inside of him, how it made him want to write me, sculpt me with language, mould me, define my edges like his hands used to trace my angles and curves and hollows.

"I have you here," he said to me, and held out his fingertips.

Then he stood up, looked at me for a long moment, and stepped back to the window.

Then Harley came. My little brother Harley. He ran in through the curtains and sat at the same spot that Ben had and talked to me. He told me about horses. Spirit Dogs, he called them, and how he was learning to call them from across the wide prairies. They'd come to him, their hoof beats like a drum song, and encircle him, nickering and neighing, and he'd tell them stories. Stories about their human brothers and sisters and how they needed the Spirit Dogs to carry them, to help them, to make them more. Then one would always choose itself and offer its back. Harley would ride. Ride wild and free. Ride with the spirit of the Old Ones.

"We get to go back to it," he said to me, and smiled.

Then he made room for John. John. My big brother John. He walked in and sat beside Harley and draped a big arm around his shoulders. He was wearing Grass Dancer regalia. There were long tufts of prairie grass tied to his arms and legs and waist and he wore elegantly beaded moccasins on his feet. A single eagle's feather stood in a headpiece made of a porcupine's tail and his face was painted in the old way, a rich ochre from the earth in three wavy lines down his face. He talked to me about being sent out to dance with the rest of the young men, to bless the gathering place of the People, to make it ready for their feet to come and pray and sing and dance in celebration of life. He talked about being blessed with the dance.

"You become a protector," he said to me.

Then Frankie walked in. Frank One Sky. He had a drum in his hands. It was an old drum and he showed it to me in great detail, explaining how it was made of a single ring of tree trunk, how burning-hot rocks were used to hollow out the ring, to burn away the inner wood. Then he told me about the elk skin stretched across it. He hit it once or twice and spoke about the high tone of the elk skin, about the blessings within its song. A marten was painted on its face. Frankie told me how those without a clan become Marten Clan when they enter the Circle of the People.

"It's a Warrior Clan," he said. "We get to be warriors."

"Spirit warriors," my brother Irwin said as he walked in to sit beside his brothers. "You get to heal the people."

He carried a water drum. He smiled when he showed it to me. The drum was old and he held it like he would a Grandfather: gently, tenderly, respectfully. He told me about the old songs that were sung around campfires and how the spirit of those songs got right to the inside of things and made them smoother. He told me that everyone got to sing together. All the People. Everyone got to be healed by the unity around the fire and the spirit of the songs. Everyone.

And suddenly they were all there. All of them, standing at my window looking at me and dressed in ceremonial garb like I'd never seen before. Old. Simple. Honourable. Eagle feathers few and far between. Sacred symbols carried proudly in their hands. Hair tied in prayer braids. Grandma One Sky, my mother, father, everyone from Big River who I'd seen depart—and behind them I could sense a thousand more, the shadowed ones who'd allowed me to witness their search, their prowl, their desire, their reach for life. They were all there. They were all there and they reached their hands out to me, palms up, and offered me comfort. Comfort. I closed my eyes and felt the waves of their beckoning, waves and waves and waves of it, pouring down like silver, telling me it was fine, it was okay, there was peace to come, peace—and I slept hard until morning.

When I woke up, I knew.

Granite

"THEY FOUND HIM," James said.

I stared at the telephone in my hand in the early morning light and shook my head to clear it. "Pardon?" I asked.

"Dick," he said quietly. "They found him."

"Oh, good. Finally. Where was he?"

"At the Hilton. He's dead."

I felt the world stop. I didn't move. I couldn't. Margo looked at me from the bed and put a hand slowly to her face.

"How?" was all I could say.

"He drowned. There was a bottle of pills and a bottle of vodka beside him. He vomited in his sleep and drowned."

I sat down heavily on the edge of the bed. I couldn't think. "Jesus. Jesus."

"The police are saying accidental overdose. I spoke to them. He had my card in his wallet and they called. No concern about suicide. It looked too casual. No note, no nothing. The officer said it looked like he'd been studying a map."

"Do the others know?"

"No. I don't think it's something I want to tell them alone."

"Jesus. Dick. God," I said, struggling to find language amid the numbness I felt.

"The papers are going to be all over this. I don't see that there's a lot we can do to stop it. We need to get over to the house and prepare them."

"No one's spoken to each other since that blow up. I'm not even sure they'd let us in. Digger, anyway."

"He's going to have to."

"Yes."

"Margo there?"

"Yes."

"You'll be okay?"

"Yes."

"Are you sure?"

"No. I'm not."

"I'll be there in fifteen minutes. Can you be ready?"

"Yes."

I hung up the phone and slumped back on the bed. I closed my eyes and felt Margo's hand on my chest. Without opening my eyes, I told her what James had told me—straightforward, direct. I heard her cry. She collapsed against me and we lay there, her tears moistening my skin.

We dressed without speaking. As I watched her in the mirror, I marvelled at the improbable, unbidden meetings that shape us. She had changed me. She had come unbidden, through the improbable union of my life with those of the rounders and of Double Dick Dumont. I owed him so much. I thought about his childlike grin when something touched him and how I had always been envious of his ability to be charmed by the ordinary stuff of living. He taught me to see again, really. Then, as I buttoned my shirt and watched Margo pull on her jeans, I thought of all the questions he asked and marvelled at how incredibly easy it had been for me to simply stop asking questions of life. Double Dick Dumont brought my mind forward again. Strange. An illiterate. A man constantly chasing words and ideas to corral them, capture them, stop their motion so he could see them and come to understand. An unversed beggar taught me that words have a life of their own, and in them, when we take the time to corral them, is the stuff of our own life, the keys to vision. Walking down the stairs, watching the bounce of Margo's hair in the glow from the skylight, I thought about how sad he'd become at the turn of a tale or the giddiness he'd move into when stories shone with ebullient conclusions or the sombre look he offered at tragedy and loss. He taught me how to respond again. To move out of the twilight.

Timber

THE FIRST THING that told me things were going to be different was the doorbell. Anyone who was part of our circle knew that you just walked into the house and found us wherever we might be. When I got to the door, I was surprised to see Granite, Margo, and James standing there. They'd never had to ring before. I wondered how much a measure of the shouting this was, or if it was something else. They looked as awkward at the change in routine as I felt opening the door for them.

"Timber," James said. "Are the others awake?"

"Yes, I believe so."

"Could you get them, please, and meet us in the kitchen?"

"Yes. Sure." None of them wanted to look right at me and I felt a shiver in my belly. "What? Is it Dick?"

"Get the others, please," James said, and the tone of his voice sent me hurrying out the back door toward the garage and the garden. Digger was looking at the workings of a radio splayed apart on his table. I hadn't been to his door since the night of the shouting and I suddenly felt timid.

"Digger?" I said quietly.

He looked up. When our eyes met, I felt absence like a tear in my chest. He felt it too, and I saw his eyes soften from the initial glare of intrusion.

"Yeah?" he replied.

"Granite, Margo, and James are here. They want to see us in the kitchen."

He nodded and rolled a small spring between his thumb and two fingers. When he placed it on the table, he kept his hand there a moment unmoving, then looked up at me again. "Okay," he said. "Guess there's some things that need saying."

"Guess," I said.

We walked over to where Amelia was nipping dead leaves and buds from her plants. She heard us coming, and when she looked at us there was a strange little smile on her face. She reached down and put the handful of pickings in a small pile in the dirt, patted it softly, held her hand there a second, and stood to look at us. "It's good to see you side by side again," she said. "It's the normal thing. The best thing."

Digger and I exchanged a look. It did feel good. "Yes." I said. "The others are here. They want us in the kitchen."

"Yes," she said. "Can I show you something first?"

"Sure."

She motioned for us to kneel beside her and pointed to a plant growing at her feet. It wasn't much. It was a raggedy little thing, really, and I wondered why she had it in the garden that she took such pride in and cared for so diligently. Her fingers caressed the underside of its pale green leaves and she smiled as she touched it.

"See this little thing?" she asked.

"Yeah," Digger said, wincing at the unfamiliar crunch of kneeling in the garden. "It's a plant. In a garden."

"Yes, but it's very special," she said.

"How come?" he asked, and I could feel the distance the argument had built between us melt away. "Don't look like much to me."

"No. I suppose it doesn't. Not compared to the tomato plants and the potatoes and the corn. They're so regal. So full of purpose. This little guy is just a plant. I don't think he does anything special."

"So why have it here?" I asked.

"Because he needed a place to grow."

"Huh?" Digger grunted.

"I found him laying in the grass over by the fence. I suspect he was a clipping from the neighbours trimming their hedges. He was just laying there, all helpless and lost, and I took him to my room, put him in a glass of water, set him in the sunshine of the windowsill, and watched over him."

"And?" Digger asked.

"And he grew roots. He wanted to live. When he was strong enough, I brought him out here and planted him with the rest of the growing things. Now, he's starting to reach upward again."

"So?" Digger asked.

She looked at both of us and smiled. "Oh, nothing," she said. "I just wanted you to see it, that's all."

Amelia looked at me then and I felt seen, recognized, known, and understood. Digger watched us, and as our gaze shifted to him he met it, pressed his lips together and nodded.

"Let's go," she said.

We walked to the back door silently but together. It felt right except for the notable absence. When we walked through the door into the kitchen, the other three were sitting silently at the table. Something in the air told me to sit, and I pulled out a chair for Amelia while Digger went to lean on the counter. I sat down across from Granite, who looked at his hands folded in front of him.

James cleared his throat. We all looked at him. He swallowed and rubbed his jaw with one hand. Then he exhaled long and slow.

"Don't friggin' say it," Digger said. "Don't you friggin' say it, you son of a bitch. Don't you friggin' say it!"

His face was contorted, red with anger, and his eyes blazed. At his sides, his hands clenched and unclenched and he swept his gaze around the ceiling of the room for some place to fix it on.

"Digger," Amelia said quietly. "It's all right. It's all right."

He looked at her and his face shook like his chin would tumble to the floor at any second. He swallowed hard and then looked at James. They met each other's gaze before James dropped his to the table.

"Son of a fucking bitch!" Digger yelled, and slammed a hand down on the counter. "Fuck. Fuck. Fuck. Fuck!"

Margo cried quietly, tears rolling down her face like rain on a window. Granite looked at Digger, who had turned and was bending over the counter clenching his fists hard against its surface and groaning. His face was loose with grief and his hands shook on the table. Amelia sat silently, calmly. I just sat there numb, not shocked, not surprised, not caught totally off guard, just frozen in place, in time.

"They found him at the Hilton," James said quietly. "There were some pills and a bottle of vodka beside him."

Digger turned to look at him. "If you try to tell me that he offed himself, I will walk right over and smack you in the fucking head, you fucking shyster bastard."

"No. He didn't," James said. "The police say it was an accidental overdose. He was reading and he fell asleep."

"Dick couldn't fucking read, dipshit," Digger said. "Or didn't you ever pay enough attention to know that?"

"Well, he was looking at a map. An atlas."

"An atlas?" Amelia asked.

"Yes. There was a town circled on it. Tucumcary. Tucumcary, New Mexico. Does that mean anything to anyone?"

We all shook our heads.

"Maybe he heard it in a movie," I said. "It has a kind of ring to it that Dick would like. He liked the sound of words."

Margo smiled at me.

"Where'd he get the pills?" Digger asked.

"There's no way to know," James said. "Probably from a street dealer. A friend, maybe."

"We're his friends," Digger said. "We wouldn't give him no pills."

"Other friends, then," James said. "Ones he met while he was gone."

Digger glared. Looking at him, I knew that I would not want to be the person guilty of handing Dick a bottle of pills. "I'm going over there," he said.

"Digger, I don't know if . . . ," James began.

"You don't have to know nothing. Nothing. All you have to know is that I'm going over there. He's my pal. I want to see him."

"They moved him, Digger. He's at the morgue."

"There's nothing in his room? No stuff? No nothing?"

"Well, according to the police there are some personal effects but nothing big. Clothes, I suppose. Toiletries."

"I wanna see him."

"Well, someone needs to make a positive identification but I thought I would do that," James said.

"You? Why you?" Digger asked.

"To spare you all the hardship."

"Spare me nothing. I'm his fucking family. His fucking family."

"Okay," James said. "Okay."

"I'm going too," Amelia said.

"Me too," I said.

Digger looked at us and nodded. "Fucking rights," he said. "Family."

Digger

I NEVER FELT NOTHING like that ever. I stood there looking down at the face of my winger and it was like he shoulda moved, shoulda winked at me, shoulda let me know it was all a big fucking gaffe. But he never did. He just lay there all cold and quiet. He just lay there like a little kid, sleeping. It tore the heart right the fuck out of me to see that. The others didn't stay long. The old lady touched his cheek with her fingertips and said his name all quiet and sad, Timber reached out to touch his hand, and me, I just stood there. Just stood there. Looking. Thinking. When they left, I kept right on standing there looking at Double Dick Dumont. My winger. My pal. My brother.

"Digger," Rock goes, peeping into the room. "Are you coming? We're finished here."

"Well, fuck off then," I go. "I ain't done here."

"We'll wait."

"Whatever."

He closed the door. It was chilly in there and I pulled my coat closer around me, then reached down and tucked the sheet snug around D. It didn't seem like enough so I walked over and got a few more from a pile on a table and covered him up good. Nestled him in on accounta he never did like being cold, hated it, really, but put up with it without bitching like any good rounder would. Slept in a fucking doorway when I met him. A doorway. No warm air grate, no empty warehouse yet. Just a doorway. A hard-core rounder getting by. I pulled a metal stool over to the side of the gurney he was on, put my feet up on the rungs of it, and looked at him.

"Amazing fucking thing, ain't it, D? We spend all that time learning how to move around with people and we still end up all alone in a cold fucking room. Hardly seems worth the fucking trip, you know what I mean? No. No. You wouldn't know that. You was always the one that wanted people around you. You was always the one that talked me into letting anybody near me. Why'd you do that, D? How come you did that? How come? I was doing good. I was getting by. I didn't need nobody. Fuck, I even told you to take a hike at first, you fucking loogan. No. I don't mean that. I never meant that. Not never, D. I never thought you was a loogan. You were just a little short on the upstroke but you were always stroking. Always. Fuck, I admired that. I flat out admired that you never gave up even when the stuff was too fucking deep even for a whiz-bang guy like me. You never gave up. I looked up to you for that. Did you know that? I looked up to you. I never told you, though. Never told you on accounta it was soft, the warm and fuzzy kinda shit that drove me crazy. I never told you until now, and now it's kinda late. Guess I'm the loogan now, eh? Keep that to yourself, though, D. I still got a reputation down here.

"What the fuck am I gonna do, D? I ain't got no one to watch over no more. I ain't go no little brother, and you was always my little brother. Always. Them others, they don't need me. Not now. It ain't no tough life we're living. Not like then. Not like when we hooked up. Remember that, D? Remember? Remember how we'd be shivering like a dog shitting razor blades, all huddled up in the alley by the Mission, and we'd suck back a few swallows of hooch and carry the fuck on? Or around old Fill 'er Up Phil's oil drum fire with the hot dogs on the stick that one of the boosters grabbed from the market? Steak on a fucking stick. Right, D? Steak on a fucking stick. Or remember the rain trick? You liked that one. Remember? How the rain'd run over a lip on the gazebo in Berry Park and we'd all get a free shower? Fuck, that was funny. You thought we meant like a real shower and they caught you all naked with a bar of soap in the rain. Jesus, I laughed. That was a good one. You even laughed like hell whenever we reminded you. I liked that about you, D. You could always take a joke, a trick. Who the fuck am I gonna joke with now, D? Who?

"It don't matter. I remember how to operate alone. I guess I could go back to that. Yeah. I guess I could go back to that. But you know what, D? You know what I fucking wish? You know what I wish more than anything? I wish our life hadn't fucking changed. I wish we'da never won that fucking money on accounta I'd still have to look out for you and you'd still be here. You'd still be here, 'cause I looked after you good, D. Best I could. No one ever got on your case with me around. Never. I don't know what you had inside you that made you kinda crazy but I'da looked after you through it. I woulda. But the fucking money changed everything and it took my attention away. I wish we'da never won.

"But you know what else? You know what else, D? I wish I could fucking fly. I wish I could fucking fly, and I know that sounds crazy coming from me, but if I could fly I'd take off right now and fly to wherever you are and be your winger again.

"Guess I can't, though. Guess you'll just have to wait while I finish up here, however long that takes. Stubborn son of a bitch like me'll probably live to be a hundred and fucking fifty just out of pure cussedness. But you'll wait, won't ya, D? I know you'll wait. Can I tell you something, D? I'm pissed at them. Not all of them. Just the Square Johns. Just the ones who never really tried to see us. The ones who figured we lived somewhere else. The ones who thought we were trespassers, that we weren't supposed to be here. I was never big on the Square Johns anyway, was I? But I'm pissed 'cause I think they coulda done more for you. Shoulda done more on accounta it's their friggin' world and they're supposed to take care of the ones that ain't got the tools. They're supposed to look out for the weak ones, the ones who need a hand making it around the world. Like me. Like I did looking after you. I'm pissed and I don't know if I'll get over it. Is that okay, D? Is that okay?

"I guess I gotta go. See you, buddy. You let me know if you need anything. Anything and it's yours. It's yours, pal."

That's what I said to him as close as I can remember. Then I reached down and kissed him. Kissed him and said goodbye.

Granite

DIGGER WALKED OUT of the room where Dick lay and right past all of us. He didn't wait for us. Instead, he walked down the street and I watched him hail a cab, get into it, and disappear. There are distances you can feel. They say that the middle of the ocean and any spot in space are similar. They say that the view is the same in all directions. Isotropic. Everywhere you look is water, horizon, and sky or else stars, planets, and space. I knew then, as I watched the tail lights of the taxi ease around the corner, that the world becomes an isotropic place when pain and sorrow and hurt define the topography of things. It's all you can see. Everywhere you look. I didn't know what power was needed to alter that. My experiences in life had never granted me that education, but I did know that people are like stars or continents sometimes: distant, removed, unreachable, the holes between them as deep as space or seas sometimes, and cold as emptiness can be.

"Where do you think he's gone?" Timber asked me.

"I don't know."

"Will he be all right?"

"Digger? Yes. That's one guy I wouldn't worry about."

We climbed into the car. There didn't seem to be anything to say, so we drove in silence, James guiding the car slowly and easily down the street. Everyone seemed to want to watch the street flow by. I know I did. The city felt emptier somehow, and I kept looking at the people on the street, wondering about their stories, where they came from, how they managed a day, a life, a history, how they felt walking along sidewalks filled with strangers and untold tales. Continental drift. It's a phenomenon that happens unsuspectingly, minute fractions at a time, the polar opposite of the Hubble constant, the rate of expansion of the universe. People drift apart like that. Minutely, fractionally, or else accelerated to light speed and beyond. But the universe was compacted matter once, and the earth was Pangaea; one continent, one world. Separation was the nature of things, it seemed. But it was the coming together of things that amazed me right then. Watching all of those people moving, orbiting each other, I marvelled at the randomness of colliding worlds. When Double Dick Dumont came into my life, it was outrageous fortune. Improbable. Unbelievable. But the more we edged closer, the more magical it became. Every movie we saw together was a joining. Every wandering conversation was a tie. Every joke, every story, every sight was another entrance we made together into a land that had never existed before, a land you learn to travel without maps, conversation your only compass to shores edging closer and closer, seamlessly, becoming Pangaea. I knew about it then. Understood. Knew for dead, absolute certain that some people are a country you come to inhabit gradually, their shores and yours touching, merging, unifying, and their departures dislodge you.

We filed into the house and settled in the living room. Margo busied herself making a pot of tea and the rest of us sat silently, wondering what to do next. It was James who took control.

"There are a few things that need to happen right away," he said. "The first is that we need to have a plan for the media. Frankly, I'm surprised they're not here already. Second, we need to discuss how to handle the arrangements."

"I'll handle the press," I said.

"How?" James asked.

"I'll handle the questions. I'll also talk to my editor at the paper and tell him I'll write the story."

"You will?"

"Yes. Not a story, really. A column. A eulogy."

"An honour song," Amelia said.

"Yes."

She nodded. "I'd like him to have the very best," she said. "He deserves that. He always deserved the very best."

"I know a good funeral director. I'll inform him right away," James said.

"Shouldn't we try to contact the family?" Margo asked, returning with a tray bearing tea and cups.

"We are the family," I said. "Technically, he was indigent."

"Imagine. An indigent millionaire," she said. "Strange, isn't it?"

"Yes," Timber said. "The whole thing's been strange. The whole trip."

"I would never have missed it, though," I said.

"Me neither," he replied.

"He needs a place to rest," Amelia said. "He needs a place where he can be at peace. A nice site overlooking a river."

"Why a river, Amelia?" Margo asked.

"Because it was his favourite hymn. 'Shall We Gather at the River.' Remember, Timber?"

"Yes," Timber said. "I remember."

"We used to go to chapel at the Sally Ann. The Salvation Army. They'd put on a big breakfast afterwards but you had to go to chapel first before you could eat. Most couldn't stand the service but Dick really loved it. Especially the hymns. He'd sing really loud even though he didn't know all the words. Of course, he couldn't read but he'd try to memorize them and sing really loudly."

"And terribly," Timber added.

"Yes. Terribly. But with a lot of gusto anyway," Amelia said. "*Shall we gather at the river, the beautiful, the beautiful river.* He really liked the idea of that. He said it was like meeting all your friends for a picnic, and I think he's probably right about that."

"Well, I think I'd best call the newspaper and start things moving there. I'll stay here, if you don't mind, just to head off the hounds when they call or arrive."

"You're always welcome here," Amelia said.

"May I stay too?" Margo asked. "I'd like to be around as well."

"My sister," Amelia said. "You're welcome here too."

"And when Digger comes back?" I asked.

"When Digger comes back, I'll speak with him," Amelia said.

"Then I guess we should begin taking care of things," James said.

And all of us moved forward together. Like continents.

Digger

"DOUBLE JACK BACK and two drafts front and centre, Ray," I go, striding up to the bar.

"You got 'er," Ray goes.

There's a fair crowd for the Palace and the bar seats are almost all taken. Looking around I see the usual gang: the talkers busy engaging their invisible pals in politics or the drama of life; the gazers staring at one spot on the ceiling or the floor; the glass rubbers stroking the frost on their drafts like a lover, nursing it, making it last; and the sharks either enjoying the booty from a scam or a score or in the set-up stage, getting enough liquid courage to do their deed. Typical old-man-bar, middle-of-the-afternoon kinda crowd.

"So what's shaking?" Ray goes, settling in for a talk.

"Damndest shit," I go.

"Yeah?"

"Yeah."

"Like what? Anything I should know about?"

I look at him. I've known Ray for years and I've never really taken a good look. He's an old fucker now. Still got the leftovers of a ducktail in his hair, still combs it back and slicks it, but there's a lot less to fucking grease. Wears glasses now that kinda bob on the end of his nose, the half-glasses that people figure give you the egghead look but really just bring out the bozo in you. Wears them on a rope around his neck like he knows he's gonna forget where the hell he put them. Jesus. I shiver thinking about how easily the friggin' years get by you.

"How fucking long've I known you, Ray?"

"Let's see. I come here right after the merchant marine so that's a good thirty years, so probably twenty-five, thereabouts."

"That's a friggin' long time to be staring across a bar at somebody."

"I guess. Only you were never that much of a talker. You were a draft-and-dash fucker for a long, long time."

"Yeah?"

"Yeah. Only really started doing the good-neighbour routine once you hooked up with those friends of yours. That's when I started to really know you."

"And how long's that been?"

"God. Fifteen years, maybe. How the fuck are they, anyway?"

"Good. Most of them."

"*Most of them* means there's a story there."

"Yeah. You ever really like me, Ray?"

"Like you? What the fuck kinda question is that? Haven't I always done you good here? Haven't I always let you be?"

"Yeah. Yeah. Sure. But that's not liking someone. That's taking somebody's loot and doing your friggin' job. I wanna know if you liked me. Really."

He looks at me over the top of those bozo glasses and I see how the years have made his eyes all watery-looking. But they're steady. They're strong and they're looking at me with a look I never seen there before. "You okay?" he goes.

"No. I ain't. I wanna know, Ray. I really wanna know."

He pours me a fresh draft, sets it down, and fires up a smoke. "You're a tough guy to figure. I never could. Not really. You only give what you figure you need to give, and that makes knowing somebody real tough. Still, you've always been a solid type and I like that. So, yeah, yeah, I liked you."

"Yeah?"

"Yeah. Given the special fucking circumstances. I mean, this place ain't exactly your basic highball lounge, you know what I mean?"

I smirk. "Yeah, I guess."

"So what's to it, Digger?"

"Dick."

"Dick?"

"Yeah. D. He's tits up. Right now. I just seen him on the fucking slab."

"Fuck me. Really? How? When? Here, have another round. On me," Ray goes, looking back over his shoulder while he gets my round. He hurries back and leans on the bar to get the goods.

I blow air through my lips, then drain the Jack. Burn. I cool the fire with a swallow of beer. "Cops say he overdosed on pills."

"Fuck," Ray goes, all solemn. "I only met him a few times but he didn't seem like no pillhead."

"He wasn't. Someone gave them to him. Someone he was with."

"Where was he?"

"The Hilton," I go, eyebrows raised.

"The Hilton? Fuck. Times have changed."

"Yeah. Sometimes I think so."

"And other times?"

"Other times it's the same shit in a different bowl."

"Got that right. So what happens now? With the money, I mean."

"I don't know. The Square John lawyer'll figure that out along with his Square John friends."

"You split it, right?"

"Yeah. So?"

"So you should ask for it back."

"How come?"

"How come? I don't know. Just sounds right. Like that's what Dick'd want."

"You figure?"

"Sure. You guys hung tight for a long time. He wouldn'ta had the life he had if it weren't for you."

"Yeah. I figure the fucking Square Johns'll be all over it, though."

"Yeah?"

"Fuck, yeah. Why the hell else were they hanging around?"

"Maybe they liked you."

"Fuck you. You just said you had a hard time liking me. Why should they?"

"Hey, who can figure out the straights? They seemed like good folks when they were here. I mean, they came *here.* And that was before the money."

"I guess. But what pisses me off is how they think they're in a friggin' movie all the time. They walk around like every fucking thing is gonna be explained for them. Like everything is gonna be what it is and all they gotta do is hang. They don't gotta do nothing."

"Whatta ya mean?"

"I mean they knew D was up shit creek a long time before this and that he couldn't swim and they didn't do nothing for him. Just waited and fucking waited and now he's fucking dead and I hate those cocksuckers," I go, and wave at Ray for more.

"You saying he offed himself?"

"Fuck, no. I'm saying they're the ones with the world by the ass. They're the ones got the tools and shit. They're the fucking shrinks and quacks and goody-goodies who're supposed to help guys like him and they didn't. They fucking didn't. All they did was try to pass it off on me."

"You? How?"

"Said I should talk to him. Like I'm a fucking shrink. Fuck. What was I supposed to say? What the fuck do I know about why a guy won't sleep at night?"

"Don't know. What *do* you know?"

I look at him and feel the old rage inside me again like I hadn't felt for a long time. Feel it building in my belly and pushing at the sides of my head.

"I know that shit is shit and the only one who can clean out your stall is you. Me? I got no business in someone else's head. I got enough fucking problems dealing with my own."

"Sounds just like them," Ray goes.

"Fuck you," I go, draining my draft but wondering why I feel sucker-punched all of a sudden.

One For The Dead

I SAW THE FACE of a shadowed one. I saw it in the fashioned wood of the carving Timber had made of Dick. Once the others had gone to take care of the funeral and the media, Timber took me to Digger's store and showed it to me. It was lovely. I could see how it had once been a big log. I guess that's what caught me first, the curious feeling of seeing the missing parts first, the log in its original form and then the magical unveiling of the man. I wondered if all art is like that, or if only those things that are hewn from love are graced with that particular magic. Anyway, I stood in the hushed light in the back of the store and saw it. Dick. He was wrapped in a blanket and staring across the open space in front of him in the way that your loved ones do when you catch them in private moments and they don't know you're there. Stark. Open. Naked. He was beautiful.

"It's like he was here," I said.

"Thank you," Timber said. "I was afraid that maybe I'd missed him."

"No. This is definitely Dick. His hands. Even his hands the way they're holding the blanket seem alive, like they're ready to clench tighter."

"Yes. It's nearly done."

"What else is there? It looks finished to me, Jonas."

"You call me Jonas more now. How come?"

"I guess because I know you more now and you feel more like Jonas to me instead of Timber. Sometimes I think Timber is gone."

"Where?"

"I don't know. Back where he always belonged, I guess."

"Where's that?" he asked, sitting on a stool.

"In the past," I said. "Everybody's past."

"Everybody's past? Is there a past that belongs to all of us?"

"Yes. It lives in the forget-me place."

"Where's that?"

"Somewhere in our journey together where someone was left behind and it was shrugged off like it didn't matter, like that person didn't matter, and the rest just carried on. Every tribe has a moment in their history like that. All of us. That's where Timber belongs. Not here. Not now. This is where Jonas Hohnstein lives."

"I like that image. The forget-me place. Is that where Dick is?"

I looked at him. He looked like a brother trying to cope with loss, all sudden and complicated. "No," I said. "Even if he was once, you've just moved him from there forever with this carving."

"Yeah?"

"Yes. Definitely. This is beautiful. It's like a song."

We looked at the piece together and he talked to me about Double Dick. Told me about the lessons he'd learned from being in his company, from seeing his struggle and his small victories. He told me about how in the beginning he'd doubted that there was a friendship under all of Dick's half-formed thoughts and questions. He told me how he'd watched him grow and how he'd wanted all of that to go into the piece in front of us. He told me how he'd loved him.

"It's all there," I said. "All of that is there in that wood."

"Do you think so?"

"Yes. You can feel it."

"Is it enough?"

I walked over and put my arms around him and hugged him. I felt his sorrow in the way his arms hung loose at his sides, like they couldn't lift a feather. "Love is always enough," I said.

Granite

I WAS PREPARING the tabletop for a few hours of writing: notepads, pens, water, and a waste basket. I'd made the necessary arrangements with Mac, and although the paper would run a short story on Dick's passing, the bulk of it would come from me. There was a big commotion at the front door. Margo and I exchanged a look and then headed out.

It was James. He'd dropped his briefcase and he and Amelia and Timber were scrambling about trying to retrieve things, made more difficult by a very tipsy Digger who was two-stepping around them trying to get out of the way.

"We all have to talk. Right now," James said when the papers had been returned to his case.

"What's going on?" Digger asked, squinting one eye shut for focus.

"We need to talk," James repeated.

We moved into the living room and made ourselves comfortable. James took an extra moment to compose himself and in that instant we all looked at each other, plumbing for clues. We had none.

"Dick left a will," James said, clearing his throat.

"What? How the hell did he do that? He couldn't friggin' write," Digger said.

"He didn't need to," James said. "He put it all on this tape recorder." He pulled a small hand-held recorder from his pocket. We all stared at it like pilgrims at a shrine.

"I'm gonna need a drink," Digger said.

"Me too," Timber said.

"Might as well make it three," I said, and James nodded in agreement.

I crossed to the bar and began preparing glasses. "Is it really a will? If it is, if he took the time to outline his wishes, it makes the accidental overdose angle hard to sell," I said.

"Hey, fuck you," Digger said angrily. "I've really had enough of your shit."

"Digger," James said firmly. "Enough. This is important and you'd best hear what's on this tape. You need to know that this will stand as the last will and testament of Richard Dumont. It will stand because he gives specific directions as to how and where he wants his assets to go. He makes specific, clear reference to where they came from, how he acquired them, and therefore no contest can be made regarding the state of his mind at the time. Certainly there's the question of intoxication, but he's coherent enough. Ready?"

Margo moved to sit beside Amelia. They held hands and leaned their heads together.

"Ready as we'll ever be, I suppose," I said, and James played the tape.

Double Dick

I NEVER WANTED YOU to worry. I guess you did anyhow on accounta you always worry about me. But I hadta walk. Sometimes it helps me to walk on accounta my head don't gotta focus on one thing an' I can look around and feel less trapped by stuff. That's how I felt that night. Trapped. I been trapped a long time an' I had to leave so I could figure out how to get myself free. See, I done somethin' bad one time. Somethin' real bad an' I ain't never been able to really get away from it even though I left where I was when I done it. I can't talk about it now. But maybe when I get back from Tucumcary I will. Maybe when I spend some time in the sun an' walk around down there I'll be able to find a way to get away from this an' tell you all on accounta right now it's hard an' scary an' I don't know where to start. But it's how come the *Ironweed* movie freaked me out. On accounta it was almost the same an' I thought it was talkin' to me. But I ain't got no place to go back to to try'n make things right, not like the man in the movie when he went an' talked to the woman after all that time. I ain't got no place where anyone ever wants to talk to me again or see me walk down the street on accounta what I done was so bad. All I got is Tucumcary. So when I come back I'll try'n have more to say about that.

But that's not how come I'm doin' this. That's not how come I'm talkin' into this tape. I wanna tell you all about what I'm thinkin'. I wanna tell you what I wanna do on accounta everybody's got somethin' they do now except maybe One For The Dead, who looks out for us an' that's kinda been what she done all the time an' she still wants to do it so she does, but me I got nothin'. Nothin' except watchin' movies, an' I wanna do somethin'.

I like talkin' to people. Sometimes they figure I'm a loogan on accounta I don't get stuff right off the hop but I like talkin' anyhow. So I thought I could be a visitor at the Mission an' the shelters an' drop-ins an' stuff like that. Just go down an' talk on accounta more than anything people wants to talk an' I know all about the life on accounta I was a rounder for so long. Am I still a rounder, Digger? I get confused about that on accounta the money an' the house an' stuff. I hope so. Bein' a rounder's all I know about. That's how come I could be a good visitor. 'Cause I'm a rounder. Anyhow, I figure that's what I'd be good at an' it don't take no school or nothin' an' I don't gotta make no money, so why not?

That's what I wanna do. But first I'm goin' to Tucumcary like I always wanted to do from the time I was a kid. Tom Bruce said it was a dream place. So maybe goin' to a dream place means I can swap the one I been carryin' for another one. A better one. Like swappin' a movie you watched too many times. I done that a few times an' it worked out good.

But when I get back I wanna do somethin'. Somethin' important. Well, more than one thing but I gotta talk about one first on accounta talkin' about two or three'll just confuse me an' I don't know how long the batteries last on these things. Okay. Let's see. Oh, yeah. Digger.

I know you don't need nothin' an' you probably don't want nothin' neither on accounta you like things simple like you always said, but I want you to buy a Ferris wheel. I want you to take some of my money from Mr. James an' get one of them things an' put it up where people can ride it an' you can run it like you done before. I know you miss that. Buy some land somewhere an' put your wheel up in the sky again an' ride it like you done before. Ride it like the best wheelman in the world. Then you can show me how to run it maybe, an' I could give you a ride an' other people could ride it too, whenever they want on accounta Ferris wheels always make people happy an' if we're not usin' all that money to help make people happy then I figure maybe we didn't learn nothin' from all the time we was rounders on the street an' didn't have nothin'. That's what I think anyhow, an' wouldn't it be nice to have a Ferris wheel in the neighbourhood to go an' ride any time we wanted? Maybe it would give people dreams like the kind they had when they was kids. That's a nice present, huh? For everybody.

Next is One For The Dead. I always wanted to buy you a dress. I used to look at you when we was rounders an' think to myself that you really needed a nice dress. A really nice dress kinda like the ones we seen in the movies sometimes. The ones that make women look like dream women on accounta most dresses don't got that kinda magic. Purple maybe, on accounta you told me one time that purple is a special colour in your Indian way but I forget what that is on accounta I don't remember stuff like that for very long no more, but purple would be nice anyhow. A nice light kind of purple like you see in the sky after the rain goes away an' the sun comes out to set an' remind us that there's always one more comin'. One more day comin'. Nice light purple. Like hope feels sometimes when you get it. You always give me hope an' even though a dress ain't nearly a big thing like a Ferris wheel I know you'd think it was on accounta you always think like that. An' you could wear it when we go ride Digger's wheel. An' maybe I could get one of them suits like the dancer guy wore in that movie with one of them fancy kind of hats, the gloves, an' the little cane thingamajig. Yeah. That's what I'd get you an' I want you to have. Miss Margo can help you look on accounta she's so pretty an' knows about all that stuff.

Anyhow, before I forget what I'm doin' I gotta talk to Timber. Timber, you gave away all your money on accounta you wanted to take care of your missus that you never done all them years on accounta you was a rounder and you forgot to do that. I thought that was nice. She's a nice lady. Kinda quiet an' scared kinda, but a nice lady anyhow. You gave her all your money because you remembered that you loved her an' that it was the right thing to do. Me, I don't need no money on accounta I can't figure what this millionaire thing is supposed to be all about anyhow an' I never did wanna do nothin' but watch movies an' now go talk to people an' that don't take no money no more. I got a house to live an' I won't ever be hungry on accounta One For The Dead wouldn't let me, so I wanna give you back what you gave away.

Get it from Mr. James on accounta he takes care of my loot. I want you to have it an' get everythin' you need to make your carvings. Maybe even get your own place like Digger's got an' show people what you do. That's what I want.

The rest of my money goes to Granite. Whatever's left. You never say much about your life an' sometimes I think you're just like me on accounta you got people you carry around with you too. An' you sold your nice house. So I wanna give you my money so you can buy it back an' go there with Miss Margo an' be happy. See, when I used to walk around all alone them evenings after we split up an' went our own ways, I used to kinda spy in people's windows while I was walkin' an' try'n get a little glimpse of what they was doin' in their houses an' see how they was livin' on accounta the house I lived in wasn't like them big houses at all an' livin' in a shack has gotta be different than what goes on there or even in the nice house made out of stone that you lived in. I thought maybe if I figured it out that I could get that for myself too, sometime. But I never could. Maybe I just didn't see enough when I looked. I don't know. But I do know that people like you don't got no business not havin' a place that's just for them. You ain't no street guy an' you don't think like a street guy even though sometimes you kinda feel like one of us on accounta you lost so much. But people like you need to be where everythin' ever happened for them. It's history. I like that word. *History.* Did you know that if you kinda split it into two it makes "his story"? Well, when I got to thinkin' about you I thought that for Granite that big stone house was "his story" an' I figured that he hadta be where his story was. When you got somethin' that's part of your story, you gotta hang on to it as hard as you can or it'll go away an' you'll spend all your time from then on tryin' to get it back but you can't on accounta time don't work that way. You gotta go home, Granite. You gotta go home on accounta you gotta finish your story. When you got one, you don't gotta look for any other ones on accounta you got the only one you ever need to tell. So have my money on accounta I don't got no home an' I don't got no story to finish but maybe I could come there sometime an' be a part of yours. Go home, Granite, go home.

Digger

"GET WHAT YOU WANTED, Rock?" I go once the tape stopped.

"What?" he goes.

"The money. You got the money. You been hanging around waiting for your shot and now it's finally come. Happy?" I go, heading to the bar for a refill.

"I never wanted anyone's money, Dick's or anyone's, and I deeply resent you suggesting that it was all I was after," he goes, all huffy and puffy.

I swallow a gulp of Scotch. "Deeply resent whatever the fuck you want. But the patch is in, you scored, and that, my friend, is the name of the game."

"There was never any game."

"Fuck you, Square John."

"Is that supposed to hurt me?"

"What?"

"The whole Square John thing?"

"What whole Square John thing?"

"This whole tidy little 'us and them' game you've played right from the moment we met. Like the only worthy person in the world was a rounder. Anyone else was surely in on some scam—some dodge, as you say—some nefarious purpose."

"Nefarious? Nice word."

"Apt. Another nice word."

"Yeah, well, I'm apt to throw you right out of here."

"You don't need to throw. I'll walk."

"Then git. Pick up your cheque at the counter."

He stands up. I give him credit, he had some sand. The old lady stands up too but he raises a hand slowly and motions her to sit like he don't need to hide behind her, so she throws me a look and sits back down.

"I pity you, Digger," he goes.

"Shove your pity. All you Square Johns ever got is pity and it ain't needed. Never was, never will be."

"Oh, I don't pity you your life. You created that. You made it what it was all by yourself, and you stayed in it as long as you did by choice. So pity would be wasted on you and your rounder life."

"Fucking rights."

"But what I do pity is your failure to see what's in front of you, all because you keep the barricades up at all times. You think life is an ongoing confrontation. You react to things as though someone, somewhere, wants to take something away from you. You prowl the alleys and find the castoffs that other people deem unimportant and fix them up. Not because you're so gifted a repairman and not because you have such an exquisite eye for the value of things, but so you can shove it in their faces with a price tag when you're finished and say, 'See. See what I can do. See what I can do with your world. I can make you buy back your own friggin' garbage.' For you, it's the ultimate thumbing of your nose at the Square John world.

"But what you don't see is that it makes you an artist. It makes you a channel to everyone's common past. A channel to those days when everyone's life was simpler and there were no barricades between us. You make that happen. People buy your fix-ups because they remind them of a time when life wasn't all about the hurry and the scurry of making it. They remind them of common things like home and welcome and reunion. But you miss that connection because you're too busy making a fucking point.

"And you miss it with the people you call your friends. You're so busy being Digger you don't know how to be sensitive. And I know you're sensitive. I know you're gentle inside all that huff-and-puff bullshit you throw at people. I've seen it. We've all seen it, and that's why we admire you and it's also why we put up with the huff-and-puff crap from you. Because we, unlike you, are willing to see beyond what's in front of us. But there's a time when you have to dismantle the front, Digger. The rounder rules don't apply to life here. They only work on the street. Maybe if you'd seen that, you'd have been a better friend to Dick."

I feel the hot swell of rage at my temples and step closer to him. "Don't tell me about my friend," I go. "Don't make that fucking mistake, mister."

"Or what? Or you'll club me senseless? Is that your answer any time someone challenges your thinking? That's a rounder rule, Digger, and it doesn't wash here."

"No?"

"No."

"Well, you've had your fine little speech. Now let me give you one, Mr. Granite Harvey. You only see what you imagine to be there. You only see what your goody-goody heart says is there. You see everyone sharing the same friggin' city. Like it belongs to all of us. Like it's all our home. Like we're all fucking neighbours or something. But we're not. We never fucking were. You Square John motherfuckers fight to protect what you got, and rounders—wherever the fuck they might be, on Indian Road or skid road—are only fighting to protect what they don't got. If you could see that, if you could just get that, maybe you'd know how to be a better friend yourself. But you can't, because you're so convinced that you fucking know. You fucking know about what's wrong. Wrong with us, wrong with the world, wrong with everything but how you friggin' see things. You only see what you think you know and, mister, you don't know shit. Me, not a friend to Dick? Fuck you. At least I rode the changes through with him. At least I stayed true to the way we were, the way that got us through everything. At least I was an example of how to be tough enough to survive. I didn't hang around in the shadows and only come out at feeding time."

We look at each other. There's more he wants to say but I can tell he's chewing over what I just said. I look around the room and the others are all waiting for something to happen, something to give them a fucking clue about what to say next, how to move or what the hell is even going on here. It makes me sick all of a sudden. I have to get away. Go where things make sense.

"You figure out what to do," I go to all of them. "You're all so tight. You're all so touchy-feely. You figure out the moves. I'm outta here."

The old lady stands up as I move toward the door. I stop and look at her. She just nods. That's it. Just nods at me as though she knows what is going on inside me, and that pisses me off more than anything.

Timber

THERE DIDN'T SEEM to be a lot to say after Digger stormed out. We sat there in the living room and I really believe everyone felt the absence of both of them, Dick's weighing heavier perhaps, but Digger's disturbing and heavy too. James, in his steadying capacity, made inquiries about our choices for the memorial service, and somehow we mumbled replies. It would be at the Salvation Army chapel in the downtown core. Dick liked it there. Sometimes it seemed like it was the only place he could ever really feel at peace with things other than being at the movies. Amelia and Margo would meet with the funeral director and choose a spot for Dick to rest. Me? I'd try to finish the man in the chair, and Granite would write the piece for the newspaper. Once we'd made those choices, we moved away to our separate places.

When I got to the store, I thought that maybe Digger would be there. He wasn't. We'd arranged a small spotlight to light up my work and I gasped when I saw the piece. My Christ. It was him. It was Double Dick Dumont as I had seen him, not only on the veranda that day but many times on the street. I wondered why it had never affected me back then the way it did that afternoon on the veranda. There were so many times we huddled in alleys, in gazebos in parks, under bridges, behind buildings, or under expressway overpasses with the same desperation, the same need for comfort, and I never ever saw it until that day. Never saw him until that moment. We only see what we think we know. Digger said that. At first I thought he meant the world around us, but I knew in that moment, staring at the living wood that embodied Dick, that he meant the people we call friends. I thought I knew him as a rounder and that was all I saw all those years. But there was always more. Always. Tucumcary. I wondered what dreams lay unsatisfied in that small New Mexico town. I wondered what hopes he'd carried through the years, hopes he'd wanted to unload against a desert sky. So much to see that I hadn't. So much to know that I didn't. So much to learn that I couldn't. I picked up my blade and tried to put those feelings into the wood.

Amelia and Margo were sitting on the veranda when I got back to the house. It was late evening. I carried the piece wrapped in a blanket and they stared at it in my hands.

"It's finished?" Margo asked.

"Yes. If it's ever really going to be finished, anyway," I said, and set the piece on the veranda and leaned against the railing to smoke.

"What will you do with it now?" she asked.

"Take it to the service. After that, I don't know."

"I think he'd want you to use it," Amelia said.

"Use it how?"

"To get attention for your work. You're really talented. He'd want you to use it to let people see what you can do."

"Hm. Maybe. I haven't thought that far ahead. I just wanted to get it done. What about the site? Did you find one?"

Amelia smiled. "Yes. It's glorious. Just what he'd want, I think."

"On a curve above a small stream. Under a big elm tree," Margo said.

I grinned. "Yes. He'd like that. Remember where we used to go before they started kicking us out? That little park? You used to tell us stories under that big tree. Dick loved that. I think it was his favourite thing before we discovered the movies."

"Yes. Digger loved it too," Amelia said.

"Heard anything?"

"No. He wasn't at his place, I take it?"

"No. He's pretty upset. How's Granite?"

"He's okay," Margo said. "He's in Dick's room right now writing his piece. It's so good to see him doing that. He's a pretty incredible writer."

"I bet. Tough way to get back into it, though, isn't it?"

"Yes. But a storyteller is a storyteller. Isn't that right, Amelia?"

"Yes. Yes, it's true. It's an honour to carry stories and honour's gotta breathe," she said with a small grin.

"How are you?" I asked her.

"I'm fine. I'm a little lonely. Sad. Wistful, really."

"Could you use a movie?"

She smiled. "Yes. I could certainly use a movie."

"Good. Me too. Dick would like it if he knew we weren't spending all our time being morose and sad."

"You're right. Let's find something in his collection. Will you pick something for us, Margo?"

"Certainly. Granite won't be disturbed. I'll go see."

We sat there in the cool air of the evening and looked at our street. It was hushed and quiet except for the bubble of distant voices that faded quickly into the dark. I sat beside her and she took my hand. We sat there together, me and Amelia, and looked at the neighbourhood we lived in.

"He loved it here too," I said.

"As long as we were together he loved it anywhere," she said.

"True enough. Do you think Digger will be back tonight?"

"No. I think Digger is busy sorting himself out. He'll stay away to do that," she said, and squeezed my hand.

"You're sure about that?"

"Yes. I'm sure. I saw it in his eyes as he left."

"Saw what?"

"Questions. Lots of questions he never took the time to consider before. He needs quiet time and space to get at himself."

"Or get drunk."

She laughed. "Or that."

Margo returned with a movie in her hand. "Well, I think I found something we can all enjoy. Something wistful."

"Wistful?" I asked. "What is it?"

"It's called *How Green Was My Valley.*"

"How perfect," Amelia said. "How perfect."

One For The Dead

IT WAS PERFECT. A perfect tale about longing and looking back. I'll never forget it. The magic of the movies fell down around me one more time. I watched and I fell in love all over again. It was a story about changes. It was a story about how hard we cling to things sometimes, and how rubbery and slippery our grasp becomes once time has had its way. It was also a story about memory, and how we become eternal by being held in memory's loving arms. Dick would like that. I remembered a poem I read in school where the poet says that the world's first gold—its richness, its treasure—is green. The green of that valley shone in that man's mind like spun gold, and Double Dick Dumont and the life we had shared glimmered in mine the same way. In all of time, there was none so beautiful.

"I liked that," I said after it ended and the three of us sat in candlelight waiting for a sign to tell us where to move to next.

"I loved it," Margo said. "I read the book when I was a girl, then saw the film in my twenties, and it touched me the same way both times."

"Nice," Timber said. "Touching. Wistful, like you said."

We heard Granite moving down the stairs and turned to look as he entered the room. He carried a sheaf of paper. He nodded solemnly at us and made his way to the bar. As he poured, he looked at the street through the window.

"Any sign of Digger?"

"No," I said. "Did you expect any?"

"Not really, I guess. I suppose I just wanted to know that he was back and safe."

"You're a good man," I said. "Thanks for caring."

He swallowed some of his drink and moved to the couch where I sat with Margo. "What did you watch?"

"*How Green Was My Valley,*" I said.

"Ah," he said, "the classics. Nothing better."

"Not right now, anyway," I agreed.

"Is that your column?" Timber asked.

"Yes," Granite replied. "I think it's finished."

"'Think'?" Margo asked.

"Yes. Sometimes I never really know. I put the period at the end of what is conceivably the last sentence and I wait."

"For what?" Timber asked.

"I don't know. A bolt of lightning. Thunder, maybe. I don't know. Something to tell me that all of that time spent pulling words and phrases and sentences from the cosmos was worth something. That it matters."

"I know how that feels," Timber said.

"Do you?" Granite asked. "Is it finished? Your carving?"

"Yes," Timber said. "At least I think so."

The two men grinned at each other and it felt good watching them connect in that way. "Maybe we should see it and then after, maybe we should hear the story too," I said.

"What about Digger?" Timber asked.

We all fell silent. There was the whisper of a car passing outside. Everyone stared at the floor. Distance. I knew then how far people can travel from each other in the amount of time it takes to form a string of words, and how the echo of those words plays across the great stretches of our departures. Digger. We all missed him. We just didn't know how to say it.

"I think it will be okay," I said finally. "Digger's never much for sentiment anyway. Too touchy-feely for him."

"Okay," Timber said. "I really want you all to see the piece."

He set it in the middle of the room and began unfolding the blanket he'd wrapped around it. We watched like kids at Christmas. Granite switched on a table lamp and the room was lit in a hazy gold as Timber carefully unveiled it.

It was a statue. It went far beyond a carving or a sculpture. It was a statue. Three and a half feet high and ablaze in the hues of wood and a light stain. When I'd seen it in the shop it had looked complete to me, but now, in the golden light of the living room, I saw how much more had been coaxed from it and I marvelled. The lines had been smoothed and the face that previously had borne the look of rough weather and wind had been sanded to the point where it was the face of an old, well-travelled man. A sad man. A man with secrets behind his eyes but a world of small joys at the corners of his mouth, which looked like it could spring into a boyish grin and erase all the suggested woe in a heartbeat. It was like Dick. Exactly like Dick. Only the hands spoke of hard living. Timber had tattered the blanket, made it rough about the edges, and there was a pilling texture to it that gave the effect of an old cloak, a gypsy cloak, a rambler's wrap. His posture in the chair was like a thinking man instead of a crying one. Dick had been a thinker. He'd been a sponge trying desperately to soak up and hold the world, and the look that Timber had given him told the tale of a man looking back at the valley of his youth, the changes in landscape, the alterations of time, the shine of memory like spun gold.

"He's magnificent," I said.

"Yes," Margo said quietly beside me. "He is. He was."

"Amazing," Granite said. "Simply amazing. It looks as though you loved him very much."

"I did," Timber said. "I do."

"It looks as though you really saw him. You really saw him, really knew who he was and who he wanted to become."

"I did. I do."

We sat and looked at the statue for a long time, each of us lost in our recollections, each of us longing for the man in the chair who looked as though he could speak to us, and each of us hoping against hope that he would.

"I suppose the only thing left is to hear what I've written about him," Granite said. "Although I don't think I've done him as much honour as this work of art has."

"There's only one way to know there, chief," Margo said.

"Let's hear it, Granite," I said. "Please."

He unfolded the papers, cleared his throat, looked at the three of us and began.

Granite

I BELIEVED that I was a worldly man. I spent my life on pages like this, telling you how I see it. Telling you how this world is made, how it moves, how it works, how it shines at certain times and sits silently in the deep, spectral shadow of our choices at others. I have known this world: travelled it, explored it, studied it, written about and explained it. But only recently have I learned that I never really knew it at all.

Double Dick Dumont taught me that. His name is a street name, a nickname, an alias—a dodge, as his cronies like to say. Because Richard Richard Dumont, as his birth certificate identifies him, was a homeless person, one of those people we pass every day and never give a thought to beyond an exasperated epithet or the pitying doling out of dimes or quarters or dollars on the days we feel particularly generous. I likely walked by him a hundred times and never saw him.

But he was one of the greatest teachers I ever knew. Dick saw the world through the eyes of a child and never tired of wonder. He was illiterate. What he gleaned of this world he picked up by asking or by shrewd observation. Words confounded him. Principles, paradigms, systems, and ideas eluded him.

But he gave me the world.

We met in the movies during one of the deadliest cold snaps this city has endured. Homeless people died in that freeze. Many more were hospitalized, and Dick and his friends sought the shelter of a movie house. They weren't cinephiles or even particularly attracted to the prospect of film. They were just cold and seeking shelter wherever shelter could be had.

I was horrified. Homeless people did not belong in the territories I inhabited. My world and theirs were separate, created by disparate gods and never meant to meet. That's what my civilized, educated, liberal mind told me, and it was how I reacted.

But the minds of gods are tricky things, and we not only met but became friends. Good friends. When Dick and his pals won big on the lottery a couple of years ago, they called on me to help them. That story has been told and there's no need to retrace it. It's the story of what came after that matters.

Double Dick Dumont was a rounder. In the language of the street, a rounder is the top of the heap, a survivor, a Ph.D. in living off the avails of the alley, the street corner, the missions, shelters, and hangouts of the ill-fortuned. Unlike us, rounders see the city from the concrete up. We moneyed folk only ever learn to see it from the heights of our privilege, our homes, our neighbourhoods, our guarded possessions—and because of that, we never really see it at all.

But rounders do. Dick surely did. So when Dick and his friends bought a home in a nice, stable neighbourhood and removed themselves from the street for good, the physical properties of their house didn't matter a whit. Not to Dick. Not to his friends. What mattered was the idea, the one idea that Dick's questing mind could latch on to and, ultimately, give to me.

Dick taught me that home is a truth you carry within yourself. It's belonging, regardless. It's the place where you never need to qualify, measure up, the place that you never have to fear losing. It's bred in the heart and germinated by sharing, spawned by community. It's through the solidarity of humanity, as tight and loyal and steadfast as a rounder's code, that we all make it through together. He taught me that with his open acceptance of me. Regardless.

Dick had never had a home. Not really. Not ever. But he gave me one. When he died tragically, he bequeathed a portion of his money to me so I might reacquire the home I sold. My family home. My heritage. My history. The one place that anchors me. I sold it because I had come to believe that I didn't need it anymore. But Dick knew differently. He knew that I needed it. He knew that I hadn't got the idea yet. I hadn't yet understood that home is a truth you carry within you, a place you can return to always when you stop long enough to breathe. He knew that I needed to return to my physical home in order to finally learn that lesson. So he bought it back for me.

He took care of his friends, too. He made sure they got whatever it was they needed, because what they needed was what he wanted. He kept little for himself, because he said he didn't need much to be happy, and I believe him. I wonder what kind of a world this would be if we all shared that sentiment. I wonder how different we all would be if we learned to see beyond what we think we know. I wonder how poor the rich would become and how wealthy the poor would be if we could do that for each other. I wonder if we can.

Double Dick Dumont could. All that ever mattered to him was being warm, being fed, and being with people. He never put a price on that. He valued it too highly. His absence has left a great hole in my world, but I am more because he was once here, because he lived. He taught me to see beyond what I think I know and, in that, he gave me the world.

His funeral will be held at the Salvation Army chapel downtown, tomorrow at 2 p.m., and donations toward projects to aid the homeless will be accepted.

Do you know how it sounds when your heart skips a beat?
No. But I remember how it feels.
That's good. But it has a sound.
What does it sound like?
You've heard it. You've heard it a thousand times. But if you can't remember, all you have to do is listen to the drum. Listen to the drum when the singers do an honour song.
Okay. I've heard that. I still don't follow, though.
Well, there comes a time in an honour song when there's a break between choruses, and since an honour song is designed to rekindle our memories, to make time real again, the lead drummer expresses that longing with a louder, harder, slightly out-of-rhythm beat. It's called an honour beat and it's meant to remind us that when we've been connected to someone and they're gone, we can always recollect them through memory—and those memories are sometimes so special, so real, so close, that our heart skips a beat because it feels like that person is right beside us again.
That's lovely.

It's true.

But you know what the secret is?

No.

The secret is that you don't have to wait until you hear the drum.

You don't?

No. The secret is to make your life an honour song.

Digger

I GOT THE SAME ROOM at the Hilton. I don't know why. I guess I kinda wanted to feel like I was closer somehow. Closer to where the friggin' shoe dropped. Not that I could do any fucking thing about it, but I just wanted to be close. It wasn't spooky. It wasn't much of anything at all except a nice hotel room with a heck of a view. I walked around a while and I touched things. Touched the table, the chairs, the TV, the remote control, and poured myself a drink from the bar. There wasn't nothing of the man here. Just the shadow of him. I sat at the window and drank, looking out over the tops of the buildings and walking in my mind down all the streets I knew by feel from down below but felt so distanced from way up there. The street. I used to feel like I was part of it. Like having sawdust in my shoes when I was a carny, only out there it'd be more like dirt and dust and some fucker's spat-out bubblegum. I didn't miss it. Fuck, it was good to sleep in a comfortable bed and have the only wind you ever felt at night be the wind of a good fart in the darkness. I smiled at that. Such a friggin' poet, I was. Dick knew that. He liked my lingo. My rap. My spiel. I watched the sun go down at that window, only moving away to top up my drink. Once darkness settled over the city, I rented some movies off the hotel system, sat back, drank, and watched movies like I figured Dick would do. *Total Recall, Pacific Heights,* and *Mr. Destiny.* That one got me. *Mr. Destiny.* This friggin' guy's car breaks down and he goes into a bar where this bartender's all kinda magical and sends him back to his life. Only, the life he goes back to is the life he woulda had if he'da made another kinda choice way back when. Fuck. It bugged me but I couldn't stop watching.

Sure coulda used a Mr. Destiny at some points in my life. If I'da stayed with the farmer, maybe I woulda got myself some land and learned how to be a farmer myself. Maybe if I'da chose a good city job after my wheel days ended, I'da been a Square John myself by now. Fuck that. Fucking Square Johns. No, Mr. Destiny was fucked up enough to turn a guy like me into one of them heartless fucks. Square Johns always figure they're top of the fucking roost and they can move in wherever they want and be welcome. Not in my friggin' world. No way. Not ever. Then I thought that maybe a Mr. Destiny coulda sent me back to that evening we seen that fucking *Ironweed* and Dick walked out. Maybe a Mr. Destiny coulda sent me back to say something, to chase after him, to be a fucking winger and not leave his side. I drank a little harder after that thought.

I woke up with a king-sized hangover. The clock said 2 p.m., and when a couple of those little hotel bottles didn't do nothing for me I headed out for the Palace to get fixed up proper. I stopped in the doorway before I left. Dick. He'd passed out here just like I did. Only he never woke up. Poor fucker. I closed the door on the hotel room and walked away.

"Hey, old timer," Ray goes when I walk in.

"Fuck you," I go. "I'm still young enough to go at the drop of a hat. Wanna try me?"

"No way. I got too much to live for."

"Yeah. All this."

"Hey, it's a life," he goes, and drops me a double Jack back and a beer. "Have some lunch."

"A steak in every glass, my friend. A steak in every glass." I drain the shot and chase it with a swallow of beer.

"You seen the paper?" he goes.

"No. I ain't seen shit but the back of my eyeballs up until half an hour ago. Why?"

"You better read this," he goes, and sets the paper down in front of me.

My eyes are all blurry and I can't get a focus on the words. I rub them a bit and they clear as Ray plunks down another round. I give him a heartfelt thank you with my eyes and smooth the paper out on the bar in front of me. At first I don't see nothing. Fucking editorial pages. Nothing for me there, I figure, and then I see Rock's picture. Only after that do the words jump out at me.

"Teachings from the Streets" by Granite Harvey. I swallow some more hooch and start to read. When I'm done, I fold the paper up, hand it back to Ray, and walk out. Not word fucking one to anyone.

One For The Dead

DIGGER DIDN'T COME BACK all that day. When he didn't return the night before the funeral, I started to think that maybe we'd lost him too. Not to the ground, just to pride. I woke up that morning and the house was quiet, but when I walked downstairs everyone was up. James was there too, even though it was early morning. He'd brought suits for Timber and Digger and a dress, gloves, a veil, and shoes for me. He handed them to me silently and I held him close for a moment or two. A good man. A good, kind man. I wished that Digger could see that. As the morning went by and we all prepared ourselves, a few people began dropping by to pay their respects. Granite's editor and his wife arrived about noon and stayed to make the trip downtown with us. Our realtor arrived and asked to accompany us as well, and shortly after that Sol Vance from the lottery office arrived and also our banker Harriet Peters with her husband. By one o'clock we had a houseful, and I felt awed by this show of affection for Dick from people whose lives he'd barely touched. James, typically, had arranged for cars, and as we walked slowly out to them I stopped at the sidewalk and looked at our house. It sat on its plot of land like a regal old lady and there were all sorts of tales she could tell, all sorts of stories held in the arms of her joists and timbers and stone, tales for long winter evenings by the fire and the elastic twilight of summer on the veranda. A very regal old girl. I grinned and settled into the car.

"Problem?" Margo asked.

"No," I said. "No problem. Just looking at her."

"The house?"

"Yes."

She looked right into my eyes. Studied me. "Yes. I would too," she said, and settled in closer to me.

There was a traffic jam at the corner of the block where the chapel was and I worried briefly that we'd be late, but it cleared soon enough and we drove on through to the front. I couldn't believe my eyes. There was a line of people through the doors, down the stairs, and halfway down the block. There were rounders, street people, Mission and shelter workers I recognized, Fill 'er Up Phil, Heave-Ho Charlie, and others. But there were also strangers. Strangers dressed in elegant mourning clothes. Others in sombre suits and dresses, blue jeans, sneakers, leather jackets. Children, teenagers, elderly folk, and couples standing there staring up at the eaves of the building, as if waiting for a sign. I saw the major scurrying about near the doors, trying to accommodate everybody as best he could. When he saw me he blew out a breath and walked hurriedly to the car.

"Amelia," he said. "I had no idea to expect this many. It's wonderful."

"Yes, it is wonderful," I said. "Where did they come from?"

"The article," he said. "They all read the article Mr. Harvey wrote in the newspaper yesterday and they've all come to pay their respects."

I almost cried right there and then. Almost broke down and wept in the street, but instead I stood proudly, straight and tall, and led my friends to the chapel. As we walked, the rounders and street people stepped forward to shake hands and offer soft words. Others nodded, smiled, and looked at us in the sad way people do when words elude them. There were easily a hundred, likely more, but when we walked into the chapel itself it was crowded. People stood everywhere. Seats were reserved for us at the front, and as we made our way there I looked for Digger, but he was nowhere to be seen. We settled in our seats and I closed my eyes and said a tiny prayer for Digger, wherever he might be, and for Dick, who lay in the open coffin at the front of the chapel. I missed them both dearly.

Then I stood, straightened my dress about me, and walked to the coffin. I heard the others fall into place behind me. It was like something in a dream. Time slowed, I could hear my breathing in my ears, each step had a slushy feel against the carpet, and the coffin was growing larger, clearer. Dick. He lay there in slumber, hands folded on his chest, a nice suit and tie with a neat little handkerchief tucked into the breast pocket. He was dapper. I touched his hands and felt the hugeness of my grief wash over me. A tear plopped down on his wrist and I smoothed it dry. Then I bent forward and placed a kiss on his cheek like I'd done a thousand times through the years and waited for the smirk and giggle that didn't come. I looked at him and admired his peacefulness. I pushed his hair back from his forehead and then placed those fingers to my cheek, feeling him against my skin and missing him immeasurably.

I looked for Digger again when I sat down, but he was still nowhere to be seen. The major started the service and although it was touching and serene, I missed most of it. I was too busy walking the streets with Double Dick Dumont. I was too busy recalling the shards of the life I was left with, holding them, feeling them, allowing my skin its memory. Only when the song began did I resurface. Only when the band kicked into the marching tempo of the hymn did I return to my place. When the voices picked up the lyrics it was the most splendid sound I had ever heard and I turned to face all those people, to recognize them, honour them, share with them the words of this song that had meant so much to Dick. I sang through broken vocal cords, salty tears running down my face, easing across my breast where the hurt and absence, grief and sorrow, lay. I sang. Sang like I had never sung before, and saw a slow march of shadowed ones ease through the door and make the honour walk past the coffin. Lots of them. Shadowed ones. The homeless, derelict, and forgotten. *Shall we gather at the river,* I sang, *the beautiful, the beautiful river.* I closed my eyes and saw Dick beside that river and it was glorious.

Timber

My Christ. All those people. All of them touched by words on paper. All of them bearing some degree of sorrow born of one man's sentiment for a friend. It amazed me and I cried again as that old hymn was carried on about two hundred voices to wherever that river might be. Granite, James, Sol Vance, Fill 'er Up Phil, Heave-Ho Charlie, and I carried our friend to the hearse, and if there were a few fumes of whisky in our wake, no one said a thing. As we rolled down the street, following the hearse to the cemetery, I looked out the back window and saw a long line of cars following too. Headlights shone dimly in the mid-afternoon haze of downtown and I watched as we passed familiar landmarks, places where we'd stood, places where we'd gathered ourselves for the effort of the day or bade each other a kind goodnight during all those years when night's privacy was our only treasure. People stopped and looked as we passed. Many waved. Many nodded, perhaps touched by Granite's words too, and I thought about the irony of all those people seeing Dick on the street for the first time when it was his last time. I wondered where Digger was right then, and if he was okay. As we turned to make the final approach to the cemetery I looked out the back window again and saw that the line of cars stretched over three blocks. Amazing.

The interment was simple. I set the statue to the side of the coffin. There was a large throng of people all around us and they gave a collective sigh when they saw it. I trailed my hand across it, then looked at the coffin. It was like I touched him too, just then. When I looked up again there was silence and it moved me greatly. Two hundred people standing and waiting in perfect silence.

"Dick would want to tell you all a story if he could," I began. "Truth is, he loved stories. He loved them when they were told to him and he loved them most when they were on a movie screen and shown to him. I think it was the words. Words amazed him, mostly because he'd never learned to read or write and the power of words to give us the world amazed him. Simply amazed him.

"I don't know what words to offer him now except to tell a story. He'd like that. We were standing on the corner once, a long time ago. It was windy. It was cold and we didn't have a place to go. The Mission wasn't open all day back then like it is now, and we hadn't hit upon the idea of hiding out in the movies yet. Dick had a little bottle of rum and I had some vodka. Our other friend Digger had whisky, so we were pretty much okay on that front."

There was a ripple of laughter from the crowd.

"We're shaking and shivering and getting anxious for shelter. Anywhere but where we were. It was Sunday, so the stores were closed. Sunday afternoon. Dick spies this vacation place across the street and gets all excited and starts pestering us to walk over there. Finally, more to quiet him than anything, we do. There're posters in the windows showing blue waters, beaches, smiling girls in bikinis, palm trees, the whole deal. So we stand there in the doorway of that travel place and Dick passes around his bottle and we drink. Digger asks what the hell we're doing there and Dick, well, Dick just gives him this look like he's surprised Digger doesn't know. Then he says, 'Permeate.' Just like that. 'Permeate.'

"I asked him what he meant. He looked at me, eyes all wide and excited, and said, 'It's what happens when you imagine.' Then he tells us to look at the posters and imagine we're there with rum drinks on that hot sand. Then he passes his rum around again, tells us to drink and imagine real hard that we're on that beach as we drink. We do, and right away we feel warmer. From the belly on up, we feel warmer. I told him that and he smiled. 'Permeate,' he said again. 'You imagined and it permeated you.'

"Now, I know it was the burn in the belly from the two shots of rum we'd just had back to back, and being out of the wind in that doorway, but I never told him that. I never told him because a part of me wanted to believe in the power of that word like he told it. I don't know where he heard it or where he got its definition, but it worked for me then.

"So from now on, whenever I'm in a park, I'm going to imagine we're still walking around and telling crazy stories to each other. Every time I go to the movies I will imagine that he's sitting there with me. Every time I see something simple and charming and gentle, like kids playing in the sunshine, or two old people walking down the street hand in hand, I'm going to imagine he's seeing it too and smiling that little-boy smile he always had for such things. I'm going to imagine that. I'm going to imagine that so he can permeate me, become a part of me again.

"Let the people around you permeate your life. That's what Dick would say. That's what he'd want for all of us. *Permeate.* It's a rounder word. Or at least, now it is."

I sat back down and watched as they lowered my friend into the ground, into the curve of a hill overlooking a small stream, and I imagined him sitting there in that shade looking over it too, smiling, at ease, at home. Imagine that.

Granite

After the service we rode in silence, each of us lost in our private thoughts, content to simply be in each other's company knowing that we were joined by a common thread now and always. A ragged thread. A common, simple thread. But I wrestled with that feeling of union. I struggled to feel calm and at ease with knowing that Dick had been cared for and tended to very carefully and lovingly. I struggled because there was an important element missing and I felt responsible in some way for the fact that Digger had not appeared. In some way I had created a great rift in the company of friends, and despite not being completely aware of how that had been accomplished, I felt guilty and ashamed for my ignorance.

"Are you okay?" Margo asked once we were back at the house.

"No. I'm not okay."

"What is it?"

"I don't know. I feel dislocated. Out of joint. Out of balance somehow."

"Digger?"

"Yes. I wish I knew what I did. What I said."

"You did everything you could. It was a marvellous piece you wrote, and look at the reaction it got. It was so incredible to see all those people. You touched them. You affected them. You altered their lives."

"I altered someone else's, too."

"You don't know that."

"He didn't even show up to his friend's funeral."

"That's a lot of weight you're willing to bear, without knowing the whole story."

I looked away. We'd changed from our funeral clothes in Dick's room and stood there amid the jumble of all those movies, all those stories, all those imaginings, all those possible worlds. I missed him. Terribly. I missed both of them.

"I need some time," I said. "Driving always helps. Driving around and thinking. Settling."

She kissed me, a rich and gentle kiss, and let her hands stay on my face a while, looking deeply into my eyes. I kissed her again and walked out.

I drove. Steered the car unthinkingly as I mulled over the years since I'd walked away from a stone carver's house and the tales it contained. I drove and watched the buildings as they slid by. Drove through rich, swanky estate areas, then neighbourhoods of small neat bungalows, row after row, and down streets full of worn facades, tumbled staircases, peeled shingling, and tattered eaves. I drove through market areas, recreational zones, corporate and commerce areas, derelict areas, and on into the industrial zone. All of them held stories, and as I wondered about the lives there and how lost they become in the maze of motion that is a cosmopolis, I suddenly realized that I'd driven to Dick's warehouse.

I'd never seen it in daylight. It was long and squat, made of rippled sheet metal with a narrow row of glass windows at the top. There were heavy chains across the doors and weeds sprung up along the seam where the frame met the ground. Derelict. Deserted. No one to hear its song. I got out of the car and walked along the wall shielded from view from the street and found the peeled-back edge of sheeting that allowed entry. Stepping through, I felt the silence immediately. This was a lonesome place. This was a place of shadow and darkness. I imagined Dick stepping through that triangle of space in the sheeting and walking through to the middle where he'd piled wood and furnishings and detritus high enough to cover the light of his small fire. I felt him. He permeated me and I walked to the middle.

There were bottles on the ground from the party Digger had thrown after the lottery win. Dust. Dirt. Spiderwebs. It appeared that no one had yet discovered this hideout. I cleared a small patch of dust from a turned-over wooden crate and sat. The light was diffused by the height of Dick's pilings, taking on an almost bronze texture and giving the shadow a curious depth. I closed my eyes and thought about all of the nights he'd come here, alone, drinking enough to sleep by the light of his fire, a man haunted by ghosts I could not even begin to imagine, incapable of repelling them and therefore settling for the thick sludge of drink that would ease him into sleep. Dick. I wondered what I might have done differently to keep him with us. I wondered how I might have changed the way I spoke, the way I moved, the way I thought, in order to really hear him, to really see, to really feel the man I called my friend. I wondered how I could have closed the gap that existed between Square John and rounder, between the derelict and the privileged, between the lost and the secure, between Dick's world and mine.

I thought about his smile. His laugh. I thought about the slack-jawed way he sat and watched movies. Amazed. Always amazed and surprised by the world and by stories. For him there were always stories, real or imagined, unlike myself, who had allowed bitterness and anger to close me off. There were no real stories left, I'd told Mac. Not for me. But I was sitting right smack in the middle of one of the greatest stories I had ever heard, and it was real. It was real. It was painful and hard and joyous all at the same time and it had changed me, brought me back, made me able, perhaps, to re-enter the home I sold, to hear its songs again, to write, to create, to tell the stories of this city for those willing to listen, for those who would imagine and try to see beyond what they thought they knew and let the lives around them permeate them. Double Dick Dumont had been an integral part of that great story, and right there in the shadowy world he had come to every night before fortune offered him more substantial shelter, he'd slept and drank and staved off demons, alone and frightened with no stories to comfort him. But he was at peace now. Now there were no alms to beg. Now there was no chill wind to thicken the blood, no cold rain to pucker the skin, no snow to freeze those big, flat feet, no storms to endure. Now there was only light, the eternal light on the banks of that glorious river where he walked. When I thought of him there, walking there, slack-jawed in amazement, I cried. Cried long and hard for him. Cried long and hard for myself. And then when my throat eased sufficiently to allow the air its movement, I sang.

"*Shall we gather at the river, the beautiful, the beautiful river,*" I sang in a whisper, tears flowing freely down my face.

"*Gather with the saints at the river,*" sang another voice, gruff and hard and out of tune. Digger stepped from behind the pilings where he'd secreted himself. He was carrying a bottle and dressed in the same clothes I'd last seen him in, unshaven, rumpled, and weary-looking.

I stood up and we looked at each other across that dim space of warehouse. No words. I didn't know where to put my hands.

"Rock," he said, wiping his face.

"Digger," I answered.

"I read the paper."

"Oh."

"I seen all them people at Dick's service, too."

"You were there?"

"Yeah. I went but I was too ashamed to go in."

"Ashamed?"

"Yeah. You loved him, didn't you?"

"Still do."

"Yeah. Me too. I guess I never really saw that. How much you cared. About him. About us. Big part of me never could believe it. That we were worth it. That I was worth it. Thanks," he said, and extended his hand.

I took it. Neither of us made a move to shake. We just stood there, clasping hands firmly, looking at each other.

"You're welcome," I said.

"Drink?" he asked.

"Yeah, that'd be good."

We sat down on crates and he unscrewed the top from the bottle. He held the bottle up to the light and we each looked around at the place where Double Dick Dumont had come for shelter. He looked at me and poured a small dribble onto the ground.

"There's one for the dead," we said together.

One For The Dead

IT WAS DICK that stopped all the dying. I don't know why, but the shadowed ones let me be after that. I found that curious. I wandered around the downtown core like Dick had said he wanted to do and visited people at the Mission, the shelters, the places they gathered, but I never saw them anymore. Just like that. Instead, I saw the people. Saw the way they could become a part of you if you let them. Saw the way their stories made your own richer, more meaningful, less a burden at times, all because you listened. That's all they ever wanted, the shadowed ones, to have their stories heard, to be made real. When Granite told Dick's story, as he did in his new column and in the book that came later, he told the shadowed ones' stories too—and they let me be. I didn't miss them. Not really. Instead, it was a comfort to know that story was doing what it was always meant to do: light the fire of imagination so the things you didn't see could permeate you. Dick's word. So perfect.

Digger kept the store going. He started a training program for men who wanted off the street. They came to his shop and learned how to repair things. When Granite wrote about the program, scores of volunteers signed on to teach specific skills like wiring and metalwork. The money from everything sold through that store went to the Mission, and the part of the program that Digger stressed most was having the men go back to volunteer at the shelters and missions they came from. In turn, they learned skills, ways of earning money, how to work again, how to be responsible, and, especially, how to laugh again. Walking into Digger's was to be drowned in waves of laughter coming from the back of the shop as he regaled everyone with wild tales of his rounder life.

"Guy needs a friggin' yuk now and then," Digger said. "What the fuck good is living through something if you can't laugh?"

He put up a wheel, too.

It was something. It took a long time to find a ground-mounted Ferris wheel but James came through for him. They found it buried under straw in a barn where it had been abandoned by a show that had gone under some twenty years prior. They used the shop to clean it up, mend it, and prepare it for use again. Piece by piece. Length of steel by length of steel, you could see the magic working through Digger's hands, bringing that old wheel back to life. They bought a piece of land near a playground in the downtown core and raised that wheel up into the sky one bright summer day with a crew made up of me, Timber, Granite, James, Margo, and the boys from the shop. Digger was majestic. He knew that wheel by heart, and as it reached upward into the sky I watched his face change. It went from old man to young man right in front of me, and I smiled to see it. When all of the arms had been placed and the braces, wires, and turnbuckles tautened, he put his hands on it. Placed his hands against one of the towers, leaned on it, closed his eyes, and I watched as his shoulders trembled slightly. When he opened his eyes again there were no tears there, just a light I had not seen before. And when he showed

Granite how to work the clutch and spin the wheel slowly around, then climbed onto a brace and stretched his arms and feet across it, I was thrilled for him. He nodded. Granite slipped the clutch and Digger rose into the air, spread-eagled on an arm of the great wheel. Granite slowed it to a stop when Digger reached the top and we all stared upward in amazement at the sight of the greatest wheelman in the world standing proudly against the sky again.

I don't know what thoughts passed through his mind that day. I don't know where he went as he stood there so strong and free, the breeze rippling his grey hair. But I hope he went to the horizon he always sought, stepped into it and found the world he'd been looking for all his life. When he came down, he punched Granite lightly on the shoulder, squeezed Timber's hand firmly, and looked at me. He looked at me and I saw right into him. Saw Digger at home. He runs that wheel three times each week now. He goes for hours and gives people rides for free. You can hear them laughing. You can hear them chatting excitedly as they pass backwards by the old wheelman on the stool. You can hear them reliving old days when Ferris wheels were the highlight of the carnival shows that passed through their towns. You can hear them telling stories, talking to each other, making new memories. And you can see Digger smiling.

The statue brought Timber much attention. After the funeral, several gallery owners called and asked to see more of his work. James found him a studio space of his own and he set to work. He was marvellous. He concentrated on people. Many days he would take me with him on long walks through different parts of the city and we'd watch people, we'd talk to people, we'd listen to their stories, and Timber would sketch quietly and quickly. Then he'd go back to his studio and bring those people to life in wood. He sold plenty. He became well known. But it was the two pieces he didn't sell that made his name.

The first was a mural carved in wood. It was a street scene, a downtown street scene, and at first it seemed plain what it showed. But you had to get closer. There was a power and a magnetic pull to the lines of blade and hewn surface that attracted you. As you moved closer, it began to feel as though you moved into it, that you were a part of that scene. Finally, you stood there and were absorbed by it. Only when that feeling sank in did you begin to see what you hadn't at first glance. There were faces in the concrete, faces in the walls of buildings, faces in profile, faces in cameo relief, faces everywhere that you had to inhabit the mural to see. Looking closer, you saw people in the corners, people hidden by line and edge and action. Ragged people. Rounders. Street people. It captured you. Snared you with the power of the invisible people you missed while you were busy trying to take it all in. He called it *Shadowed Ones* and it was sublime.

The second was a statue of Sylvan. She held a jade plant in her lap while she rocked in a chair. The detail was stunning. Her eyes were melancholic, squinted slightly, and her focus was far away, beyond you, over your shoulder to some place only she could see. Or not see. The lightness in her hands was compelling, the fingers laced around the pot that held the plant. The word was *grace.* They spoke of a grace carved into the fine lines of her face, the set of her shoulders, and the delicate placing of her feet. But the mystifying part was how he managed to suggest something missing. Something off to the right of her shoulder that spoke of a longing, an absence, an unfilled space. I knew what went there and every time I see it, I see Jonas Hohnstein standing proudly beside the one true love he carried all his life. Saw that space filled forever. It was where he belonged. She sits in the Richard R. Dumont Gallery in a special window framed by smoked glass, looking out at the world, at the street.

Granite bought the stone house back. He and Margo moved there and he wrote a column for the paper. Not political pieces. Pieces about people. He told Digger's story after the wheel went up. He told about Fill 'er Up Phil, Heave-Ho Charlie, and a lot of the other rounders we introduced him to. Then he told stories about the barber who'd had the same shop on the same corner for forty years. He told about the immigrant man who reunited with the love he thought he'd lost in the Second World War. He told about the engineer who retired and built an enormous miniature railroad in his basement for the neighbourhood kids to enjoy and learn about days long gone. He told real stories because he discovered there were a few of those left after all.

He hears the songs again. He feels them. He raises his face to the beams and timbers, closes his eyes and feels all that history envelope him like clouds, he says. I'm happy about that. When I see him now, I see a man surrounded by time and place. He wears it like a soft wrap and he's comfortable.

Me? Well, I used my money to make a special place for women. It's called Deer Spirit Lodge. In my people's way, the deer is a gentle spirit, healing and nurturing. The lodge is a place for women to go to learn to nurture themselves after a life on the street, in prison, or just life in its toughness and difficulty. Wawashkeezhee Manitou. Deer Spirit. It's what I wish for them. I bought a nice building on a quiet street in a family-oriented neighbourhood and filled it with soft furniture and warm things. Margo and I worked together to set up a program that has spirituality built into every facet, and then I stepped aside and let her run it. Oh, I drop by as often as I can to talk to the women, make a soup maybe, or go on a movie outing, but mostly I leave it in Margo's hands because I'm busy elsewhere.

I'm busy on the street. See, it wasn't enough for me to just drop by and visit. No, I know a rounder's ways and I know that there's always a big lack of trust of someone from the outside. Always suspicion. Always a perceived lie. So I went back. I left the house on Indian Road and went back to the street to live among them again. They need me. They always needed me. The boys are okay. They're strong now. They have lives and they don't need me to lean on or tell them how things are supposed to go. But others do. I sleep outside. I make runs for them. I listen to them. I'm one of them. I always was. I always will be.

But now and again I come home to Indian Road. I come home and sit on the veranda with Timber, Digger, Granite, Margo, and James and we talk about the old days, about Dick and cold snaps, Square Johns and rounders, shelter and fortune, and dreams and home. We talk a lot about home. Then we go to the movies to sit in the hushed atmosphere of magic and let the light of someone's dream light up our worlds again.

Quite the story.
Quite the journey.
Quite the life.
Yes.
I wouldn't change a single part of it.
Me neither. Going back to it always fills me up again.
Me too.
So where will you go now?
I don't know. I never know. I just sort of arrive somewhere and inhabit that place for as long as I feel like it.
That must be nice.
It is. It truly is.
Do you have a home now?
It's all home. Everywhere. It's all home.
You sound so different. I know that it's you, but you sound so different.
Well, the truth is that when you make it home, everything that made life difficult out there disappears. You become whole. You don't stutter anymore, you think clearly, your body's not old and tired. You're healed.
That's so comforting to know. But there's one thing that bothers me.
What's that, old friend?
What do I call you now? Do you have a different name there?
Well, I will always call you Amelia. And you can always call me Dick.
Yes. Dick. So long, Dick. Travel well.
I will. And I'll see you again.
I know. I know.

THE BEGINNING